FIREFOX . . . AND NOW . . .
SNOW FALCON.

"One of the slickest, most action-packed books you are going to run across this year . . . Thomas misses no tricks and tension is sustained from first page to last. He is a very good writer." These are the accolades used by *The New York Times* to review Craig Thomas' bestseller. And, in the opinion of many, *Snow Falcon* is even better.

FIREFOX . . . AND NOW . . .
SNOW FALCON.

Someone is plotting to undermine the Soviet bureaucracy. Someone is conspiring to explode the delicate, tense negotiations for a third SALT agreement—a treaty bitterly opposed by the Red Army. Someone is planning moves that will affect not only the stability of the Russian government, but also the future of world peace.

FIREFOX . . . AND NOW . . .
SNOW FALCON.

Someone has written a stunning novel
of international espionage that hurtles the
reader toward a shattering climax . . .
CRAIG THOMAS

SNOW FALCON

Craig Thomas

BANTAM BOOKS

TORONTO • NEW YORK • LONDON • SYDNEY • AUCKLAND

SNOW FALCON
*A Bantam Book / published by arrangement with
Holt, Rinehart & Winston General Book*

PRINTING HISTORY
Holt, Rinehart and Winston edition published April 1980
A selection of the Book-of-the-Month Club August 1980
Bantam edition / June 1981

2nd printing . . . . . . June 1982		4th printing . . December 1983	
3rd printing . . . . . . July 1983		5th printing . . . . March 1983	
	6th printing . . November 1986		

ISBN 0-553-26605-5

Published simultaneously in the United States and Canada

*Bantam Books are published by Bantam Books, Inc. Its trade-
mark, consisting of the words "Bantam Books" and the por-
trayal of a rooster, is Registered in U.S. Patent and Trademark
Office and in other countries. Marca Registrada. Bantam
Books, Inc., 666 Fifth Avenue, New York, New York 10103.*

PRINTED IN THE UNITED STATES OF AMERICA

KR   15 14 13 12 11 10 9 8 7

*For my Mother and Father
and In Memoriam
John Knowler—simply the best*

ACKNOWLEDGEMENTS

I wish to express my gratitude to TRJ, who assisted in the matter of helicopter accidents, and to KPJ, who acted in the capacity of officer commanding those units of the Red Army which feature in the book.

I am also indebted to various publications, especially to two works of reference, namely *The Soviet War Machine*, edited by Ray Bonds, and *KGB* by John Barron, and to that indispensable travelling-companion, *The NAGEL Guide to the U.S.S.R.* The quotation on page 273 comes from *A Division of the Spoils* by Paul Scott, published by William Heinemann Ltd. and William Morrow Inc.

I would also like to express my thanks to the Embassies of Norway and Finland for their help in time and materials during the period of research for this book.

Finally, I would wish to acknowledge my immense debt to the late John Knowler, who worked as my editor on this novel shortly before his untimely death, and who first enabled me to become a professional novelist. I owe him a debt I could never have repaid, even had he lived. As an editor, a counsellor and friend, he is irreplaceable.

Craig Thomas,
Lichfield

"The situation at the moment is such, the Soviet Union's economy is on such a war footing, that even if it were the unanimous opinion of all the members of the Politburo not to start a war, this would no longer be in their power."

Alexander Solzhenitzyn
1 March 1976

PRINCIPAL CHARACTERS

THE BRITISH

Kenneth de Vere AUBREY	:	Deputy head of SIS (British Intelligence)
Maj. Alan WATERFORD	:	Attached as instructor to 22 SAS
Alex DAVENHILL	:	Foreign Office Special Adviser to SIS
Lt. Allan FOLLEY	:	22 SAS, seconded to British Intelligence
PHILIPSON	:	SIS Staff, Helsinki

THE AMERICANS

Charles BUCKHOLZ ANDERS	:	Deputy Director, CIA
President Joseph WAIN-WRIGHT	:	his chief assistant

THE RUSSIANS

Maj. Alexei K. VORONTSYEV	:	Special Investigations Department (SID), KGB

Feodor KHAMOVKHIN	: First Secretary, Communist Party of the Soviet Union (CPSU)
Yuri ANDROPOV	: Chairman of the KGB
KAPUSTIN	: Deputy Chairman, KGB
GROMYKO	: Foreign Minister of the Soviet Union
Mihail Pyotravich GOROCHENKO	: Deputy Foreign Minister
Ilya Maxim Alevtina Pyotr	: Junior officers of the SID
Marshal PRAPOROVICH	: O.C. Group of Soviet Forces North(GSFN)
Admiral DOLOHOV	: Red Banner Northern Fleet
Col. Gen. OSSIPOV	: O.C. Far East Military District
Lt. Gen. PNIN	: GSFN
Capt. NOVETLYN	: GRU (Military Intelligence)
Capt. Yevgeni VRUBEL	: KGB Border Guard
Maj. Gen. VALENKOV	: Commandant, Moscow Garrison
Capt. Ilarion V. GALAKHOV	: GRU
Anna DOSTOYEVNA	: former Minister of Culture
Natalia GRASNETSKAYA	: wife of Vorontsyev

PRELUDES

At the border between the Federal Republic and the DDR west of Eisenach, the E63 ceases to be an autobahn, and becomes merely a main road for the sixty or more kilometres through the Kaufunger-Meissner Wald to Kassel. At one specific point along that more twisting metalled strip, Kenneth Aubrey had decided upon a road accident involving a container lorry and three cars—one of them a Mercedes, the others Volkswagens.

He stood under the shelter of dark trees above the level of the road, the rain sweeping between him and the scene below. Behind and to his left, in a lay-by, the squat white shape of an ambulance waited, seemingly inappropriate to the erected carnage he was watching. The ambulance was still, its engine turned off, a fug steaming its windows.

Aubrey watched the mobile crane lowering the crushed bodies of the two Volkswagens painstakingly into the middle of the road. Small wet figures scurried around it, arranging the two wrecks as if in some display of modern sculpture. After perhaps twenty minutes, during which time he began to imagine the damp from the needle-coated earth under his feet was seeping into his Wellingtons, as he rested on a shooting-stick, the Mercedes was towed up by a break-down truck, unhooked, and men pushed it towards the two Volkswagens. Aubrey heard the rend of torn metal as it was edged into a grotesque three-pointed star against the smaller cars.

3

The German alongside him coughed. Aubrey glanced to one side, lowering his glasses, and said in German, "Yes, that will do very well, Herr Goessler."

"I am pleased, Herr Franklin," the German replied without humour or enthusiasm. Punctilious, but reluctant, Aubrey decided. He smiled at the use of his cover-name. Silly—but new regulations at every turn. Goessler knew him as Aubrey—had done for years.

He turned back to the road, gleaming like the PVC jackets and capes of the men down there.

The container lorry, SAUER AG large in yellow on its cab and cargo, was being driven slowly towards the mobile crane which hung above the wreck like a sinister carrion vehicle. One man in a cape was directing the driver with precise indications. Aubrey looked at his watch—plenty of time. Rain spilled from the brim of his hat as he bent his head. It wetted the knees of his suit, and he clucked his tongue in disapproval.

He watched as the mobile crane, gently at first, then as if delighting in its own strength, raised the body of the trailer, then jerked like an animal breaking its prey's neck, so that the container toppled upon the wreckage of the three cars.

The metal shrieked. Aubrey winced, as if he had seen the weight topple upon himself in some dream. When the great truck had settled, he nodded, satisfied, and looked again at his watch. Late afternoon, perhaps an hour more to wait, and the day drawing in under heavy grey cloud.

The wind changed, blowing rain into his face. He rubbed the wetness away.

"It appears to be very convincing," he offered.

Goessler said, "It's as good as you will get—without *driving* all the vehicles together at high speed."

"A reasonable facsimile will suffice," Aubrey said stuffily.

He watched the mobile crane move off, and the shiny figures of the men gratefully clear the road, heading for the mobile canteen he had ordered for the purpose. Their bent shoulders, ducked heads, suggested gratitude.

Then, suddenly, the road was deserted. Towards Kassel there was a diversion sign, and east down the road, two miles away, there was another sign directing traffic onto the 487. That sign would be removed quickly when the

4

time came. He could faintly hear the helicopter that was spotting for them. God knew what the visibility was like—but he had to trust . . .

He focused on a bend in the road, perhaps fifty yards away, towards the east. From there . . .

Less than an hour.

The driver of the container lorry travelling west from Jena and the Zeiss factory, carrying cameras and camera parts into the Federal Republic, was about to remark on the absence of traffic on that part of the E63 to the man seated alongside him—a man perhaps somewhat too old to be convincingly a driver's mate—when his truck rounded the bend on which Aubrey had focused his glasses.

The wreckage was bundled high in his vision like some grey bonfire ready to be ignited. He stamped down on the brakes, gripping the wheel as he felt the skid beginning. He eased off the brakes, eased them on again—but there was too little time and distance, and he knew it.

"Cover your face!" he had time to shout, and then the windscreen was filled and the cab dark with the monstrous heap of tangled wreckage.

Aubrey watched the impact shift the wreckage as if the oncoming truck were a bulldozer. The noise assailed him, tearing, crying sounds that belonged to no human experience. The whole mass of metal, to which he had now added perhaps three hundred and fifty pounds of human material, slewed across the road, almost into the ditch below him.

Then it stopped. Silence. He was grateful for that; he could sense Goessler crouched into shock beside him. A whistle blew, and Goessler's team went into action.

The ambulance, headlights gleaming off the road, blue light flashing, siren wailing, turned out onto the road. A police car appeared round the bend in the road, and parked broadside-on, blocking oncoming traffic. Its red light swept continually across the road. A red fire-engine appeared from the trees, as if lost, then drew out alongside the container lorry.

The cab door had to be cut open with torches which flickered blue off metal and wet road, sparked and blazed. When the first of the men, the driver, was lifted

5

from the twisted intestines of the cab, it was evident he was dead. Aubrey did not need the white face of one of Goessler's men looking up towards them, and the shaking head.

"Why have they bothered with the driver?" he snapped. Then, raising his voice, he called, "The other man—he is the one. Is he alive?"

A fireman had clambered into the cab, and now he appeared, his hand raised towards them. Aubrey could see the extended thumb clearly in the glasses. The man was alive. A shiver of success, and relief, possessed his old frame for a moment.

"We shall go down, Herr Franklin," Goessler remarked, with the first urgency he had shown all afternoon. Aubrey raised himself from his stick, letting the glasses hang from their strap.

He was irritated by having to hold on to Goessler's arm for support as they descended the muddy slope.

The second man, the driver's mate, was extracted from the cab in half an hour. His legs were obviously crushed by the impact, and the German doctor continually shook his head. He administered morphine to keep the man unconscious. When he was finally lowered onto a stretcher, and the black bags had been inflated round the crushed limbs to form splints, the doctor glared at Aubrey with what seemed to him to be dislike, even momentary hatred.

"Don't waste your sympathy, Herr Doktor," Aubrey snapped at him across the stretcher—its red blanket and white, strained face. "This man is a senior Russian tank officer. *Not* a German—as you well know. Now, get him into the ambulance."

When the driver's mate was loaded aboard, Aubrey climbed into the rear of the ambulance, Goessler following him. He slammed the doors shut behind them. A nurse, water from her wet cape joining the pool from the umbrella Aubrey had folded, began giving a transfusion to the unconscious man on the stretcher.

As he watched the tube redden through its length, reach the arm like a quick red snake, and the bottle begin to empty, Aubrey was suddenly afraid. It was as if a hand had swept down the house of cards he had built—or someone had laughed at something he had thought, or written or composed in secret.

"How bad is he?" he asked the doctor, sitting beside the patient.

"Bad."

Aubrey tapped the floor of the ambulance as it jerked into motion, its siren accelerating up the scale as it headed for Kassel. His umbrella protested drops of water onto his trousers.

"He must live," he remarked. "It is imperative that this man makes a *sufficient* recovery." There was a hissing, almost threatening urgency in his voice. The doctor was quelled, rather than resentful. "The man must live—he *must* live."

The *Kasseler Zeitung* carried a news item on the accident, and what it claimed were exclusive photographs. There was a vivid description of the wreckage, and the weather conditions. The main burden of the article seemed to be an attempt to reopen discussion on extending the E63 autobahn from Eisenach to Kassel through the Kaufunger-Meissner Wald, which stretch of road had proven once again fatally inadequate for the present volume of traffic.

A further item on the same page informed the readership of the death of the driver's mate, one Hans Grosch, of Stadtroda near Jena, after an unsuccessful operation at the Kassel Central Hospital. His body, the authorities had informed the *Kasseler Zeitung,* would naturally be returned to the DDR for burial, in due course.

That evening, twenty-six hours after the accident, an RAF Hercules took off from an airfield outside Hanover. When it landed at RAF Brize Norton, an ambulance was waiting for one of its passengers, who was then driven to a small private hospital outside Cheltenham.

Cunningham looked down at the red file on his desk, then up into Aubrey's habitually ingenuous blue eyes. The face round those eyes, once child-like and unageing, now appeared drawn and thin. Age, Cunningham decided, did not become Aubrey. It seemed to have wasted him more than others. Unless the weariness, the stretched skin, could be put down entirely to his interrogation of Smoktunovsky.

"A great pity the man died," he observed. It was not a criticism.

Aubrey looked at the bright wintry day outside in Queen Anne's Gate, over Cunningham's shoulder.

"I quite agree."

The warmth of the room was stuffy, dry, belying the weather, which possessed such an agreeable sharpness that Aubrey had walked part of the way to his office that morning. "However, perhaps convenient, since his body may now be returned to the DDR, in compliance with the official request by the family Grosch." He smiled thinly. "Colonel Smoktunovsky of Group of Soviet Forces Germany—I wonder how he liked playing the part of driver's mate? I quite forgot to ask him."

Cunningham flicked open the file. Aubrey was always bitter after a prolonged interrogation; as if hating something in himself.

"Satisfied—in broad terms, Kenneth?"

"I think so. In broad terms. Colonel Smoktunovsky knew a great deal."

"False alarm, then?"

"I think so. The military analysts are taking their time coming to the same conclusion—but I think they'll get there. No, the sending of perhaps the most senior tank officer ever into the Federal Republic to do his own routine reconnaissance was—well, perhaps an expensive luxury, or a piece of bravado. An old warhorse, feeling his oats . . . ?"

"Rather an expensive jaunt—for him."

"Quite. No, for the moment I don't think we have to worry about GSFG starting the next war just before this Helsinki business reaches an admirable conclusion. However, with Smoktunovsky coming over to survey the Federal road system disguised as a driver's mate of humble origins—one can't take chances."

"And you enjoyed your elaborate trap?"

"A hit—I do confess as much." Aubrey nodded. The gesture was almost sanctimonious, certainly smug; yet there was a flash of something Cunningham almost described as self-disgust, just for a moment. "However, perhaps you would turn to page thirty-six of the interrogation transcript. I have marked the passage."

Cunningham took his spectacles from his breast-pocket, then flipped through the typed pages. Typescript, done with Aubrey's neatness of touch, on an old manual

machine. A Russian had lived and died in those pages—
Aubrey himself his only comforter and confessor; perhaps
the most successful and remorseless interrogator Cunningham had ever known. There was nothing of the cramped,
close intensity of those hours and days suggested by the
double-spaced type.

As if reading something in Cunningham's face, Aubrey
said, "I could admit that the whole thing was quite awful,
if you wish." Cunningham looked up sharply, "But it is
over now. And there may be something of interest for us."
He nodded at the typescript and, as if bidden, Cunningham
began to read. When he had finished, he looked up
again.

"Mm. I am to make something of this?" He sounded as
if he thought Aubrey was making the false judgement of a
tired man.

"I'm not that tired, Richard," Aubrey said softly. "You
may understand better, with a little perspective. Smoktunovsky was almost certainly GRU, Military Intelligence,
as well as senior GSFG tank tactician. His rank at fifty-
two was an affectation. As such, he was hard to crack,
despite his injuries and poor morale. What I have underlined there came only towards the end, when he had
broken almost completely, was rambling, trying to cover
tracks, that sort of thing. But still he tried to hide this
from me. I formed the distinct and certain impression
that he thought it was what I was after all the time, and he
certainly did not render it without the fiercest struggle."

"So?"

"Ciphers—code-words. Little else. If I had so much as
caught a whiff of it earlier, I would have gone for it—as
it was . . ." He lifted his hands in a shrug. "Nevertheless,
what Smoktunovsky considered *most vital* to conceal was
encapsulated in those phrases, and that number. *Group
1917—Finland Station* and the twenty-fourth. The last is
presumably a date, though it might be something else. I
am convinced that he thought it most important, and
highly secret."

Cunningham was silent for a moment as he re-read
the underlined passage. When he looked into Aubrey's
face again, it was evident he was sceptical. There was
sympathy in his eyes that could only be for Aubrey's tiredness.

"Wasn't the man just rambling—his prayer-beads, perhaps?"

"I considered that. No, there is a later stage when he does that—a dead wife, I gathered, sons, his own father. His wanderings around himself were personal, not political."

"And you want—?"

Aubrey rubbed his eyes, as if assailed by the weariness of the interrogation again. He saw his suspicions with Cunningham's eyes, momentarily.

"I—should try to explain my feelings about this, Richard. I don't want to be accused merely of a womanish intuition." Aubrey smiled briefly. "It's the language that's being used. The whole *revolutionary* evocation—"

Cunningham smiled. "I see. This is a semantic intuition, then? We are to be concerned with language, with meaning?"

"You're dismissing the whole thing—but you weren't there, with him. He was down in his belly, escaping me in screams, Richard!" Aubrey shuddered, as if someone had opened a door and let in cold air. "No, you weren't there. This was *so* important to him, he had to hide it. Wainwright and the Soviet First Secretary are to sign the SALT3/MARS agreement early next year. The Red Army is, we are certain, violently opposed to the Politburo over the whole package—they've even gone into print arguing for an *increase* in defence spending."

The words tumbled out now, as if he had struck some rock in his mind and a long-carried cargo was being spilled. The last hours with Smoktunovsky had been desperate, wearing; he had shortened the Russian's life by perhaps more than a day because he would not let him rest. In the end, he had had to lock the door against the medical staff while he went after what the crazed mind was still trying to keep from him.

Cunningham was shaking his head.

"Opposed, yes. That is to be anticipated—"

"Richard, I put Smoktunovsky in the bag because we were afraid of what Exercise '1812' could mean on the NATO central front. It turned out to be a false alarm. But that snatch was the result of well-founded suspicion on our part that the Army was engaged in a bitter quarrel with the Kremlin. Smoktunovsky didn't tell me that they'd kissed and made up."

10

Cunningham rubbed his chin for a while, then nodded. "It all seems very slim to me, Kenneth. Perhaps you were in there too long with him—" Aubrey's old blue eyes flared. "No, I withdraw that. Very well—talk to people, send in a man if you wish. Where might you begin?"

"I'll talk to a couple of people at MOD—the less dense among them. As to a penetration mission—I accept that I have nowhere to send someone at the present. But, the Red Army is not going to lie down and let its balls be cut off by Khamovkhin and the rest of the Politburo. I'm quite certain of that."

"Kenneth—I do hope you're wrong about this."

"Exactly my own sentiments. *Exactly.*"

"Very well, play it back. If it's any good, then we'll send it upstairs for analysis." The tape-operator made as if to rewind the spool of the tape on the recorder, then his team-leader stopped him. "Who did you say this old man was?"

"His name's Fedakhin—Bureau of Political Administration of the Army."

"Are we interested in him for any reason?"

"No. He just used a Secretariat telephone, that's all. He wouldn't have expected it to be tapped, but it was. I was just playing through last night's efforts after I came in, and I heard it. He's talking in code."

"OK, Misha, the floor is yours. Impress me."

"Captain."

The younger man switched on the rewind, and they watched the spools changing their weight of tape, and the numbers rolling rapidly back. Misha stopped the tape, checked the number with a list at his elbow, then wound back a little more. Then he switched to "Play" on the heavy old German recorder.

The captain noticed that, as usual with taps done as routine, the installation, and quality both left much to be desired. The voice was tinnily unreal, and distant.

"Our man for *Group 1917* is in place," the old voice said.

"Good. But you should not have called."

"I apologise. Let the illness of an old man excuse me."

"Very well."

"You need have no worries concerning *Finland Station*, my friend. It has been settled, in terms of personnel, and it can now proceed satisfactorily. I shall be able to retire a happy man, and await the great day."

The captain's nose wrinkled at the clichés, and he tossed his head, Misha being invited into the contempt he felt. He knew with certainty that contempt for the old fart on the tape was driving out curiosity, but the knowledge didn't worry him. Old men—his wife's father—talked endlessly of *great days*, and *happy retirement*, and *golden ages*, come to that—

"Thank you, old friend. Take care of yourself."

Misha let the tape run for a few seconds, then switched it off. He looked up eagerly into the captain's broad face, so that the older man felt obligated to feel interest.

"Well, sir?"

"Yes—tell me, then. Who was the other man?"

"Unidentified."

"What number was dialled?"

"Wrong sort of tap—no record."

"A name was asked for?"

"No. I'll play it, if you like—" The captain shook his head, lighting a cigarette. "Only an extension. Could've been anyone."

"So—what's the excruciating importance of all this, Misha?"

"I don't know, sir. But he was talking in code, obviously—and people who do that have something to hide, don't they?"

After a silence, the captain said, "Usually, they do."

"Stig, old boy—it's you."

The heavily-built, florid Englishman who never spoke Finnish if he could avoid it, looked up from the newspaper he was reading, recognised his visitor—unsurprising since he had been waiting for him in the bar on the Mannerheimintie for half an hour—and gestured him to another seat at his table. The bespectacled, fur-hatted Finn sat down, briefcase across knees pressed primly, and tightly, together. The Englishman watched him peer nervously into the less well-lit corners of the bar—a nervous tic that Stig had always demonstrated, at every meeting over the last five years. He'd probably done it with his predecessor, Henderson. Poor little sod—

"I—you always choose these public places, Luard. Do you have to?"

12

The Finn's English was excellent; unlike Luard, he had no distrust of a foreign tongue, speaking four languages other than his own. Luard's Finnish was improbable at best, Stig considered.

"Sorry, old boy. Standard procedure. And no one follows you about, old boy. No one has done for years—" It was as if Luard suddenly became irritated with his companion. "Everyone lost interest in you years ago, Stig. They wouldn't care if they knew you passed stuff onto my lot—I should think Finnish Intelligence *hopes* someone does, just in case they ever get hold of something of importance."

Stig's narrow, tired face with its doughy complexion suddenly sharpened, took on a vivacity of anger.

"You need not insult me, Luard. I asked merely on this occasion because I have something that you must see— and this is not the place to start passing round infra-red photographs."

Luard's narrow eyes slid into their creases of fat. Then his features went bland as the waiter approached. Stig ordered a beer, and Luard another Scotch. When the waiter had brought the drinks, and Luard had made a patronising show of paying, he said, "Infra-red. They must be good. What of?"

"The Finnish-Soviet border area, south-east of Ivalo."

"Oh—those." Stig appeared puzzled, bemused. "Are your lot still taking them from those high-wing monoplanes, so the Russians don't suspect they're doing something your government has agreed there's no need to do?" Luard was smiling broadly, his face seeming to be enveloped by the fat cheeks, the heavy jowl—nose, eyes being pushed into a little fist of lumps in the centre of the globe of fat pink flesh. Stig hated him.

"They are still using private aircraft, if that is what you mean." Luard laughed, raised his glass, his little eyes twinkling, and presumably drank the health of the Cessnas and their pilots from Finnish Intelligence. He watched the antagonisms chasing themselves across the Finn's features, and decided to give Stig a rest.

"All right, old man. Let's see them."

"Here?" The Finn appeared outraged, violated.

"We're in an alcove, aren't we. Don't be such a virgin. Holiday snaps, dirty pictures—doesn't matter. No one's going to care."

13

"Perhaps you could explain, Shelley, why this has taken two months to reach me?"

Kenneth Aubrey looked at the sheaf of infra-red photographs fanned open on his desk, then up at his aide. The young man appeared disconcerted, but confused more evidently than distressed.

"Sir, it was passing through my hands as routine. I didn't think you needed to see it."

"Very well." Aubrey sighed. "I accept that I was being inordinately curious when I removed them from your tray. But—now that I have them, pray enlighten me."

"They came in the Bag from Helsinki. With a note from Luard denigrating his contact as usual, and making light of these."

"And what are they meant to represent?"

"I checked with Helsinki, because the explanatory note was unsatisfactory." Aubrey nodded in compliment. "Apparently, it's a practice roll from one of their covert border-checks. We don't have the later rolls they took of the Russian side of the border. This lot was on its way to the shredder when our contact sidetracked them."

"Why should he do that?" Aubrey picked up one print, and Shelley another, in order to direct Aubrey's attention. He knew that his superior disliked anyone who stood at his shoulder to draw attention to something he was studying.

"The smear of infra-red sources in the top left-hand corner is Ivalo, the cold spot beyond is Lake Inari—apparently." Aubrey nodded, impatiently, it seemed to Shelley. "Towards the bottom, the other smear is the small town of Raja-Jooseppi. The mystery resides, apparently, in the fact that there should be another, smaller smear down near the bottom right-hand. A village called Rontaluumi."

"Yes?"

"The practice roll appears all right—except that there is no heat-source whatsoever from the village."

"What?"

"Our contact's superiors rejected the film as partially damaged, or wrongly developed. The rest of the film, the over-the-border stuff, was quite satisfactory."

"What other explanation might there be?"

"Luard said, with scarcely disguised contempt, that it frightened the life out of our contact."

14

"And is he a man given to panic?"

"No."

"Then what is his explanation."

"He says that *not* to make an infra-red impression of any kind means that the village was empty of life—human and animal. And must have been for several days before the film was taken."

"Sir, there's no contact from Brunton."

"How long is he overdue?"

Shelley was puzzled. Aubrey knew, probably to the minute. Nevertheless, he said. "Four days, sir—and a couple of hours."

There was a long silence, then: "A very strange empty village, then. What was the weather like?"

"Nothing to speak of."

Another silence which seemed to oppress Shelley, then: "Very well. Mark his file for disposal. Make out an instruction to Pensions, would you?"

Shelley recognised the brusque commands that habitually masked shock in his superior. He saw how old Aubrey suddenly looked; and he saw also the gleam of curiosity in his eyes, and the set of the mouth which revealed a kind of anticipation of Shelley's news. In some way, Aubrey had anticipated that Brunton might not come back, that there was some considerable degree of risk in checking out the duff roll of infra-red film from Helsinki.

As he made to leave, Aubrey called at his back: "Get Major Waterford over here as quick as you can. And pass the news on to Alex Davenhill at the FO."

"Sir."

"You realise what this could mean—this whole empty village and disappearing agent thing?" Waterford said.

"Enlighten me, Major."

"If the Red Army wanted to use the one good road to Ivalo—the *one road*, in fact—then it would have to remove the inhabitants of the village first, before it crossed the border."

Aubrey studied Waterford's face. It was characteristically expressionless; except insofar that it portrayed honesty. When Waterford spoke, his features, direct and without subtlety, assured his listener that he was giving

15

what amounted to his real—and presumably honest—opinion.

"Very well—suppose I entertain that hypothesis for the time being. I would simply ask why? Why should they want to use the one good road to Ivalo."

Waterford appeared impatient. Asked to rehearse once more lines he knew by heart and which were more than familiar to his audience—even to Aubrey from SIS. Robotically, he began.

"The Russians advised, and assisted, and partly funded the new cross-Finland road system. Finland exists at all by permission of the Kremlin—"

"Waterford, I know the political background. Strategic matters, if you please."

"If the Russians wanted to close the Baltic and the North Atlantic, or shut down the North Cape monitoring stations, or required more deep-water, ice-free outlets and harbours—any of those things, which might suddenly become urgent necessities, would mean the annexation of Norway. And to get to Norway, part of the force would go via Finland. Through to Ivalo, first stop. The Norwegians have just one enlarged division up there, while the Russians can call on twenty—and planes from eighteen airbases, and the Red Banner Northern Fleet."

"But, is there in existence any necessity for the invasion of Norway?" Aubrey appeared unperturbed, calm and reassuring behind his cluttered desk. "To support this strange piece of surveillance film that has come our way."

Waterford shook his head.

"I shouldn't think so. There's one thing, though. Just a theory, you understand?"

"Go on."

"The theory is that if the Red Army wanted to give NATO its marching orders, then it might not do so on the central front—it might try its luck in Norway first off, just to find out whether we'd hold together."

"You take this roll of film seriously."

"It doesn't matter to me. If I were *you*, though, I'd take it seriously. I'd get someone to take a look—soon."

PART ONE

FINLAND STATION

15th to the 18th of . . . . , 19 . .

"The tasks of the Party are . . . to be
cautious and not allow our country to
be drawn into conflicts by warmongers
who are accustomed to have others pull
the chestnuts out of the fire for them."

—STALIN

ONE

THE FALCON

The brief period of daylight had again passed, and the sky was hard with stars. A soughing wind flicked at the snow, wiping it in quick flurries from the ground and pattering it against the walls of the tent. Folley awoke refreshed, stiff with the cold and still with the image of the retreating helicopter in his imagination, the tail-light winking as if in valediction.

He opened his eyes, shook himself, and climbed out of the sleeping-bag.

He appreciated from the tiny rodent noises of the snow against the tent that the weather was holding, glanced at his watch, and then unstrapped the tent-flap. He knelt there, listening with his whole body, head cocked on one side.

Eventually he seemed satisfied, and went out into the air which seemed to grasp at the lungs from within. He stretched, easing the stiffness. The ski-ing of the previous night, after dropping from the helicopter which had come skimming in under the radar net into Finnish Lapland, had taken its toll—not of his strength, but of his youth, it seemed. He was aching in muscles he never considered. He rubbed at the backs of his thighs, easing them under the white camouflage over-trousers.

Then he seemed to decide that further delay was pointless, and there was an urgency about his repacking of the tiny white tent and even in the eating of his rations. He considered coffee, and at once rejected the delay it would involve.

He was a little less than thirty kilometres south-east of Ivalo, the Lapland town at the southern extremity of the sacred Lake Inari. He was well away from the single main highway from Rovaniemi in the south, and from the single airlane between the two towns. A light plane had passed overhead soon after he had been dropped, its lights winking as it made its approach to the airport.

He was in a country desolate with snow, a lunar landscape without real features, even so close to the foothills of the Maanselka, the mountain chain crossing the body of Finnish Lapland. All the previous night he had passed through the ghostly landscape, heading south-east, and this night, too, it would be the same. Winter exercises inside the Arctic Circle had taught him what to expect in terms of terrain—but even then that had been northern Norway, where the slopes of the land were knife-cuts to draw the eye and hold it, where the fjords broke the snow like fingers spread on a white page.

He shook off the sense of deadness. Here, he was less than twenty miles from the Soviet border.

As he pushed off, digging in with the ski-sticks, putting his bulky, laden form in motion, he knew that this first mile might be the last one, just as every mile he had travelled might have been the mile of arriving.

The large-scale map of Finland that Waterford had pinned to the wall of his cramped hotel room in Hereford remained clear in his mind. He could see Waterford clearly, four days previously, pinning up the map, then sweeping his hand down the Soviet-Finnish border. Waterford had stressed that the location could not be precise.

He sensed, suddenly, the isolation, the loneliness. Waterford's room had been as redolent of it as this landscape. The experience was emptying. At the same time, the hours on the long cross-country skis increased his awareness, like some drug. Emptiness almost tangible in the snow-bound tundra, its tips of small trees jutting like the fingers of buried hands. Or the thin pine forest, always threatening to die or vanish—straggling away from him to expire on the distant slopes.

He passed deeper into the night, and the only sounds were the constant wind and the ceaseless and rhythmic hissing of the long skis.

Beneath the Arctic camouflage of his winter combat clothing, he wore the uniform of a lieutenant, his own rank, but a *Yliluutnantti* of the Lapland Rifle Battalion. His uniform was Finnish, the Russian-style fur hat jammed on his fair hair under the camouflage hood. Badges of rank on his combat dress were accurate. Across his shoulders, free of the heavy pack, was lying a 7.62 mm M/62 assault rifle, the Finnish copy of the Russian Kalashnikov; in a hip-holster, a 9 mm Lathi pistol, regulation firearm for Finnish officers. And there were the papers, and their false identity. He was engaged in a cross-country endurance and survival test, part of his final examination before acceptance into the exclusive and semi-secret Finnish Special Force—a body equivalent to Folley's own British SAS.

Eventually, deep in the night, he stopped to rest, his breathing laboured as if to impress him with the body's exertions and the distance he had travelled. He unslung the pack and the rifle in its canvas sleeve, and set up the tiny gas heater. He brewed coffee, hunched in the darkness behind a fold of the land. The burdened trees leaned over the lip of the dell, as if in some fish-eye lens. He felt enclosed by the trees from the flatness and the flowing white curtains of the forest.

He cupped gloved hands round the mug and swallowed the coffee, grateful for the pungent taste. It shocked the palate, unfroze the mind. He could hear Waterford talking in his steely, precise tones, suggestive of a masked or restrained power—even a deep and bitter fury.

He knew something of Waterford's cavalier and even brutal army record, his connections on more than one occasion with the SIS. He allowed himself to laugh, a sound sharp as cracking wood in the silence and cold air, as he recollected the small, childish excitement he had felt as the briefing had begun. He had understood the crude exploitation of information in his CPP (Complete Personality Profile) by the senior man, yet he had been unable to quench the sudden warmth of the belly or control the shallowness of his breathing as the words separated him from others, acknowledged that he was the only suitable selection for the *Snow Falcon* thing.

Ski-training in Scotland, the hours in the gym, the shooting practice with unfamiliar weapons, the hurried Finnish instruction from a professional type—for a long month he had lived with that. And it had all been un-explained until that last meeting in Waterford's room. Then transport by Hercules to the NATO base at Tromsø.

He had tumbled through the door of the Wessex even as snow billowed out and blinded him and the helicopter pulled up and away, banking severely and heading back into Norway.

"*What we want,*" Waterford had said, "*is evidence, and the harder the better. That's why you have the camera. And you are expendable, Folley, and so is the mission in this instance. There'll be as many Snow Falcons as we need to find the answer.*" The hard blue eyes had stared into his at that point. "*This isn't just suspicion, or pissing about trying to resurrect old networks or anti-regime movements in Eastern Europe. This may be now, and tomorrow. So, don't be too easily convinced, and don't miss anything, either. Find out if there's more than rein-deer and a few Lapps in fancy dress in Finnish Lapland these days!*"

As if he heard the voice now, insistent in his ear, he woke himself from the narcosis of his rest and the coffee. He could be close now, and the empty landscape might not be as empty as it seemed. Soon it would be light again, the time of caution. He threw away the dregs of the coffee, and stood up. He had more miles to cover before he pitched camp.

Alexei Kyrilovich Vorontsyev pushed the files away from him, leaned back in his chair rubbing his eyes, and the persistent nightmare flashed against his lids almost in the instant that he closed his eyes. His wife—Natalia Gras-netskaya, mezzo-soprano with the Bolshoi, a rising opera-tic star. He could see her clearly, as if she were in his office on the Frunze Quay, above the book repository. He wanted to remove his long fingers from his eyes, but he did not. She still fascinated him, even after the years of her infidelity. He could not rid himself of the persistent obsession with her, even after her body passed into the possession of others, and she had rendered him, he be-lieved, faintly ridiculous to the wide and privileged circle of their acquaintance.

He pulled his hands away with an effort, and blinked in the harsh strip-lighting. He got up from behind the desk, galvanised by some current of thought, and went to the window. He looked down from the third floor, along the almost deserted Frunze Quay, the cold Moscow evening kept out by the double glazing and central heating.

He was thirty-six. He jiggled the coins in his pocket, a small comfortable sound that seemed to interpose itself between his awareness and his recriminations. He held the rank of Major in the KGB. More than that, he had transferred from the 2nd Chief Directorate five years before, at the age of thirty. A meteoric performance to have become, so early, a member of the Special Investigations Department, to move out of the Centre on Dzerzhinsky Street into these more discreet offices.

A hollow success.

The department was the most exclusive and powerful in the security service. It investigated the Politburo, the armed forces, the KGB itself—if and when necessary.

He had avoided social occasions during the past few weeks. He could not explain why the pressure upon his ego, his self-confidence, had grown so acute and painful during that time. But it had happened. So that he expected his suits, expensive and non-Russian, not to fit him when he put them on in the mornings. There was this physical sense of being *smaller*, diminished. And he could not speak of it to anyone.

Only Mihail Pyotravich might understand—but even he would be without sympathy, would despise him. The lip would curl, and something like a cast or cataract possess the eye. He could not tell his step-father—though undoubtedly the Deputy Foreign Minister already knew the full extent of the estrangement.

His stomach twisted with the knowledge, and the body revolted again against the surge of thoughts and imaginings. He was truly powerless; the woman dominated him, humiliated him, treated him with contempt—lately lived apart from him, paraded her lovers in public; and he was powerless.

Sometimes, he thought he might go mad. It had been as if he could smell other men on her skin when she came home. And, should he taste her skin now, he would taste there other mouths that had explored her, teasing at each secret part of her he had once believed only he possessed.

The thought of her body tormented him—it was an accurate description; tormented. He still wanted her.

23

Impossible.

His own infidelities disgusted him. He was amazed that he still felt he was betraying her and the vows that he had made silently, though the Soviet ceremony did not require them. His mother had claimed that the father he had never known had made such vows. He could not have done otherwise.

He turned from the window. There was silence beyond the door of his office. His secretary would have already left, and perhaps the others on his floor would have abandoned their offices. He turned the files on his desk with his hand, flicked at the spools of tape. He had been transferring recorded reports to cassette prior to storage in his files. And then the assessment of that week's documentation for his superiors. An assessment that would go directly to the Deputy Chairman of the KGB responsible for the SID.

He would leave it until tomorrow. The reports of the agents seemed unpromising. The movements of a Red Army Colonel-General during four days' leave in Moscow seemed of little significance. And the man would be returning to his duties at HQ, Far East Military District the next morning. Deputy Kapustin had laid emphasis on its importance, but it seemed little more than routine.

He yawned, a nervous reaction. He could sense the details slipping from him even as he dwelt on the matter.

He went back briefly to the window. The sodium lamps along the quay were hazy globes of light. An icy fog was beginning on the river. The Moskva slid beneath it, flecked with lights from the Gorki Park on the opposite bank. Beyond its dark patch he could see the straight ranks of the lights along the Lenin Prospekt.

He sighed, bundled the tapes and files into his desk, and locked the drawer. Then he let himself cautiously out of the office, as if he had no honest business there, his body adopting involuntarily a humiliating posture—cowardly. As if it feared laughter in the shadowy corridor.

The Kremlin office of the First Secretary of the Communist Party of the Soviet Union was a large, somehow bare, room. It was screened from the apparatus of government by two outer offices. As he paused at the last door, his hand raised to supply a perfunctory knock—the night security staff had informed the First Secretary of his arrival—Chairman of the Committee for State Security Yuri Andropov could already envisage the room. It bore none of the terrible blankness of the office in the days of Stalin, when the room had a plasticity to its visitors that could make it cathedral or oven, depending on the Leader's mood and the force of the visitor's imagination. Now it was simply a large room, with a huge and ornate desk at the far end. Carpet now silenced the footsteps of those who approached the First Secretary, and there were armchairs, some occasional tables—a visible concession to the decade, and to the character of the man who waited for him.

He opened the door. First Secretary Khamovkhin turned from the huge carved fireplace where a pile of logs burned brightly, and Andropov noticed the drink in his hand. There was Scotch for him, too, in a heavy tumbler on one of the small tables. The two men shook hands warmly, and Khamovkhin gestured Andropov to a chair. He sat down heavily himself, his double-breasted jacket undone, flopping open to reveal the swell of the stomach beneath the striped shirt. Sensing the Chairman's eyes on him, Khamovkhin smiled tiredly, raising his glass and encouraging Andropov to drink.

There was a formality about the occasion inseparable from any meeting between them. As if their minds minced carefully round the obstacles in the room, flicked between the lumber that scattered their responsibilities and their public lives.

Khamovkhin suddenly focused his eyes, and rapped out, "Am I—too suspicious, Yuri?"

Andropov was silent for a long time. If he gave the correct answer at that moment, the matter would recede, no one would be blamed, and the whole business would be forgotten.

"No," he said finally. "That would be the easy way out—for both of us. Would it not?"

Relief, and regret. The First Secretary rubbed his prow of a nose with thumb and forefinger. He stared into his glass, then looked up.

"I suppose not. No easy escapes, eh?" He laughed. The firelight flickered on the steel frames of the Chairman's spectacles; made the lenses two blank moons for a moment. Then Khamovkhin saw the determination of the eyes as the head adjusted slightly.

"We—have to take it seriously, don't we, Feodor? You sign a document in Helsinki in nine days' time whereby the Soviet Union agrees to significantly reduce its nuclear arsenal, strategic and tactical—and cuts the throat of its own conventional forces. We know it, the Politburo has agreed it, and the army is beside itself with anger."

Khamovkhin was puzzled by the tone. His brows drew together, and his eyes became lidded. Andropov thought him an animal retreating into cunning as its enemies surprised it.

"You are a member of the Politburo—you agreed to it."

"Naturally. We have no choice. Two bad harvests in three years, crippled by the defence budget—China determined to supplant us bidding for the favours of the West . . . What else is to be done but follow President Wainwright's line of least opposition?"

"Secretly, you don't like it?"

"Do I have to? It's all right, Feodor, it's not my direction in which you need to look. The army hates the KGB as much as it hates the Politburo."

"We are agreed on that, at least—my friend." He smiled, but almost immediately his face darkened once more. "But—nothing? You still know nothing, with time so short?"

He stood up, and loomed over Andropov suddenly. Then he took their tumblers to the cabinet, filled them, then sat down again. He stared into his drink, into the fire, then into Andropov's eyes.

"We cannot show our hand, Feodor. How many of us are there? Even the whole of the KGB . . . Not sufficient, if we push them to some precipitate move."

"When will they make their move—dammit, *when?* You should *know!*"

"The most appropriate time would seem to be, Feodor, while you are engaged upon your State visit to Finland, when you leave Moscow in three days' time!"

Khamovkhin was stung by the concealed accusation. His hands, bunched on the material of his trousers, worked there for a few moments as if throttling something invisible. Then he forced himself to sit back in his chair, appear relaxed, certain.

"You may be right. I—have to go. Very well, Yuri, I

shall be well out of it, if anything—happens. I admit that. But I am known to be going. I cannot alter my arrangements . . ." He tried to laugh. "It might be considered braver to be skulking in Helsinki than in Moscow!"

"It might. But it is the excuse they may be looking for. The Army High Command . . ." Andropov continued, breaking the moment of false confidence like a stick in his hands ". . . will see it as an opportunity not to be lightly missed. At least, that is my opinion."

"Then find them. Find the leaders—arrest them!"

"And provoke the very thing we wish to avoid? The High Command is edgy—I might almost say *desperate*, about this Helsinki agreement. If it is signed, there will be no going back for us. The army will be melted down—a missile become a shotgun. That is how they see it. And America is waiting to see us go through with what we promise. We're in the cleft stick, Feodor. At least, I will be when you have left for Helsinki."

"Then find them. Find a way of proving who is involved—what exactly they plan to do, and when. Then— *finish them!*"

"Easy to say," was Andropov's reply as he sipped at his whisky. "Easy to say."

Alex Davenhill switched off the engine of the Porsche, and Aubrey was grateful for the silence. The swishing of the rain under the tires, the throatiness of the engine— even the speed at which Davenhill drove—had all conspired during their journey to Hereford to irritate and depress him. He resented inhabiting the sleek, expensive shell of Davenhill's car, just as he resented the cheerful flamboyance of the man's conversation and behavior. He had decided that he felt old tonight—and determined not to be roused from his irritated contempt for his companion.

"Right, Kenneth, shall we go up and see the sinister Major Waterford?"

"I see no other reason for having travelled for two hours in this wingless jet aircraft."

"Don't be so crabby, Kenneth dear." Davenhill laughed, opening the door and climbing out. The noise of the rain loudened, and Aubrey felt cold. Davenhill came round the car and opened his door. Aubrey made an old man's fuss

27

about climbing out of the low, comfortable seat, Daven-hill holding his arm. "Come along, Auntie," he said with a grin.

Aubrey straightened himself, and turned up the collar of his dark coat. Davenhill looked at the façade of the small hotel, across the street from the car park.

"I agree," Aubrey said, as if mind-reading. "Not a very prepossessing place. However, Major Waterford prefers it to SAS HQ just up the road."

"He must have a penchant for the Gothic."

"Bring those papers from the back seat, would you, Alex?" Aubrey replied, scuttling off at a surprising speed to the shelter of the hotel porch. Davenhill took out a briefcase, locked the car, and crossed the splash of wet-lit street after Aubrey.

They climbed the stairs, Aubrey still in the lead. Alex Davenhill, unbuttoning his leather coat, smiled behind him, pleased to feel himself Aubrey's messenger-boy as an alternative to the unnatural stuffiness of most of his professional life as Foreign Office Special Adviser to the SIS.

Aubrey paused before a door that was merely a dull veneered sheet of hardboard, and knocked. Davenhill could see the tic of interest at the corner of his mouth, and composed his own features into an intelligent supe-riority. Aubrey had warned him not to bicker with Water-ford; Davenhill eased his animosity towards the soldier into the back of his mind.

Aubrey heard a muffled voice through the door, and pushed it open. Davenhill followed him through into the cramped room with the hideous wallpaper, purple trum-peting mouths of flowers and wreathed stems on a yel-low ground. The sight of it made him shudder.

Waterford was sitting in an armchair with soiled and frayed loose covers. He did not get up when they entered. Davenhill noticed that the single-bar electric fire was less efficient than the heater in his car.

"Mr. Aubrey—Davenhill." Aubrey took a chair oppo-site the SAS instructor. Alan Waterford was a big man, threatening the chair he sat in with his bulk. Davenhill de-cided once again that it was that fact that was most potent about the man—*threat*. A barely contained violence. His face, even now, was angry with a grimace that occupied mouth, eyes, jaw. The moustache seemed to jut at them,

28

as if they had trespassed. Yet there was interest in the blue eyes, too. Davenhill perched himself on the edge of a rickety cabinet, the briefcase clutched, as if protectively, across his chest.

"What's the news?" He lit a cigarette, seeming indifferent to any reply.

"The Falcon is loose," Aubrey said. Waterford nodded. "No contact as yet."

"Tonight's the night, then."

"Possibly."

Davenhill wondered why they had come. Aubrey seemed tense with doubt.

"Are you *sure?*" he blurted out.

"Of what?" Waterford asked, staring at a patch of damp on the ceiling. "Bugger upstairs has just had a bath," he observed, suddenly glaring at Davenhill. "Sure of what?"

"He'll get back," Aubrey confessed reluctantly.

"No. What's the matter—lost your nerve?"

"Not at all. But—I must know. Things may become—more urgent than I supposed. I need definite proof, not speculation."

"Then Folley will have to dig for it, won't he?"

Davenhill suddenly sensed the underlying mood possessing Aubrey. Almost as if he had seen the man's real age, highlighted by shadows from the standard lamp. Aubrey *was* old, and they had come from London because he felt at a loss—perhaps even felt he was making a complete idiot of himself. And he wanted to blame Waterford.

"I came to you and Pyott in StratAn," Aubrey began with a bluster designed to conceal the lack of confidence Davenhill had perceived, "to interpret infra-red photographs that ended up on my desk. You—both of you— placed a *weighty* interpretation upon them which caused me to act as I have done."

Davenhill could see Waterford's rising anger, and wondered whether Aubrey was aware of it. He felt rather pityingly towards the old man, and disappointed.

"Not forgetting the gentleman you picked up on the road outside Kassel," he said softly. Both men seemed to turn to him immediately, as if resenting his interference. "You can't shuffle off—"

"I am not shuffling!" Aubrey snapped. "I merely wish to confirm our suspicions in this matter. But now I will need proof of some kind—*irrefutable proof*. Both of you must understand that. It may be a case of the Pentagon, and therefore the White House, having to be convinced by hard evidence. There is no cause for alarm, ladies and gentleman. Now—is there, or is there not?"

There was a silence, then Waterford said, "There is— oh, yes, there is cause for alarm. Don't worry, Mr. Aubrey. Folley will find you something to wave under their noses."

It was deep night now, and Folley was having to get up periodically, move about to ease warmth and feeling back into stiff, cold limbs and joints. He had established himself the previous dawn in the shelter of an outcrop just beyond, and overlooking, the village of Rontaluumi, half a mile from the Soviet border. Below him, one narrow road led through the village and away behind him towards Raja-Jooseppi and Ivalo.

He had watched the village for hours—eerie, he thought it, the way there was no movement, nothing down there. When night had come, no lights; in daylight, not a footprint, no sounds even of animals. He had stopped watching hours ago—now he had turned his attention to the border itself. *Check that out, and make sure you're thorough*, Waterford had said. And bugger all more revealing or useful than that! Normal normal normal—the Red Army's gone to bed, he thought, and almost laughed aloud because boredom made easy irreverence amusing and he wanted to hear a noise—other than those drifting from across the border.

In front of him, clear through the Star-tron night-vision glasses, he could see the watch-tower that overlooked the road. There was a fence, high and barbed but seemingly fragile; then, beyond that, the huge electrified fence that marked the Russian side of the border. Across the mere hundreds of yards separating him from the Russian tower he could hear a radio, tuned to some all-night European pop programme. Occasionally, shadows passed across the windows of the hut atop the spindly tower, and the searchlight swept across the snow in a hungry pattern on both sides of the border.

Quick look back at the village. Silent, deserted. In the morning, or before, he would have to go down there, and check it out—*thoroughly*. Not a bit like Goldsmith, he thought—comfortable Gothic. It *was* sinister—better

30

watching the border. Where have all the reindeer gone—and the Lapps? And the chickens and the pigs and dogs?

He was bored. Now, with the USSR once again in his night-glasses, the hard starlight gathered and magnified, he had lost the edge of danger. Nothing but the routine of border guards, the innocuousness of buried mines and the still wire. There was no watch-tower to guard the Finnish fence, only the fence itself pretending that Finland was defensible.

He heard someone cough, and his ears, adjusted to distance, knew that the noise came from the tower. Shadows bulked beyond the swing of light across the snow, but they were unthreatening. He yawned. The inevitability of routine had captured him.

He slid back over the lip of his outcrop, the snow slithering under him, and brewed coffee out of the small wind, out of sight. He sipped, tracing the warmth to his stomach. He began to wonder at the vacuousness of his own thoughts—to smile at the idea that he was being reduced in IQ with every hour he spent in that place. As if his brain were vaporising in the cold air.

When he finally slid back over the lip to take up his position again, it had already begun.

He picked up the night-vision glasses, focusing anew for something to do, and saw that the searchlight had ceased to slide across the snow. And the watch-tower was darkened, and silent. It was as if the glasses were not working. He could see nothing. He swept across the space of snow, ghostly now, for some sign of movement, a light.

Then he saw them. Tanks. He experienced a moment of total disbelief; then a moment of pure terror. Tanks. Even as everything in him rejected the information of the eye, he went through a trained process of identification—T-72 tanks, front-line, latest model. He identified them by the 115 mm cannon, the six road wheels, the turret similarity to the older T-62.

Coming through the border wires that were no longer there—across a minefield he knew had to be there. He could not understand it; cold had invaded the brain, clogging it like thick oil.

Tanks, in single file down the one narrow road, were crossing the border into neutral Finland. He refused to believe it. He began to count them, his mind fumbling over instructions, cold fingers turning the huge, clumsy pages of some manual. He was shivering. The village below had been *emptied*—in preparation for this.

He could not use the transmitter, not now. He had to reduce himself to the role of spectator. The first of the tanks rolled beneath him, and he had somehow got the camera sighted, with its infra-red attachment like the barrel of a weapon. He began to photograph, the film winding on automatically, silently. He held his breath.

He watched the tanks pass away through Rontaluumi, and he knew the lights would not come on, doors would not open to the sound of engines, and the strange squeaking of the tracks on the iron-hard snow.

No lights; the tiny hamlet was deserted. It added to the quality of nightmare the scene possessed.

He counted a regiment of tanks, and after the first few he did not bother to reload the camera. A regiment. Then what was obviously a motor rifle battalion, a support for the armoured column. In Finland.

His thoughts circled the inadmissible. *Invasion*.

And then perhaps, after an hour, two hours—he had not looked at his watch once, and did not do so now—the road was empty again. He saw the lights go on again in the tower, and the searchlight take up its pacing gleam. The wire on the Soviet side was closing, a great hinged section of gate which crossed the road—the Finnish fence was magically already reconstituted.

It was a massive effort to stand up, to move strange limbs as if under water, to strike camp. He went through the routine with leaden hands in thick gloves, fumbling over the tasks.

He had to follow. He had to find the destination. The column had passed out of sight and sound into the fir forest beyond the hamlet, still following the single narrow road. He had to follow.

He kept returning to one idea—it wasn't like an invasion. It was orderly, swift, silent—but it was . . . *transport*. Yes, that was it. He had been watching troop movements, and only he knew they were Red Army, and the terrain they crossed was that of Finland.

Otherwise it was normal. One hundred and twenty tanks, BMP combat vehicles, mortars—and the silent troops in winter combat clothing, riding the tanks and the transports. It was no attack formation, no indication of a front along which the column was advancing, deploying. A movement between two circled points on a map, along the single possible road. No one would attack Finland with a single regiment of tanks and one support battalion.

He pulled the pack to comfort on his back, felt the balance of the long skis strapped to his body, and then moved off cautiously. He picked out his trail with great care, down the slope of the outcrop. He had to follow the road, to overtake the armoured column; to discover its purpose.

TWO

EVIDENCE OF CIRCUMSTANCES

It was a cold, bitter morning in Moscow, the Moskva like a sheet of opaque, slaty glass under a sky threatening more snow. Only the previous day had the Frunze Quay been cleared of the last snowfall. Vorontsyev had again taken up what threatened to become an habitual position at the window of his office. His back was to the two other men in the room as he listened to a tape-recording from the hotel suite of Colonel-General Ossipov, obtained by a bug and recorded in an adjoining room. The two SID officers with him were responsible for the recording. Ossipov had demanded, as was his right as commandant of a Military District, a suite free from bugs; only the SID was permitted to override such a demand.

There was something actively unpleasant, depressing, in listening to Ossipov's old-fashioned seduction of a high-class call-girl. It was out of place, and clashed with the vigour, and vulgarity, of his engagement in the physical act.

Vorontsyev did not turn round as the girl, well coached, achieved her climax in a way most calculated to flatter the ageing General; he did not want to meet the eyes of the two young men, to know what they thought of the animal noises from the tape.

Glasses clinked, after a long silence which seemed still impregnated with sexual release—Vorontsyev could almost smell the semen; the girl had miscalculated, the General had suffered a premature ejaculation . . . Vorontsyev formed the pseudo-medical description of the old man's failure with a feline pleasure. The girl had been apologetic, the General gentlemanly in his reply. The scene, it appeared, had drawn to a satisfactory conclusion.

"That was two nights ago," Vorontsyev said. "Is there any more of it?"

"You don't think the General . . .?" The words cut off. One man had nudged the other, more sensitive to Vorontsyev's mood. "No—he is alone for the rest of the night, and sleeps quite well."

"OK." Vorontsyev turned as he heard the tape switched off. "Let's have a look at the pictures."

Maxim, the younger of the two junior officers, switched off the light and drew down the blind. Pyotr, his partner, operated the small projector on Vorontsyev's desk, and a monochrome image of the Colonel-General appeared on the screen against one wall of the office, walking down the corridor of an hotel with a girl. Vorontsyev stared hard at the girl, then the slide-cartridge clicked. Entering the general's suite, then later, the girl coming out again.

"We took film through the two-way," Pyotr offered. Vorontsyev shook his head.

"Offer it to Tretchikhin diwnstairs. He collects that sort of thing since his wife left him." He winced, as if his tongue had returned to an abscessed tooth. He attempted to smile, and added, "Send in the duty-team from yesterday—let's see if they have anything slightly more out of the ordinary."

"I would have thought this was pretty . . ." Maxim began, but Pyotr dug him in the ribs with his elbow. They took with them the cartridge of slides and the recorder.

Vorontsyev knew the girl. She was often used for the amusement of high-ranking officials or officers like Ossipov. Strict medical and security checks—one of a small, exclusive coterie of professional tarts, unlike the enthusiastic amateurs such as Natalia Grasnetskava.

The second duty-team was also young—Ilya and Alevtina; he called all his juniors by their first names. He had begun to suspect that his tone had changed, become slightly ingratiating, not preserving the distinction in rank.

"Well?" he snapped, at the young man and the girl, recent transfers and still much in awe of their new power. "What have you two to report?"

Ilya ostentatiously consulted a black notebook. "Do you want the lot, Major—or just the edited highlights?"

"*Thoroughly,* whatever you do." He turned again to the window.

"The general passed the morning at the Pushkin Museum of Fine Arts," Ilya summarised. "As you know, Major, he has a personal collection of ivory and jade statuettes—he spent a lot of time inspecting the Egyptian collection this time . . ." Vorontsyev nodded. "He visited the Hermitage collection in Leningrad many times, before he was transferred to Far East District . . ."

"Yes. Go on."

"He was alone throughout this time. Before lunch, he took a taxi to the Alexandrovski Gardens—he walked there, in the sunshine, until he lunched at the Metropole in Sverdlov Square. We . . . have an expenses claim . . ." he finished lamely.

"For *both* of you? Was that necessary?"

"Just for—one . . ."

Vorontsyev knew they were lying, but it did not matter. They would learn that expenses were come by the hard way, or not at all.

"And the afternoon?" he asked.

"The Tretyakov Gallery—all afternoon." The young man sounded bored.

"You must learn, Ilya, that not everyone is as much a Philistine as you are. I'm sure the tour of the gallery was good for you."

"Yes, Major."

Alevtina said, "Sir—is all this getting us anywhere?"

Vorontsyev thought for a moment. He was not on the point of describing his conversation with the Deputy Chairman late the previous night. He said simply:

"It all may be of the utmost importance. Always understand that, both of you. We don't get called in unless it's already a serious matter." He looked at them both in turn, until they signalled their understanding. "Very well. Let's see the films."

He twitched down the blind, shutting out the leaden *view* from the window. His interview with the Deputy had been urgent and short. He *had* to find something—apparently, there was something very nasty to find, and he had to find it—no, he could not be told what it was he was looking for—and he knew then that they did not know; but it *did* exist, and Ossipov was a possible suspect. So were the other officers they had been watching on their periodic leaves in the city. Men from every military district, none of them below the rank of regimental Colonel.

The light dimmed, and the cartridge case clicked. Pictures of Ossipov in swift succession passed across the screen. Bending to look at an oriental statue, the collector's greed clear on his smooth, heavy features. In the gallery, face lit by the glow from illumination above a huge canvas by Repin—then bending to an ikon, almost in worship.

Then the Gardens, the features pinched by the cold, bathed in the pale sunshine; his back to the camera as he paused to speak to a woman, to raise his dark hat . . .

Vorontsyev looked at Ilya, who shook his head. He waved his hand, and the monochrome procession continued. Even entering the male toilets at the Metropole, after lunch.

"You checked?"

"He left nothing but his urine," Ilya replied softly. "Do you want to see the rest, sir?"

"Not if they're all like this."

The beam of light died, and Vorontsyev tugged up the blind. Ilya turned to face him.

"What official functions has he attended in the last four days?"

"None, sir. He's on leave."

"What about the officers' clubs, that sort of thing?"

"We could only get in there officially—you didn't want that."

"No, not yet."

"Sir?"

"Yes?"

"This operation, sir?"

"Yes, Ilya?"

"Is it—look, sir, are we looking for evidence to get rid of him, or is there really some *specific* thing we have to discover?"

Vorontsyev glowered, then smiled and nodded.

"Very well. As far as I can see, it isn't just for the sake of it. Not one of those operations. He hasn't offended. No, it's for real. Something is going on, and it's probable

37

centre is the army, and high up. We're supposed to find something—a clue might be enough, a few names. At the moment, we don't know who or what. Clear?"

Both seemed relieved, as if they preserved some vestige of private conscience which had to be appeased.

Ilya said, "Thanks, sir." Alevtina merely nodded her agreement.

"Good. But it would be useful to find out who he met, talked to, in the clubs. You got a list?"

Alevtina handed him a sheet of paper on which was scribbled in the hand of the KGB man who doubled as a waiter at the principal Moscow officers' club, the names of the men to whom Ossipov had spoken. For SID—even when the officer was an attractive young woman rather than a bully-boy—for the blue ID card, he would have watched, and noted, without question. Vorontsyev glanced down the list. One or two generals, old acquaintances being watched by other units of the SID, one or two juniors now or previously under his command.

"Vrubel? KGB Border Guard—Finland border. Is that odd, or not?"

"Vrubel. We wondered that, sir. We checked. His father was an officer with General Ossipov during the war—killed near Berlin, in the last days." The girl was concentrating on the conscientiousness of her tone. Vorontsyev thought she might not yet have lost her sense of herself as a woman in a male-dominated élite. To him, she was one of his junior officers.

"I see. Does Vrubel frequent army clubs very much?"

"Don't know, sir. I think he came by invitation this time—the General's invitation."

"Mm. Leave it for the time being. What other contacts, of any kind?"

"A cousin, sir. Vladimir Ossipov, an official in the Foreign Ministry. Not very important. He called on him and his family, just before we came off duty yesterday. He's a fanatical Party member, is Vladimir."

"Very well. Let us go back to the day before—and go through this process again. Just for a change, show me the pictures first."

Once more the blind was dropped, and the slides flicked on the screen. He felt no irritation at the lack of substance emerging from the surveillance, and little responsibility other than that of the automaton, checking and double-checking. The routine soothed, refreshed. Even in the SID there was the humming of obedient, unthinking machinery.

"Who's that?" he asked. The background was the Museum of the Revolution on Gorki Street. Ossipov was engaged in conversation with a man in a dark overcoat and hat.

The slides flicked on, the projector humming slightly with warmth. More pictures of the two old men, still in conversation.

"No one special. Ilya was able to listen. It was about politics."

"Politics?"

"Nothing controversial. In praise of Soviet achievements—especially the Revolution itself, and the war." The girl, too, seemed bored, answering for Ilya.

"Is that it?"

"Yes, sir."

"Very well—go on."

More slides—out of doors. Snow, caught on the shoulders of the General's dark overcoat, and curtaining the clarity of the picture. Vorontsyev squinted.

"What is this?"

"After he left the museum—it's Pushkin Square. I took one here because he waited a bit, as if to meet someone. . . ."

"And?"

"Nothing. Caught a taxi—and we took another, to follow him."

"Where?"

"Hotel—a couple of drinks."

The scenes flicked, as if accompanying the narrative. Back of the man, then the taxi, back of the man outside the Moskva Hotel, entering the foyer . . .

"You followed him in?"

"Yes. He stayed in the bar, then went to the toilet, then caught another taxi . . ." Both of them were bored, it was evident now. Brushing aside a minor irritation, Vorontsyev watched the screen. Back of the man, entering a taxi.

"Where next?"

"The cinema. On the Marx Prospekt. Some epic extolling the usual virtues, school of Eisenstein. Wartime stuff, I think. I almost went to sleep."

"But you watched him throughout?"

"Yes. He went to the toilet again—must have a bladder problem, or it was the cold—then took his seat, sat alone for two hours, came out, oh—went to the toilet again, then caught a taxi back to the Moskva for a light meal . . ."

Slides. Back of the man entering the cinema, grainy with snow, head bowed, hat held on head. Back of the man coming out of the cinema. Other people.

"Back!"

"What?"

"Back! The shot of him going in—then this shot again."

"Sir."

Vorontsyev watched, felt the tension close on his bowels, then ungrip again as he sensed an error. The two young officers had hardly risen from their languor, except that the girl whispered the time to Ilya.

"No—" Vorontsyev whispered. "No."

"Shall I go on, sir?"

"Yes. How close were you when he went into the cinema?"

"A bit back. Not many customers at that time."

"And he went into the toilet?"

"Yes, sir."

"You're sure? On the way *in?*"

Alevtina consulted her notes. "On the way out . . ."

"You said on the way *in!*"

"I—no, only on the way out."

"Quickly, go back to the Moskva—to the shot of him leaving the hotel, getting in the taxi. Quickly!"

Ilya fumbled with the cartridge; stuttering clicks, then the smoother sound as images flashed on the screen in quick succession.

Back of the man entering the taxi. It was inconclusive, Vorontsyev recognised, as if he had hoped for something clearer. Yet he sensed how it might have been done.

"What is it, sir?" Alevtina asked, craning forward in her chair, staring at the flecked expanse of overcoat. Snow, the flurried curtain.

"Where were you when he came out of the toilet—the hotel toilet?" Vorontsyev snapped.

"Recess in the foyer."

"At the bar," added Ilya.

"Where did he put on his coat?" Vorontsyev enunciated the words slowly, carefully. They sensed the importance of their answer. They screwed up their faces helpfully.

"In—the bar," Ilya said finally.

The girl added eagerly, "He was wearing it as he crossed the foyer."

"And you were *behind* him all the time, from the moment he left the toilet until he got into the taxi?"

"Yes." Her voice held an apprehension of failure, but puzzlement was more evident.

"Then that's it!"

"What is?"

"What's the next slide?" Vorontsyev calmed himself, afraid of his leap of insight, the certainty of suspicion. *"Before* this one, I mean."

"Entering the hotel—there." The cartridge clicked like the bolt of a rifle, Vorontsyev thought, his imagination gleaming with effort.

"Back again . . . back again . . . back again. See it?" The two slides were swiftly interposed—back of the man, entering in a comic juxtaposition. In and out of the revolving doors of the foyer of the Moskva Hotel. A television trick, Alevtina reminded herself, stifling a smile.

"What—sir?"

Vorontsyev, an impatient parent, yet happy in his own secure knowledge, crossed to the wall, and his finger jabbed, mottled monochrome, at the back of the dark overcoat.

"See the tilt of the shoulders here?" The hand wiggled impatiently, and another back appeared, leaving the foyer. "Now here . . . If you enlarged the hand . . ." He squinted at the hand holding the dark hat down on the head—the snowflakes were huge, like irritating butterflies on a specimen slide, obscuring some scientific data. "If you enlarge the hand, I've no doubt you will find a different one—fatter, shorter fingers, or shorter nails."

He turned to them, grinned, and dramatically crossed to the window and let up the blind. Strong morning light now, not so grey.

"It's not the same man. The man you sat behind in the cinema was *not* the Colonel-General! You spent two

41

hours following the wrong man." In the pleasure of confirmation, Vorontsyev was uncondemning. "So—why and where did the General go?"

"How did they switch back, sir?"

"The cinema toilet. I'll bet you were given a good look at the face, coming out of the cinema . . ." Alevtina's face betrayed a childish sense of being made to appear stupid by an adult. "Of course. Now, go back to the man in the Museum of the Revolution—the one with the dark coat and hat, about the General's age. And place your bets, my children—place your bets!"

Folley fumbled a new film into the camera, the cold stiffening, thickening his fingers in the few seconds since he had removed his mittens. Already he had six rolls of film—infra-red the first two, then a change when dawn came—in his pockets, but he seemed possessed now to record everything he could. He was overwhelmed by the evidence, and by a disbelief that made him collect every scrap of it he could; perhaps he already heard Waterford's mocking tones, or those of the superior, affected queer, Davenhill.

He closed the back of the camera, raised it to his eye, focused, checked the exposure, and pressed the stud. The camera began to photograph, silently and automatically, a group of soldiers erecting a camouflage net beneath which rested, somnolently evil, three T-72 tanks, the gun of each seeming to point straight at him.

He had been there for three hours, and he knew he should have left long before. Whatever luck there was had to be disappearing rapidly. Twice already, patrols had almost stumbled upon him as he skirted the fringes of the camp beneath the forest roof, pointing his camera like a gawping eye wherever he could—a child in a huge military exhibition.

All the time, he felt an irrepressible urgency to continue taking photographs—snap, snap, snap, move on, snap, snap, move on—he wondered whether he was acting out some caricatured parade-ground behaviour in order to avoid considering the reality of what he photographed.

Snap, snap, snap—tanks, two guards lighting cigarettes, erection of an HQ hut; snap, snap, snap, move on—a man peeing behind a tree, lifting the skirts of his winter overcoat, head with its fur hat bent in solemn inspection, motor rifle transports; change lens to telephoto; snap, snap, snap—smoky distance brought nearer, the ranks of T-72s stretching away, giving a sense of the size of the area they occupied; he sensed he was even beginning to compose the shots.

Voices. He stumbled backwards, ducking behind a tree, straining to catch their direction, number. Three, four? Coming closer, moving from the left, calling so they were spread slightly apart, having to raise their voices. He felt nothing, nothing more than alertness to every tiny noise of movement, below the clear voices. He dropped the camera into a deep pocket of his combat clothing, the long lens hard against his thigh, and brought the rifle slowly round to a position where he could fire it through the canvas sleeve. He flexed the cold index finger.

Four of them. Sweep patrol, round the perimeter. One of a number of teams, perhaps as many as six. Coming with the dangerous morning. Twenty yards—he caught a flash of whiter whiteness, less smoky than the vague distances of snow-heavy trees. A guard, rifle held slackly but ready for use, wending through the tight-standing pines.

Another, away to his right. They would pass just beyond him, if he slipped round the tree, just a little . . .

Footprints. Deep holes in the thick snow. His footprints, coming to the tree, from the direction towards which they were moving. He couldn't hide them. He eased the rifle level with his waist, reached for the barrel with his left hand.

Something in one of the photographs—quickly, quickly, he urged his cold brain. A stream of urine, smoking in the freezing air . . .

He turned his back to the approaching men, fumbling in his over-trousers, bending his head, visualizing the picture he had taken. He tried to urinate, concentrating, wanting to giggle with nerves and the urge to verisimilitude. The feeble stream splashed against the tree, washing the snow down the trunk.

"Don't let it hang out for too long, son," the nearest man called. "You might need it again!" Someone else laughed. He laughed too, and the sound was ridiculously thin and pretended to his ears.

"Thanks for the advice," he called back in Russian, and stood there, all awareness now in his back, the great stretch of white between his shoulders—target.

Then he let himself look round. He had long finished urinating, and he was freezing cold, the iciness spreading through his loins, his thighs. The nearest man who had passed ten feet from him, was moving away again, into the trees. He heard him laughing, calling out some obscenity—not back in his direction, but to one of the others. A laugh like an animal's bark returned from someone hidden further in the trees.

Folley adjusted the rifle, slipped on the mittens, looked around him carefully. He had to go now, get out quickly before the next sweep-unit came upon him, following the last one round the perimeter in an anti-clockwise direction. He moved away from the tree, treading carefully, placing his feet in the deep snow as if he might have to move quickly, would need extra purchase, at any moment.

There was one thing left to do—check the village, Rontaluumi. He wanted photographic evidence that it was empty.

Away from the camp, near the road they had turned off to hide in the forest, he buckled on his skis. As he bent to do so, the reaction hit him, and it was a long time before he could even stand upright on limbs suddenly watery and without strength.

Eventually, he was able to move off; gradually, pushing deeper with the ski sticks, he gathered strength and speed on the long skis, and headed for the village.

Alexei Vorontsyev felt tired, but satisfied. Replete, he considered, as if after a heavy meal and good liquor. The day's work had proved eminently satisfactory. Blowups of the slides proved that Colonel-General Ossipov had gone missing for more than two hours, without trace, and that a man he had met in the Museum of the Revolution had substituted for him. Vorontsyev still retained in his mind gigantic images of two hands, both curled to clutch the brim of a dark hat, pinned side by side on the wall of his office. As a photographic expert had confirmed for him—the hands were not the same. And the *wrong* hand belonged to the man in the museum.

Vorontsyev had informed Deputy Kapustin, who had commended his work. Other units of the SID, also assigned to the matter, had not proved so successful, checking back over their files. But, with his lead, they

44

would recheck, and Kapustin was certain something of real significance would emerge.

Vorontsyev put the car into gear, and pulled away from the traffic lights before turning into Kalenin Street, where he had shared an apartment with his wife. One side of the wide street still contained the old houses, many of them turned into government offices. However, new luxury blocks of apartments had been built, unadorned slabs and façades of grey concrete, without aesthetic value yet possessing a degree of social elevation that attached to few new developments in Moscow.

It was only as he tugged on the handbrake, as if the noise of ratchets awakened him, that he realised he had returned from old habit to a place where he no longer lived. There was a sharp, nauseous taste in his mouth. He had moved out months before, when the strain of living with Natalia's infidelities, all the time becoming more and more blatant, had proved too much for him. Because in the end she had not even bothered to lie. He closed the door of the car again, his mood evaporated.

His work appeared unsubstantial now, and the voice of the Deputy in his memory was tinny and unreal. All that he saw was the hard, assured face, carefully made-up, of his wife, smiling at him. And the crown of dark, groomed hair he had once possessed with the rest of her. He opened the door again, and got out into the noise of traffic travelling out of the centre of Moscow, towards the north-western suburbs; he had parked the car, unthinking, where he always parked it, opposite the foyer door to the apartment block.

He leaned against the car for a time, and lit a cigarette. He did not bother with his overcoat, despite the cold wind, and his hands shook as he cupped them round the flame of the lighter. When he drew in the first smoke, he leaned back and looked up towards the lighted windows. Fourth floor, fifth along—yes, she was there.

The mood of the day crept back into him—the power he had exercised in setting in motion the investigations he had ordered was too impregnated in his personality, like a scent in his clothing or his skin, to be got rid of by the betrayal of memory. He could still see the hands pinned to the wall, betraying the substitution of Ossipov by someone as yet unknown—but who had been photographed, and who would be found. The power of achieving secret

45

knowledge of Ossipov made him bold now. He had a desire to confront his wife—and anyone else who might be there.

It was as if he were drinking from a flask, standing there in the cold, and his head had begun to spin, and he had deadened the defeated ego—recovered himself. When he finished the cigarette, he walked towards the foyer door.

There was a porter he did not recognise, a new man. To him he showed the blue ID card, which obviated explanation. The man was likely to be an informer to one of the departments inside the 2nd Chief Directorate, anyway. The man, impressed, seemed to shrink back into the uniform he wore, saluted, and disappeared back behind the glass partition that separated him from the residents. Vorontsyev crossed to the lift.

He rode to the fourth floor, stepped out, and walked slowly down the carpeted corridor. His principal fear at that moment was being seen by a neighbour who knew him and his circumstances.

He stood in front of the door, despising his weakness, and the involuntary wiping of his hands on his coat. Then he took out his key, which he had not returned to her, and inserted it in the latch. She had not bothered to have the lock changed.

His teeth gritted, and he pushed open the door, into the tiny hall. At the door of the lounge, which overlooked Kalenin Street, he could hear her voice inside—the laughter so like music, but false, as opera falsifies words into beautiful sounds. She had made her laughter attractive, enjoyable—but nothing more than a sound.

He pushed open the lounge door. There was a man in the room. Her head turned to him as he was taking in the KGB Border Guard uniform, the distinctive shoulder flashes. It was, he thought, vulgarly like his wife that she would want her uniformed lovers to wear their uniforms. The man appeared disconcerted. But not his wife. She was merely angry.

She said, "Alexei—what the hell are you doing here?" Then she puffed dramatically at her cigarette, blowing the smoke audibly in his direction. He stood at the door. The KGB officer appeared distressed now—something officer-like and stupid had entered his face, Vorontsyev noticed, disliking the man. Natalia said, "Alexei—allow me to introduce Captain Yevgeni Vrubel, on leave from

46

border duties. Yevgeni, this is my husband, Alexei." Natalia, Vorontsyev noticed in the moment before the name struck him fully, seemed suddenly amused by the confrontation.

The brief daylight was giving out again, and yet Folley remained in the empty village of Rontaluumi. In some inexplicable way, he had wasted the few hours of daylight, acting as if he was unable to deal with the tanks that had crossed the border during darkness, with the camp he had photographed, preferring the smaller mystery. What had been done with the villagers?

He had searched every house, every store and shed. Nothing, not so much as a cat or dog, no sign of life anywhere. It was as if some plague had swept through there, and the bodies had been afterwards removed. Empty rooms, empty chicken-runs—fodder untasted, tins still in the cupboards and on the shelves. As the hours passed he became desperate to find some clue, as loneliness more suffocating than that of his journey overcame him.

Finally, he settled himself in a battered armchair in the living-room of the largest wooden, single-storey house. He kept his white winter combat dress on, and cradled the gun on his lap. He was tense and worn with waiting and searching. He had sufficient evidence—yet he wanted more, an answer to this empty village and its pressing silence.

The whole idea of invasion had become ridiculous—forced to the back of his mind by the emptiness the village emitted like a gas. The implications of what he had seen were buried—he refused to consider any of them.

Empty.

This room—he had the sense of invading other lives, but no sense of the lives that had been lived there—and himself; he could catch sight of himself in a smoky mirror over the huge fireplace. Out of place; rudely forced upon this place, squatter or looter. He had touched nothing, acutely aware of his intrusion. What had happened to the people of Rontaluumi? There wasn't a single sign of violence.

Then he must have dozed—a false light sleep.

He woke to the sound of voices outside, the calling of orders; a tone of voice that reached down into him, pulling him awake. He was out of the chair in a moment, the taste of sleep still sticky in his mouth. He dribbled, wiped it away, blinking his eyes, straining to hear . . .

As he moved to the door, the door opened. He had forced the back door, next to the log store, but the man outside was using a heavy key to turn the lock.

The heavy door swung open.

A figure, in winter combat dress, hood thrown back to reveal the Russian fur cap on the dark hair. A face twisting with surprise, and the hand moving to the holster.

Folley shot the Red Army officer twice, the rifle still at his hip, the sudden noise of the gun bellowing in the low-ceilinged room, echoing back. The doorway was empty, wiped clean of the man's form as it fell into the snow outside.

For a single moment his body was frozen, the aftermath of unpremeditated violence. A boot stuck across the doorway, belonging to the dead man—the echoes of the two shots from the rifle dying away. Then he gathered up his pack, slung it over one shoulder, adjusting it on his back as he forced himself through the narrow door to the kitchen; he collected the skis from their propped position against the back door and opened it silently.

Behind him there was a cry, orders barked in distant voices like the call of foxes. He stepped out into the darkening evening, alert for movement.

Beyond the initial rise, the ground sloped away from the back of the house, towards a narrow frozen river, and dense firs already looming and dark as the light faded rapidly. He clambered up the slope, then stopped to buckle on the heavy, long skis, then pushed off. Behind him, as the wind of his passage began to louden, he heard a shout, then the explosion of a gun. Something whined past his head, then again—a sharp, unreal cracking noise, as if he had crossed thin ice. Then he was shielded by the rise.

He jumped into a stop that spurted snow away from him—efficiently braking at the foot of the long slope. There were trees now between him and the pursuit, and the sheet of the river just below him, the banks heavy with icy grass. He unbuckled the skis, stepped away from them, hoisted them across his shoulder. He slithered down the bank, almost losing his footing as his boots met the smoother ice of the river. He trod carefully, moving lightly and surely, the darkness comfortingly drawn around him,

48

his passage silent. There was more shooting, then silence; he knew they would pursue him now.

He guessed that the armoured column had sent back some kind of patrol, for a reason that remained obscure. He could only think that they were to hold the village as some kind of crossing-point, that other columns were expected that night. And perhaps they had been intended to look for him. Ski-tracks, leading away from the camp—

He spent no time, even as he clambered up the opposite slope, in considering his own death. They would not let him live, he believed; but the priority of his survival had become uppermost now. He had to make some report, present some evidence of what he had seen. He could not, except in extreme emergency, use the transmitter now. That had been impressed upon him. Violation of Finnish neutrality.

As he settled on the far bank, hunched into the hard snow at its edge, the rifle with its night-sight aimed across the already glimmering sheet of ice, his lips twisted in a smile. Waterford and Davenhill, and whoever was behind them—they would know something had gone wrong by his inability to report or return. But not the size of it!

A white-clothed figure, ghostly, appeared at the other side of the river. He fired. The figure dropped away, merging with the snow. In the wake of the single shot, he heard a moan, carrying distinctly across the space between them. Another figure ducked back behind a thin tree-trunk. He fired twice, could see through the sight the white chips appear on the trunk. He fired twice more, grazing the bole of another tree. Nothing moved.

But he had the pictures now, the rolls of film and his mental count. One hundred and twenty tanks. A motor rifle battalion in support. In Finland. Enormity of simple statistics. And his impression of the column merely at a transit camp for the moment. It had to be reported.

In a day's time, the helicopter would return to the dropping point, but would not wait for him. It would return only once more, the following night. Then he would be presumed dead, effectively out of the *Snow Falcon* operation.

He wondered whether Waterford had known what he had found, already. Known that it was Russian armour. He had proof the Russians were invading Finland.

49

He had *proof*. He fired again, and a man staggered back behind the trunk that had concealed him. Wounded, but nothing more than that. He fired again, twice, a warning pattern. Then he slid backwards, towards the skis. The lip of the bank hid him from them as he fitted the cross-country skis, and pushed away silently, the skis slithering on the firm snow, the wind beginning to sing in his ears as he gathered speed.

For a moment, he felt a sagging of his knees, a heaviness against his back, as if he had carried the pack for long hours without rest. Then he dug in with the sticks, beginning to stride as the land levelled and he wound through the denser fir trees, gliding like a ghost. He shook off the weariness and the image. He was vulnerable. Already, they would have crossed the river; and they would have called up reinforcements. He was the tail of the comet streaming away from them, but pulling their mass surely behind him. And leaving a clean, new set of tracks for them to follow.

He struck south-west, in an opposite arm of the forest to that which followed the road to Ivalo; he followed the course of the river, its southern tributary, keeping well within the firs. When the trees died as the land rose again, he would strike westwards, towards the main north-south highway. He tried to comfort himself, as the body laboured and the legs tired, with the thought that the deeper into Finland he moved, the safer he became.

It was a difficult consolation.

Natalia had disappeared into her bedroom, complaining of boredom and a headache. The small clock on the wall-shelf showed the time to be almost seven-thirty. Vrubel's dark, handsome face appeared to Vorontsyev to be puckering with irritation—yet there was a frown of nervousness created by the knowledge of Vorontsyev's rank and department. Vorontsyev had savoured the young man's discomfiture, his apprehension—not as something professional, but as a diet on which his sexual jealousy could feed. He believed that the KGB Border Guard officer had slept with his wife, and he used his professional weight to disturb him.

Vorontsyev smoked an American cigarette—ostentatiously, he had offered one to the uniformed Vrubel. He had refused, smoking instead a Russian cigarette in its

50

cardboard holder. The cheap, dark tobacco was pungent in the room.

"Why did you meet Colonel-General Ossipov at the officers' club, Captain?" A professional tone of voice, the interrogatory flatness, the absence of the man's name, as if he were already a cipher.

"Why? Because he invited me to, Major. He was a comrade in arms of my father—at Stalingrad. He has always —favoured me with his friendship, ever since my father was killed." Vorontsyev noticed the cold tone, which was without fear. He was talking to someone who belonged to a special class, an élite; the clique that the army had always inspired. Yet he was struck by the likeness of their separate biographies—he, in Mihail Pyotravich, possessed a guardian, an influential substitute parent, as this young man did, apparently, in Ossipov.

He dismissed the thought. He did not wish to identify with Vrubel in any way.

"What did you talk about?"

"Old times—the future. The things *friends* talk about." Vrubel was smiling again, unafraid. Once again, Vorontsyev was struck by the assurance Vrubel displayed. It was unexpected, despite his rank in the KGB. SID officers were not met with confidence, with secret amusement.

He said, "I understand what you mean by friends, Captain." Vrubel's left eyelid twitched, as if a secret nerve had been struck. Vorontsyev became irritated by the smile on the other man's lips. Sexual dominance, which he had enjoyed over Natalia and her lover for the past hour was vanishing, evanescent as steam. He was being laughed at again.

"Of course, Major." The tone was patronising.

"You met the General again?" he asked.

Vrubel shook his head. "Our tastes do not coincide, Major. The General likes museums, art, sculpture. I prefer . . ." He spread his open hands on his knees, smiling. "Other pleasures," he added.

Vorontsyev became cold. He saw the man's intact ego, the sexual arrogance—and something more. Secrecy, the enjoyment of unimparted knowledge. He saw how the balance of their relationship had swung like a pendulum, in minutes. He used his insight.

"I see," he said, looking down. "You—where did you meet my wife?"

"We were introduced by—another friend of mine. A mutual friend."

The amusement was evident.

"Who was that?"

"A member of the Bolshoi—a dancer."

Vrubel was not lying—it was obvious that he was enjoying presenting himself as the stallion of the Bolshoi, and Natalia as a cheap tart.

"I see." He looked up, snapping: "When do you return to your duties, Captain?"

"Alas, tomorrow." He stubbed out his cigarette, and looked markedly at his watch. Vorontsyev saw the confidence ooze, the skin of the face now smooth again, the look untroubled. "I have tickets for a show—at eight," he said pointedly.

Vorontsyev squeezed anger into his face.

"I see." He stood up, robotically. "I shouldn't waste your valuable time, then! I'll leave you." He bunched his hands. Vrubel was unmoved. "Tell my wife I'm sorry I interrupted you, won't you."

"I will."

Vorontsyev sat in the car, trying to recapture the professional mask that had slipped from his face in the lift; a moment of pure rage had smothered his coldness. Now, he regained something like composure. He picked up the microphone under the dashboard.

"Centre—go ahead Moscow Unit Nine-Six-Four," he heard in reply to his call sign.

"Put me through to my office—night duty-staff."

He waited, then he heard Ilya's tired voice.

"Yes, Major." There was no amusement, only a peeved deference, and frustrated boredom. A broken date, probably.

"Don't sulk!" he snapped. Then he hesitated. "I—I'm at my wife's apartment, on Kalenin Street."

"Yes, Major?"

"A—Captain Vrubel is being entertained there . . ." The words came out, dragged up, each with its separate soft explosion of breath. His chest seemed to hurt with exertion. "I want a tail on them—on the *man*, understand?"

"Yes, Major—isn't he the—?"

"He is. I want a team out here, and another car for myself. My wife knows this one."

"You're going to tail them yourself, Major?"

"Yes. Anything in the rules against it?"

"No—sir."

"Right, then! Anything on that *bastard* in black, yet?" He let the accumulated venom into the question, as if expelling saliva that had filled his throat. He spat at Vrubel in the emphasis of the words.

"Nothing, sir. The computer doesn't know him. We're waiting for time on the central records computer now."

"Get that time! I don't know what Vrubel knows, but he knows something. But he won't be easy to question, or to break." He understood how he had chosen the word —the personal life leaping over the snake of professional procedures. "We *must* have that man who imitated Ossipov. He must know *why* he did it."

"Yes, Major."

"Get those cars over here, on the double. They're leaving soon."

"On their way, sir."

He almost wanted to plead that Ilya send men who would not laugh at the humiliating prospect of Major Vorontsyev trailing around the city after his wife and her lover, using the Centre's vehicle and manpower resources to do so. Instead, he clipped the mike back under the dashboard.

He gripped the wheel, noticed that he was cold. He took one ragged breath, then started the car, and drove some way down the service road to the flats. There he parked with a view of the foyer, waiting for his wife and Captain Vrubel to come out.

Folley crouched, exhausted, behind a spindly fir, his ears straining to catch the sounds of his pursuers. Nothing. For a few moments, he was safe. He drew in the cold night air in great heaving sobs, and his body began to shake with reaction to the demands he had made upon it. There was no impression of loneliness, of fear or loss of hope. Only the body, pleading with him, already wanting to curl into some foetal rest.

He looked at his watch. He had been travelling, with only two short stops, for four hours. He was on the very edge of the fir forest, the trees tiny, misshapen, dwarfish. He had climbed steadily, wearily, up out of the bowl in which the taller trees grew, and were dense, into the higher country, the bare landscape on which he would move like a white fly towards the main Ivalo road.

He could not use the radio; it would pinpoint him, since the frequency available to him was that used for ordinary NATO traffic. The Russians would be monitoring that; and the chopper that was airborne in order to pick up his reports would not be airborne until the morning.

He had lost the brief, illusory comfort of moving further into Finland—he wasn't safe, could not be until the chopper made the first of its dashes across the Finnmark, bearing Finnish markings, the pilot in Finnish army uniform, to the pick-up point. And it would happen only once more after that; exactly twenty-four hours later. If he did not appear, he was to be presumed dead.

Or captured.

Folley wondered, weakly, whether he was the first *Snow Falcon*; or had there been others, as there would be others after him if he did not return? Had any of the others learned what he knew? Snap, snap—had the pictures been removed from their bodies?

It would not matter, his limbs and joints persisted, if he was caught; lie down. It wouldn't be long before they caught up . . .

He pushed with his hands, but his body refused to rise from the snow. It was as if everything except his mind was straw. Even the way his legs stretched out, comical, like a scarecrow; ridiculous.

He attended to the body, in a compromise—as if bribing it with the chocolate from his pack. And he pressed the canvas sleeve of the rifle to his face, as if as a reminder.

So far—so far . . . No airborne search. He didn't think it likely, not yet. But he knew they would have to risk it after dawn. Perhaps they would use Kamovs or MILs to hunt for him—drop troops ahead of his possible and predicted course. They must know he would head for the road, had to be going west.

His thoughts tailed off into a lysergic acid photography, fed by the adrenalin of weary fear, in which the tactical moves of the day to come were vivid with terror and exhaustion and capture.

He knew they would do it; they had to. They understood what he had seen. He had to be stopped.

His left leg was twitching. A feeble attempt at movement, he wondered, or a protest at thoughts of continued flight.

He wasn't sure that he slept, but the taste of sleep was in his mouth; yet it might have been minutes only. He jerked awake because a cry to attention sounded within him. Something as imperative as a dream of falling . . .

The cry was outside himself, he realized with a bright, tearing pain of betrayal and fear in his chest. A voice had spoken, only a few Russian words after he recognised that it was not his dream speaking. Close.

He rolled onto his stomach. It was that close. As if the next step of the foot would place it on his chest, smother his face . . . He slid the canvas sleeve from the rifle, and aimed. Into the telescopic sight, gathering the feeble light of stars and snow, walked the Russian soldier. And he was that close, close as the body had recognised, moving instinctively as it had done.

The rifle boomed in his ear, twice, and the Russian collided with the tree-bole he was carefully skirting. Folley even saw the lips distort as the cheek was dragged down the rough bark—body sliding into a silly, ablutive crouch. He rolled away from the tree, then fired again on his back as he saw the second man turning towards him, surprised by the sudden noises. He fired again, and the aim was poor; two more shots, and the man was staggering, his own rifle, a stubby Kalashnikov, discharging into the snow. A bright spittle of flame. Then the dull concussion of the white-clothed body into the snow.

He stood up with no sense of weariness. He slung the skis over his shoulder, and, ducking into a crouched run, scuttled like a crab across the uneven ground, away from the trees. He heard again the cries of foxes behind him, but no shots. He had, he sensed, been caught in the middle of a file, grown ragged as it was sweeping the forest skirts, and now they could see one another as they re-grouped and they dared not fire in case it was one of their own. But they would sense his general direction.

Snow pucked from the tree branches, stinging his face wet. Trees no higher than himself. He felt as if he were wading out of deep water, into shallows that exposed him as a target. Snow—dusted up from dwarf trees by the brushing of his pack, the pumping of his heavy arms—splashed across his white clothing.

Few trees, a lip of bare rock almost without snow, then nothing except a land tumbled under the starlit sky, soft, illusory folds of country fading out of eyesight. Before him, a long, gentle slope. He stopped, out of sight behind the lip of rock, and fitted the skis. Then a single moment in which the body seemed to fail—and he dug in with the sticks, pushing away.

Shots behind him, but distant, not even the insect noises of bullets passing close to him—only the sighing wind, the cold stars, and the hiss of the skis as he wound down into a high valley.

He almost sensed, in some para-normal manner, when they too fitted skis, dug in, and began to pursue him. He did not look behind. Ahead of him in the darkness was the north-south road, like the border of another country.

For a moment, he thought he heard, distantly, the buzz-saw whine of a helicopter.

THREE
PURSUITS

"Can you be certain—certain of *these* names at least?"

Khamovkhin waved the list of names in front of him. He was sitting at his desk, away from the fireplace where they had sat the previous night, and Andropov had had to pull a chair to the other side of the desk. He understood the First Secretary's need to establish an aura of self-confidence, and did not resent the subordination forced upon him. He had played the same game with three of his Deputies that morning.

"I think we can—Politburo members who have consistently supported the moves towards greater *détente*, arms reductions—objected to the increases in defence spending . . ." Then something seemed to snap in him, letting the tight calm elude him. "You know most of these men—have known them for years—Feodor. *You* can vouch for their loyalty!"

Khamovkhin appeared challenged for an instant, then he relaxed into his chair.

"Perhaps you're right. The last thing we need is paranoia. Yes, yes . . ." He put the list aside. "These, at least, should give us no cause for concern."

"Good."

Khamovkhin seemed suddenly to relax. He got up, went to the cabinet, and brought back the bottle of whisky and two tumblers. He poured two generous measures, and passed a tumbler across the desk to Andropov. Andropov looked at the glass as if at something that vaguely threatened him.

"We must wait and see, then. My performance this morning should have stirred something up—I *was* right, eh, old friend?"

"On balance—yes. Though we conclude we are certain of those names on that list—there are others whose loyalty might be called suspect—who have links with the High Command, sympathies or records that tie them to the army. Yes—" Andropov sipped his drink. "You have worried them. One of them may make some move, give himself away."

"Why does there have to be someone in the Politburo in league with those bastards in the High Command?"

Khamovkhin swallowed greedily at the whisky.

"You mean—why not a simple army take-over?" Andropov shook his head. "No. *Too* simple. *Group 1917* is *inside* the Party machine—it has to be. If anything like a complete coup is being organised—against the Committee for State Security as well as the Kremlin—then it could not be done, for example, without the assistance of GLAVPUR inside the army. The loyalty of the Political Directorate would have to be swayed or circumvented. Not to mention the GRU, and our other checks and balances."

Khamovkhin nodded.

"I know you're right. It was the only way, smoking them out. But—what a farce. I thought I was going to laugh at some of the things I was saying—and the way they were taking them!"

"Indeed. Your style of leadership helped. They would not expect to be accused of treason by you. I wonder you didn't remove a shoe and bang the edge of the table."

Light glinted coldly on the Chairman's spectacles. He appeared to be smiling. Khamovkhin, doubt still rankling like creases in his bedclothes, shifted in his chair.

"How much good will it do, Yuri? To say we have details, confessions that point to a huge plot against the Party leadership—"

"If they want to know what we know, then they must come more into the open. Especially if their effort is as close as we suppose it is. They must institute enquiries of their own." Andropov spread his hands on his knees. "Panic? No, perhaps not so violent a reaction. But something may emerge—something precipitate?"

58

"I suppose so. Can we trust the SID?"

"We can trust no one else. They, at least, have brought this sliver of hope—the substitute for General Ossipov. The Special Investigations Department is all we have."

"Will they find this—substitute? Now that we have let Ossipov return to the safety of his hide-out in Khabarovsk, six thousand miles away!"

"We *could not* move against him. But he has helped us. We can begin to recheck every piece of documented evidence on senior officers—and their contacts with senior Party officials—during leave-periods in Moscow. It is something."

"Not enough. Too little, and probably too late."

"Calm yourself, Feodor. If the apparatus turns on us, we are finished. We have to accept that, before we begin. We also have to accept that the KGB is an investigative organ, not an army. They will move against us with the army—which part of it, or *all* of it, doesn't matter. We can only defend ourselves if we know *who* is behind it. *How* won't matter, if we can get hold of *who*—those who will give the orders. If they are silenced, then there will be no orders given. If they are not, then—" Andropov raised his hands. Whisky slopped from the tumbler onto the trousers of his grey suit. He looked irritated, mopped at it with his silk handkerchief.

"As fragile as that," Khamovkhin observed. "Your thesis can be spilled just as easily, with a shrug by the army. And lots of other liquid besides. Most of it ours." The cynical superiority drained from his face as he gazed towards the fireplace. "We have no more than *days,* Yuri. What the hell can we do just in days?"

Vorontsyev sat alone in the car they had brought for him. The second car was parked across the street. They had followed Vrubel and Natalia after the performance of some dreary comedy at the Mossoviet Theatre on the Bolshaya Sadovaya—the sort of play an officer would want to see on leave from the Finnish border, a weak satire on provincial life in the Soviet Union that everyone seemed to want to see, so that the tickets were at some kind of premium.

Now, the cars were parked in the Arbat, a short distance from the apartment in the Kalenin Street. Vrubel and Natalia were enjoying a late supper and drinks in the

Praga Café. There were still people about to distract his thoughts as he watched their faces, lit like those of fish in a tank as they patrolled the narrow pavements, stared into darkened shops.

But his attention kept returning to the curtains across the windows of the Praga on the other side of the street, dimly lit from within. The sight possessed him because he and Natalia had often eaten or drunk there, in the early days, when he had waited for her to finish a performance in the chorus of the Bolshoi. A time before many things.

It was evident that Vrubel had chosen the Arbat because of its proximity to Natalia's apartment. He was to be forced to witness, from his car, the laughing, meaningful exit from the café, the summoning of a taxi, perhaps the heads leaning together through the rear window, even the grotesque cliché of merging shadows thrown onto the drawn curtains of a bedroom.

He had forgotten the surveillance purpose of what he was doing; so much so that he was on the point of ordering the other tail-car to go off-duty. He could not bear the thought that other men would sit outside the apartment-block on Kalenin Street, watching the same shadow-dance on the curtains. The thought left a vile taste in his mouth, and a creeping sensation in his genitals, as if they were threatened with pain or damage. He picked up the handset.

"Maxim," he said.

"Yes, Major."

"Forget it—go home."

"Home, Major?"

"Yes, dammit! Go home. I'll take care of things here!"

There was a pause, then, with a tone in which he could sense the pity: "Yes, sir." Then, formally: "Moscow Unit Seven-Oh-Four-Seven going off-duty in the Arbat. Returning to central garage. Good-night, Major."

"Good-night." He jammed the handset into its clip under the dash, rubbed his chin hard, a rasping sound in the car; it was as if he were rubbing something clean. Then he looked at his hand, to see if it trembled. It was steady, and he was thankful.

They came out of the Praga, laughing as he had anticipated—he could almost tell from the slant of her body, the way her fur coat was wrapped against her, the pressure of the slim form against Vrubel's uniform . . . she was inviting him without words. It was as if he had seen her fornicating in the harshly-lit street, so naked were her intentions. When the taxi moved away, he switched on the engine, and followed at a distance. There was no necessity to keep close. He knew their destination.

He parked quietly, with a view of her bedroom window, as the taxi drew away. Vrubel's tip, in anticipation, had no doubt been generous. Then they had gone inside—a part of his mind shared the lift with them. Then he picked up the handset, and called the Centre, requesting to be put through to the SID offices on Frunze Quay. All communications from mobile units were relayed through the central control room in Dzerzhinsky Street. Eventually, Ilya replied. His voice sounded more bored than before. Vorontsyev, as he waited, his mind on the Ossipov-substitute, had been unable to distract his eyes from the bedroom window. The light had gone on, the curtains tugged across. It was as if she knew he was down there . . .

"Vorontsyev," he said, and his voice sounded thick and strange.

"Yes, Major." There was some effort to attend, to sound interested.

He saw the figures moving in an old dance, against the lighted curtains. He could feel her body . . .

"Anything on that bastard yet?"

"Er—no, sir. Not yet."

"Why not, for shit's sake? You must have something!" The bodies swayed—he could see the imperceptible movement towards the bed. "Get your fucking finger out, Ilya! You're wasting time!" He wanted to go on shouting into the handset, shouting obscenities, berating his subordinate, purging himself. Orgasm of jealousy, hot in his dry throat.

"Yes, sir." Ilya was abashed, shocked.

"Get—on with it, then. I want something by the morning. Something *definite!*"

"Sir."

He pushed the handset down into the passenger-seat, leaning his weight on it unconsciously. He was shuddering, as Vrubel would be, soon. The heave of the final thrust . . .

He got out of the car. He could no longer watch the darkened window. He drew in the air, gratefully, and

61

made himself walk. He walked up and down, a sentry to Natalia's infidelity, his hands thrust in the pockets of his overcoat, his face a set, grim mask.

Vrubel, as he left, almost bumped into him, paid no attention except to mumble an apology. Vorontsyev, looking up, saw the officer's back walking away from him—uniform purpled beneath the street lamp for a moment, then the form shadowed again. He watched, hating.

He had been surprised when Vrubel and Natalia had taken a taxi from the apartment to the theatre, and wondered why Vrubel had no hire car. He saw him now fishing for a key, opening the door of a Zil, looking back up at the window, then starting the engine—a sudden loud cough that seemed to waken Vorontsyev. He looked at his watch. Twenty minutes—Vrubel had been with his wife only twenty minutes.

Even as the laughter began to bubble acidly in his throat—the image of temporary impotence sketched in his mind like a cartoon on a lavatory wall—he sensed that Vrubel was leaving with a purpose. He wasn't running *away*, but *to* . . .

He ran to his own car, seeing the Zil turn out of the service road, heading north up the wide thoroughfare. Towards Arbat Square, and perhaps the Sadovaya motorway ring. His own engine fired at the third hasty attempt, he flicked on the headlights, and screeched away. There was satisfaction now in action, for the first time that night. He roared across the Kalenin Street, in front of a taxi which sounded its horn at him—Vorontsyev recognised with a smile that the man was probably KGB; he would otherwise have shown caution in remonstrating with a car so obviously in pursuit of something or someone.

Vrubel's black car was well ahead of him, crossing the Arbat—he caught a glimpse of it as he weaved out of the stream of traffic for a moment, into the path of an oncoming lorry. He ducked back in, then surged out, overtaking three cars before having to squeeze back into the heavy flow across the square. The night-life of Moscow, flowing back out to the new suburbs.

He did not catch sight of Vrubel again until they had both turned left onto Tchaikovsky Street, part of the inner motorway ring; then right through the Smolenskaia, and suddenly out across the Borodino Bridge, the water sluggish, dark ice perhaps as its edges—he could not be sure; certainly it was much colder.

As he crossed the bridge, it was as if he left the apartment behind him. Now thought, accelerating with the car, focused ahead and he began to sense that he had inadvertently panicked Vrubel. Something about his visit to the apartment had made him suspicious; perhaps the man could not believe that it was entirely fortuitous. But where was he going? Out of the city altogether? Had he arranged, perhaps, some meeting because he sensed that the SID suspected him?

Vrubel's Zil swung west onto Kutuzov Prospekt, and Vorontsyev found himself only two cars behind. Flanking the wide avenue, the pink-bricked blocks of apartment were grubbily washed by the sodium flares. There was a frost in the air; Vorontsyev turned up the heater of the car. The railway bridge, then the glass and aluminium cylinder of the Kutuzovskaya metro station. Vorontsyev wondered whether, since they were in a quarter where many diplomats of foreign countries resided, Vrubel had a call to make along the Kutuzov Prospekt. He stayed two cars behind him, hidden from the rear-view mirror.

There appeared to be no deviation as they drove through the quieter suburbs. Cars dropped away from the file, a stream running dry; the street lighting less insistent. Vorontsyev, who rarely had cause or inclination to visit the outer suburbs of the city, felt himself in a strange country. Only one car separated him from Vrubel now. He did not think that Vrubel suspected his presence— the way he had left the apartment on Kalenin Street indicated that he had no suspicion that he was under surveillance—but he suspected that the KGB officer had indeed set up a meeting. Either he wished to pass on something he had received from Ossipov at the officers' club— or he wanted some kind of reassurance about Vorontsyev's apparent interest.

As the lights died behind them, Vorontsyev switched off his lights. He felt a sudden chill as the road disappeared, and the flat countryside winked out. The road was becoming icy, and the night was hard with stars. Gradually, he became accustomed to the pale gleam of light reflected from the snow still covering the fields. And he followed the lights of the car ahead of him, which still masked his presence from Vrubel.

As far as Vorontsyev could tell, they were heading for the excursion spot, Arkhangelskoe; they had taken the Minsk road, the continuation of the Kutuzov Prospekt, then turned right onto the Rublevo road. When they turned left again, it was towards Uspenskoe. And the car between the Zil and Vorontsyev turned right at the crossroads. Vorontsyev waited, then pulled out, lights still off. Moving away from him, he saw the red rear lamps of the Zil. Unsuspicious acceleration.

Gradually, they slid together into a country of slim trees lining the road, and shimmering, snowbound fields. There was something sufficiently beautiful about it to affect Vorontsyev. They crossed the Moskva, heading southwest, and then the Zil turned off the main road, into the trees. Vorontsyev stopped the car, saw the small sideroad, unmarked and unsurfaced, and slowly turned into it. Ahead of him, winking suddenly through the trees then lost again, were the rear lights of the Zil. He wondered for a moment whether he was being led into a trap—then he sensed that the meeting-place was to be one of the many wooden *dachas* built in the Arkhangelskoe district—summer and weekend homes for prominent members of the Party and the bureaucracy. He smiled. SID had investigated, in its time, a number of peculiar reports concerning social and personal behaviour in *dachas* like the ones dotted through the woods.

The *dacha* was appropriate to conspiracy, as well as to sexual perversion, he considered with satisfaction. Then he saw the brakelights go on ahead of him, and he stopped the car immediately. He wound down the window, and listened. In the clear frosty air, he heard the door of the Zil slam shut like a rifle shot. Carefully, he got out of the car, taking the Makarov pistol from the glove compartment before he did so.

The ground was covered lightly with snow, masking sound but masking also any sticks that might betrayingly snap. He trod carefully, keeping to the deeper shadow of tree trunks, heading for the spot where the Zil had stopped.

His feet were cold through his thin shoes by the time he reached it. Its lights were off—and it was empty. He wondered for a moment whether it was indeed a trap as he looked around him swiftly, gun held in front of him—then he saw the dim light, from behind curtains, a little way

64

ahead. As his night-vision improved, he saw that he was at the edge of a small, man-made clearing, on the other side of which was a low wooden *dacha*—a large one, he noted with a creeping excitement he could not altogether restrain or disapprove. He enjoyed the sensation of crouching against the Zil, watching the destination of his journey just fifty yards away. He did not notice the cold now, except as a sharp sensation in his nostrils.

He circled the clearing, watching for signs of movement at the lighted window or the almost invisible door set back beneath an over-hanging porch. Nothing.

The young trees grew close to the side of the *dacha*. He paused in their shelter for a moment, checked the Makarov, and slid a round into place. Then he moved swiftly across the strip of moonlit ground, his feet crunching on snow that had begun to freeze hard. He slipped over the rail, onto the wood of the porch. He steadied the rocking-chair that remained there from the summer, felt its material damp beneath his hand, then moved quietly towards the door, ducking beneath the curtained window.

He drew what seemed his first breath as he paused outside the door—and experienced a moment of doubt, the sense of traps laid and about to be sprung; how many were there inside the *dacha?*

The door was open. He pushed it gently wider. A narrow wooden hall, a strip of dull carpet, the feel of rough wood under the hand he used to guide himself in the darkness. Ahead of him, and to the left, a glow of light from beneath a door. He listened for voices, but there was a deep silence about the house. Nothing, not even his own breathing.

He stepped back from the door, raised his foot, and kicked at it. The thin door swung open, the lock tearing, and then he held it open as it swung back towards him. Through the door, gun ready. There was no one behind it.

No one in the room. The dim light, he saw suddenly, had to be a decoy, and he turned swiftly, as if sensing soneone behind him. Again, no one.

He moved cautiously out of the room, closing the door so that the light would not outline him, and began a search of the remaining room.

The body was in one of the bedrooms, at the rear of the *dacha;* it was still dressed in the formal black overcoat, and he almost expected to see the homburg hat

65

resting on the bedside cabinet. Someone had folded the arms decently across his chest, and there was, he saw, a dark hole in the white forehead, near the hairline. White hair. The face, staring up at the ceiling, was reposed, still with lack of expression. Chiselled. He moved closer.

There was no one living in the house. Not now. He looked out of the window, saw nothing; listened for the noise of the Zil's engine starting up. Silence. He looked down at the body.

It was the Ossipov-substitute. He felt disappointed—even cheated in some obscure way. He leaned over the face, as if demanding an explanation. The dead face stared sightlessly up at him, seeming now irritated that he had come between the open eyes and their concentration on the ceiling.

The body was small, like that of Ossipov. The tight, drawn skin appeared unreal in the moonlight—the face of an actor. He looked nothing like Ossipov; if only surveillance team had seen the face, they would have raised the alarm. But only the back—the black overcoat, the hat. They had made only one mistake—to be seen together at all; no, not even that—only the mistake of the substitute having his features recorded in the museum.

And that error had been corrected. Vorontsyev, with distaste, touched the hole of the wound. Dry blood, what there was of it. And cold skin. The man had been dead for some time. How long?

He raised an arm. Stiff. Dead perhaps more than twenty-four hours. A careful anticipation, the discarding of something soiled by wear or faded with exposure. A liability.

But, why was it here?

Because the sense of the trap returned at the precise moment, as he felt the delicate cold wire running from the hand up the sleeve of the black overcoat—he understood what it meant.

He turned and ran, out of the bedroom, crashing against the wooden wall so that it shook, cannoning off, seeing the patch of starlight from the open door at the end of the corridor. . . .

And then the bomb that had been so carefully wired to the body, and which he had triggered when he moved the arm—exploded. Something shoved him in the back, through the frail wooden fence in front of the porch—he felt the rail bite into his thighs, and then he was tumbling over it, bringing it down after him. Snow—just the merest sensation of wetness as his face ground into it, and the horrific noises that deafened him, and the after-shock wrenching through his body. Then black silence, even as the pain began.

The restored house was on Kropotkin Street, and suitably spacious for a long-serving and respected member of the Politburo. Ilarion Vikentich Galakhov sat opposite the man he knew as *Kutuzov,* and from whom he took his orders. Galakhov, at thirty-three, was a Senior Lieutenant in the GRU, Military Intelligence. As such, there were many superior officers to whom he was, apparently, responsible. For two years now, however, he had covertly obeyed only this man, the leader of *Group 1917.* He and those deputed by him to issue orders. One of those, Yevgeni Vrubel, he had obeyed earlier that night, only to find that the order had come not from *Kutuzov,* but was a panic-measure by Vrubel himself.

Kutuzov was angry, the rage of flouted authority barely concealed; and also beneath the striven-for calm there was hatred of a man who had jeopardised a strategy the extent of which could only be guessed by Galakhov. He watched the old man carefully, studied the strong face with its deep lines of concentration and authority, and silently cursed Vrubel for tricking him into the killing of the Ossipov-substitute and rigging the bomb that had almost killed the SID Major. How *Kutuzov* had heard, how he knew Vorontsyev was still alive, he could not guess; but he had.

"Where is Vrubel now?"

"A safe house."

"You know which one?" Galakhov nodded. "Good. Ilarion Vikentich—we must cut our losses. Get rid of Vrubel tonight, before you leave Moscow." It was said without emotion, as if the projected action had cleansed the old man of his feelings. Except for one final mutter, almost an aside: "He tried to kill the SID man—to save his own skin. When there was no need. That is unforgiveable."

"Yes, sir," Galakhov acknowledged, and found himself

the immediate subject of a keen stare from the old man. The heavily furnished lounge, lit only by the soft glow of one standard lamp in a corner, seemed to menace him.

"Very well. You were deceived, Ilarion Vikentich. I accept that." Galakhov could not restrain the sense of relief he knew must show on his face. The old man smiled in satisfaction. "As for your task—the arrangements are made. Your flight to London is booked, under your new cover-name. You know what you are to do at Heathrow—I need not reiterate it. However, understand me clearly. You *must* kill the traitor Khamovkhin in Helsinki. There can be no failure, no excuses. The present First Secretary of the Soviet Communist Party must not—*must not*—be allowed to survive our operation. On the 24th, kill him."

Galakhov nodded.

"Yes, sir. It will be done."

"Good. Now find Vrubel, and dispose of him."

The MIL helicopter beat overhead, low enough to shower him with snow disturbed from the pine-tops. They had used a helicopter after all, and in the bright moonlight followed his ski-tracks as easily as following motorway signs. There was nothing he could do, he realised, except wait for the helicopter to go away—and it would not do that because it knew his general location, and was acting as a spotter for the pursuit.

Folley was deadly weary; only as the helicopter moved away a few hundred yards to the west did he realise how ragged his breathing had become, and sense more clearly that the shivering of his body had nothing to do with the throb of the rotors over his head.

He was not going to get away. Not going to—no chance.

"Christ!" he muttered, his face lifted to the branches above him, dark now that the snow had been blown from them. There was nothing he could do, nothing.

Except go on, run until they ran him down, cornered him. He was in a forest of pines now, in a deep valley, and the helicopter was blind. His ski-tracks had entered the trees, then disappeared. It could only wait until he re-emerged. Soon it would begin to skirt the edges of the forest, anxious not to miss him, anxious to prevent his having a head-start on the pursuers.

The helicopter was useless now, he told himself. Useless, useless. It did not matter about the veracity of the idea, only its efficacy, a nostrum of power for the flagging body, the eroded will. Useless. He had the rest of the long night in which to run.

The helicopter's noise died away, and its threat diminished. It was searching—needle in haystack, spy in forest, it couldn't find him—

Silence. He strained to catch a sound, any sound. Nothing. He could move again. He unzipped his combat suit, and pulled out a folded map protected by a polythene jacket. Then he flicked on a small torch, focusing its pencil of light on the map, nodding to himself as he understood the contours of the land lying ahead of him. He checked the compass on his wrist, then flicked off the light, stowing the torch and map quickly as if they had already betrayed his whereabouts.

All night to run.

He moved two paces from the tree, and the rifle rang out from away to his left. He felt a searing pain across his ribs, and groaned aloud, stifling the noise almost as it began, blundering head-down towards the nearest trees as two other shots bellowed after him. Night-sight, he thought, unslinging his own rifle, tugging at the canvas sleeve as he jolted his arm against the safety of a trunk, breathing shallowly with fear and the pain in his flesh-wound. Then he whipped round the trunk, and fired three shots in the general direction of the Russian who had found him.

How many? Care, *care*. He brought the rifle to his shoulder, and traversed the area, squinting into his own infra-red sight. Hollow dark spaces, lit as if by a dull fire. Nothing moving—and the growing, creeping sensation that someone was watching him, searching for him, through an identical night-sight. His finger curled on the trigger, and he had to consciously stop himself loosing off any more betraying shots; whistling in the dark.

Then the voice. Finnish first, which he barely understood. Then, after a pause in which admission was decided, English.

"You can't go any further. Give up. It's impossible for you." Distortion of a loud-hailer, metallic voice wearing him down with its magnified confidence. He had to stop himself firing. "Give yourself up. We'll make sure your wound is treated."

69

He winced at the reminder, dare not look at his side now. They had him. Traverse, traverse he told himself. This is a bluff, they're moving in—

Shadow of a winter uniform, red-lit by the sight. He squeezed off two shots, pulled back behind the tree as fire was returned from at least half-a-dozen Kalashnikovs.

All from the same general direction. Perhaps a half-circle, only a crescent yet; *move!* He pushed away from the tree, crouching as if under the weight of the skis and pack, rifle banging against his thigh, left hand pressing for the first time against the burning side. Shots, ragged as they searched for a target. He began to weave and dodge, still hunched, breath labouring almost at once as he galloped awkwardly in the snow, great heaving steps like a wild, but tiring, horse.

He turned, shielded by a tree, and raised the rifle. He waited for the first ghost to shimmer in the red circle, until the cross-hairs settled on the middle of the carefully moving bundle of winter uniform—then fired once, and immediately struck off to the left as fire was returned.

Breath ragged, side hurting like hell—noise of the helicopter returning from the north—strength running out, and the day still ahead of him. He itemised his hopelessness as he kept running, knowing that he would never tell anyone what he had seen, that he had failed already.

After Galakhov had left him, the old man took his dog for a walk in the small triangular park which had once been known as the "Field of Virgins." He passed on the east side of the park a bust of Frunze, hero of the civil war, one of the founders of the Red Army, and almost raised his hat to the stern face as he passed. An unhabitually comic notion; perhaps his decision regarding Vrubel had lightened his mood, he thought. He paused for a moment, while the big old hound capered like a pup on the frost-sparkling grass, and looked back at the Frunze Military Academy. He could even see the low-relief hammer-and-sickles decorating the stern concrete façade; not given to admitting, or indulging, moments of nostalgia, he allowed himself to remember his own training there, soon after it was built in 1936—an over-age cadet who had temporarily rejected the political life. The war, too—that time came back in brief, flickering images.

Then the dog rubbed against his trousers, and his mood was disturbed. The lines in the face hardened again, became stern with anticipated business. He kept to the glinting path, his footsteps loud and clear, his stick tapping almost in a marching rhythm; the noises of the dog on the stiff grass were the only other sounds, as if all traffic had stopped outside the park. The park itself was empty of other people.

The eccentricities he had cultivated for years, the apparent harmlessness and geniality that age seemed to have lent him, now served him well; he had not been tailed from his house, as he was sure other, less apparently loyal, members of the Politburo had been that night, and on other nights.

There was a twist of contempt in the smile on his lips. A smile which vanished again as he stood before Merkurov's giant bronze statue of Tolstoy. Immediately, he felt the size of the statue as an expression of power—his own, or that of Tolstoy, he was uncertain, even indifferent. He shivered slightly, with anticipation rather than cold. The dog continued to scamper, and his thoughts were suddenly stronger, imitative of a younger man, not the respectable, waned figure he had chosen to become.

Party man. Peel away the layers. Party man. Yes, he was that; except that now the Party was in the hands of the sweepings of the Revolution. Non-Party men. Compromisers. Schoolmasters, economic experts, balance-sheet men—men interested only in personal power. Khamovkhin and his crew. The anger coursed through him, mesmerising his attention; his litany.

Khamovkhin the clown had tried to panic his unknown enemy by his vague denunciations in the meeting of the full Politburo. Khamovkhin and his hyena, Andropov, had caught some whiff of *Group 1917*—nothing more. They were the ones close to panic. And he was safe—on the safe list, no doubt; unsuspected.

When he had been silent, as if in homage, before the statue for perhaps ten minutes, he said, softly but clearly, "Well, my friend. What have you to tell me?"

From the shadows beneath the statue, a voice full of disgruntled respect, and cold, said, "Pnin's tanks have been seen, sir."

"What?" He felt cold, at once recriminatory. "How?"

71

"An agent, the General thinks. Probably not Finnish."

"He's dead?"

"Not yet—they are in pursuit. I was told it was only a matter of hours."

"Who sent him?"

"The Americans—the British?"

"Damn!"

"General Pnin considers that you were ill-advised to order a full-scale rehearsal of the border crossing."

"Damn Pnin! His security is—*non-existent*. How did the man get close enough—what did he see?"

"Certainly the village—probably the crossing itself."

"They must get him, then."

"General Pnin sends his assurances as to—"

"Pnin is a fool."

"Sir."

The younger voice retreated into silence. *Kutuzov* stared up into the giant bronze face, aware of the frost that sparkled like eyes above the beard. He tried to draw strength from the statue, and calm rationality.

"The British sent a man before—the one who was killed before he could talk. Pnin should have been more alert. Vrubel is dead," he added to the courier. "He will have to be replaced by his second-in-command for next week. Tell Praporovich that."

"Sir," the courier replied.

"Are there arrangements for taking this agent alive?"

"The General is aware of the importance—"

"He'd better be. Are there arrangements to keep me informed, as soon as a—result is achieved?"

"Sir. By tomorrow night, there will be word."

"Then that will have to do. Tell Praporovich that SID knows nothing—though Vrubel did his best to give them a lead. And give the order for Pnin to withdraw—at once. As soon as he has captured the agent."

"Yes, sir."

"What of Attack Force One?"

"Ready to move up to the Norwegian border on D minus One, sir."

"Good. Dolohov and the navy?"

"All the ships required for *Rabbit Punch* are at sea, or refitting at Murmansk, ready to take troops aboard on D minus One."

"*All*—at last?"

"All, sir."

"Better news—better news. Very well. When is your flight?"

"Another two hours."

"Very well. Tell Praporovich that the agent, when captured, must be transferred at once to the Leningrad house, and interrogated thoroughly. We must know what the British know—if anything. It must not upset the timetable."

"Marshal Praporovich asked that the timetable be confirmed, as of now."

"Assuming word comes from Ossipov not later than five days' time?" As if sensing the grandiloquence of the moment, the old man stood erect before the bronze statue, staring up into Tolstoy's blind face. "Yes. One week from now. D-Day is the 24th."

As he swung down into a great fold of the Maanselka, the central mountain range, he could see, to the northwest, the peak of Kaunispaa; he was only a mile, perhaps, from the main north-south road and the village of Lannila. If he could make the road, he might again have a choice—north towards Ivalo, south towards Vuotso—west along the road to Kuttura. Places that offered rest, and help, however illusory.

His side ached intolerably, his body pleaded for him to stop, ached with effort and hunger—even so, it was spurred by the proximity of the road, the destination he had travelled towards all night and into the first daylight.

The MIL helicopter, a squat, droning beetle, had hugged the slope of the land, then descended on him suddenly even as he first picked up the noise of its rotors. It was barely light; but the helicopter was black against the grey sky. It rushed upon him, flurrying snow in its downdraught as it hovered, then moved ahead of him, skimming the ground. He watched as white-clad soldiers dropped from its belly, laid like mines across his path. He tried to stop, jumping so that the snow surfed up. The nearest man was less than a hundred yards away, and the noise of the MIL, and its skirt of snow, were deadening, oppressive.

He looked round, and the pursuers, dog-weary as he

was himself, topped the last slope, and fitted skis again or rested for a moment. One of them waved, and Folley could hear a thin cheering.

The helicopter lifted away again, swinging above him so that he could see the grinning face of the pilot. His wave was an insult, perhaps even a recognition. Then the shadow was gone, a paralysis deserting his limbs. He unslung the rifle.

The men in front of him had fitted snowshoes, and walked clumsily, inexorably, towards him in slow-motion. Each of them carried a Kalashnikov. And behind him the first of the tired skiers was thrusting down the long slope, only hundreds of yards away.

He could have angled his flight, thrust off towards the left or right and outdistanced the men on snowshoes. It appeared that they wished to take him alive rather than kill him. But his body revolted at the idea, and his legs were finally and suddenly without strength so that he knew he was not going to move any more.

Then a second MIL lifted above the slope that had masked it and its noise.

He pointed the gun uselessly at the ground. He swayed, felt he couldn't stand long enough for them to reach him. He kept turning his head as they closed on him. Kept turning it until they stood around him in a wary ring. Someone took away the rifle, examining it.

He kept looking not at their faces, but at the red stars on the fur caps they wore beneath their camouflage hoods.

FOUR
BEACH HEAD

Kenneth de Vere Aubrey settled into the somnolent, contemplative mood that he usually enjoyed in the Public Gallery of the House of Commons. As he grew older, he was aware that the sounds that rose from the floor of the House, especially those made, as now, by a poorly attended Question Time, threw his awareness back upon himself. He had almost entirely lost an earlier, youthful sense of the business of the world being done there. The Chamber had become a club.

He had reported to the Foreign Secretary, after lunch, on the security procedures to be put into effect, by the SIS in cooperation with the CIA and the Finnish Intelligence Bureau, for the culminatory stages of the Helsinki Conference on Mutual Balanced Arms Reductions, one week hence. The Foreign Secretary himself would head the team of British observers at the treaty signing; the United States' partners in NATO would be signatories only to the second, and supplementary stage, of the conference, to be held in Belgrade in the autumn.

An opposition speaker was on his feet, requiring a junior minister at the Foreign Office to explain what assurance the government, and the President of the United States, had been given as to the sincerity of the Soviet Union with regard to arms reductions—a late, and rather naïve, attempt to stir doubt; or perhaps to draw attention to the speaker. There were a few half-hearted murmurs of derision from the government back benches. The front benches on both sides of the House were conspicuously bare.

Aubrey came to the House more often in these last days of his employment with the SIS than he had done in earlier years. It irked him that he could not precisely explain his motives; but it was tolerably warm. An obscure sense of desire for legitimacy nagged him, as it often did. Perhaps he was disillusioned after sitting below the salt for so long—enter Third Murderer, he thought. Here, at least, it was tolerably above board—at least, it gave that illusion. Perhaps that was also the reason he spent less and less time with the operational side of the service, and preferred administration and oversight of intelligence gathering.

Perhaps he was growing senile, and ought to begin attending the Upper House. He shifted in his seat, and cursed the ailing circulation that so swiftly made him cold and cramped when still. And, aware of the physical, he thought of other men of stronger sensual passions than himself; their horror at the growing inoperancy of limbs, their sense of desire unabated, but more futile and humiliating with the onset of age.

They had spoken no word of retirement to him as yet; for which he was grateful. If anything clouded his general self-possession, his satisfaction with his lot, it was the idea that one day the neat, uncluttered flat in Sussex Gardens would become a bare, unfurnished cupboard to be inhabited, with growing dissatisfaction, for the long hours of endless, successive days.

He wondered how cold it was in Finland, and whether to delegate the organisation to one of his senior assistants —perhaps even to Davenhill, whose standing with the Minister, though not immutable, was at that moment satisfactory. And it would do the young man good.

Then he saw Davenhill, still in his leather topcoat, looking around at the Gallery, and Aubrey sensed that he was looking for him. Snow had turned to gleaming wetness on his hair and shoulders in the lights of the Chamber. He did not feel irritation—perhaps something about the younger man's attitude, an eagerness of body and face, intrigued Aubrey. He felt a swift pluck like mild indigestion at his stomach, and smiled. Then Davenhill saw him,

76

and waved the newspaper in his hand, stepping immediately down the aisle to him.

". . . The facilities for mutual inspection, by satellite and by military delegations, written into the terms of the Treaty, are surely all the Honourable Member could require, even for *his* satisfaction . . ."—the junior minister droned, raising two languid supporting breaths, and a mutter of denigration. Davenhill, who was looking extremely serious as he sat down, could not forbear to smile.

"Dear, dear—standards down again, I see. I don't know why you come here, Kenneth."

"And to what do I owe the pleasure of your company?" Aubrey asked drily. "To answer your remarks—I come because I find it all so reassuring. Don't you?"

"No intimations of mortality, then?"

"None at all. An abiding somnolence—I'm sure the map is still mostly pink, you know." He studied Davenhill carefully for a moment, then added: "What is it?"

"Folley . . ."

"What about Folley?" Aubrey found it suddenly difficult to control his interest; perhaps even panic—and knew that he was getting old.

"No contact."

"What?" Something had been disturbing his calm—now he knew what it was. There had been an edge of concern that Folley had not reported in by the time he left his office to come to the House. He should have done—should have been picked up. "What does Waterford think?"

"I've got him waiting downstairs—will you speak to him?"

"Yes, I must. Come."

Aubrey cast one swift glance down at the floor of the House, then turned and made his way out of the Public Gallery.

Waterford was waiting for them near the Members' Entrance. Again, Aubrey was struck by his bearing; despite the military officer's civilian overcoat and the trilby hat, he still appeared like a prizefighter masquerading as a retired soldier, so looming was his presence, so marked his features by extreme experiences. He was a rogue operator—which was why he and Davenhill had chosen him. Waterford merely nodded to Aubrey as the little man

77

gestured them through the doors out into New Palace Yard. The commissionaire saluted Aubrey as they passed.

Aubrey put on his bowler hat, and turned up the collar of his dark overcoat. It was still snowing, and beginning to lie. Davenhill belted the leather topcoat. The lamps in the Yard were great, faded billows of light; their footsteps were muffled by the thin layer of settled snow.

They patrolled the Yard once. Aubrey became irritated with their silence, the sense of them as machines who would not speak without his command.

"Well? Waterford—what's happened to him?"

"He's dead—or caught."

"How can you know that?" Aubrey felt himself protesting too strongly; but he felt an obscure sense of danger, threat, which placed what might have happened against the polite remarks inside the Commons in a chilly perspective. "Weather?"

"Nothing to kill him off."

"Delay?"

"He was to report *if* he needed more time."

"Unless it would endanger him to do so—the helicopter is going back again tonight, isn't it?"

"Yes, it is," Davenhill said, speaking for the first time. "But—shouldn't we have a contingency plan?"

Aubrey was suddenly reluctant. His mind kept placing what he was being told, and what was surmised, in the blackest contrasts with the report he had made to the Foreign Secretary that afternoon—even to his recent conversations with Buckholz, Deputy Director of the CIA, talks with the Finns—he realised he was shivering; not with cold, not for Folley, not for any specific thing. But at a vague, oppressive sense that he had, simply *had*, to consider the Helsinki Conference in direct relation to the possible disappearance of Folley, and the certain disappearance of Brunton, and one test roll of unproven infrared film.

"What's the matter, Kenneth? You look absolutely awful." Davenhill touched his elbow, and Aubrey straightened, and said:

"Contingency plan. Very well. There is only one—no time to brief anyone new, get them trained—you two will have to go."

"What?" Davenhill was aghast; squinted nervously up at Waterford's bulk.

Waterford merely nodded, then said, "With *him?* That's a risk."

"Kenneth—I'm not a field-agent. How the devil can I go?"

"You can—and will. Don't you see—if Folley is lost to us, then we may be dealing with something very serious indeed—so serious that the protocol of sending a Foreign Office Special Adviser no longer applies! You will prepare yourselves to leave tonight—unless we receive a report from Folley after the helicopter's second trip across Finland."

He stood looking at the two of them, then looked up at the façade of Westminster Hall. He could see only dimly through the slanting snow the statues of English kings ranged along the building. And the lights seemed distant, too. He shivered again. He looked at Waterford, and added:

"Very well. If Folley is missing, I will admit the feasibility of your hypothesis. The Russians are in Finland, and probably in force. It will be up to you to prove it!"

The car had left the road at the northern end of the Ustinsky Bridge, smashed through the thin layer of ice on the northern bank of the Moskva, and sunk beneath the dark water, early that morning. Only at noon was the lifting operation got under way, two bright red mobile cranes manoeuvred into position on the Kotelnicheskaia Quay, when Vorontsyev's office obtained a priority order signed by Deputy Chairman Kapustin.

The frogmen could work only minimal shifts in the freezing dark below the surface, and the work proceeded with painful slowness under the titular direction of Police Inspector Tortyev, who was KGB, but who had been reluctantly forced to accept the authority of Alevtina, to the policeman a much-too-young junior officer in the SID. But he was not prepared to argue with her signed authority; he satisfied his sense of inferiority and truculent envy of the girl's position with pleasure that she at least kept out of the way, mostly in her car, or near the tea-wagon that was also doling out generous measures of vodka to divers coming off shift.

The girl sensed Tortyev's sullen hostility, and the surprise of the other policemen, and enjoyed the reactions she created. She was aware of herself as a diminutive figure in fur coat and hat, and long boots, as if she were a fashion model posed against some unexpected industrial background. And, since she rarely doubted her abilities or her instincts, she knew that no mere drunk had crashed a black Zil saloon into the Moskva, despite the impressions of the only witness, a policeman on foot patrol along the quays, looking for dossers or black marketeers and the like. She knew that Vrubel was in that car, and that he had been put there dead. Even if the policeman who had seen it had seen only one man, being below the level of the bridge, on the Quay, he had heard the car start up, and accelerate. Alevtina knew they would find a jammed accelerator when they got the black saloon out of the river.

The late afternoon was bitterly cold. She wanted more strong tea, but sensed that Tortyev, briefing the crane operators near the tea-wagon, would misinterpret any movement on her part, and instead lit another cigarette. The car's ashtray was almost full of stubs. Long English filter-tips; she never smoked Russian tobacco. Major Vorontsyev was recovering in hospital, they said: if they got the car up soon, then she would report to him personally later in the evening. She did, she decided, believe the doctors, and her smirking colleagues who well knew her concern for their chief, when they said he was all right; but she would like to see for herself.

She was half-way through the cigarette when Tortyev came towards her car, opened the door, and slid into the passenger seat, rubbing his gloved hands together, and blowing ostentatiously with the cold.

"It's ready. The divers have rigged up the lifting gear, at last. They can't see a body inside . . ."

"What?" she said sharply. "The doors are open?"

"No. Neither doors nor windows. He has to be in there —if there was anyone in there."

Alevtina smiled in a superior way, exhaling smoke which rolled under the roof of the car. "Just wait and see, Inspector. There's someone in there."

"I hope you're fucking right—otherwise it'll have been a very expensive piece of salvage work, won't it?"

Alevtina continued to smile broadly, understanding the motive behind the obscenity. Doubtless Tortyev had already imagined what she would be like in bed, and come to the conclusion either that she was the same as any other tart with her SID knickers off, or a cold fish who worshipped her work and was frightened of men. The conventional grooves in most of the male minds around her in the KGB amused her. Women were spy-bait, or secretaries; not much more to most of the officers she knew. She had been accepted by the rest of Vorontsyev's team, after an initial period of sexual innuendo and proposition, as a police officer. It was all she asked; she knew that Vorontsyev respected her abilities, and that was a bonus.

"Let's go and have a look, then, shall we?" she said, reclaiming the initiative and getting out of the car. Tortyev slammed his door when he, too, got out. Alevtina shivered, despite the coat and fur hat, and thrust her hands into her pockets. She walked down almost to the shelving stonework of the edge of the Quay, and looked up at the mobile crane, its head dipped out over the river like some African bird drinking. Tortyev, standing beside her but a few feet away, raised his hand, and shouted an order. The crane-driver raised his thumb, and then put the crane into gear. The second crane had withdrawn, as if ousted in some rivalry between the two machines.

The black saloon, roof first like the back of a whale, came up out of the water, swayed, and hovered above the river, water streaming from panels and underbody, mud thick on the wheels and sills, then the crane traversed, and for a moment the dripping car hung over the girl, soaking her. Someone laughed—not Tortyev though it was doubtless his idea—as her coat was soaked. Then the car was lowered onto the Quay behind her. She stood furiously still, her back to the policemen and their sniggers and grins, not even taking her hands from her pockets. She dipped her head, and filthy river-water dripped from her hat into the pool around her feet.

"Get a torch, then!" she heard Tortyev snap at someone, and the sound satisfied her. She would wait—after all, she *knew*.

She heard the blow-torch start up, sizzle for a little while, then a rending of metal as the door was heaved open. She listened to the sounds of men scrabbling with something in the interior of the car, waited still, then turned on her heel even as Tortyev was starting to come to her, strode up to the car, and looked once at the white dead face staring sightlessly through the windscreen of the car. The body had been reseated upright in the driver's seat. She recognised the face—it was still sufficiently similar to the one in the photographs in her car.

"It's him. Have him taken to the morgue, *Inspector.*"

The doctors told him almost as soon as he came round that he would not have frozen to death, wrapped in his topcoat as he was; he was told in the same neutral tones that they used to inform him that there were no broken bones; only a badly-sprained left wrist and multiple bruising. The deafness had worn off slowly, although they diagnosed one perforated eardrum, and the buzzing in his head and the dizzy sickness both left him during the afternoon. By the evening, he could sit up in bed in the private room of the small hospital in a rural suburb of Moscow—an aristocratic house in the old days—and consider his good fortune.

The bomber had not wired for instantaneous explosion presumably for his own safety when arranging the body on the bed. It was a ridiculous way to have avoided death; he could still feel as a sensation in his fingertips, the delicate cold wire, the strand that had linked him for a moment with death.

As the hours passed, he found his attention returning to the minutes of his occupancy of that cold, small bedroom at the *dacha,* and the face of the Ossipov-substitute. He had been found, facedown in the slush, by a senior member of the Central Committee Secretariat, who was cohabiting in his *dacha* with a woman not his wife. Vorontsyev retained a dim impression of a man in pyjamas and Wellingtons and a silk dressing-gown round his shivering form—before he had passed out again from the pain of being turned over.

Why? Why such—*extreme* measures? What was he so close to that a bomb had to be used to stop him? Vrubel —they would not see him again, unless he re-emerged in the last condition of the Ossipov-substitute. According to his wife's statement, Vrubel had made two telephone calls before leaving her flat. She had overheard neither call. How many men would it have taken to organise the operation that quickly? A lot—trained, expert men. The ruined *dacha* belonged to an unimpeachable member of the Council of Ministers. It was impossible that he should be involved. He was not even in Moscow at the time, but at a trade conference in Leipzig.

Vorontsyev lit one of the cigarettes at his bedside, coughing on the raw smoke. Then he lay staring up at the ceiling for a long time. Thought became, gradually, suspended; he almost dozed. Cigarette after cigarette disappeared from the packet, and the most conscious thing he seemed to do was to stub each butt in the metal ashtray advertising some awful beer.

It was late in the evening when he received a visitor— Deputy Chairman Kapustin. The bulky man with the broad, expressionless face settled himself on a chair at the bedside without enquiring after Vorontsyev's health. Vorontsyev tried to sit more upright; Kapustin seemed not to notice his efforts.

"I want to discuss your—accident, Major," he said. Vorontsyev sensed the pressures of other voices, issued orders. Perhaps even from Andropov? He felt a quickening of thought, almost in the blood. "I have to be completely frank with you," he added as if he disliked the idea, and wished to disown it.

"Yes, Deputy?"

"From the report you dictated this morning, it is clear that you have stirred up something rather nasty and far-reaching. Though you can have no idea what it is." The final phrase was heavy with seniority. Vorontsyev could not like Kapustin, but was too intrigued by what he might learn to resent the man's proximity. Yes, he decided, he was flattered by the promise of revelations, of being fully informed.

"Your investigations," Kapustin continued, his homburg hat still balanced on his knee, but the fur-collared coat now unbuttoned, "were intended to add to our knowledge of the movements and contacts of senior army officers. This surveillance was ordered by . . ." He paused, as if forcing himself to overcome the habits of years, ingrained, then he managed to say: "By the First Secretary and the Chairman, in joint consultation. Similar surveillance has, as you are aware, been carried out during the past year on a number of generals and military district commanders. What you in your section of SID do not know is that similar surveillance has been applied to senior members of the Politburo, the Praesidium, the Supreme Soviet, and the Central Committee Secretariat . . ."

Vorontsyev was shaken. He said, "All with the same—suspicion in mind, Deputy?"

Kapustin nodded. Vorontsyev lit another cigarette, and saw that his hand was trembling with excitement. Whatever was going on, it was huge, out of all proportion to the small sliver of the totality that he had glimpsed, that had embedded itself in his flesh as surely as if it had been a splinter of wood from the ruined *dacha*. The compartmentalisation of all the security organs of the state extended even to the SID. He had had no idea that perhaps half the force was working on the same operation as himself and his team.

Kapustin said, "You talked with Vrubel—what impression did you get of him? Did he know who you were?"

Vorontsyev, because his mind raced to the possibilities, ignored his private humiliation, so much so that he said immediately, "He found me comical as a cuckolded husband . . ." Kapustin remained silent. "But he was cocky, and not just with sex . . ." Vorontsyev concentrated, seeing the man's face, hearing his voice. "He knew who I was, and that if I wished, I could make trouble just because he was having my wife. But he didn't seem to care. It seemed to make him more confident."

"What do you conclude from this, Major?"

"I don't know. At the time I suspected something—some secret knowledge or power that made him—*immune?*"

Kapustin's eyes lit up. He said, "Exactly! That is what I suspected from your report. A great pity that you did not take other men with you . . ." He waved aside protest, and went on: "Whoever is behind this, they are suitably ruthless. One must admire them for it, if for nothing else."

"What do we know, Deputy? So far?"

"Mm. I am permitted to tell you—ordered, in fact. The earliest clue was a tapped telephone call from the Bureau of Political Administration of the Army; a senior member of that department of the Secretariat who was about to retire, due to inoperable cancer. Perhaps he made a slip just because he was old, or ill—or confident. He used a phone that he would not know was tapped, but he might well have suspected it. His name was Fedakhin. He talked in what was obviously code, and he mentioned two strange things. He referred to *Group 1917*, and later in the conversation—that was his call-sign, we think—he referred to *Finland Station*. He was responsible for that area of the border, and the north-western military district. Apparently, this *Finland Station* was proceeding well, and he could look forward to retiring a happy man —to await the great day, as he put it."

"Vrubel referred to nothing like that," Vorontsyev murmured unhelpfully.

"I didn't suppose he had," Kapustin observed. "But what do you think the terms might mean, eh, Major?"

Vorontsyev wrinkled his brow, looked at the Deputy, and said, "I can't think what they might mean—I know what they do mean, the date of the Revolution, and the destination of the train from Switzerland . . ." His mouth dropped open. "You don't think . . . ?"

"I think nothing. Chairman Andropov's thoughts are what I convey to you." There was a solemn emphasis in the words. *"Revolution?* Seems hard to believe doesn't it?" There was a bright glint of perspiration on Kapustin's forehead, above the heavy creases of age and office. "I would prefer not to think—but I have to, and so do you."

"Very well, Comrade Deputy." Vorontsyev felt that the situation required formality. "What happened to the man Fedakhin?"

"He died. Apparently the disease was more advanced than was diagnosed. We put maximum surveillance on him, but to little or no effect. It appears that somebody was suspicious—no one went near him again."

"But—his contacts before. How much do we know about them?"

Both men seemed to accept the collusion that the situation forced upon them. Both relaxed into the tense informality of their common business. Kapustin said, "Not very much. Typical Party background—kept his nose clean. Ready to change sides and loyalties when Kruschev was swept away, had never identified himself with that regime, except when he had to. A second world war soldier, political indoctrination—then returned to his duties in the Secretariat. Clean record—until this chance telephone intercept." Kapustin shrugged.

"Family?"

"Know nothing."

Vorontsyev persisted, as if he were interrogating the Deputy. Kapustin, hotter still it seemed in the airless room, acquiesced; as if it were easier for him to be questioned than to volunteer a briefing to a subordinate—and one in a hospital bed, at that.

"What else is there, Comrade Deputy?" Vorontsyev did not question his own eagerness—whether revenge, or the burial of private worlds.

"Not very much. For the expenditure of so much effort, very little indeed. We have a dossier . . ." He patted the briefcase that rested by the chair, and to which he had not referred since his arrival. "Of all movements and contacts of officers and bureaucrats under surveillance during the last year. All the teams are going through them, as you did with Ossipov, checking for some new lead, or some connection."

"The—suspects? Are they confirmed, or not?"

"No. They are—*everyone* who might possess the power or the influence was put under surveillance. Automatically."

"Power for what?" Vorontsyev asked after a while.

"Revolution. That is the broad picture. The assumption that a revolution is being planned . . ."

"Ridiculous!" was Vorontsyev's first reaction. Then he stopped short, abashed at his indiscretion.

Instead of anger, Kapustin said, "I might agree with you, Major. If I knew as little as you do. But—fantastic as it is, I have to consider the possibility. So do you."

"But—why? And how? With the Committee for State Security so effective. It would need cooperation—converts —in the Politburo, the High Command, the Praesidium, the Secretariat, the KGB itself."

"I quite agree. As to why, I don't know. As to how—it could take ten years to plan, and execute. And it would need the army—and the navy, too, perhaps. Certainly elements in all the organs of government and control in the state. It would be—huge."

"I *can't* believe it!"

"Perhaps not. But—something is going on. Generals don't have to have substitutes in order to visit prostitutes, of either sex. And the substitutes don't get killed on the merest suspicion that discovery may be just around the corner! Think of that when you're reading these files . . ."

Again he tapped the briefcase with a hand that was backed with dark, curling hair—dark as the hair that curled from his wide nostrils. "And think of this, too. If it would take say ten years—and it is happening—where are we in their timetable, at the present moment?"

Folley watched the guards carefully; it had become a habit so to do, as automatic as glancing in a driving-mirror at precise intervals. There was no possibility of escape connected with it. The two young Red Army soldiers, a corporal and a senior private, seemed content with his company. During the hours of the short day, they seemed comfortable, even approachable—as if they had received no orders against fraternisation. Folley realised that it was an illusory state, and it was designed to make him less troublesome to his guards.

The small tent was cold, but he was still warmly clad in his winter combat clothing, boots and mittens—the Finnish uniform beneath it they had disbelieved, especially when his command of the language had been discovered to be rudimentary by a Senior Lieutenant who interrogated him in Finnish; but they had allowed him to keep it, and his supposed identity. Except for the papers, which had disappeared. They had spoken to him in English after that. His silence was a tacit admission. He had not answered their questions, but they knew his nationality. He had to ask for the toilet, for food and drink, in English, before they would respond. Yet still they had not beaten him.

The three of them sat round the oil-stove, feeling its warmth on their faces, the fronts of their legs. In the hours that he had been held in the camp, they had done little else. They had allowed him to exercise, of course.

They had interrogated him, but not physically. He had told them nothing; though he was evidence by his solitariness of the level of suspicion that had despatched him to Finnish Lapland.

They did not take him seriously. That was his impression of the regimental commanders, colonels both; and the impression given by the small, neat, precise man with the one large silver star of a major-general on his shoulder-boards. He had met the General only once, when he had been taken to be questioned in the wooden hut erected to serve as headquarters for senior officers.

During the night of his pursuit, another regiment had arrived; this time a Motor Rifle Regiment, comprising a tank battalion of forty older T-62 tanks, a battle recce company, three motor rifle battalions, whose vehicles were mainly BMP and BTR-60 armoured personnel carriers; field artillery and anti-aircraft batteries; the medics and technical support group. And a chemical platoon and its vehicles.

Folley had been unnerved by this latter more than the assembled firepower and personnel; it was the most real of the sights, the most vivid in imagination. For many hours afterwards, he was not sure that he had seen it. He tried to persuade himself that it was not the case; he had pieced together the skeleton of the major rifle regiment from the vehicles he had seen, and the men; and within that context, he knew he had caught a glimpse of the vivid yellow vehicles of the chemical platoon.

No one had explained the presence of the Russian armour in the forest south-east of Ivalo. And there was a comfort in ignorance—until what he knew of current war games, the conversation of a friend on the War Studies Team at Cranwell, and his own tactical sense, pressed upon him the conviction that he was amid only one spearhead. There had to be others, concealed on either or both sides of the Soviet border, along its length with Finland.

And the main armoured strike would be to the north, along the single main road to Kirkenes, into northern Norway. And that strike would be preceded by chemical attack; that much he could be certain of.

The Finnmark, therefore, was the target.

Russia was going to war in Scandinavia. It was a simple, brute fact.

Sitting there, watching the two guards, he sensed that he was still numbed by the fact; he had no urgent desire to return to Tromsø, then to MOD, with the knowledge of what he knew. He felt himself strangely *identified* with what was happening here, in this place. As if the events were those of a nightmare, and he could not quite believe in it; nor escape it. The nightmare was so real, but confined to these acres of forest and camouflaged vehicles and disciplined men, that he could not see beyond it. It was easier, much, simply to sit, to wait out the hours of daylight, sleep out the night; perform his bodily functions—exercise, urinate, defecate, and adopt the subdued, waiting tension of the camp.

He had heard how hijacked airline passengers identified with their captors, came to hate those outside who tried to help them. It had happened to him. He was almost one of these soldiers now—who questioned nothing, who simply followed orders, and left the niceties of Armageddon to their superior officers.

He guessed that this force was intended to take Ivalo, and its airfield, or perhaps to strike across the north of Finnish Lapland into Norway. All that he had ever understood of Soviet tactics was that some kind of airborne assault would have to be made on selected targets—to hold them until armoured columns arrived. Perhaps, he wondered, these men were to hold Ivalo as a forward airfield for transports which would lift men into Norway.

Now, when he spoke to the guards, it was as if no distinction of loyalties divided them. They were men in uniform; circumstances had thrown them together. He said. "Can we walk for a little?"

One of the two men spoke reasonable English—the corporal. He nodded, and replied, "I think so. A little stroll, yes?"

"Yes."

It was the end of the short afternoon; the weather was grey now, threatening snow. All around them, the scene had a smoky and indistinct quality. Men's breath smoked around their heads, like white scarves. Vehicles, dusted with snow, under camouflage netting, were still, unthreatening. Folley was pleased with the peace of the scene—its painted stillness. It accommodated him and it did not threaten his mood. Men still looked at him, between and slightly ahead of his guards; their stares disturbed him, but only a little. Already, it seemed, they were used to him.

He crunched through the deep snow, rutted with tracks and prints. There was little to explain, it seemed. He was merely *there*. A random thought of their initial anger at the deaths he had caused disturbed him now, as if he had been accused of some unkindness—or a different colour of skin pointed out.

He watched the Senior Sergeant approach almost with indifference. The man halted in front of him, his square face framed by the hood of the winter combat outfit, star just visible on the fur cap, and spoke in Russian to the two guards. Folley was able to distinguish only the military ranks referred to, and assumed that he was to be taken before the General again. The sergeant preceded them, his boots crunching heavily in the rutted snow over which heavy vehicles had crossed and recrossed.

They passed perhaps only fifteen or twenty of the hundred and sixty tanks, and a handful of the armoured personnel carriers before they mounted the steps to the wooden command hut, a low, single-storey barrack of a building erected by the crew of one of the workshop vehicles. There were command trailers, of course, just as in his own army—but this general had chosen something closer to a house. He struggled with the idea that this had a meaning, something to do with a lack of urgency. But he dismissed the idea as they passed into the outer office.

The guards snapped to attention in front of the lieutenant. Folley did so too; erect, face front, eyes above the officer's head, staring at the fugged window behind him, its rime of frost on the outside thickened by the closing circles of mist inside. There was an efficient stove in the room.

The lieutenant waved the guards away. After they had gone out, he stood up and offered Folley a cigarette.

"Lieutenant?" he asked, holding out the cigarette-case. Folley shook his head, and the young man added: "They are not as bad as your propaganda makes out, you know." Folley was forced to smile, hardly on his guard, hardly sensing that he was being deliberately put at his ease.

He stood there for some time, while the lieutenant walked round him, as if inspecting his kit. Folley had the sense of basic training again, or returning to that when he joined SAS. It was uncomfortable because it reminded him that they were on opposing sides. The atmosphere began to menace him in its silence.

"How much do they know, Lieutenant?" the Russian asked, his English accented but assured. There was something in the tone that made Folley take note. Looking at the man properly for the first time Folley saw that he was not wearing the motor rifle or armoured flashes on his shoulder boards or collar tabs. This was something new. The truth was slow in revealing itself, so retreated had his brain become from the realities of his situation.

90

"I—my name is . . ." He began it automatically, the eyes expressionless and the voice mechanical. The Russian officer hit him in the stomach, and as he fell against the wall of the office, it appeared that this was the signal to two other men, two NCOs, who came in from the inner office. Folley, surprised, looked up at them. The two men were looking at their officer, who was perched on the desk, smoking. As the truth seeped into the front of his mind, as from behind an almost watertight door, Folley began to laugh at the melodramatic posture of the officer. Like something out of an old film.

The taller of the two NCOs kicked him in the thigh as he sat there, and he rolled away, into the flying boot of the other man who had got onto his other side. The blow caught him in the side of the head, and the pain screamed in his temple and his neck.

The Lieutenant, who was from the GRU, Military Intelligence, like his two NCOs, watched dispassionately as the beating began.

Galakhov disliked botched or hurried work. The death of Vrubel, whom he had been forced to execute immediately upon *Kutuzov*'s orders, had been such a performance. No difficulty—but too much haste. Just as in the case of the mirror above the washbasin into which he now stared; almost coming away from the wall because someone had not bothered to do the job of mounting it properly. The screws were pulling out of the plaster. His tongue clicked against the roof of his mouth in disapproval.

He studied himself critically. Fur hat, sheepskin coat, English shoes, leather briefcase, battered suitcase behind him on the chequered floor. Yes, it would do. He signified acceptance as if to a tailor, nodding at his reflection. He glazed his stare—better. Something about his eyes—Vrubel had seen it, hadn't wanted to come with him, had had to be cajoled into not suspecting. The killing itself had been easy; and the dumping in the Moskva of Vrubel and his car—well, perhaps that was bravado, or irritation with *Kutuzov* for the way in which the old man presumed his services were acquired only by a nod, or a command, like turning on a tap. Let the KGB find the body, and start searching for the killer.

He turned, picked up his suitcase, and left the washroom in the principal Departure Lounge of Cheremetievo

Airport. As he passed out into the fuggier warmth of the lounge, he heard his flight being called, as he had known he would. A charter flight to London, with the last of the winter season tourists to Moscow. On it, he would be unremarked. His English was excellent, his papers good.

He clicked his fingers—the duty-free shop. He should have a polythene bag, and some cartons of cigarettes or a bottle of spirits. Tourists' last roubles, which they could not export, disappeared satisfactorily in the duty-free shop.

As he passed the main stairs to the restaurants and the Diplomatic Lounge, he glanced up at the two heavy KGB men at the top of the flight. He smiled, not at them, but at the knowledge that First Secretary Khamovkhin was leaving from Cheremetievo later that evening in his Tupolev Tu-144, for Helsinki.

Galakhov intended to arrive in Helsinki later the next day, as part of the drafted security staff surrounding the Soviet leader. Without pausing in his stride, he continued towards the duty-free shop.

Feodor Khamovkhin sat in a corner of the Diplomatic Lounge, and tried to arrange his limbs in a relaxed position. He felt nervous, and his arms and legs seemed to have some kind of cramp, so that it was difficult to sit still, not to be restless. He saw Andropov watching him as he chatted to some of the Party that had assembled either to fly with Khamovkhin to Helsinki, or to be present at his departure. Most of the Politburo were there—one of them at least not sorry to see him go.

He tried to press down on the thoughts, as if replacing the lid on a foul-smelling dustbin. But there seemed to be no pressure in his mind which could contain the suspicions. There they were, rings and lumps of dark coats, eddies of laughter or talk. All little men—no, some better than others—all part of the system, the same system as himself, all knowing the facts, none of them blind . . .

He stirred in his seat again, the restlessness of impotent fury irresistible. Andropov, as if recognising a danger signal, excused himself from his conversation with Gorochenko, the Deputy Foreign Minister, and crossed to him. He waved the two security men to further seats as he sat down.

92

"Relax, Feodor," he murmured. "You look far too nervous to be leaving for a State Visit which will culminate in your greatest political triumph."

Khamovkhin looked at him suspiciously. "Your humour is rather acid tonight, Yuri."

"Perhaps my own nervous reaction to the situation?"

"Nothing will happen here . . . ?" The thought had occupied the vocal chords almost before he was aware of it. *He hadn't thought it before!* "Sorry."

"Nothing, Feodor. I picked these men, just as I have selected the security staff who will accompany you. I give you my word—as far as I can be sure, and I have been *thorough*—that the men who will guard you can be trusted. Wherever I have had to draft them in from."

Khamovkhin patted Andropov's thigh, a gesture the Chairman seemed to dislike.

"Thank you, Yuri." Then he looked up into Andropov's ascetic, emotionless face. *"You* are in effective charge now. It's your job—to find these people."

"It always was, Feodor," Andropov replied sharply. "I know what is at stake here. But I can't move until I *know!*" Some reserve broke in Andropov suddenly. For so many years he had been unconcerned with power; his power had been evident, and unchallenged. Now, he was impotent, and looking into a mirror of impotence in the face of Khamovkhin. It was a precise, but visionary, moment, which he loathed. "I have to know," he added more calmly. "So, I have to keep my nerve, eh, Feodor. Perhaps it's a good thing that you won't be here—mm?"

Khamovkhin's face darkened, as if bruised by the stinging remark. Then, strangely, he nodded. "Perhaps, perhaps. You play a better game of knife-edges than I do, Yuri. I admit that."

Andropov bowed his head mockingly. "I shall need to."

"Let me know—anything, let me know."

"Of course. My men will rig the transmitter for you. I will be available—either myself or Kapustin, at any time. Regular reports will be made to you. If it happens, you'll hear it on the news. If not, you'll hear it from me."

Khamovkhin nodded. Restlessness again—yet some other movement than a cramped stirring seemed appropriate, even necessary. He stood up, and straightened his body. Like someone going out to execution, he thought, then smiled. No, someone bluffing his way across a border. Leaving his friend, but *subordinate*, to face the firing-squad. As everyone there knew, he had always played a good bluff.

He looked at the little groups of dark coats, and the white or bald heads—very few dark ones, a game of old men—and wondered which one of them it was.

"Which of those bastards is it?" he whispered, and Andropov touched his elbow in a warning gesture. *Old men,* he thought with contempt that did not entirely disguise self-disgust. Thinking aloud, dribbling while we sleep, creaking when we bend, snapping like old sticks when we break. A stupid, desperate game of old men—ancient, toothless figures who have to wear long underwear all year, and waistcoats and woollens—Politburo, High Command, Central Committee, Secretariat. Full of old men.

"Which of those bastards is it?" he asked again, bending slightly towards Andropov. "Find him, and kill him—then kill the others."

Andropov touched his forehead in a mocking salute.

FIVE
SCHEMES OF THINGS

The underground OPCO-ORD (Operations Co-ordination) room of Group of Soviet Forces North was surprisingly understaffed, or so it seemed to Admiral of the Red Banner Northern Fleet Dolohov, as Praporovich ushered him through the door, so that the two elderly men stood looking down from a gallery over the huge electronic map-table below. Only a few staff officers fussed around its perimeter, like billiards players assessing some future shot. He looked towards Praporovich as if for some explanation. Praporovich smiled.

"Bare, isn't it?" he said gruffly. "With a purpose. And not just to demonstrate what things might be like if—" Marshal Grigory Ilyich Praporovich, commander, GSFN, cut off the sentence by an effort of will. A moment of silence in which calm reasserted itself in his features, then: "We have moved normal strategic exercises and war games to OPCO-ORD TWO at Murmansk. There have been various computer malfunctions here in the past weeks which made such a move imperative."

Dolohov, the smaller, neater of the two men, smiled at the Marshal.

"And those officers down there—your *Rabbit Punch* team, I presume?"

Praporovich nodded. "They are all *entirely* trustworthy, Admiral."

"I don't doubt it."

"Come," Praporovich instructed, the arm he placed about Dolohov's shoulder oddly at variance with the inflexibility of command in the voice. "Come and see what you came to see."

He walked the Admiral along the gallery, their shoes ringing on the metal walkway, then ushered him into a control-booth, glass-fronted and empty except for two junior officers, which looked down over the huge map, its surface like opaque, slaty glass, devoid of features, reflecting only, and in a diffused manner, the lights in the ceiling of the high room.

The two junior officers sprang to attention from their chairs in front of a massive command console, and then Praporovich motioned them to sit. He guided Dolohov to the window, and then said:

"Very well—begin. Placements for dawn on the 24th. Set it up."

Dolohov could see the lights winking on and off on the control board behind him, and noticed, too, that the staff officers below had donned headphones, picked up cues so that they were more like billiards players than ever. More lights reflected in the glass in front of him, and he heard the rapid clicking of instructions being typed into the computer. Winking lights.

"You have recalled Pnin, then?" he said, as if to make conversation with Praporovich, staring grimly down at the unlit table below.

"Yes. It is done. Tonight."

"Tell me—you consider that *Kutuzov* made a mistake—?" He tailed off as Praporovich glared at him.

"No, I do not. It must be right. *Kutuzov* wished to ensure that nothing can go wrong. Pnin's timings had to be got right. Unknown territory for us—virtually. We don't rehearse the invasion of Scandinavia very much, even in GSFN!" Praporovich laughed deep in his chest, almost a threatening sound, and without humour. "The timetable is vital—the North Cape installations have to be taken out, and the Allied Mobile Force has a timetable we must be certain *we* can beat. *Kutuzov* understands this—" There was an implied slight, but Dolohov ignored it. "Now, the timings are right."

Dolohov nodded. Below him, the table sprang to life—a huge map of the north of Russia and northern Scandinavia appeared, melting into sharp focus, having, through the thick glass of the table, the appearance of three dimensions—brown mountains, green forests, blue sea. It delighted him, and he did not despise the almost child-like pleasure, though he thought Praporovich would have disapproved. Praporovich considered him, he knew, a weak link, a prevaricator. Perhaps he was; but it was his head, once the Northern Fleet put to sea on its own initiative.

Dolohov, in the silence of the OPCO-ORD room's control booth, his sense of Praporovich's presence both disturbing and reassuring, was prepared to admit a certainty beneath his prevarication. But only to himself. The navy would suffer as acutely as the army in the wake of the new SALT agreement. He, as a vocal opponent of such arms reductions, would be put out to grass, and a yesman brought in. Dolohov could already name the man who would succeed him.

But not that, he reminded himself. Not that—

He had moved uncertainly, and with darting, uneasy self-consciousness through a political maze for much of his life. From practical sailor to flag rank to administration, to Fleet command—for thirty years he had ceaselessly wondered why he never heard the language of revolution, the tone of Leninism, except in public utterances. He had kept his thoughts private, so that people believed he had none to think and none to share—but there had been a secret. He had stood, for a generation since the Great Patriotic War—on a rising mental ground, watching for the movement of armies, the spread of the creed to which he had given himself. Until now, it had never happened, or seemed likely to happen.

He could not speak for the army—even for the big man beside him—and its motives. And he clung, against suspicious, chilling moments of differing insight, to the idea that *Kutuzov* believed as he did.

Prevarication was, for him, a need to ensure that it would work. He was gambling his ideology, his secret self.

So, prevaricate—let them prove it, once again.

Lights on the map now. Dolohov recognised the colours which represented his own vessels—red for submarines, yellow for destroyers, green for cruisers, white for troop transports. On the map, the Northern Fleet had already set sail, and was in position. Along the northern coast of Norway, troops were to be landed from transports, each of them flanked by red lights, backed by yellow or green. Varangerfjord, Tanafjord, Laksefjord, Porsangenfjord, Altafjord—each deep inlet of the Barents Sea having a loop of the one main road from Kirkenes running at its edge. And that road had to be held so that the massive armoured thrust, preceded by chemical attack, could move effectively across the border into Norway, and along that road. The armoured force was a vivid concentration of blue light on the border, seeping already, it seemed, into Norway.

"Your principal dispositions," Praporovich said unnecessarily. Dolohov nodded.

"I can reasonably go no further down the coast than that—except with submarines," he observed. "That is what I wish to discuss with you. I think your targets illdefined, in some cases wrong. I agree with the North Cape monitoring systems. I have to move units of the Fleet *very* carefully until they are disposed of. I accept the operation against the fjord targets, however, with much more reservation. I think we should move to close the Baltic, *and* the northern Atlantic shipping lanes—"

Praporovich seemed surprised, even irritated, as at a persistent but untenable request from a child. His voice was carefully modulated, however, as he said, "Not yet— we threaten *only* Scandinavia directly. The rest is implicit. We have discussed this topic often before, Admiral. There is nothing new to say."

Dolohov felt no reservation concerning Praporovich's anger. He had decided, in advance, that he would promote the sense of his importance to *Group 1917* by this challenge. Praporovich was too careful, and too thorough, to steamroller his opinions, or dismiss them as the waverings of a weaker man.

"Very well. I want assurances that you can reach Tromsø and Bodø and Bardufoss during the hours of daylight on the 24th. And you can't do it by road, and I can't do it for you."

"I will have available—wait!" He turned to the two console-operators, and snapped: "Put up dispositions for 24:00, on the 24th."

Dolohov turned back to the view through the window, watching the lights of his naval force wink out, wink on again in different locations.

"Sir—which variant?" he heard one of the two young men ask.

"Variant Four," Proporovich replied. Then he said to Dolohov, "Variant Four anticipates the strongest possible resistance, and the slowest build-up of forces on our side. It assumes the arrival of units of the Allied Mobile Force, to support the Norwegians, in strength. It is an extreme unlikelihood that they could stiffen resistance as much as we have posited here. Also, in this variant, we have considered the worst kind of weather and road conditions along the entire length of the road system we persuaded the Finns to let us build."

Dolohov masked his satisfaction behind a nod. This is what he had come for. After months of more peripheral vision of the invasion—oh, yes, they had told him the details of the coup against Khamovkhin's gang, but treated himself, and the Fleet, as something dog-like to be given its orders, round up the sheep, and sit panting at their heels until they patted it on the head. He was at last being put fully in the picture now. Thus, he ignored the seaborne lights on the map-table as they winked out then came on, clustered around the seaward ends of fjords or threatening Tromsø and Hammerfest and Narvik and Bodø, and watched the landward lights. Like minor explosions of current, thick purple light bloomed around Kirkenes, Tromsø, and points between them—a chain of purple clouds—until the computer adjusted to the time-factor, and the purple became a dissipating fuzzy haze. Chemical attacks, taking place ahead of the main column, now being stabilised by the decontamination teams, rendered safe for the passage of armour.

"You have taken more than a hundred and fifty kilometres of the Kirkenes road?" Praporovich nodded. "And the other targets—*desant* operations?" Again, Praporovich nodded, but remained silent. Dolohov sensed that he disliked imparting the information. Perhaps GSFN had been secretive for too long.

As he watched, child-like at some celebration full of coloured lights, he began—even as he masked any satisfaction that might appear in his features—to believe that it would work. Work—yes, the great work. It was beginning, down there where the staff officers fussed around a chessboard of coloured lights.

Kirkenes was now distinguished on the map as an orange light; so was Bodø, and Bardufoss—and Ivalo, Dolohov noticed as his glance strayed eastwards from Norway. Airfields, he presumed, taken and being used to accelerate the inflow of support troops. Or to launch other *desant* operations towards the south of Finland and Norway.

"Look—" Dolohov began, irritated by the Marshal's silence. Praporovich turned to him. "I accept everything you've shown me—but my vessels are sitting in fjords all that day, and for days to come. What guarantees have you to offer?"

"None. We will be at war."

"I want to know about *response*, dammit!"

"None. Not until we stop. Annexation of Finland, and the north of Norway. Then we consolidate, and then we talk to the Americans."

"You're very sure of Wainwright."

"We are. He has no time for flexible response, no time for a conventional force to encounter our forces. And he won't use the nuclear force. Nor shall we. That's your guarantee. When we are in power, he will deal with us, because he will have to. On our terms—"

Dolohov, studying his companion, sensed, in a peculiar way, the voice and person of *Kutuzov* himself—a quiet, deep fanaticism, an abiding self-assuredness insisting on reality only in the terms that the voice described. Praporovich ended: "We shall succeed, because we must. It is the last throw. *This*—" He waved down at the map. "This is our show of strength, just as much as the capture and trial of Khamovkhin and the others, and the stamping out of those shits in the KGB." Suddenly, he seemed to relax, almost as if amused at the portentousness of his own words. "Come down, Admiral, and have a closer look. And—" Dolohov saw that it was as if the soldier had read his mind, had been reading it over the past months. "No secrets now, eh. Too late for secrets between us."

Again, he put his arm around Dolohov's shoulder as he led him out onto the gallery. Admiral Dolohov felt no resentment and no sense of pride to be reasserted. The long, high room, the echoing of the footsteps, most of all the map that glittered with a myriad lights, suggested a community that could not be broken, and of which he was an essential part.

The meaning of the display was success. Of that, he was at last convinced. He was among men who shared his secret dreams, and not amidst opportunists, lackeys, self-seekers, revisionists. The revolution was taking up arms. *Jihad.* He did not know why the Arabic had popped into his consciousness, but he smiled at its appropriateness. *Jihad.*

The biting wind chilled Khamovkhin immediately he stepped out of the comfortable warmth of the Tupolev; it seemed to have waited for him, for he saw the quick grabbing of fur hats, the sudden discomfort of those waiting for him on the tarmac of Seutula Airport. Two security men went down the steps in front of him, and took up their positions—and he felt himself reluctant to follow. The flight had been a respite, almost a reprieve. The sense of crossing the border *from* a foreign country to somewhere safer. Now, nothing of that—just the wind buffeting him, shrinking his sense of safety until he was aware of every inch of his old flesh.

Behind him, Gromyko murmured something to an aide, and Khamovkhin stepped forward, one gloved hand holding the rail of the passenger gantry. Immediately, the Finnish army band began the Soviet anthem. Its strains sounded tinny and unsubstantial in the wind, and the little figures of the President and Prime Minister of Finland, and the official party, too far away from him and quite unimportant. It was as if the bulk of the Soviet Union pressed at his back like a palpable thing, and he had the sense of Andropov's last mocking glance and the idea that he had run away.

He shook hands—more old men, he thought. The President welcomed him, they embraced in the Russian style. He felt old, leathery skin against his cheek. Then stepping forward again, down the two rows of the guard of honour, the cold eating into him, the faces of the Finnish soldiers white and stiff like those of dolls, the slim rifles bisecting their chilly features. He wanted it to be over.

A strip of red carpet, its edges ruffled by the searching wind, leading towards the podium, and the microphones. The flash of cameras; he remembered to smile at them, facing the battery. The press of the West, of course, all of them booked into comfortable hotels in Helsinki and waiting for the 24th. He climbed the three steps to the podium in front of the Finnish President, and composed his features to listen to the speech of welcome. He looked at the airport buildings, and saw only a few watchers, and some security men, all unnaturally still. And the television cameras—pictures to Finland, America by satellite, and of course, Russia. Persistent flashes from the photographers below the podium, and the sense of others crowding behind him. Ridiculously squashing onto something much too small to accommodate them. He almost wanted to laugh.

The President remarked the historic nature of the visit, the fittingness of the time and place, the wished-for completion of the treaty in a week's time. Until that time, he was their honoured and welcome guest in Finland. His own reply was brief, memorised even though he held the notes in his hand—the extra-large type of the IBM machine, specially manufactured with the Cyrillic alphabet, required because of his weakening sight. He promised a successful signing of the Treaty, and looked forward to his visit. Two metaphors of a long journey occupied the central part of the text, which had already been distributed to the press.

Thankfully, he stepped down from the podium, where the wind seemed worse, and climbed into the official Presidential limousine which had drawn up alongside. More flashes of cameras in the strengthening morning light, and then they were lights and faces behind him, sliding past the windows. He was alone in the car with the President of Finland, and they both smelt of the cold, and of heavy overcoats. He sat back in his leather seat, and closed his eyes. The President stared straight ahead, as if he had been warned not to look in his basilisk direction. Khamovkhin was thankful for that. The chill, this sense of every inch of himself, began to dissipate. He began to feel comfortable.

Galakhov went directly through the nothing-to-declare corridor for UK citizens at Heathrow. An uneventful flight in company with a motley group of British tourists —half-an-hour's boring conversation with a Trade Unionist and his wife about the cosy picture of Russia they had seen, venturing as far as Novosibirsk on their round trip. And the restorations to Leningrad, and the hospitality they had been shown.

"At last we can begin to learn in Britain," he remembered the man saying. "When this Treaty's signed, nobody can go on pretending Russia's still something to be afraid of—eh?" He had smiled, and nodded, and agreed, and had himself, in his English persona as a bank clerk, been most impressed with everything he had seen, including the women. The presence of the Trade Unionist's wife had restrained her husband's replies, he felt.

Two men were waiting for him when he had passed through the customs barrier. He nodded to them, and then went into the coffee shop in the passenger lounge. He queued for coffee, then sat at a vacant table, and waited. He watched the business of Heathrow through the windows, idly sipping at the coffee. He looked often at his English shoes, and marvelled at the insipidity of the security both at Cheremetievo and Heathrow, and the fact that people believed what was written on pieces of paper pressed between cardboard covers.

When he looked up from staring at his feet, the two men had joined him. Both of them, to his eyes, appeared far more English than he did himself, expensive suits displayed beneath open top-coats.

Without looking at either of them, he said quietly, "We are running to schedule, I take it?" His tone implied that it would be their fault if they were not.

"We are." The taller of the two men, and the one appearing more distinguished, more moneyed, seemed undisturbed by the tone of command in Galakhov's voice. His voice implied that Galakhov was in their hands now, and that they knew their part—did he?

"Where is he now?"

"On his way here—the flight leaves in two hours. He left the Embassy a short while ago, driving himself here. There's a radio car downstairs, and he's being tailed." Only in the exhaustive detail of the operation was the distinguished man betraying his subordinate role.

Galakhov nodded. "Good. Where is the gun?"

"Concealed in the toilet—third cubicle along from the door. I still consider a gun the wrong method—"

"*You* consider? Just do as you're told."

The tall man was silenced. Then his companion, who

103

seemed to have observed the exchange with truculent boredom, said, "The blood on the floor, *Comrade*." And Galakhov realised that the squat, dark-haired, badly-shaven man was effectively in charge of this part of the operation. He bridled at the insulting tone, but held his tongue. "We do not want to have to explain, or to clean up after you. You will be up and away, *Comrade*, but we will still be here."

"What do you suggest?" Galakhov said quietly, restraining all feeling. "And where?"

"That's better." Galakhov winced inwardly at the reversal of roles now so evident, and enjoyed by the dark man. Another of those occasions when he was nothing but an executive, a tool to be used by little men with hair coming from their ears and nostrils, and the cunning of foxes. All of them taking a temporary royalty borrowed from *Kutuzov*. "Stick to the original plan, Galakhov. You have an important message—trick him into the toilet, and kill him there—you've got two useful hands, if your file isn't out of date."

Galakhov looked down at his hands, and looked up again, grinning.

"You're a pair of shits, you know that?" he remarked, still grinning. The tall man bridled, but he saw an element of new respect in the way in which the dark man looked at him. Then he nodded.

"Very well. But do it our way—mm?"

"Naturally. Where is the briefcase?"

The tall man handed it over. Galakhov looked inside. A couple of slim files, and a sealed envelope bearing the stamp of the Trade Mission at the Soviet Embassy in London. It would lure the man they wanted to somewhere quiet so he could open it.

"You tell him there's an answer required."

"Yes. What's his cover—what we expect?"

"As far as we know, yes. You'll recognise him, anyway?" Galakhov nodded, placing the briefcase by his seat. "He's still travelling as a Finn, returning to Helsinki, and his business. Export saunas, that's the line."

"Good." Galakhov looked at his watch, then said to the tall man, "Get my change of clothes, and find out where he is as of this precise moment."

There was no more than the hesitation of a moment

before the tall man got up, and left them, heading out of the coffee shop with an admirably military bearing.

"Good front man," Galakhov's companion murmured. "Spent years in England. You should hear him in a pub."

"Really?" Galakhov remarked. "I wondered what it was he did to any useful purpose." He looked at his hands, then picked up his coffee cup, cradling it. The dark man, too, looked at Galakhov's hands.

Vorontsyev had not shaved. He was uncertain as to whether he had shaved the previous day or when he had left the hospital and returned to his cold flat. It might originally have been lassitude, or boredom. Now, he prowled the bare room that he called his study, the walls of which seemed to have enclosed him further, pressing on him with a brightness of maps, diagrams and his scrawled handwriting. He had not had time to wash, or clean his teeth. He was unsure as to how much sleep he had had, or the time at that moment.

His mouth, he noticed as he ran his tongue over his teeth, tasted awful. He had smoked too much. The air of the cramped study was thick and blue, and smelled of ashtrays—there were two big ones, one on the arm of an easy chair, the other on his small bureau, full of ash and stubs; and there were deposits of ash on the worn carpet, like the droppings of some desiccated bird.

He was still dressed in his old woollen dressing-gown —but he had replaced the thick striped pyjamas they had given him in the hospital with his own silk ones.

He was, strangely, not tired. Even though his head was thick, and seemed at times close to seizing like a cold engine; he was too excited, a tangible feeling in his stomach. He was no longer aware that he was merely duplicating what must be happening in dozens of offices in Moscow and other towns. With better facilities, better sources of information more easy to tap. He was alone, on sick leave, defined in a situation where he had surrounded himself with the blueprint of a system—the Soviet Union reduced to a problem to be solved on paper.

It satisfied him. His study, which seemed dusty and airless when he had first opened the door—hours, days ago? —had become familiar again; almost a part of him. There was no private experience any more—no feelings at all except for the barometric effects on him of his deliberations. He was rid of self; he was merely a brain, a memory, an imagination—operating upon known facts, assumed realities.

One plain wall of the study was decorated with something that resembled a genealogical table. The power infra-structure of his country, his state. He had drawn it on a huge tablecloth of paper, held together with sticky tape, pinned high on the wall. It was carefully drawn in red felt pen—with touches of green and blue here and there.

Each box in the branching table was clearly labelled. It was partly for information; and part of its function was a treasure-map, a cipher.

Near the ceiling—he had had to climb painfully onto a hard chair, his bruises protesting, sweat breaking out because of the simple, repeated exercise—were four boxes, representing the Praesidium, the USSR Council of Ministers, the Politburo, and the Central Committee of the Party. The four organs of control. Around the Politburo and the Central Committee he had drawn blue boxes—the organs of decision making and real control.

The branches of the table that interested him, descending from these two boxes, were the Ministry of Defence, below it the main military council and the First Deputy Ministers; then, spreading like the fertility of some medieval king, the general staff, the High Command of the armed forces, and the various branches of the services, details describing their sub-divisions more hurriedly scrawled beneath the boxes—because by that time he had become convinced that the military structure alone could not supply the answer to his problem.

From the Central Committee he had drawn a vertical line downwards to GLAVPUR, the Political Directorate of the armed forces, which was the Party's means of control over its huge war machine. An arrowed line descended from the GLAVPUR box, then slid leftwards beneath the sections of the services, dropping like seeds at each one, a symbol—the letters "PS." Each arm and branch of an arm of the Soviet armed forces possessed a Political Staff, responsible to GLAVPUR.

At that point, as he completed it, he left it; he did not need to add the GRU, Military Intelligence, which operated on the same infiltrated system as GLAVPUR; not the KGB, the Committee for State Security. He knew, too well, how that diagram would read, and he knew its intimate, unavoidable entanglement with the armed forces as with every aspect of Soviet Life. In the Politburo, the effective governing body, the KGB was represented by Andropov himself; on the Central Committee sat at least one KGB Deputy Chairman at any time; in the Praesidium and the Supreme Soviet, the titular government, the KGB was present. In the Secretariat, the Party's civil service and therefore present in every Ministry, there were KGB officers in civilian guise. And the GRU was operated by the KGB, subordinate to it.

He thought for a moment that he might have a clue, there and at that point. But it did not work. The *whole* of the GRU would have to have been suborned.

At that point, he had rested, sitting back in the armchair, staring at the system reduced to a chart—like the one that had been at the end of his hospital bed. This one measured the temperature of the state. He returned to the image of the king's genealogy. The fertile son was the KGB; his children were everywhere. And, because of that, nothing made sense. He had smoked, made a scrappy sandwich lunch, and drunk some beer.

The beer had grown warm and flat in the room, despite the temperature in the grey street outside the fugged window.

He tried to enter the matrix at a different point—went back to the files left with him by Deputy Kapustin. He had drawn the diagram, he admitted, out of arrogance. The brilliant candidate who requires no revision, no cribs supplied by an earnest, dim bookworm. But it had been stupid. He sorted the files, selected another wall, and pinned the photographs, one by one with a gallery's neat spacing, labelling each one with the name he found printed on the reverse.

It was as if Kapustin was an examiner at the training school, where Vorontsyev had first shrugged off the oppressive influence of Mihail Pyotravich Gorochenko, his adoptive father; where he had forgotten, for the first time, the privileged position that had made him envied, and disliked, at school and the Lenin University—which had paralysed his ability to decide his own future. Gorochenko had enlisted him in the KGB—engineered it. The man, his real father's oldest and best friend, had made him safe. That had always been the strange feeling he had had —of being *protected* by Gorochenko, placed where he could inflict rather than be inflicted upon.

It *was* an examination, he thought, staring at the photographs later in the day, when the galleried neatness of rows of faces had become edited, and there were large gaps above scribbled names as the least suspect were removed, lying in a discarded, spread pile on the floor. And it had been as at first—when he had first revelled in the power of mind, of reasoning, and—yes, he admitted it, the secret nature of the work, the intrusive, *spying* quality of it. After the training school, he had found his identity, and could once more love his adoptive father, whose name he had never been forced to take. He was himself.

Until Natalia, and the way she rubbed off the acquired skin, wearing his identity away as she made him a cuckold, a jealous, suspicious, agonised fool whose work suffered, whose reputation began to decline.

He brushed aside the thought.

Ten photographs. Ten case-histories.

He had selected them carefully, only removing a face from the wall after much deliberation, cross-referencing in the files that had come from the cheap briefcase as from a cornucopia. Endless riches of detail; a ceaseless diet of collected observation. Six military men. Two members of the Politburo. Two members of the Secretariat. Not all the suspicious ones, just those best placed. Samples, really. If nothing transpired, then others . . .

Then that, too, seemed complete, and he blenched before the mass of documentation stretching back over twelve months. He sat in his chair, looking at a discarded photograph that had slipped from the arm. He picked it up, and smiled. A dead man; he had been the first to come off the wall, with a laugh at the hidebound attitude that included corpses in the ranks of the suspected.

Twelve months of detail—periods of leave, all journeys within the Soviet Union or countries of the Warsaw Pact; all committees, all social engagements, and contacts. Sexual indulgences. Digests of tape-recordings; contacts leading back to the old man who had spoken over the tapped phone of *Group 1917*. Private habits, reading

108

material, exercise of the bowels, the dog, the digestion; holidays; second homes, financial records . . .

He had baulked at it, for the moment. Instead, he let his mind assume another tangent. The couriers.

For there had to be couriers. There could be no written or recorded messages or instructions. Word of mouth. Had it not been for Ossipov, then he would have concluded that the cell was tight-knit; after all, to achieve a coup, sudden and certain, would take only troops stationed in the Moscow Military District; no need to include Ossipov. Yet he was the one who had dodged his tail—been *aware* of it in the first place. Far East, based on HQ, Khabarovsk. Why was he necessary?

The local KGB Resident had been alerted, but as yet there was no report. It was one-horse outfits, in the East. Like frontier lawmen in American films, he thought. Far East was a military business, altogether. And suitably masked from heavy surveillance, therefore.

Couriers?

Civil servants, GRU personnel—back to the problem of subversion. Not soldiers, no real freedom of movement there. Not the senior officers, too attractive to the magnet of surveillance, they. Someone, some group—able to move freely?

Which was why his soldiers on the wall all came from different military districts—in their grainy blow-ups which savoured of secrecy and the power of unseen watchers. Odessa, Kiev, Central Asian, Siberian . . .

They might tell him something about the methods of communication, if they had anything at all to tell.

Substitutes? Still no ident on the Ossipov-substitute, that infuriating figure whose dead hand he had held. He could still feel the thrill of the cold thin wire, running into the sleeve of the black overcoat with the fur collar. Were there others?

It meant going back to the photographs—he would need his team, and here in the flesh not at the other end of a telephone, to do the same thing as he had done with General Ossipov.

And why Finland? Why Vrubel, who was dead?

He wanted to go to Finland. For whole minutes, the idea possessed him with an impatience great as that of any child. He knew that someone would be checking; he

109

wanted it to be himself, or one of his team. The egotism of the small room, the dusty light of it and the work there, was strong. Why Vrubel? Was he a courier?

The doorbell rang, startling him. Automatically, he looked at his watch. Four o'clock. In the afternooon? He had been staring at a picture of Marshal Praporovich, just about to step into a Moscow taxi. He had no idea how it came to be in his hand, nor the cigarette he had been absently smoking.

He got up as the bell summoned him again. Reluctant, he felt, then quickly aware of the dishevelled state of his appearance. He locked the door of the small study behind him, and went out into the narrow hallway.

Mihail Pyotravich Gorochenko stood on the doorstep, snow glistening as it melted on his shoulders. Vorontsyev's face immediately creased into a smile of welcome.

"Mihail Pyotravich—how wonderful to see you!" The two of them embraced, the younger man feeling the rough skin against his cheeks, the paternal fervency of the old man's kisses. Then he ushered him into the lounge— sparsely and unconcernedly furnished from some warehouse which stocked furniture of a standard kind for KGB apartments. Gorochenko sat himself near the electric fire, switching it on—then he glanced quizzically at Vorontsyev, sensing that his adopted son had not inhabited the frosty lounge that day.

"Busy, Alexei?" he asked as Vorontsyev poured vodka for them both, then set the bottle between them on a low table, scuffed with storage, nicked with wear. There were rings from wet glasses on it that he had not polished away.

Vorontsyev glanced at the locked door, wanted to tell the old man, but said, "A bit. There's no leave, you know!" He laughed. The old man nodded safely, and downed the vodka. Vorontsyev refilled the glass.

The Deputy Foreign Minister of the Soviet Union watched his face carefully, as if for signs of pain or age.

"I'm sorry I have not been to see you earlier, Alexei, my boy," he said. "Politburo business—things are buzzing . . ." Vorontsyev felt a twinge of shame at his own reluctance to confide. It was a habit he automatically obeyed. And the old man expected it. "You were badly hurt?"

"No—father." Vorontsyev enjoyed the ease with which he used the word these days. Not so well, perhaps, when the old man periodically tried to patch things up between himself and Natalia—he wondered whether the old man would use the visit as an excuse to do so again—but today, with a lot of preliminary work done, he could relax into an older familiarity. He smiled, and the old man's bright blue eyes smiled back at him from the strong, square face.

He leaned over and patted his thigh. "Good. Just bruises, the doctor told me. I rang the hospital yesterday. Comes of having a thick skull—like your father!" They laughed, recalling the same dead man. No hint of a gap between them because of their lack of propinquity.

Gorochenko lit a cigarette, and expelled a blue funnel of smoke towards the ceiling. Then he said, "It's a pity you haven't a woman about the place, to help you get well . . ." He held up his hand as Vorontsyev's face puckered with displeasure. "Oh, I know what you are going to say. I meant *her.*"

As if his mind turned a hunched, protective shoulder towards the old man, Vorontsyev said, "I don't want to discuss my wife—*father!*" This time the word was a plea.

"No, no. I have no wish to give you pain, my boy. But —you were once so happy, eh? And—Natalia has been to see me—yes. Little Natasha who went so far away from you. She came to me, and told me about—the other night."

It was as if his ribs protested; Vorontsyev drew a sharp breath of pain.

"What?"

"Yes, my boy. Today. This morning she called to see me at the Ministry. A private interview."

"What for?" Vorontsyev winced with suspicion.

"She—asked me, to arrange an interview. She wants to talk to you."

"About what? She's never needed my *permission* before for the things she does!"

Gorochenko's face darkened. He said, "Don't sulk, Alexei! Listen to me. Your calling there the other night— it disturbed her. And I think she felt humiliated. And even sorry that it had to happen." He spread his hands for silence. "I'm not saying she's changed, or that she wants to begin again. Just that she wants to see you." He patted Vorontsyev's thigh again. "I want to help you—not her, but *you*, Alexie. You believe that, don't you?"

Vorontsyev fought back something akin to tears. He felt young, brittle as glass, foolish. And he did want her back. He had always known that, as Gorochenko knew it. He knew he would agree to it, agree that they meet. He nodded.

"I believe it."

"Then I'll say no more. You can think it over. Then let me know. I said I would—let her know what you decide. A meeting with no promises, on either side."

"Very well," Vorontsyev said stiffly, sitting upright, starched by the emotion beginning to move in him. He poured two more vodkas with a perceptibly shaking hand, then said, "You look tired, father. You are working too hard."

"May be, my boy." He played with the thick white moustache, his homage to Stalin as he called it, and smiled. He drew on the cigarette, coughed, and added, "That cunning old bastard, Feodor, sniffs treason—as usual!" His eyes seemed suddenly to focus on Vorontsyev's face.

"Treason?"

"Don't worry. I'm not digging. Merely telling. The last meeting of the full Politburo. A performance of exceptional merit from our First Secretary. Plots against him, against all of us—inspired by the West, naturally. And he was hot on the trail! Quite like the old days."

"You—discount the idea?"

"Not necessarily." He barked with sharp laughter, and in the sound he was a powerful man, and unafraid. Wisely cynical, wordly-wise. "But I have heard the whole thing before. I think it comes with age, like prostate trouble or sciatica." He laughed again. Then he said suddenly, "Who tried to kill you, Alexei?"

"I—don't know," Vorontsyev said, seeing the hard anger in his adoptive father's eyes. The old man looked at him for a long time, then, seemingly satisfied, he nodded and looked at his watch.

"I must go, Alexei. I have an important meeting." He stood up. "You—take good care of yourself," he added gruffly. "Understand?"

"Yes, father." The words were so sombre, so charged with parental domination, that Vorontsyev felt as if the old man were rehearsing him in his school learning, or overlooking his mathematics. Or perhaps in the days of his student arrogance, arguing with him.

Gorochenko said, as if divining something, "To try to

112

kill an SID man means it is serious. Whatever it is—take care of yourself. You know what it would do to me if anything happened to you—eh?" Vorontsyev nodded again. "And—think about that other matter. Natalia. I don't like things as they are . . ." A hint of inflexible command in the voice, then: "Try to allow yourself to see her. Try to solve things, eh?"

"I—I'll try."

When he had seen the old man out, he had no desire to return to the study. Faces on the wall or relegated to the frayed carpet. He wanted—yes, wanted, he admitted, to think about his wife.

Folley was in little condition to register tangible scenes. Only the sense of personal movement, the grip of mittened hands on his arms, and being bundled into the back of a small, cramped vehicle, roofed with tarpaulin; he registered the change of environment with painful concentration. The aching body adopted unsuccessfully the hard outlines of the cold metal. Lights. He could remember lights, and the din of tracked vehicles waiting to move. Moving.

He tried to notice, to absorb and retain impressions. A litmus imagination. But it was difficult, because the gouts of pain from the broken ribs, the bruised flesh, still overwhelmed him. He slipped in and out of awareness, as if hiding from something. Yet someone might ask him to remember; so he tried.

It was snowing—the snow blowing into his hanging face, or flung as noisily as gravel against the tarpaulin. Two men in the seats in front.

The swollen tongue rasping thickly against the broken craters of teeth. Real, that.

The jolting of the journey—he raised himself to look out from the flap of the tarpaulin, once; saw a succession of tanks winding down a slope of the road behind him. And at the speed of his vehicle, they were not being left behind. Racing, almost, in that weather. A ridge in the road jolted him down again, and he passed out. After that, he did not attempt to look out again. Snow, blinding like a curtain—orange haloes of headlights, from somewhere behind. That was all.

He had no distinct awareness of time, or direction. And little idea of his context within the Russian column as it

113

moved back towards the border. He believed he had told them nothing—but as the shocks of pain went on, all he wished was that the journey would end, or the vehicle stop for a little; he could not remember the interrogation clearly at all. Did not remember its object.

Only the movement, then; after an undetermined time, it was only the next jolt, the next protest of the body, that concerned him. The minute changes of position, finding unbruised parts of himself that might cushion the shocks as the vehicle careered down the road to Rontaluumi; no longer just a vehicle, flapping tarpaulin or screaming, chained wheels or plastic seating thrust against his cheek —his whole world, now.

He had, in fact, passed out once more when the column began to pass through the border wire east of the village; his own vehicle, driven by Lieutenant Shapkin of the GRU, was near the lead, behind the advance Motor Recce Company, because orders had been received from Leningrad that the Englishman be returned to Russian soil as soon as possible. Pnin, the General in command of the Ivalo strike force, "Finland Station Six," had obeyed each of his instructions, relayed from Praporovich in Leningrad; even the one concerning Folley. By the morning, which would come late and dark with the convenient storm, the only Russians remaining on Finnish soil would be a covering party left in the deserted village.

Folley was unconscious for most of the helicopter journey to Leningrad. The brief and violent storm had abated sufficiently to allow a helicopter to set out from the deep forest that now concealed "Finland Station Six" on their own side of the border. Folley had slept in stillness for a few hours, in a wooden hut, of which he had perceived little—shape of planking, and the heat from the stove. Then, when they hauled him to consciousness, in darkness still, the snow thick against the windows, he had cried out once, as if robbed, and passed out.

Galakhov waited until the Finnair flight to Helsinki was called, and his target had begun to stir in his seat in the Departure Lounge in the Queen's Terminal, before making his approach. He required the distraction of time slipping away to cover any suspicion by the target. He was dressed in the uniform of an Embassy chauffeur; a disguise which would excuse his unknown face but supplement a fiction that he was KGB. The tall man had taken away the suitcase and his travelling clothes, then returned. Both of his contacts were seated elsewhere in the lounge, waiting to follow him and the target.

Ozeroff, GRU Military Attaché at the Soviet Embassy in London, drafted by special order of the Chairman of the KGB to security duties in Helsinki, was just gathering up his topcoat and suitcase when a chauffeur snapped to attention in front of him, and saluted.

"Sir—" the young man began, when Ozeroff snapped, "You bloody young fool, what do you mean by drawing attention to me like that?"

"Sorry, sir," the young man muttered, shuffling his feet, rigid stance collapsing into nerves. "Urgent communiqué from Moscow Centre, sir—I was told to catch you before you left. There's a reply expected—"

"Dammit!" Ozeroff glanced in the direction of the overhead loudspeakers, then at the departure board. "Important, you say?"

"Sir."

"Very well, give it to me." He motioned towards the briefcase in the chauffeur's grasp.

"Not here, sir—" the young man said respectfully.

"Very well—where?" He looked about him. "Hell, the toilets, then. Follow me."

Galakhov picked up, despite the movements of many passengers, the movement of the two contacts—the "dustmen," as he had called them, much to their annoyance. Ozeroff, the whole operation, was in his hands at this moment, and he enjoyed that. He scuttled behind the striding Ozeroff, only a few years his senior but stiff with military service and self-importance. His appointment to the security staff surrounding Khamovkhin had been made because of his fanatical loyalty to the regime, and to the KGB, for whom he worked, despite his titular appointment to Military Intelligence. Galakhov watched his bearing carefully, on two levels—to imitate, and to overcome.

Easy to kill, even without the gun that had already been removed from the cubicle by the dark man.

Ozeroff swung open the door of the washroom, letting it swing back towards the ignored Galakhov. Galakhov stopped it gently, and pushed it open as if protecting the sensitivity of his hands. Then Ozeroff was facing him, ignoring the two men washing—one of them using an elec-

115

tric razor, its buzz like a warning—his hand held out for an envelope that Galakhov fished for inside the briefcase. One of the men moved to the roller towel, and began to rub at his face—an Arab, puffing with cold, humming as if nervous, as if picking up some hidden tension. The shaver, check shirt and well-tailored jeans, who might have been American, or European, ignored everything except his reflection in the mirror. Galakhov backed a little towards the door of one of the cubicles. None of them appeared to be occupied—yes, one near the Arab was closed. He motioned with the envelope, and Ozeroff, conscious only of delay, and of possible changes of plan, took the envelope and passed inside, beginning to close the door. Galakhov saw the Arab about to turn, saw the shaver pause to inspect the side of his jaw, rub at it—and pushed into the cubicle with Ozeroff.

The GRU officer leaned back against the cistern, even as his eyebrows raised in surprise. Galakhov put his finger to his lips, and proffered a notebook and pencil and mouthed the words: "Your reply, sir." Ozeroff nodded, and tried to move away from physical contact with the chauffeur. And, as Galakhov had known he would, he half-turned in the secrecy of childhood or examinations, away from the intruder upon his privacy. Galakhov listened. The humming Arab passed the door, which he reached behind him to lock silently, and the noise of the battery shaver started up again, long louder strokes as the man worked at the last rough places.

Galakhov raised his hands above his head, pulling at the strap of his watch, stretching out the thin wire until he clasped it with both gloved hands—the gloves were padded, to protect the fingers—and then Ozeroff was beginning to turn, having been puzzled by the forged letter—

Loop, pull. He was slightly to one side of the man so that he could not exert the knee in the back, and would have to choke him. The letter fluttered to the floor, and slid under the door of the cubicle, and Ozeroff's hands were trying to scratch at the biting wire around his throat. Galakhov could see the eyes, the way they asked questions still even as they protruded more and more—the mottled skin turning a satisfactory purple, the hands scrabbling, tearing the skin on the neck, the body and legs doing nothing, nothing—

They never did, never did, he thought. Too much concentration on the attacked area, no rationality when a man is being choked to death. Ozeroff reached out one hand to the wall, obscuring a scrawled bit of graffiti, as if steadying himself. Already Galakhov was taking the weight of the body as it began to slump, while tightening the wire still further. Feet of Ozeroff trying to maintain balance, instead of lashing out.

All the time, for every moment, Galakhov could hear the noise of the battery shaver. Ozeroff made no noise, pressed rigid between Galakhov and the wall, no scrabbling, no breath. When Galakhov released the wire—he felt Ozeroff's body slump further, and saw the eyes roll up under the lids—he began to whistle tunelessly, as if in embarrassment at being overheard by the man shaving. The shaver paused for a moment, then continued to buzz. Galakhov leaned forward, and guided Ozeroff's limp arm with his elbow.

The toilet flushed.

Galakhov released the body, caught it against the wall with his hip and stomach, and lowered it onto the seat. Then he leaned back against the wall, feeling hot, stifled. He did not look at Ozeroff's face, but listened. The buzz of the shaver had stopped. No one else had come into the washroom. He looked at his watch as he rewound the wire. In another two minutes, his two "dustmen" would arrive to take away the remains.

"Hey—in there." American!

"Y—yes? What is it?"

"You dropped a letter, or something?"

"Yes—yes I have."

"In Russian?"

"Yes." All the time, Galakhov had spoken with a more pronounced accent than he normally used when speaking English. "Business—I am from Finland." He looked into Ozeroff's dead face, and smiled.

"Sure. None of my business. Here—"

The letter appeared at his feet, pushed under the door. Next to the notebook and pencil that he had dropped— Galakhov realised he hadn't heard them fall.

"Thank you—thank you very much."

The washroom door swung shut behind the American. Galakhov relaxed, staring at the high ceiling of the room, ignoring the body slumped on the seat. Then the door of the occupied toilet swung open. Water flushing, then hands

117

being washed, then the click of the roller towel—the washroom door opening, sighing shut, then opening again, the footsteps of two men.

Water running.

"All clear," he heard in the tall man's excellent English.

He opened the door, saw the man dressed in white overalls, and took the suitcase that was handed to him. He changed in the next cubicle, listening to the noises of Ozeroff's body being bundled into the linen basket on wheels, covered with dirty linen. The other man changed the roller towels.

The men were gone before he finished changing, taking the suitcase with the chauffeur's uniform when he passed it out to them, leaving another suitcase, Ozeroff's, for him to employ in his cover.

Galakhov made the final flight call for his Finnair jet to Helsinki. It was the evening of the 18th.

PART TWO

MAIN FORCE

18th to the 22nd of . . . . . ., 19 . .

"A civil war is inevitable. We have only to
organise it as painlessly as possible."
—TROTSKY

SIX

THINGS FALL APART

He was left now, on the A40, the driving, persistent sleet obscuring vision and inducing lethargy, with nothing more than a desire to stop. Only when the small delivery van stopped would he begin to think of a drink, or food. He and the tall man had finished the flask of coffee—and he knew he could not drink anything more from the silver hip flask without falling asleep.

The M40 had been bad enough—lunatic drivers over-taking, spraying the windscreen, and the sluggish wipers, with slush; but the A40 was worse. He and the tall man and the body of Ozeroff seemed to have been imprisoned in the delivery van for an endless time. He was irritated, and careless, with the fatigue of long having completed his task, and not being able to relax from it. They had not even stopped at a pub; something stupid, even supersti-tious—pushing their luck—about leaving Ozeroff in the car park while they drank whisky by a fire. He shrugged, amazed at his own surrender to the conditions of this af-termath. After all, the signal had gone off to *Kutuzov* di-rect; all they had to do was to lose this body for the space of less than a week. By that time, it would all be over—and they would be out of the country, anyway. Stupid.

Kutuzov, of course. Old Magnet-man—Svengali. If he said it was important—*vital*—then you did it, no matter how gritty your eyes were, or how your stomach protested.

He glanced at his companion, heaped uncomfortably

in the narrow seat, and trying to doze. Then he stretched his eyes wide, and concentrated on the flying sleet, the fuzzy headlights, the sudden slow rush of other lights out of the darkness.

He saw the other lights, realised that they were high up, as on a truck, and swerved. He was aware, in the few seconds remaining to him, of a noise as Ozeroff lurched like something resurrected in the back of the van, and his companion stirring as he was jolted awake, mumbling through a dry, sticky mouth for him to take more care. He was aware, too, quite certainly, that he was going to die, and that the betraying Ozeroff was lying in mock state in the back of the van—and he hoped the local police were very stupid men.

Then the car-transporter, having strayed across the white line because the driver was tired, and hurried, flipped the van over on its back, as a child might turn a tortoise upside-down with the aid of a stick. The van, apparently that of a towel service firm, ended up in the ditch at the side of the A40 just outside Wheatley, after somersaulting twice. The back doors burst open, sliding out, almost as in a farce, the body of Ozeroff, feet first, onto the roadside verge. The driver was crushed against the wheel—the passenger flung through the windscreen. The driver of the transporter, uninjured, was sick when he inspected the wreck and the three bodies. Then he called the Oxford police from the nearest telephone box.

Kenneth Aubrey was chilled, angry, and fascinated. Traffic on the A40 had been reduced to a single lane, and a canvas screen erected to shield the accident from the inquisitive. Behind this, spotlamps glowed in the sleet, shining down on the sodden bundles, side by side now, and covered with grey blankets, themselves sodden wet; policemen directed the moribund queues of cars coming home from pubs and parties, or analysed the events of the accident. Aubrey alone, perhaps, now that he had been introduced to the three bodies, remained still, and contemplative.

"So much stuff on them, sir, we got in touch with the Branch. They must have thought of you."

"They did, indeed, Inspector. My thanks for your promptitude," Aubrey had replied stiffly to the Inspector, who was bending to peer under the umbrella Aubrey carried. And *such stuff*—chauffeur's uniform, British passport for someone, with a face not identifiable among the dead here, another change of clothes, and one of the dead murdered with a rather out-of-date, though still effective, KGB tool, the watch-wire—Timex Cravats, he understood were their popular name. It *was* KGB, that was evident—the one security machine above all others that enjoyed the gadgetry of violent death, the little toys that killed.

And towels from the airport—strange that they had not rid themselves of them, or the white coats. Aubrey thought he understood the lethargy of aftermath. But—who was dead, and who killed him? And—Aubrey could almost taste the feline pleasure of the mystery—who owns the face on the British passport?

"Inspector?" he called.

The policeman, disgruntled and wet, hurried up.

"Sir?"

"I have some instructions to give. Perhaps I might use your car radio?"

"Certainly, sir."

"And I shall have need of photographs of these three—not here, but when they've been cleaned up. As quickly as possible—you can get them removed now. All papers, anything you remove, will be collected for our own investigation, early tomorrow."

"Sir."

As they walked bowing to the windy sleet, the Inspector grateful for Aubrey's offer of a crescent of the umbrella, Aubrey had a sudden image of the crash outside Kassel, months before. And he sensed an excitement he could not quite explain, certainly not define with any precision, that here was coincidence pointing in a certain direction. He hurried his steps, unconsciously, to the police car.

"You'll want it rigged through to—London, sir?"

"Yes, use the number you would normally use—I'll take it then."

It took little more than two minutes for the police radio to be patched into the receiving station on one of the floors of the Euston Tower, and from here Aubrey was connected directly with INTEL-CORD, the SIS's co-ordination and evaluation section, housed in Queen Anne's Gate itself, unlike many of the service's units.

"There you are, sir." The Inspector left without pause,

handing the mike to Aubrey, shutting the car door on the sleet and the traffic. As the window misted almost immediately, Aubrey felt quiet, and calm, with a little tickle of excitement beginning somewhere in his stomach.

"Who's that?"

"Callender, sir."

"Good. Callender—send someone out here to collect some pictures, some bodies, and some evidence, would you? One of your customers has some nasty marks on his neck, which one of our foreign counterpart is responsible for. I—shall want a lot of clearance time for this Callender. I shall want to know who the men are, and whose picture I have in a fake passport."

"Sir, we're right up to here with co-ord work—"

"No, Callender, you are not. Not as of early tomorrow morning. Hurry things up, would you? Out."

He sat for a time in the fuggy car, warmth not apparent, but cold less so. A great nuisance that he was booked on a morning flight to Helsinki, to act as Waterford and Davenhill's control, and to oversee security, in conjunction with the CIA man, Buckholz, for the Treaty Conference's final sessions, when Khamovkhin and Wainwright would both be present. A great pity. Here, on this Oxfordshire roadside, there was a real mystery—and, with an instinct he would never have trusted as a younger man, he knew it was important.

Galakhov knew that his picture had been taken at least twice during the time he spent passing through Passport Control and then Customs at Seutula Airport. It would have been done by the CIA, by Finnish Intelligence, even perhaps by the KGB. It did not matter. To any foreign intelligence service, he was simply a native Finn returning to Helsinki, then travelling north; and to the KGB, he was expected. And they would be expecting Ozeroff to look like *him*, not like the body in the Heathrow toilet. Records had been changed, the computer doctored, everything required already done. Thus, it was with confidence that he passed through the controls, out into the lounge, and waited to be contacted.

He could not restrain a small pulse of excitement beating in his chest, making his breath flutter. There had been little reaction on the plane to the killing of Ozeroff —he had had a couple of drinks, true, but only for the pleasure; no, but he could not help, as he stepped onto Finnish soil, realising how deep into the operation he already was, and how close to the real simplicity of the thing. Preliminaries were almost over—he and Khamovkhin, soon. All he had to do was to pass the interview with the Head of Security where Khamovkhin was being kept during his visit, then act his part until Khamovkhin was no longer required to be alive.

"Have you a light?" a voice asked him at his side. He turned slowly.

"What?" he asked in Finnish. "What do you want?"

Nonplussed, the young man said, "Have you a light?" He spoke in Finnish.

"I am a non-smoker—it is a filthy habit," Galakhov replied, bored, even amused at the kind of rubbish the KGB still considered viable operational procedure.

"Where is the toilet, please?" the young man asked. Though he spoke in Finnish, this time, instead of the word *toaletti*, Galakhov heard the Russian pronunciation, *twalyet*. He almost burst out laughing.

"Wait till you get home," Galakhov said; then, when the young man's face appeared suitably pained, said, "I believe the toilet is on the next floor."

The young man could not quite disguise his satisfaction before he made his face expressionless, and said, "Follow me, please." He took Galakhov's suitcase, and walked away towards the glass doors to the car park. Galakhov, seeing his neck still red above the coat collar, even though cautious by nature, and careful of indulging his abiding sense of superiority, could not help but consider how easy the whole thing was going to be.

Vorontsyev had rubbed a small round clearness in the mist of the window, and was staring down into Pyatnitskaya Street. People on their way to work, huddled in heavy clothes, shunted against each other on the pavement six floors below. It was a bitter day, frost bright on the road, the trails of tires black on its silver.

He had got up at six, washed and shaved, and eaten a good breakfast. The work, and drink, of the previous night had left him and he felt refreshed.

The faces were still on the wall—the diagram of the State on a second, and a huge map of the entire Soviet Union on a third, lapping down over the bureau. He was

125

waiting for the duty officers of his team to arrive. When he briefed them, they would be taken entirely into his confidence. Then he would talk to Kapustin, and seek permission to go to the Finnish border, to discover what Vrubel had been doing.

He posed himself before the faces, and stared up at them. Old men, most of them. Men of distinguished loyalty to the Party, men about whom no questions had been asked, not even during the Kruschev regime. And yet, if they were guilty, it was precisely during that period that they would have been forming this *Group 1917*, working out its strategy.

He looked at General Ossipov. It was an older photograph than the ones he had studied in his office, and the man was in a light suit, and it was summer in Odessa. He knew the place, had holidayed there with Gorochenko and his wife, just before he began his studies at the Lenin University.

He did not allow himself to idle over the memory, though it was pleasant. Marya Ilyevna Gorochenka retained a special, perhaps sacred, place in his memory.

Vorontsyev smiled at the simplicity of his attitude—like so many other simplifications, or unthinking responses he had made over a lot of years—conforming, accepting, belonging; and yet he could not despise such a sleep of reason. They were good people, both of them. He had wept at her funeral, and many times the prick of tears had come to him when he thought of her. It might have been a luxury, but she had been his mother, childless and grateful for the opportunity; his own mother had died soon after the war, soon after the death of his real father. He remembered her as a faded, untidy, shabby woman. Something that hovered in corners, and did not go out—like a ghost, or something left over that no one wanted.

He skirted the procession of images, and focused again on Ossipov. Why the Far East? And the reference, he suddenly remembered, to *Finland Station?* Did that mean Finland itself, or Leningrad? Was it a reference to the return of Lenin to Russia, in the sealed train—a symbol of what the coup wished to do ideologically? Was Vrubel's attachment to the Finland border confusing him?

"You cunning old shit," he said softly to the photograph. "Where did you go, and who did you meet? And what for?"

126

He looked above the photograph, to another. Praporovich, commanding Group of Soviet Forces North, a strong man, old-style Communist; he had a blunt, violent language which expressed his hatred of the West, his commitment to the eventual, and military, spread of Communism. Who could be more loyal a servant of the State—on the surface?

Vorontsyev crossed to the chair at the bureau, and pulled out of the old briefcase the file on Praporovich. Then he moved a sheaf of papers from the armchair, and sat down, opening the buff folder on his knees. He had not been seized by a definite idea—merely by the logic of beginning at the top. The Marshal was the most senior man on the wall in front of him. He would require to be investigated first, as was his right, Vorontsyev thought with a smile.

Praporovich was a widower, with two sons, both of them in the army—Vorontsyev checked them immediately shuffling through the loose papers until he found photostats of their army records. One was a Major in an Airborne Division, the other a Colonel in command of one small section of the northern missile chain—"Firechain." Little there. He went back to the old man, looking up once at the hard, square features appearing to regard him with contempt from the wall—a portrait of an old and terrible Tsar. He winked at the photograph, wondering why the Marshal could not smile even at a party following a large-scale military exercise in the DDR. Perhaps he was an habitual stoneface?

The Marshal rarely took holidays—he had a *dacha* outside Leningrad, and spent a great deal of his off-duty time there, or in his suite of rooms at the expensive Baltiskaya Hotel. He rarely entertained women at either residence, preferring his huge collection of gramophone records and his books—and his persistent hobby of woodcarving. Vorontsyev studied, briefly, pictures of two statuettes in polished wood, and seemed to touch the old man's private self. A boy and a girl—the girl on a small pony.

There were sheets of small prints supplementing the written records. They were less talismanic than the cartridges of slides he had watched of Ossipov, but he studied them carefully, noting the faces he did not know, the possible contacts—though he did not compare them

127

with the supplementary sheets which explained their identities. Not at that moment. He was interested in the Marshal.

Praporovich's movements had been exhaustively documented. Military conferences at the highest level in Moscow, Leningrad and various Warsaw Pact capitals—Prague, Berlin, Budapest, Warsaw. Vorontsyev wondered for a moment whether there was sufficient freedom of movement . . .

But no. He could not be his own courier. He was present at the annual exercises of Group of Soviet Forces Germany—though not at the most recent winter exercises, which were the largest for five years—"1812."

Vorontsyev felt chilled, as if a door had opened, but no light, only cold flowed from it. He checked back, his fingers clumsy and gloved with haste. No—Praporovich had not attended *every* exercise over the past years—seven, eight, ten years; he checked off the references on the grubby photostat compiled by Leningrad SID. He usually attended the summer exercises—had been on the 1968 exercise that had led to the intervention against the Dubček regime—but he had attended . . . two, four of the last seven winter exercises in the DDR. As part of the necessity for all senior Group Commanders to be aware of overall strategy. In case of illness, resignation, death—transfer was easy.

Why not?

Was his staff there?

Vorontsyev scribbled the query on a fresh page of his notepad. He would have to check. He wondered why Praporovich had not been at "1812." And did it mean . . . ?

He refused to countenance the idea that acceleration was taking place, that there was any *vital* reason why the Marshal had stayed at his headquarters in the Soviet Union. Nevertheless, as if in answer to some subterranean explosion, his hands shivered with the ground-shock. The solid structure of the investigation appeared on the point of subsidence sliding into something horridly real.

He began to cross-check. How closely was Praporovich acquainted with the other faces on the wall?

It was a little after nine when the doorbell rang. He looked up from the papers now spread on the floor, stretched as he rose from his kneeling crouch over them, as if trying to spark them into reluctant flame, and his

back and bruises protested. He stood up, stepping carefully over the arranged documents. He had taken the decisive
step of cutting the original documents to pieces, arranging them anew, with the help of paste and a stapler,
into sections which displayed more easily and meaningful-
ly the relationships between the men on the wall.

And it *was* interesting—if one went back far enough.
Almost, he thought, almost like discovering someone who
has patiently covered his tracks, but who had been at the
scene, or near it, at the time in question—whatever his ali-
bi, however he had burned the bloodstained clothes, tidied
the room, removed the fingerprints . . .

No. His men had arrived. He would let them see, and
ask them to decide, before he would commit himself . . .

His smile of satisfaction died when he saw his wife on
the doorstep, her face freezing into haughtiness and a sense
of mistaken action as she saw his own face change.

"Well?" he said. He was holding the door foolishly ajar;
it was like his stupid mouth, he thought, hanging open.

"I—want to talk," she said, appearing to damp down
her irritation, her embarrassment.

"What about—I'm busy," he snapped.

"You—you've seen your father?"

"Yes. I said I'd telephone."

"You might have said no. May I come in?"

He looked at his watch.

"I'm busy," he said, then: "Oh, come in!" It was graceless, and sulky. He despised himself for the immaturity
of his reaction. He could sense the smile of satisfaction on
her face as he led her into the lounge. He waved his hand
towards the sofa. Natalia hesitated, then settled herself.
She did not offer to remove her fur coat, nor the dark fur
hat she wore.

Standing by the empty mantelpiece above the electric
fire, he studied her. Her cheeks were touched with pink
from the cold outside. Her fur-lined boots, to her knees,
were new, and unmarked from the pavements. She had
come by taxi.

She said, "I had to talk to you." It sounded remarkably
superficial. As a singer, she was not renowned for her
acting ability, only for the quality of the voice itself. He
felt she was acting a part. He could not understand why
she needed to.

"About what?"

"Us?"

"*Us?* There isn't any us, is there, Natalia?" Even the use of her name seemed a concession. He *did* want her there.

She opened her coat, as if on cue. It was ridiculous. She was too smartly dressed—dark-green wool, with a high collar and excellent fit. It would have cost money—would have been given by a lover, or bought on a Bolshoi tour. They had been in Paris in the autumn. It was as if she declared herself naked by the gesture. He hated her.

"Isn't there?" she said. "About the other night—I'm sorry it had to happen. I—was ashamed . . ." She dropped her gaze.

He could not believe her. He wanted to re-establish some sense of superiority, and his voice was loud as he said, "Sorry? Ashamed? Your bloody lover tried to *kill* me—or didn't Mihail Pyotravich tell you that?"

She looked at him, and there seemed to be something real happening in the theatrically wide eyes. She was speaking to him, as well as to some imagined audience of her performance.

"I—he didn't say that . . ."

"Didn't he? He left you before you could climb all over him, and led me right into a neat little trap. For some reason, Vrubel wanted me dead! You wouldn't know why, I suppose?"

"You don't think—?" she began, and there was genuine fear in her voice. As if she sensed herself alone in the room with him for the first time.

"How the hell do I know! You're capable of it." She shook her head. He admitted: "I suppose not."

There was a silence. He turned his back on her, and lit a cigarette from a fresh packet. He heard her say: "What about us, Alexei?" It was the first time she had used his name. And the tone was old, magical. He knew it was calculated.

He turned round.

"You're here, aren't you?" He wanted to go on being bitter, recriminatory. But, though he despised his feeling, he could not ignore it. Too often he had imagined the scene, and he was now helpless before the reality. He had to concede; that had been decided when he opened the door to her. "What the hell do you want with me, Natalia? You've buggered up my life once already! Do you want the satisfaction of doing it again? Is that it?"

130

She shook her head. He was glad she did not offer to move from the grubby sofa and its dun-coloured covering. He did not want to be any closer to her. Her body, even at that distance, was tangible against his frame. The sensation was dirty, like a wet dream. He hated that—she the cinema, he the audience; her body unreeled like the frames of some titillating film. He tried to dissolve the feeling in anger.

"The hell it is? Who sent you, eh? Mihail Pyotravich?"

She looked startled, as if he had seen deep into her self, but she said, "He only helped me to make up my mind."

"Fuck you, you bitch! I don't want to be handed you like some sticky sweet! Or a bandage because I'm coming to pieces! If you don't *want* to come back, then get out—get out!"

He turned away from her again, willing her to move, wanting her not to come closer to him. He heard the sofa creak slightly as she stood up.

The doorbell rang again, releasing him. He turned round, and saw her hand a little extended. He smiled in satisfaction.

"Work," he said.

"I'll go, then." She hesitated, then: "Shall I come back —later?"

He wanted to hit her, at least banish her. He nodded.

"Yes, if you want to—" He would not offer to go to the flat on Kalenin Street—he had to preserve that much. She nodded, reached out as if to touch him, and then dropped her hand.

"Later, we can talk properly," she said.

The doorbell rang again. He acquiesced with a nod.

To the manager of the Matkailumaja-Turiststation, the only real hotel in Ivalo, they were from the Central Electricity Generating Board, studying the hydro-electric schemes in the Inari region. Philipson, the man the Helsinki Consulate had loaned them, spoke Finnish and established their cover. The staff of the nearby Kirakkakoski power station lived in their own compound, and only came into Ivalo at the weekends. By the time that happened, Waterford and Davenhill would have left, probably be back in London.

Philipson had a jeep for them, and had stocked it with supplies, had driven north-east out of the town with them,

131

and then watched them as they turned south-east, towards Raja-Jooseppi. Then he turned up his fur collar and headed back to Ivalo. He had little idea of their intention, and small wish to know. It was his role to fend off any awkward enquiries concerning the presence in the area of two British electricity experts.

They camped the first night off the single road just south of the village of Ruohokangas. Waterford, it seemed to Davenhill, paid little heed to the bitter cold, to the discomforts of travel and pitching camp, to the inadequacy of the food, or to him; while he resented, ever more bitterly, the decision that had placed him there. He had been shunted by Aubrey in the most high-handed way, and made to appear nothing but an errand-boy.

He was cold in his sleeping bag, his teeth chattering, his feet numb. He could hear the steady breathing of the other man, and hated him. He had always found it difficult to resent himself for very long, or indulge in recrimination; but he could, he knew, be satisfyingly viperous towards others. Now, that feeling towards Waterford warmed him, and eventually he drifted into sleep.

In the morning, he awoke aching with cold and senilely stiff. When he moved, his whole body protested. He reached out of the sleeping bag, and his hair was stiff with rime. He sat up, groaning. Light, grey and unwelcoming, was coming from the open tent flap, and he saw Waterford's face grinning at him without humour.

"'Your turn to cook breakfast."

"Push off!" Davenhill snapped, rolling the unzipped flap of the bag away from him, and climbing wearily to his feet. "You like this, don't you?" he asked, as Waterford allowed him out of the tent. "This Hollywood stuff—very manly." His voice was acid; but there was a bile of memory, as if they had shared an unsatisfactory physical act.

Waterford said, "I thought you were the man's man."

Davenhill's unlined face narrowed with spite. Then he seemed to control himself, and said softly, "Is that how you get your kicks? Despising people? It's a sign of weakness, you know."

Waterford walked away. He had set up the primus, and Davenhill crossed to the jeep and fished out the provisions box. Then, not looking at Waterford again, he began to prepare the breakfast. His mind came free of ice and acid at the smell of the coffee.

They shared the breakfast in silence, then Waterford stowed the tent, and they pulled back onto the road. It had snowed heavily in the last forty-eight hours, and the narrow road was clean of vehicle tracks. The chains on the wheels bit and stuttered at first, then they made better going of it as they entered thicker forest; the snow was a light covering over compressed snow-ice. Waterford drove in silent concentration, and Davenhill became enervated by the passage of silent, snow-heavy firs which crowded against the road, a flowing, dark tunnel on either side of them.

"Bloody silly," he said after perhaps a couple of hours.

Waterford appeared to digest the remark as a piece of vital information, then he replied, "Any suggestions?"

Davenhill's surprise at the alkaline tone was increased when Waterford halted the jeep. Then he found Waterford looking at him. "Well?" the older man said. "Anything to suggest?" There was the edge of contempt again, but controlled.

"Why aren't we stopping—looking?"

"This is the only road, Davenhill. I don't intend being caught, like Folley. So far, there's been nowhere anything big could have left the road. This . . ." He waved a hand at the lines of the firs. "This isn't deep cover, not enough for the kind of thing . . ."

Davenhill studied the trees lining the road. Dark and impenetrable they appeared to him.

"God—it's hard to believe in Aubrey's idea out here!"

"It isn't Aubrey's idea, and it isn't hard," Waterford said drily. "It's just the way you civilians look at it that makes it hard to believe." His breath smoked around him. He was big and solid in the driving seat. He still frightened Davenhill who, used as he was to the Foreign Office, and the professional detachment that allowed only glimpses into souls in moments of indiscretion, could see no further than the skin with Waterford. He was not a type of person he had met before; and his self appeared as hooded as his eyes.

"Well, then?"

"Well what?"

"Will we find anything?"

133

"Who knows? *Anything* may find us."

"That's a pleasant thought to start the day. I—hadn't thought of it like that before."

"You wouldn't."

Waterford started the engine, which coughed like a cry in the cold silence. He eased out the clutch, and the jeep skidded, then rolled smoothly forward, the packed surface of the road now rutted tangibly below the skin of snow.

"What are we looking for?" Davenhill asked after a while.

"Not tracks—just a clearing, or a track. Damage to trees—anything."

"Right."

It was more than another hour before Waterford stopped the jeep, a look of irritation on his face.

"You and your bloody water!" he snapped. Davenhill smiled disarmingly, and jumped out of the jeep. "Christ!" Waterford added as he moved away. "Who's going to see you? I shan't be looking!" Davenhill was already off the road and moving more clumsily through deeper snow.

When he had finished, he moved from behind the tree, and knelt in the snow. With a smile on his face, he fashioned a snowball, looking up to see Waterford with his head averted, and aimed and threw. The ball of snow spattered like a ripe fruit against the side of the jeep. Waterford looked round, brushed some snow from his sleeve, and tossed his head. He appeared as if he might be amused. Davenhill walked towards him. The white gouge in the trunk of a tree almost slipped his gaze.

Then he went back to it.

"Waterford," he called.

"My mother says I can't come out to play," Waterford replied.

"Look at this," Davenhill said firmly, already moving to another tree. A hole in the trunk, a piece of bark plucked away when something was removed. "Where are we on the map, Waterford?" he asked, his voice still un-inflected with excitement. He did not understand, as he moved from tree to tree, what the spike-marks might be. But understood they were man-made, and recent. Snow had been brushed from the places where the wind had fixed it, as if by heavy curtains or a large gloved hand.

Waterford said, close behind him: "The forest is deep-

134

er here—begins to stretch for a couple of miles, maybe more, either side of the road. Trees are thicker, too."

"What does it mean?" Davenhill said caustically.

"Not much," Waterford said quietly. "Perhaps the fixing-points for camouflage nets."

Davenhill looked at him. "What?"

"Maybe. But maybe not Russian, anyway. The Finns do have an army, you know." Davenhill suspected Waterford's habitual sarcasm, but his face was expressionless—except for a thoughtful frown as he peered at the gouge in the tree. Then he bent down, and brushed at the snow, disturbing it.

He stood up, brushing the snow from his gloves.

"What were you doing?"

"I wondered about the pin, that's all—they took it away, like good soldiers should."

He crossed to another tree, then another, working his way in a vague circle back to Davenhill, studying the trunk of each tree before which he paused.

"Well?" Davenhill was impatient now.

"Something has been pinned to these trees all right. Possibly netting—enough to cover half a dozen vehicles."

"Tanks?"

"Possibly. Troop-carriers, whatever."

"Thank God."

"Hardly. Not really evidence."

"What do you want—a packet of Russian fags, the odd Kalashnikov rifle dropped in a hurry?"

"More than this. Let's find where this unit, if unit it was, pulled off the road, shall we?"

"Aren't you going to take pictures?" Davenhill sounded childishly disappointed.

"Make a real impression on the Pentagon and NATO, eh?" Waterford said with a slight smile. "Please, gentlemen—conclusive proof that the Red Army invaded Finland—pictures of nail-holes in trees!"

As he walked back to the car, he was laughing, Davenhill trailing in his wake, his shoulders hunched with disappointment. He had perceived only then how ridiculous he must seem to Waterford.

"How could they move through those trees?" he asked as he climbed back in the jeep.

"They couldn't—not far without damage, anyway. No delightful groves to assist movement."

He started the engine, and they followed the road once more, Davenhill now alert for any break in the trees.

"They wouldn't cause damage, though—would they?"

"Not unnecessarily."

A few minutes later, Davenhill said excitedly, "There!"

"I see it."

Waterford pulled into the side, and switched off the engine. There was a gap in the tree, probably caused by a felling operation, on a small scale, the previous summer. A wedge of trees had been lifted from the forest, a slice of dark cake.

Waterford got out, and said: "Stay here. I don't want your fairy footsteps over that ground just yet."

"Why not?"

"Because I am looking for something in particular."

He walked away while Davenhill savoured the new ease in their relationship. Waterford, engaged in action, was easier. Not more human, enlarged in compassion. Merely distracted from bitterness; indifferent to his contempt for others.

Davenhill watched him kneel just off the road, and sweep gently at the powdery snow which crackled as its iced surface was disturbed. The sky was palely blue now, and high and empty. The scene, Davenhill observed, was losing its hostility, becoming photogenic.

"What are you doing?" he called.

Waterford went on brushing, over a wider area, his hand smoothing the snow aside until he exposed the packed ice-snow beneath. Then, eventually, he stood up.

"Bring the camera over here, would you?"

Davenhill joined him. Waterford had exposed, like the tracks of some strange species, the rutted ridges of caterpillar tracks. Tanks, or personnel carriers.

"Well done," Davenhill observed, capitalising on a new familiarity. "How many?"

"Just a few. Outriders. Some sort of advance guard, close to the road, ahead of the main column."

"But they're not here now!" Davenhill burst out with the pure disappointment of a child.

"I should hope not. If they are, then there could be a couple of regiments, even a couple of divisions—in there." He pointed towards the trees.

"Mm." Davenhill photographed the exposed tracks, then said, "What next?"

"Fancy a walk in the woods?" Waterford said.

"That depends. What are we looking for?"

"What we find. Come on—let's get the jeep off the road and under the trees, then we'll scout around a bit."

For more than an hour they combed the ground beneath the trees, working gradually further into the forest, taking any path that suggested itself as wide enough for the passage of tanks. The search proved fruitless, and when they returned to the jeep, Davenhill was disappointed. He understood that they would find very little—perhaps nothing. But to kneel in drifts of snow, to part the blanket or examine the bark of trees for marks was an invidious, tiring, frustrating job.

"We need to get further east," Waterford observed, swallowing from a small flask which he then passed to Davenhill. Davenhill felt the brandy warm his stomach. He said, "What happened to Folley, Waterford?"

"Christ knows." Waterford looked at him, as if appraising some reaction. "Probably dead. *We* know they've been here. He must have found them, too. And they found him—otherwise we could all be sitting in London listening to his report." He looked at the camera, still slung round Davenhill's neck. "Fuck," he said softly. "All we've got is some caterpillar tracks. I wonder what he saw?" He looked at the trees as if envisaging camouflaged vehicles beneath them.

"Where was the main body? The heavy stuff?"

"East of here." He reached over and lifted a folded map from the pouch at the side of the door. He pointed a finger. "Look, the forest is Y-shaped, stretching north and south of here. In either arm, I should think."

"Where are they now, then?"

"Gone home?"

"Because of Folley? Perhaps they've called the whole thing off?" It was not a serious suggestion.

Waterford said, "I doubt it. I think they had a dry-run. Timing would be of the essence to them—getting to Ivalo, then north-east to link up with a main attack." He traced their route on the map. Davenhill, looking over his shoulder, nodded as he saw the line of advance unfold. Waterford pointed out Kirkenes, in Norway, and the road from the Russian border. "That's where they'd cross," he said. "Down here would be the second thrust, to link up— oh, there." His finger picked out Lakselv, on the Porsangenfjord. "But they'd hop along that road with airborne troops, and land men by amphibs in the fjords." He looked up at Davenhill. "It would be a shit to stop them," he added unnecessarily.

"A few pictures of tracks in the snow won't stop them, either."

"What we want is Folley," Waterford admitted. "But he won't be in very good voice, even if we should find him." He threw the map into the jeep. "Come on, let's get moving."

An hour later, they stopped for the fifth time. At each of their previous stops, they had inspected likely gaps in the hedge of the forest that pressed in on either side of the road. They had uncovered nothing. There was something phantasmal to Davenhill in the way a simple snowstorm had obliterated any trace of the forces he now knew had been on Finnish soil. Perhaps as recently as forty-eight hours ago. Folley—he thought of him with a wince of pain, sharing the man's route now—must have found them. And as Waterford had said, they had found Folley.

He climbed reluctantly out of the jeep, and trailed after Waterford towards a star-shaped pattern of forest rides that was obviously used to allow the passage of lumberjacking equipment and the removal of felled trees. It would appear that here they were at the heart of the forestry operations.

"How would they have known about these paths?" he called as a thought struck him.

Over his shoulder, Waterford said, "Low-level photography—under the radar net, snap, snap, and off home. Easy."

"I see." He paused, as Waterford had done. Four trails snaked away through the forest. The trees seemed dense, heavy with snow, silent. "Here?" he said.

"Here—if anywhere," Waterford replied. Then he turned to Davenhill, and the younger man saw a flicker in the eyes, as if the blank mirrors had been removed. It was excitement, Davenhill thought. Perhaps love? Something strangely absorbing to the soldier. Then he understood it. The passion of the hunter close to the game. The spoor was beneath the thin film of snow at his feet. He could sense it. It did not make him like Waterford; but it added a kind of respect, and he placed himself more readily in his hands.

"What do we do?"

"Look. We'll need the jeep. Each one of these trails. And—watch out for felling work that may have taken place."

As they walked back to the jeep, Davenhill said. "Why were they here, Waterford? In my enthusiasm to believe, I didn't ask why."

"Why? I don't know." He started up the jeep, and pulled off the road, heading up the trail which most nearly paralleled the road from Ivalo. After a while, he said, "The theory is—to succeed, at high speed, entails airborne operations, air-dropped supplies, all that kind of thing. That means transport aircraft. And they may not have sufficient. If so, an armoured column would take Ivalo, to support the lightest possible airborne assault. Then consolidate at Ivalo, air-drop light forces ahead, and follow up with armour. Sending armour up these roads . . ." He smiled as they bucked out of their seats. "Like pouring a waterfall through a bottle-neck. Overcome lack of airborne transport by using armour as quick as you can. In this case, someone decided that it needed practice. The dry-run, as I said."

"Then when will they be back?"

"I don't know." He pulled off the track at that moment, into the softer snow under the trees. "A nice tunnel," he said enigmatically. Almost immediately, they came to a clearing, roughly circular. And the trees, shorn of branches, stacked as if for the spring. "There."

Davenhill sat in the jeep, absorbing the innocent looking clearing.

Waterford got out and cast about. Walking as if over a film of ice, he moved around the circle. Then Davenhill saw him stoop over the snow, brush at it with the tenderness of archaeology, then raise his hand to beckon him.

The snow beneath the freshest fall was stained with engine oil.

"This is it," Waterford said. He stood up, and waved his arms around the clearing. "Bright as a new pin."

"What's under here?"

"Troy," Waterford replied. "Get digging."

"So that's it," Vorontsyev ended, looking at Alevtina and the three men gathered in a crowded, littered study. While he had talked, they had looked at the walls, eyes straying *to* the scattered files, the pasted, clipped strips of information.

There was no relief now that there was silence, no release. Rather, all four of the junior officers seemed insistently appalled by mental digestion of what they had heard.

"Chief?" Maxim said in a small voice. He tittered with embarrassment, then cleared his throat. "We have to keep coming back to this bugger Vrubel, and who killed him. Do we know *any* more about him?"

Vorontsyev settled in the single easy chair—his team were stiff and upright on dining-chairs from the other room. He said, "Alvetina, what's new?"

"Nothing, sir" the girl said, correctly, almost primly.

"Sent the bill for your coat to Tortyev, have you?" Ilya asked.

"I have," she snapped. Then, to Vorontsyev, who was smiling: "We can't trace anything suspicious in his contacts—and no one saw him that night. This is a dead-end, sir."

"Naturally. He wasn't mugged for his wallet. All right —his history. He's been on the Finland border for two, three years. In charge of a section of the wire. Overall security. You know how the Border Guard works—compartments, autonomously run, but with a central co-ord."

"Then is he being used in his capacity as a Border Guard officer, or as something else?" Pyotr's mind seemed to unclog as he asked the question. There was just a dull patch of brain at the front of his head now, solid as an undigested dinner.

"As a Border Guard—what for?"

"Doesn't it depend what this *Finland Station* is supposed to mean?" Alevtina remarked. Vorontsyev looked at her carefully. The girl never started hares.

"Explain."

"What I wondered, sir, was whether it was just his code, or the code for something bigger."

"Bigger? In what way?"

"What are we dealing with, sir—revolution, or something else? We are dealing with the army, aren't we?"

"We are. But it's the revolution aspect that we have to be concerned with here—so where does Vrubel fit into that set-up? I can't believe that a Border Guard Captain is behind a revolution! Can you?" Ilya shook his head.

"Quite. However, we are going to divide our strength, as of now. What we have to know is what the set-up along his stretch of the wire is. Know everything. His men, their attitude, his movements, and the like."

"You know what you're saying, sir?" Maxim said. "You *are* suggesting that he's concerned in some kind of border *crossing* . . ."

"Don't talk rubbish!" Pyotr burst out, then saw Vorontsyev's unamused features. "Sorry."

"Sounds ridiculous, doesn't it?" he said. "But—is it? I want to *know*. Which is why I'm going to Finland in the morning—at least, to the border. Deputy Kapustin has placed this team in charge of the Vrubel business—run everything down. You four will stay here, and branch out as much as necessary over the next couple of days—tracking down *any* lead suggested by his contacts, his background, his behaviour-pattern."

Not one of them uttered an audible protest. Then Pyotr said, "This is while we're checking on your Rogues' Gallery, sir?"

"Yes. I want you to concentrate on Vrubel, but on the others as well, taking two each for the moment. When I get back from Finland, I'll take on the other two myself—Ossipov and Praporovich."

"We can presume that Vrubel knew a lot—otherwise why try to kill you when you tailed him?"

"That may have been already set up—witness the body of the old sod in the black coat. I wonder whether Vrubel wasn't laying for me all the time? However, I can't see it. We assume no one else knew of our suspicion that Ossipov had a double . . ."

"Hundreds of people did, by the time we started asking questions. Vrubel was in the KGB. So are a lot of others who must be helping!" Maxim said, his eyes staying fixed on the wall-chart that Vorontsyev had drawn.

"Agreed. It could be anyone. Which is why we have to turn up something, and soon. Some common factor."

"How widespread is it sir?" Ilya asked. "I mean, you don't need much to knock over the Politburo, not if you're using tanks."

"True. Moscow Military District could supply more than enough—even a nice airborne assault on the Kremlin!"

"What a bloody mess that would be!"

Vorontsyev smiled thinly, then went on: "So, we have

141

to gain some kind of inside knowledge of Moscow District without arousing suspicion. But, if it's Moscow, then why Ossipov—he's at the other end of the world? And why Vrubel—he was based a thousand miles away? And all the others. What of them?"

He flapped his hands on his thighs, an audible disturbance in the sudden silence.

"We're going to make a lot of noise doing this, sir," Ilya offered unhelpfully.

"I know. We can't afford low profile, but we have to look like a small and isolated group, just making enquiries. Remember that. We can't afford to trigger off the thing we're trying to prevent."

"But, sir—" Ilya again. "Do you really think that a *revolution* is on the cards? It's impossible, surely?"

"Is it? Not if the army does it, surely! Can you see the air force bombing their comrades in the tanks, or the fleets shelling Moscow from the Baltic? It only needs a little push—and what is there to tumble down? The Politburo, the Kremlin clique—and *us!* Do you fancy taking on a T-72 with a 9 mm pistol, Ilya?"

"I see."

"All of you—do *you* see? All they need to do is to take and hold the centre. If they're sure of enough army support from the other Military Districts. Then no one could touch them. The KGB swept away, and replaced by some military police organisation, and the Kremlin in the hands of the Marshals. It's easy—as long as it's the army doing it!'

His face had gone bright with perspiration and effort. He wanted the best out of them. They were young, and the system was their safe, warm womb. He had to show them how unsafe the whole thing was when threatened by an army. The Red Army.

"But why would they want to do it?"

Vorontsyev paused, then looked at each face—each clean, scrubbed, confident face. They seemed so young, and incapable of being hurt, or believing themselves mortal. And a mental consideration that might have been going on beneath the conscious surface seemed to clarify, achieve a peroration. Those faces in front of him in the untidy room dazzled him with insight.

"You four—not one of you believes in anything—

142

right?" They appeared puzzled, grins starting and fading like little glimpses of sunlight. Alevtina looked quizzical, but as if she teetered on the edge of his own realisation. "You don't read Lenin, you don't remember Stalin, or the War against the Fascists—think about being in Berlin, in the grounds where they found the petrol-soaked corpses —" He felt the rhetoric whirl up, speaking through Gorochenko's experiences, and what he knew of his own father's life. If he could suddenly understand, perhaps they could, too. "Or finding the thousands of lime-decayed bodies in the mass graves—Babi Yar and all the other places the SS had been. Go further back, remember the Civil War against the Whites, the hungers, the billions who've died since 1917. Think about these things when you buy your next bottle of malt whisky in the shop across from the Centre, or eat your subsidised breakfasts in the Centre canteen, or order a new suit from imported Italian cloth. Silk scarves, fur coats—" he added suddenly for the girl's benefit. "It's a cushy number, brothers and sister. Without history. But these old buggers remember—and perhaps they still believe!

"Or maybe they're just not ready for their pensions, or to throw away their SS-22 toys and new bombers and reactor-driven aircraft-carriers. In the end, does it matter a toss whether they have a motive or not? They may be doing it—and that's all that should worry us!"

Slowly, they looked at each other, then to him. Each one of them, as if present at some ritual, nodded to him. He sat back again, relieved. Then the telephone rang in the lounge. He had not switched the extension through. Ilya got up, and he waved him out.

The others got up, stretched, and began to study the faces on the wall. Vorontsyev tried to relax into the satisfaction of authority, to attend with a complacent half-ear to their comments, often ribald, frequently irreverent. Yet it was a hard quietude. What he had told them, the emphases he had placed, had frightened him, too. It was no longer easy to think in terms of wall-charts, pictures taken with the power of secret surveillance If the army was really engaged on a coup, then there was no stopping them—not if they had the agreement, even acquiescence, of the majority of senior commanders. Like those men on the wall.

Moscow would be no safer than Luanda, or Beirut. Except that the struggle would be short, and bloody—and the army could not lose it.

"I'll take that hatchet-faced bastard, Timochenko!" Maxim said with delight, tugging the photograph from the wall. "He once gave my cousin the shaft—I owe him!" It was said with amusement, and with an underlying enthusiasm.

"Don't frame him," Pyotr laughed.

"I shan't need to!"

Ilya came back into the room at that moment. Vorontsyev turned to receive the message, still smiling at the enthusiasm of Maxim as he now hunted for the files on Timochenko, one of the two members of the Secretariat he had pinned to the wall. His smile vanished when he saw Ilya's white face—as if, he thought, only at that moment had the danger come home to him.

"What is it, Ilya?"

"Sir, that report on Ossipov and his staff from Khabarovsk KGB Office—"

"Well?"

"They're all dead—the office was blown to smithereens early in the morning—the off-duty team were murdered at home. Bombs . . ."

"What?"

The silence of the room was stifling.

"The work of the Khabarov Separatist Movement—they say. They're all dead. Every KGB officer in the town."

And Vorontsyev understood.

He would have to go to Khabarovsk himself.

Ossipov had had them killed.

SEVEN
WINTER JOURNEYS

None of the Oriental carpets or embroidered sofas, not even the tall windows overlooking Dzerzhinsky Square from the third floor, nor the high ceiling, could disguise in spacious elegance the functional nature of Andropov's office. The furnishings displayed him as a connoisseur, as someone immensely privileged in his society—and the battery of telephones on his immense desk betrayed his position as Chairman of the KGB. Mahogany wall-panelling, brocaded curtains—he sat looking round the room for a few moments after Kapustin had left, then turned his gaze on the telephones. He shook his head, as if admitting a reality.

The line to the Kremlin, the line to the Politburo and Central Committee members, the lines that connected him with any, or every, KGB office in the Soviet Union. He stared at the Bakelite that, through high-frequency circuits, allowed him to control his security machine.

Dial Khabarovsk, and see who answers . . .

He did not wish the thought, but now it had presented itself, he felt an anger stirring in him, shaking a frame unprepared for high emotion. He despised emotion—feared it because it had the unfamiliarity and danger of an infection.

Of course he had approved sending Major Vorontsyev to Khabarovsk, with a forensic team. The Major's supposition was not unsound, that Ossipov had had his men killed. There, the centre of the little storm he felt. *There.* All right, in the Ukraine, before now, KGB men had been stabbed in alleys, even been blown up in their cars; but to take out the whole team?

Something else. It meant it was close. *They* had nothing to fear.

Khamovkhin had left him in charge. The apparatus of State had moved to Dzerzhinsky Street, to the Centre. Andropov perceived no possible irony in the thought. This was now the State, he thought. Here. Because nothing else mattered but that they find, isolate, and remove the enemy. And only he, and his service, could do that.

Could they?

He stirred in his desk, a sudden cramp in his legs. He looked down at them, as if they had turned against him. He did not blame Khamovkhin—only a stupid man would do that. Everything had to be as normal. Which was the trouble—no one could be told. They were sitting in a restaurant with the rest of the world, but only they knew about the bomb—and most of the staff were sick, or untrustworthy, and only one or two could be sent to search it out, disarm it—

He put aside the analogy. It was too real, too sensuous. Feodor had left him to mind the house.

The file on his desk was leather-bound. In it was material not dissimilar to that which had been scattered over Vorontsyev's floor, pinned to his walls. Material that tired and infuriated Andropov. Ridiculous not to have a perfectly clear idea of who might be involved—who *had* to be involved—and maddening, to be able to do nothing. He could not admit to impotence, not after the years of power. But he was aware that the State had shrunk to the size of this room, and that his hold upon things was as fragile as the connections made when he dialled numbers on the telephones in front of him.

He stood up, walked swiftly, as if possessed with purpose, to the windows, and looked down. The square in front of his office sparkled below him. The people of Moscow were out in great numbers, as they always were when the snow fell, or the frost glinted. Winter people, the Russians. He felt detached from them, as he always did. He felt no sense of mission, no obligation.

He went back to his desk, and opened the file, flicking through the polythene-covered pages, seeing the faces

146

stare out at him. The prime suspects. Praporovich, Ossipov, the Defence Minister, Marshal Yaroslavich, members of the Politburo, the Central Committee.

Isolate, and destroy.

But, before he could do that, he had to discover the chain of command, the heirarchy of the coup. And twelve months had so far brought nothing. If, if, if—who is behind it, who is the leader, who, *precisely*, is involved, what are the commands, the plan—*when?* His head ached with the unanswered questions, his body ached with the sense of impotence. He was not afraid, but—

Did it *all* depend on one young Major in the SID, and his flight to Khabarovsk? How could it? And how could it not? Had the Khabarovsk Office discovered something, so that they had to be silenced?

The telephone rang, startling him.

"Yes?" The *Kremlevka*, the direct line to the Kremlin. Pushkin, the Prime Minister. The business of government. He listened, and stared at the room. It was there, the business of government, he thought. In that room.

Vorontsyev was waiting for the specialists with whom he was to fly to Khabarovsk. His plane left in another hour, and he had arrived in order to finalise the briefing of Ilya and Maxim, who were flying to Leningrad, on their way to Vrubel's section of the border wire.

The three of them sat together in the Diplomatic Lounge, in that glassed-off section of it reserved for the KGB. As they sipped at coffee and watched the commercial airliners stack, descend, and touch down outside the double-glazed windows, Vorontsyev warned them, repeatedly, of the parameters of their investigation.

He knew he was being cautious, but caution was required. It was of the essence. He felt old, much older than them, a crabbed and pinched soul in the face of their almost adolescent enthusiasm. The tension was high in each of them, and they were impatient with his sober mood. Yet they had to understand. He saw Maxim's eyes drift to the TWA Boeing as it slid past the windows, and snapped:

"It's not for my health's sake, you know!"

"Sorry, sir," Maxim said, just able to resist glancing at his companion.

"You have to be undertaking an *ordinary* investigation

147

—understand? You have to convince everyone that you're doing a police job because Captain Vrubel has been murdered. His mistress reported his disappearance . . ." He lowered his eyes for a moment. The name filed on the official notification to Missing Persons was that of his wife —her maiden and professional name. But it had to be good—because he did not know who might engage himself in checking the checkers.

His own excitement had long since drained away as he set up the two-pronged investigation—Maxim and Ilya to Finland, himself to the Far East. Kapustin had agreed that the action of the Separatist Movement in Khabarovsk was unexpected, even suspicious. And had consented to his personal investigation of the bombings, together with a team from the SID who would study the forensic realities. Vorontsyev's target was Ossipov, and military truth. Because he had been able to convince Kapustin, and presumably Andropov himself, that Ossipov had to be perhaps the most important single link in a chain that they could not see. Not only had he bobbed up, a cork of suspicion, but the death of the whole KGB team was too fortuitous to be accidental.

He had slept little, his mind turning like his stomach with rising nerves. He said, for perhaps the third time since they had arrived at Cheremetievo, "We dare not trigger the thing we're trying to prevent." He knew they regarded his sombre face as that of a rather boring uncle, intent on restraint, on dampening youthful spirits. He felt the necessity to communicate to them, and the difficulty of doing so. They were being entrusted with an investigation he would have handled himself; and they understood the gravity, the weight. But they did not *feel* it as he did.

"We'll be careful, Major," Ilya said. "We know what's at stake."

"Good. Just Vrubel, then. Arouse as little suspicion as possible. But act *normally*, please! You are in SID, and that should frighten people. Don't be too low-key."

"No, Major."

He gave it up. It was like rehearsing children in a lesson. Parrot-fashion they repeated what he taught them, but they did not understand. He was filled with sudden foreboding.

They sat in silence for the few remaining minutes,

148

then their Leningrad flight was called, and he stood up with them, and they shook hands. He was despondent as he watched them move away down the tunnel towards the plane. He was afraid that they would miss something, something important. He should have gone himself.

He got himself another coffee from the machine, winced at its acrid taste, and lit a cigarette. He picked *Pravda* from the plastic bench, and scanned the inside pages. The official story of the explosions in Khabarovsk was to lay the blame where it had been claimed by telephone—the Separatists.

He folded the paper, and tossed it aside.

Kapustin had not been willing to be rushed into a premature judgement. He had not shared Vorontsyev's moment of inspiration when Ilya had repeated the telephone message. Kapustin, and Andropov saw the wider picture —which was largely grey, unformed. Kapustin wanted to know *why* Ossipov was involved, and he could not tell him. He could not even imagine a plausible explanation. Instead he clung to the fact that Ossipov had needed a double, to avoid surveillance. To meet someone, receive orders.

Another unit of the SID had begun to investigate the Moscow Military District heirarchy. The excuse was a trumped-up bribery charge against senior officers—or was it misappropriation of military equipment? He could not remember. But he was certain they would discover nothing that related to *Group 1917*.

Again, he felt an urgency envelope him, choking yet electric, spasms to his muscles and brain, urging activity.

He looked up, and Natalia was standing beside him. So unexpected was her appearance, he was disorientated for a moment. It was from the past, the scene, especially the careful smile, and her arrival was apposite.

Then he said, "What in hell's name are you doing here?"

Once more he was conscious of the way in which her smile flickered like something working from an interrupted current, then reestablished itself. She was determined not to be angered, or put off. He wondered whether that was what penitence was like.

"I came to see you," she said. "You didn't ring."

He was suddenly suspicious.

"How did you know I was here?"

"Mihail Pyotravich told me."

"Told you—when?"

"Don't interrogate me!" she flashed, and the revelation of her known temper convinced him there was no need for suspicion.

"He doesn't know I'm here," he said, as if relenting, but falling into that sullen, pouting mood and expression she so detested.

She smoothed her features before he could react to her look, and said, "He was with—oh, Kapustin, I think, early this morning. He told him."

"Oh. Well?"

"I'm coming with you—I have a few days before we begin rehearsals for *Cosi*—Mihail told me, I think, so that I could think of it . . . If I hadn't, I'm sure he'd have suggested it!" She laughed. It was false, winsome in a play-acting way. But her laughter was one of the things most unnatural about her.

"I'm working!" he snapped, but he sensed his own powerlessness; like the beginnings of a head-cold. She confused his thinking, somehow—*overshadowed* him. It wasn't sinister—rather he had drawn comfort from it, at one time. Something to do with his childhood, he assumed. Need to be dominated—mother-fixation . . .

"What the hell—?" he said, aloud. Her face narrowed, then he added, "All right. Sit down—but don't get in the way!"

"Very well, Alexei—certainly, Alexei!" she chorused, mimicking her pretence of subordination, of dutiful wife-hood, from the early days. He could not prevent the smile, even though he almost choked on the sudden sense of loneliness memory brought him; and despised, for an instant, the dependence he was demonstrating.

She moved the small leather travelling-case to her side, smoothed the long leather coat beneath her, and crossed her long, booted legs. She was desirable, even now, he thought. Yet he said, "Just don't interfere when I'm working, that's all."

"I won't. But you won't be working all the time, will you? We will have time to—discuss things?" He would not admit the suggestiveness of her tone.

"I suppose so."

It was with relief that he saw the approaching figure of Blinn, the Deputy Senior Forensic Officer of the SID; tall, gangling, hang-dog. He looked like that American film actor—what was it? Matthau. Walter Matthau. Yes. He had seen him in a film, a couple of years ago, at the Dom Kino, by virtue of his privileged rank. Behind Blinn were two others. Then minutes before their flight was called, his thoughts turned to Khabarovsk, and seven dead men.

Already—and it was the shortness of the time that terrified him—Folley was finding it increasingly difficult to retain any firm hold on experience. Even though he had not been beaten again since his arrival at the house where they were now keeping him, he was blindfolded, his ears filled with wax, thick gloves on his hands. He was kept in a cellar, he imagined, because he climbed steps when they wanted to talk to him. Already, he was grabbing the stuff of their coats—uniforms, he thought—when they took him, leaning against them, trying to make them talk to him.

He had done the things they had done to him—undergone the white noise, the spreadeagling, the lack of sleep, the hooding. He should—was—able to withstand it. They were only the techniques used on Provos, in the earlier stages of interrogation, and he had been trained to take them—*easy ride,* they called it in 22 SAS.

But, they weren't here. Didn't want to know *where* was here. They had walked down familiar corridors, into familiar rooms, before the sessions began. Not like him—not like him at all.

He did not know where he was—just somewhere in the Soviet Union. Which, he realised, was a ludicrous thought, and not at all comforting. But the worry lay deeper than that. He was not disturbed or disorientated by the interrogations. The two officers who had conducted them, using the shit-and-sugar formula, tough and pleasant, had failed to elicit the kind of information they were seeking; and though their interminable questions whirled like frozen sparks in his brain for hours, and he had not slept for what seemed like days, he had not broken. And he did not think he would.

Except for the sapping of resolve that was going on all the time, deep inside him, like the crumbling away of a cliff, or the subsidence of a huge building. Because *no one,* not even himself, knew where he was; he would already

151

have been disowned by London. *Expendable*. Waterford's word for him. And he would only have been passing on the message from on high.

It was hard, and harder all the time, to resist the sense of annihilation that crept closer to him, made him curl on the narrow cot in the cellar as if afraid of the dark. He had become afraid of wetting the bed, and he wanted to suck his thumb—or call out for the guard, who wasn't a bad sort.

No, he thought, definitely, and with an effort. It had not become as bad as that. That had been the nightmare last night. *Night?* The last brief sleep-period, he corrected himself. He walked hooded up from the cellar when they wanted to talk to him, feeling along blind corridors with closed doors and uncarpeted floors, into a room with heavy curtains always drawn. Once they had let him see it. And he had the feeling, the inhibition, that if he had moved to tug the curtains open, they would have shot him.

Only a nightmare. But, he knew they would have heard the noises—probably even now they were feeling the rough stuff of the sheets, seeking the evidence of drying sweat, or urination.

He had ejaculated once—when was that? He had been ashamed of the semen staining the sheet, and his trousers. It was weakness, even if it did not help them. Yes it did, he corrected himself—they knew that under the unhelpful surface, he was escaping.

It was Novetlyn this time. The sugar-man. The modulated voice of an actor or a queer. Insinuating, full of Russian promise . . . He formed the silly joke with difficulty, and laughed aloud, beneath the hood which was too thick for any light to penetrate. His bruised lip, which was healing slowly, cracked again, and he felt the dribble of warm blood down his chin.

He wanted to cry, wanted to dab at it roughly with a handkerchief. Everything had to be an assertion, have about it a residual toughness. He had to go on believing he was holding out, winning.

He said, "Let me ask you a question? Which lot are you in?"

"Lot?"

He heard quick footsteps, and flinched as if before a

152

stick, then the hood was pulled roughly over his head. Novetlyn's face was close to his, and he was smiling. Folley blinked in the subdued light, and was grateful. He dabbed at his split lip. Novetlyn sat behind his desk. He lit a cigarette, and laid one on the other side of the table, in front of Folley, ready for him to pick up and smoke when he felt he had resisted long enough to make his point. He smiled encouragingly, waited for the explanation.

"You know what I mean? Your partner, he wears GRU uniform—Colonel, too." Folley, as if on a treadmill, felt the volition of scorn. "But you don't. Nice Italian suit—cost a packet in the KGB shop across from the Centre, I'll bet." He sneered. The grimace made the lip bleed again. He dabbed at it furiously with his grubby handkerchief.

"Ah. Would it help you to know? Yes, perhaps it would. Therefore, I shall remain a man of mystery to you." He drew in smoke, blew it towards the ceiling, then said, "Come, let us talk again. I like talking to you."

"Piss off!"

"An English expression?"

Folley clenched the handkerchief against his groin, hurting himself with the effort of restraint. It did get to you— the consistent *superiority* of the interrogator. That when they talked—and the collapse of the will when you were alone.

He stopped his thoughts. He imagined himself, on a road, slowing down—walking. Strolling.

Stopping.

Novetlyn said, "Ready?"

It was as if he knew, the bastard. Folley, lifting his eyes, saw the smile on Novetlyn's handsome, shaven face. The blue tie, with the large silver pattern; the lightweight suit, as if it were summer. Even the suede shoes were Western.

"You're a bigger shit than the other one!"

"Come—you haven't forgotten his name already?" Novetlyn was evidently pleased with the situation.

The drawn curtains were behind him. A heady pattern of browns and oranges, which disturbed but drew the eye. There was nothing else in the room on which to focus the gaze. Just the bare desk, and Novetlyn behind it. The carpet was neutral in tone, the wallpaper drab.

Folley picked up the cigarette. Novetlyn, as if he had

153

timed the moment, had left his lighter beside it when he last spoke. Folley tried not to devour the smoke too greedily.

"You see," Novetlyn said, pressing the long fingers of both hands together in a momentary steeple, "we didn't have a chance to talk to the man who came ahead of you." He smiled. "We don't even know his name. He was clumsy, and got caught, and someone with too much enthusiasm and too little in his head shot him. Not like you—rather a good attempt, we thought. More the *professional* approach."

"All London dustmen are trained to use that rifle—and in karate," Folley said.

"Ah, the sense of humour returns—excellent. No, no. We are sure you are not a dustman—some other agent of disposal?" His English was almost without accent. "We think SAS—based at Hereford." He had never mentioned the regiment before. Folley gripped the ball of the handkerchief in his hand, pressing his knuckle into his thigh.

"Who? SAS? They don't send SAS out to do this sort of thing."

"I'm sure the Sultan of Oman would be disappointed if that were true," Novetlyn remarked drily. "Anyway, your unit is not important. We *do* want to know whether another will come, and then another. You see—it would be as well to be prepared."

"When are you going to bribe me?"

Novetlyn snapped, "When you are ready to be bribed! Which is not yet, I think."

The force of his insight struck Folley like a blow. They *knew!* They could hear the rumble as his self slid into the total isolation that waited for him like the sea. "I don't *know* anything!" he persisted.

"Who sent you? Gaveston in SO-1? The Ministry of Defence? No, I think not. Who, then? How many people are interested in you, and in what you might have learned?"

There was the slightest inflection of urgency. Folley glimpsed others, outside that room, pressing Novetlyn for results. And the man disliked haste. He grasped the tiny hope of a time-limit, regardless of the conclusion.

"Lots of people! So you'd better let me go, hadn't you, before my big brother comes to find me. He's a policeman."

"Here, everybody's big brother is a policeman—and their little brothers are in the army," Novetlyn replied.

"Variety is the spice of life."

As if he sensed the initiative slipping, Novetlyn frowned, then said, "No one will come for you."

"Sod off!" Folley replied, swallowing the gurgle of loneliness that was bilious in his throat. "You don't know that—you don't know *anything!*" He tried, and failed, to inflect his voice again with an imitation of childish sneering.

"But we will—and you know that we will. If I told you what progress we have made, what *regress you* have made—in the short time—if I told you what little time you have been here, you would realise that we shall, very soon, know all you know."

"You've got Colonel Krapalot's script today!"

Novetlyn smiled.

"It isn't even today. I shan't tell him his new nickname —it is appropriate. He's a shit when he's not interrogating, you know."

"So are you."

"Very well—back to the cot, and to the foetal position you are increasingly adopting, and no doubt the thumb in the mouth. Don't wet the blanket. Your guard might laugh."

He pressed the buzzer beneath his desk, to summon the guard.

Khamovkhin slumped in his chair, and poured himself a large whisky. He spilt some of the liquid on his waistcoat, muttered a curse, then ignored it as the dark stain spread. His mind was so exhausted by the day that he did not consider the symbolic properties of the stain.

The helicopter flight over the sixty miles from the centre of Helsinki had been a final strained weariness after the other events of the day—a hammering metal box around him, shadowed by two other helicopters, and a flight path patrolled on the ground and in the air all that day. It had drained him, so that an aide remarked on his health, behind his back, to one of the security men who had surrounded him since this morning.

Now, even the walls of the Lahtilinna—the sixteenth-century castle frequently used for prominent political visitors to Finland, even for meetings by visiting heads of state with the President and Prime Minister—failed sufficiently to enclose him, rid him of the day-long sense of *exposure*, of helplessness.

The castle overlooked the Vesijaarvi, squatting on a hillside above the lake, three miles outside Lahti itself. A fortress it still was; except to him.

He could barely remember the rapturous applause with which his address to the Finnish Parliament had been greeted. Politically, it had been a fitting climax to a day of success. Lunch with the President, in the company also of the Prime Minister and the Cabinet, a tour through the streets—here he had refused, politely but insistently, to undertake a fashionable "walkabout"—and there had been crowds, enthusiasm more marked than curiosity. Yes, it was good, and seen to be good. Everywhere the cameras, the flash of bulbs, the chatter of commentators.

A little fat old man in a little room. His imagination insisted on that, and on the vulnerability of the body, and the title, and the power. All vulnerable.

A decoded transmission from Andropov lay on the eighteenth-century writing-desk behind him. He had glanced at it, but could not turn past the first sheet, as if the paper burned him. Nothing, and more nothing. But, oppressively closer the threat—a KGB office blown up somewhere by pretend-dissidents.

A knock at the door. Smile, smile, he thought—then a moment of fear, distrust of his own voice, more whisky to unfreeze the chords.

"Yes?"

"Security report, Comrade First Secretary."

"Who is it?"

"Captain Ozeroff, sir."

"Come in."

Galakhov opened the door, and saw Khamovkhin seated at the writing-table, presenting his back to him. He knew that it was bluff, saw the deep impression of the man's body in the cushion on the armchair. Khamovkhin was frightened, had been all day from the talk of the day-time security team that had accompanied him to Helsinki. He closed the door behind him, and stood to attention. Khamovkhin went on reading something, then turned to him. Galakhov admired the strength that appeared in the square face, the ruddiness of accustomed power.

"Yes, Captain?"

"Your daily security digest, sir." He proffered the file.

"Thank you." Khamovkhin indicated a low table before the fireplace, and Galakhov placed the file on it. "I—may take a walk by the lake later, Captain. Bear that in mind in your—security patrols, would you?"

"Sir."

"They tell me it's quite beautiful here."

"Sir—but it's hard to see it that way when you're on duty."

"Hard for me, too, young man." Khamovkhin's gaze seemed to penetrate, question, understand—just for an instant. Then there was nothing but an old man's rheumy eyes and tired, baggy folds of skin beneath them. "Thank you, Captain. You may go."

"Sir."

Galakhov smiled to himself as he closed the door behind him. The officer on duty at a desk in the chilly corridor, looked up and said, "The old boy still jittery?"

"Not so you'd notice. I think he feels safer here."

"Good." The man looked at his watch. "I'm off duty in an hour. See you in the bar—you can tell me all about London. Years since I was there."

"Sure," Galakhov replied, walking away down the corridor.

The KGB office in Khabarovsk was a ragged hole in the grey façades along Komsomolskaya Square. A bitter wind blew sleet into Vorontsyev's chilled features, and scattered a lying whiteness over the charred, smashed array of spars and frames that had once been a four-storey shipping office, the second and third floors of which had been the security HQ.

The wind sought through Vorontsyev's heavy sheepskin coat, down its turned-up collar, and the damp of the ground struck through the thick fur boots. He shifted his feet again, to warm them, and the powdered fragments of glass crunched under his steps. There was no longer even a wisp of smoke from the fires the bomb had started to suggest that anything recent had happened. It was old wreckage, the black stumps of teeth in an ancient jaw.

The explosion had torn out the sides of the buildings on either side of the shipping office. He looked up, his eyes

157

squinting against the wind-blown sleet, and saw an office desk leaning drunkenly out over black space. Apparently, a secretary had been sitting there. Flying glass had decapitated her. He had not seen the body.

Alongside him, respectful and silent, stood Inspector Seryshev of the Khabarovsk Police. He was in a uniform overcoat and cap, and his ears were red with cold, like his nose. Occasionally, he murmured deferentially as if afraid to cough, and shifted his booted feet. He was a middle-aged man, careful of his pension and his prospects, and he knew that the younger man was a Major in SID and that it behooved him to stand alongside him for as long as Vorontsyev remained.

Vorontsyev said, turning to him so that his pale face was lit by the flashing red light on the police car, "Why the hell were there only seven in the KGB team here?"

Seryshev shrugged without taking his hands from his pockets.

"You should know the answer to that one, Major." He observed what he considered an appropriate deference, sensing that Vorontsyev would react unfavourably to a greater obsequiousness, and because he could not overcome the habitual lack of fear the KGB inspired six thousand miles from Moscow Centre.

"I don't know! A town of nearly half a million, and there are seven KGB men to look after it."

"Don't forget we're here too," Seryshev muttered.

"What happens in the summer—tourists?"

"The KGB come in with the Intourist guides. More of them here, then. Bloody uncomfortable, being out here otherwise. Military District, too—the GRU are more than enough to make up for the absence of your lot."

"Are they?" Vorontsyev said musingly, and Seryshev decided not to enquire. "Tell me about the Separatists. What sort of information do you have on them?" He rounded on the policeman as if he expected to be told lies, or fed excuses. His face was drawn with cold and with anger. And perhaps something, something like fear, Seryshev decided, even though he could not understand such a feeling.

Seryshev looked around at the forensic team poking among the wreckage of the shipping office while he replied. Four hundred pounds of explosive—it could be as much as that. He shook his head. There were still some bodies in there—or parts of things that had once been people.

"No fuss just lately," he said. "About eighteen months ago, one or two minor incidents . . ."

"Any with bombs?"

"One. A car blown up. No one injured."

"What else?"

"Some nameless threats—leaflets, banners. One or two arrests."

"Anybody special? What's the set-up?" Vorontsyev, despite his indifference to Seryshev, felt an anger which he could not define welling up in him, so that his throat was constricted. It was as if he suddenly sensed the distance between himself and Moscow; was one of the men who had died. Certainly angry on their behalf.

"No," Seryshev replied in a stolid, unexcited way. "Only students. Heavy sentences, to discourage others, of course. But—no leads to anything. No expectation of anything . . ." He waved a heavily mittened hand towards the wreckage. "Anything like this."

Vorontsyev rounded on him.

"The men here were *wiped out!* Someone did a very professional job on them—wives and families, too, in some cases. Each one with a bomb. Don't you have any *idea?*"

Seryshev shrugged. "No." He did not like the admission, but it was safer than bluff, he considered, at that moment.

Vorontsyev stared at the wreckage, as if willing himself to remember every detail. Then he said, "Nothing else?"

"Not for months."

Silence, then Vrontsyev called, "Blinn! Anything yet?"

The stooping forensic officer looked up, his face caught by the revolving, winking light on the police car. He looked chilled, and irritated.

"Don't be stupid, Vorontsyev! What would you expect? I'm still putting together the parts of the people here!"

"Get moving, then!" Again, the unreasonable, unreasoning anger flared, filled his throat like nausea. "Balls to the bodies! I want to know how they died, and who killed them!"

Blinn took a step towards him, casting aside a charred length of carpet. It rolled back over something humped and blackened that Vorontsyev did not care to identify.

159

"You're a prize bastard, Vorontsyev! It's *people* who died here, don't you realise that?"

Vorontsyev was shouting now, in contest with the wind and Blinn. Blinn seemed even more deeply shocked than he over the atrocity. As if the massive safety of his organisation and his office had been stripped from him like so many inadequate clothes.

The two men stared at one another across the spars and frozen waves of the ruined building, Blinn's taut, thin face reddened by the light, the sleet blowing across it caught by the same glancing light.

"I want to catch the bastards who did it! And I may not have a lot of time to do it. Can you get that into your thick skull?"

Blinn's nostrils flared. Vorontsyev saw the puzzlement succeed anger in his face. He had said too much.

"What the hell has time got to do with it? All the watches and clocks around here have stopped!"

"I—I'm sorry," Vorontsyev said. "It—look, it may be urgent," he added, stepping away from Seryshev. "Urgent. So put someone on the explosive—exclusively. And at each house that was blown up. I want to know type, amount—all of it." Blinn was already nodding in concert with the demands. "I want to know how much there was. And then perhaps we can guess where it came from."

"OK, I understand." He looked at Vorontsyev. "I wondered why they sent you out here." He turned away.

Vorontsyev looked once more at the rubbish of the building and its occupants. Where did the explosive come from? Ossipov, you bastard, he thought, this isn't like slipping a tail in the cinema toilet . . . Again the unreasonable anger. If it was you—I'll finish you.

Even then, in the street, despite the sleet, the chilling cold, and the traffic thinning in the square behind him, it did not sound a particularly stupid boast.

General Ossipov was entertaining a young man in civilian clothes in his quarters; his town quarters, a suite of rooms on the top floor of the Dalni Vostok Hotel on Karl Marx Street. The young man was standing before him, almost at attention, staring into a mirror above the mantelpiece—an ornate, gilded mirror in which he could see the back of Ossipov's grey head and sometimes the side of his face as he spoke. The young man felt angry with his orders from Moscow, and half-afraid of their affect on Ossipov.

The General had taken too much to drink already, that was evident. His tie was slightly askew, and the grey suit appeared rumpled—the collar was wrinkled to the hairline, he could see. He was feeling aggrieved that he should have to berate the General, imitating the anger that *Kutuzov* had shown when he had briefed him the previous night. He was not certain the General, in his present semi-drunken mood, would respect his status as courier.

"You dare to tell me that I have acted precipitately —that I am wrong?" Ossipov snarled, a second or two later than he would have done, the emotions muddied by the drink. The young man winced at the evident blame *he* was attracting.

"Sir," he said again, "I am only repeating what I was told to say. You know that is my function. My opinions are irrelevant."

"You arrogant young turd!" Ossipov snapped, and the young man saw the head jolt upwards, in the mirror, and refrained from meeting the General's eyes.

"No, sir," he said.

"You tell me that *Kutuzov* considers me a fool who has acted like a silly, middle-aged virgin when a man looks at her? God, I got rid of that stinking KGB gang in one night! And the Separatists will get the blame!" The General laughed, but the young man considered it was only the confidence of alcohol.

"I was told to inform you that the SID have a man here —a Major. That *Kutuzov* considers this to be an indication that the—*enemy*—have a strong suspicion that all is not as it appears out here."

"Considers? Rubbish!" Ossipov poured himself another vodka, a noisy meeting of bottle and tumbler. "We have five days, if his bloody marvellous plan works! What, pray, is there to fear?"

"You became an object of suspicion, General," the young man proceeded. "An SID unit was on to you—you eliminated your double with Vrubel's help. Now you have attracted this attention to the Far East District, just a few days later."

Ossipov shifted in the chair—the young man saw the head jerk, the whole body move, as he came out of the chair. Shorter by five inches or more, his head came into view at the edge of eyesight as the young man strained to stare into the neutral mirror.

"Attention? Attract attention? What the hell does that mean?"

The young man swallowed, then said, "It means—*Kutuzov* considers that the exercises should be suspended while the SID man is here."

There was a silence. As if drunk himself, the young man moved his gaze over the reflected room; over the ornate furniture, most of which belonged to Ossipov, over the thick, patterned carpets—returning, unwillingly, to the back of the General, the square shoulders and the bull neck.

"No," Ossipov said with difficult restraint, the glass clinking against his dentures a moment before his reply. "*Kutuzov* should have asked me whether I was *able* to suspend the tests, not give me an order when he's thousands of miles away. I will not jeopardise the whole operation because of one man. 'Exercise Mirror' must continue. There are still problems with the chemical attack to precede the armoured assault. These must be solved in the next two days!"

Ossipov regained his seat, studied his drink for a moment, then went on: "I am working *without* expert assistance—I have to, since I can't trust the scientists I could otherwise lay my hands on." The courier stood patiently at attention, staring into the ornate mirror. It was, he presumed, one of his more irksome duties to listen to these old men as they communed with their drink and their past, present and future. "And if we are to test the chemical devices, then we have to go through the fiction of the whole exercise to fool the American satellites."

He looked up briefly, but the young man did not meet his eyes and he returned his gaze to the carpet, his head resting on his chest. "They must continue to think we are once again rehearsing the invasion of China—*not* the invasion of Norway. Tell *Kutuzov* when you return to Moscow—" The General seemed to have created in himself a certainty born of reasonableness, and of reasoned argument, and was prepared to end this tirade on a note of quiet defiance. "Tell him that for his sake, for all our sakes, I will not stop now." He paused, then, with confidence, snapped, "Now, get out!"

EIGHT

BORDER INCIDENT

The MIL helicopter followed the single road from Murmansk to the Finnish border, flying at little more than five hundred feet above the narrow white parting between the heavy darkness of the trees and the strip of dull glass that was the river Lotta.

Already, the country below was boring to Ilya. Their flight to Leningrad, then the transport plane, an old Ilyushin, which had taken them to the military airfield at Murmansk, had tired him. He never slept well on aircraft, unlike Maxim, who had dozed in the seat next to him, wrapped in his heavy overcoat, snoring gently. Instead, he had drunk whisky on the prolonged flight and in the uncomfortable, sparse transit lounge at Murmansk, until the MIL was able to take off before first light and in improved weather.

He had little idea of how to conduct the investigation. Major Vorontsyev had told them, repeatedly, to be careful, to convince whoever they met that it was a straightforward missing persons case—except that the missing person was a KGB officer, and that was why the SID had been called in. But he knew that they would find out little that way.

What was there to find out, anyway?

The dark trees, the snow-covered swellings of the landscape, flowed beneath him like waves.

Finland Station. That was all.

He tapped the pilot on the arm. The young man turned to him, lifting one earphone of his headset.

"What is it?"

Maxim stirred lazily in the seat behind him, irritating Ilya. How could he sleep so soundly, with the rotors beating above them, and the insecurity of being suspended above the wild landscape below.

"Where are the tanks?" he said, grinning foolishly. The pilot smiled.

"Not yet," he said. "The divisions are pushed almost up to the border here. I'll show you some when we get there." He replaced the earphone, and turned away from Ilya. A few minutes later, Ilya again tapped him on the arm. The pilot pointed to a second set of headphones, slung over the dual controls of the MIL. Ilya uncomfortably adjusted them, and the pilot's voice crackled inside his head.

"What is it? You're like a kid!" He was smiling, however.

"Were you on Vrubel's staff—part of his section of the wire?"

"Yes," the pilot replied. "But I'm army, not KGB."

"How come?"

"Your lot don't seem very keen to fly choppers in this part of the world," the pilot replied. Ilya scowled, and the pilot added, "Don't be insulted. It gets pretty rough. I'd thank you for a Moscow posting!" He laughed. For a moment, Ilya had the feeling of some ambassadorial charm being exercised, as if the young man was more aware than he seemed behind his affability.

Then he said, "We do cover more than Moscow."

"Sure. But SID?"

"All right—you win. I prefer Moscow, or Leningrad—I don't like flying, and I'm trying to make conversation!" He shrugged.

"Great! Now, what do you want to know?"

"Just tell me about the captain. What sort of officer was he?"

"One of the best," the pilot answered. "Even if he was KGB—sorry. No, he was army, really, like you're really a policeman. Good to his men, firm, clear-headed, even when he'd been drinking . . . A loss—if he's dead."

There did not seem to be any depth of regret.

Ilya said, "You're sorry he's dead, then. If he's dead . . ."

"Of course I am. Good man." He added, after a pause: "He *is* dead, I suppose?"

"Who knows?"

"You've implied it—so did your office in Murmansk when they called for me."

"I suppose so," Ilya wondered, then: "Why should he be dead? Or, why should he disappear?"

Ilya looked out of the window, as if indifferent to the reply, and the flowing landscape appeared even more hostile. He could not be certain why that should be. Was it the landscape making the conversation sinister, or was he picking up something that made his position, five hundred feet above *that*, more insecure than ever?

He wondered, too, how strongly the Murmansk Local Resident had implied that Vrubel was dead. It was as if the pilot had known about it for some time, and had come out on the other side of shock.

And perhaps, he thought, he didn't like Vrubel and it is politeness towards the dead that gives him a stilted, practised manner. He smiled at his own suspiciousness.

"I don't know," the pilot said after a while, having screwed his face to the contortions of thought. "It has to be something in Moscow, not here. There's nothing out here—except us."

"No jealousies—nothing like that? Nothing in the line of duty?"

"Out here? You didn't know Russians had landed on the moon, did you? That's it, down there!" He pointed below with his thumb. "All it is is trees, tanks, and men. Men get drunk, play cards, read dirty books, toss themselves off because they're so bored . . . But it doesn't lead to murder. Oh, Vrubel gave out his fair share of extra duties, as punishments, but that wouldn't explain it."

"And what if he disappeared?"

"Why would he do that? Boredom?" The pilot was disbelieving. "With you lot on his tail as soon as he does? Why not disappear from here, anyway? Nip over the border. Nothing easier!"

"Nothing?"

"Well—almost." The pilot pushed the stick forward, and the nose of the MIL dipped so that the trees and the

165

river and the whiter ribbon of the road all seemed to assert themselves, reach up at Ilya. He stared at the pilot, who pointed. "Down there!" he said, pointing ahead. "You see if you can spot them—three tank regiments on permanent station."

"Finland Station," Ilya said, thankful for the opportunity, savouring his assumed indifference as he said the words.

"What was that?"

"I was making a joke," Ilya said, looking directly ahead. "Isn't that what they're for—Finland? So it's a Finland station—uh?" He simulated the huge amusement; rather well, he considered.

The helicopter drove towards the trees, and Ilya concentrated, as he had been instructed. He could see nothing. Only a single clearing, and two figures in heavy coats and fur caps—and perhaps netting.

The pilot said, as they lifted away again, "Finland station? That's good, that is. Do you think Comrade Lenin would have laughed?" Now he too, was smiling. The rapport of humour seemed to have returned to the flight-cabin.

"I doubt it," Ilya said, relaxing now that the helicopter was flying a level course once more. "No sense of humour!" He laughed.

And you, you bastard, grinning away, Ilya thought. You've heard that before—*Finland Station*. I wonder what it means to you?

They had staked out the ground as clearly as they could; tape and stakes, a weird pattern of parking spaces where they had discovered the traces of vehicles. Or where temporary wooden huts had been erected, or tents put up. And they had amassed their evidence—pitifully labelled and stored in plastic bags—cigarette-ends, oil-stained snow —this in a freezer box in the jeep—splinters of wood, empty cigarette packets.

And the photographs—roll after roll of film.

When they reported back to Aubrey, he would authorise a single low-level photo recce flight over the area. Then the hard evidence would be presented to the government of Finland, and to NATO, and to America and the Soviet Union.

Davenhill had slept an exhausted sleep, and resented it

when roused by Waterford, though it was mid-morning by the time he awoke. When they had eaten, they set off down the last miles of the one road to Rontaluumi and the border.

By afternoon they were on a rise above the village looking down on the back of the few houses that clustered around the main street and square of the village. They had been there for two hours, and they had seen nothing.

As the glasses passed between them once more, and Waterford pulled at his flask before handing it, too, to Davenhill, the Foreign Office adviser said, "It is deserted, I suppose?"

"Could be full of vampires," Waterford observed. "Sleeping off the daylight and the peculiar diet."

"What are they using for victims?" Davenhill said, feeling the long monotony thaw, resolve itself in grudging humour. He rolled onto his back, drinking the brandy, handing the glasses back to the soldier.

"How about a tank regiment of the Red Army?"

"A nice solution to our problem. Is it deserted?"

"Christ knows. It certainly looks it." Waterford scanned the silent village once more through the glasses, then put them at his side, and stretched himself, shifting his prone body. "We are going to have to find out. Fancy volunteering?" There was no longer a sneer in the voice, and Davenhill felt no offence. Their relationship had become anaesthetised in work; they were part of the same mission, and that sufficed for both of them. They relied upon each other now. Davenhill nodded.

"Come on then. I don't fancy this place after dark. We'd better go in now." Davenhill was still smiling when his tone darkened and he added: "Softly, softly is the word, Alex. You keep close to me, you take the safety-catch off your gun, and you keep your eyes swivelling like those on a bloody chameleon. Savvy?"

"OK. You're the expert. What do you expect?"

"The dead lying on their beds, hands across the chest," Waterford said. "Or mere emptiness. I don't know. What I *don't* expect is to find Russian soldiers—but then, I don't want to be surprised." He lifted his head, raised the glasses, scanned, then said, "The big house—village headman that will be. We'll make for that. Just follow me." He looked at Davenhill, and the younger man saw the features tauten, the eyes seem to become shallow yet in-

167

tent. It was as if he were looking at a sharp monochrome picture of the man, without shadows or highlights. Something etched, yet flat.

"Watch yourself," Waterford said quietly. "No heroics, and no panic. If—if there's anyone nasty down there, it'll be the time to remain normal in the abnormal situation. That's what it's about, son—being ordinary when the world goes mad."

"I'll try."

Waterford nodded, seemingly satisfied; yet Davenhill thought he caught something in the twitch of the lips that might have been pity, or disappointment. Then the bigger man got up, into a crouch, and dusted off his waterproof trousers.

"Ready?"

"Ready."

Davenhill followed him down the slope, keeping to a crease in the land as to a path, his body balanced inwards towards the slope, his eyes on the path Waterford was making through the restraining, glutinous snow. Waterford, he knew, was ceaselessly scanning the village as their viewpoint dropped lower, to the level of the ground floor of the house that steadily, jerkily seemed to move towards them.

Beneath them then was what must be the garden, or at least the strip of land belonging to the house. There were no footprints in the snow, but it had snowed that previous night, and Davenhill dismissed the relief that threatened to bubble up in him. He felt the tension, withdrawing into himself, unaware of Waterford except when he touched the body in front of him whenever the man stopped, or as he watched the sunken footprints. A little narrow frightened world that was Alex Davenhill.

Ordinary.

He understood what Waterford meant. Like entering the club, or the new bar, this should be.

No, not even that. Like the washing-up, or mowing a lawn.

Christ, he wondered, how does he manage it, to be like that when a bullet might tear the life out of him at any moment?

Davenhill tried breathing deeply, regularly.

"Do your exercises later," Waterford snapped in a whisper. They were almost at the rear door of the house, and

Davenhill saw, as Waterford pointed, the chipped whiteness against the door and the frame around it; the absence of a lock. He said nothing, however, moving instead to the window to the left of the door. He rubbed at the frost, and peered in.

"Well?" Davenhill asked after what seemed like minutes of Waterford craning and bobbing his head.

"It's very tidy," Waterford observed. "Very houseproud. And not what you might expect from someone having to leave their home suddenly." He moved back to the door, abstracted, and Davenhill felt more than ever outside what was taking place. This was a celluloid reconstruction of events—a demonstration film.

Waterford touched the handle of the door with a mittened hand. Then he suddenly had the Parabellum in his hand, and Davenhill clutched inside his pocket for the Walther. It was an instinctive, clumsy gesture. It was years since he had fired a gun, and never in anger. Unless grouse counted. He almost laughed at the idea, and hated the nerves that bubbled close to hysteria. Ignoring them for something like a minute had only made them multiply, like amoeba.

The door swung open soundlessly. Waterford glanced at him, shrugged, and put the gun to his lips for silence. Then he opened the door suddenly wide, and ducked inside. Davenhill waited for a moment, as if forgetting a cue, and feeling foolish. Then he went through the door.

Waterford was already in the big main room of the house where Folley had sat. It was empty, tidy, clean. Waterford wiped his fingers over a mirror, then along the edge of a table. There was no dust. His face was creased into a dramatic, abstracted frown.

"There *is* no one here," Davenhill said, and his voice was very loud.

"Possibly. But the evacuation is recent, and perhaps temporary. I wonder—?"

Swiftly, he checked the bedrooms, all on the one floor. Then he paused before the cellar door.

"Is that the cellar?" Davenhill asked. "What—do you expect?" He was suddenly assailed by a Gothic imagining which was stupid, and only served to emphasise the unhealthy state of his nerves.

"Not the corpses—I hope." He pushed open the door, which creaked, and reached for the light. There was only

169

the usual slight mustiness of a cellar, and the smell of stored animal fodder. He went down the steps. Davenhill waited, again with the foolishness not so much of reluctance but of incompetence. In this water, he could not swim. And he knew it before he dipped his toe.

He joined Waterford at the bottom of the steps.

"See?" Waterford said, holding a Kalashnikov rifle up for his inspection. It was neatly stacked, with three others, against one wall. Looking at them, Davenhill noticed the uniforms hanging from fresh pegs, the boots—then, near the stacked hay, a military cot.

"*Are* they Russian uniforms?" he asked.

"Not the Lapland Fire Brigade, that's for certain."

"What does it mean?"

Waterford was patient, probably because he conceived no immediate danger.

"A special detachment, left to guard the village."

"And—the villagers?"

"Settled—elsewhere."

"Well, where are they?" Davenhill pursued, determined not to move ahead of the answers he elicited from Waterford.

"Out and about—looking for us, or someone like us."

"What?"

"Folley must have come here, or been brought. They found him, and they'd expect another enquiry of the same sort. That's why the uniforms are here. And I bet they speak Finnish."

It was not a voice that they heard next, but footsteps on the bare floorboards above their heads. Waterford saw Davenhill's eyes roll comically in his head, and almost laughed inwardly at the way in which real fear hadn't even begun for the clever queer. He felt him an encumbrance, and pitied him at the same moment.

"What do we—?" Davenhill's whisper was a squeak.

Waterford covered his lips again with the gun barrel, then listened. A voice called out in Finnish, and Waterford smiled. He motioned to Davenhill to put the gun away, and slipped his Parabellum back into the shoulder holster. Again the voice called out, then the footsteps began on the stairs, and they watched two legs above high boots come into view. There was an assuredness about the unhesitating steps.

Waterford called out, "I say—can you help us?"

170

He moved swiftly to the foot of the steps, looking up into the face of the young man before he could leave the steps. The man, dark, thin-faced, was smiling openly, and yet contrived to appear surprised. "You speak English, old man?" Waterford added.

Davenhill remained where he was, confused and withdrawn. He could no longer fathom motive, even identity. He wasn't sure who the young man on the steps was, but he believed, with difficulty, that he must be Russian. And his ignorance screamd that Waterford had betrayed them by addressing the man in English.

"A little," the young man said, and the accent was no longer Scandinavian.

"Ah, how lucky, eh, Alex?" He turned momentarily to Davenhill. "We're electricity board surveyors from England—our jeep broke down about a mile from here. Do you think the chaps here might help us?"

It was ridiculous, Davenhill had time to think. Then the young man said, with difficulty, "I saw you—come here? Why are you in the cellar?"

"Couldn't find anyone, old man. Thought there might be someone down here. Not your cellar, is it, old man? Awfully sorry."

"No—I live—other house. You come up now?" There was nothing of menace in the voice, perhaps only anxiety that they come quickly.

There were wet footprints on the stone floor of the cellar, next to the uniforms and the leaning rifles. It was stupid, a farce that they should be pretending to be innocent travellers. Davenhill felt something in him collapsing. His breath smoked round him in the cold.

The young man had stood aside on the steps, Waterford, with a charming, bland smile, was passing.

He turned and said, "Come on, Alex—this chap will give us a hand with the jeep!"

He went up the steps quickly, and Davenhill, seeming to himself to be moving through an element more glutinous than the thick snow behind the house, followed. He hardly glanced at the young man, then, aware of admission in his averted gaze, stared at him, grinning foolishly; hating his inadequacy, already sensing Waterford's scorn.

That, more than the fear as soon as he was above the young man, and his unguarded back was to him.

At the top of the steps, Waterford, relaxed, smiling,

was waiting for them. His hands were in the pockets of the heavy anorak. There was, incredibly, nothing to fear. Ridiculous.

The young man was alert—Davenhill saw the tension in his frame. An inappropriate image of nakedness, remembered just for a moment, then he was standing between Waterford and the Russian who was still pretending to be a Laplander.

"Why are you here?" the young man said then.

Waterford smiled, disarmingly. "Ah—hydro-electric power." His hands went into a mime, his voice into a pedantic deliberateness, head moving in emphasis. "Water —dams, using the power of the water—we are *investigating* for the British electricity industry . . ." Pausing, while the vocabulary caught up. Davenhill was tempted to laugh, and admire. "What can we learn from your country? You understand?"

"Ivalo?" the young man said.

"Yes. Doing a bit of sightseeing—tourists?—on our own." Waterford had moved away from the young man and was looking out of the window. Davenhill saw now how lean the Russian's frame was, how fit the man must be underneath the assumed civilian clothing. He remained near the Russian, as if a token of good faith or an emblem of peace.

"Where is your jeep?" the young man asked, moving too.

"Just outside the village," Waterford said, apparently unconcerned, looking up the main street of the village. The young Russian approached him. Davenhill could see the menace in the movement, but could not be objectively certain—hating the impotence that made him a spectator of the tiny events, and concentrating, as if afraid of missing something—but Waterford seemed oblivious.

When he turned from the window, he was holding a knife, glimpsed briefly by Davenhill, and the young man's back flexed convexly as he bucked his stomach away from the point of the blade.

"One move, sonny, and I'll kill you, just one move or sound—understand?" Davenhill knew sufficient Russian to understand what Waterford had said.

Then the older man moved closer to the Russian, turning him with apparent ease, knife now across the stretched

172

white throat above the check shirt and the collar of the anorak.

"Don't kill him—!" Davenhill blurted out, as if disturbed by events on a screen that were unexpectedly real.

"Shut up!" Waterford snapped, and Davenhill almost failed to recognise the voice, as if a trick of ventriloquism had made the man's lips move. Alien . . .

Then Waterford pushed the man so that he stumbled, slipped on a loose thick rug, a splash of bright colours, and even as he turned over on his back Waterford kicked him in the thigh, near the groin, bent and pulled him to his feet, drew the gun with the right hand and hit the Russian across the cheekbone with the barrel.

Davenhill found his long fingers at his quivering lips, and a strange voice saying, "For Christ's sake, what are you doing to him?" It was his own voice, and that was horrible, too.

"*Disorientate!*" snapped Waterford, as if reciting some lesson. "Get a bucket of water—now!" There was no resistance in Davenhill. He turned and went out into the long kitchen.

He heard the sounds of tearing cloth, then slapping, and he hurried, as if afraid to be rebuked, filling the plastic bucket from beneath the sink with ice-cold water. He slopped it back from the kitchen, along the bare corridor to the main room, where Waterford snatched it from him, and flung the contents over the dazed, bleeding Russian in the armchair where he had been pushed. The man was naked, except for his boots and long socks. His torn trousers were in a stiff, degrading pool around his ankles. The check splash of the shirt was beside the armchair.

The body jerked as if from electricity as the water cascaded, shocked, froze. There was a strangled cry, and then Waterford was on him, knee on his chest, gun beneath the point of the jaw, forcing the flopping head with the lolling black hair up, to look into the blue flat eyes.

"Where are the others?" he barked, shouting almost, jerking the gun in his hand so that the Russian's jaw grated, and the head snapped up and down. Puppet, thought Davenhill, with appalled fascination.

There was no sound from the Russian.

"Where is the Englishman? Where is he?" Again the pressure of the gun—then he saw Waterford lean away,

173

and the Parabellum exploded. Davenhill found his hands about his face, plucking at his lips, wanting to cover his ears. There was nothing he could do; the Russian was dead. He heard Waterford's voice, distantly: "Where is the Englishman?" Why ask a dead man? "Where is he—you're not deaf yet!" The command in the voice was—terrible.

And then Davenhill saw the head flop, as if alive, and Waterford said again. "Where is he? Did you bastards kill him? *Answer me!*"

There was a choking sound, as if the young man was still swallowing the water thrown over him, and the head moved again, and over the hunched shoulder of Waterford he saw the eyes roll in the head, whites rather than pupils, and another groan.

Only then did he realise that Waterford had not killed the Russian.

"Speak! Now! When did you kill him? When?"

A silence. Then:

"No—not kill . . ." the voice was awful, something already dead trying to get back from somewhere impossibly far. "He—was taken back."

"I don't believe you, you little Russian shit! He's dead!"

"No, no!"

"Yes!"

"Beg you . . ." Davenhill heard, and braced himself, hands fluttering at his sides, uncertain.

"You killed him!" Each syllable broken, precise with menace.

"No! They took him back over the border with them!"

"Who!"

The voice was easier now, lubricated by some whiff of possible life.

"The tank regiment—when they went back."

"When?"

"Two—days."

"Why are they here?"

"I don't know. *Invasion!*" The last word was shrieked as the gun drew back from the jaw, then pressed against the temple. Davenhill saw the terrible eyes swivel in the head, following the gun. All whites.

Then Waterford, as if some conjuror or magician re-

174

leasing a spell, stepped back, slipped the gun into its holster. Then, his back to the Russian, he put on his gloves.

"Right," he said. "Let's get this young man outside and back to the jeep, shall we, Alex?"

Davenhill was immobile with shock, disorientation.

"Come on, Alex," he heard Waterford say, almost cringing as the bigger man came towards him. But his voice was kindly. "We haven't got any time to waste. Get him dressed."

He left the room abruptly, exuding a confidence more appropriate to a Ministry corridor, an officers' mess, than to their present situation.

Then he realised that the peculiar sound in the room was the Russian's teeth as they chattered uncontrollably. The young man was hunched in the armchair, arms wrapped across his chest, moaning through the noise of his teeth. He moved to him, helping him slowly to his feet. The young man flinched from him, and his body began quivering as soon as it abandoned the mould of the chair. The eyes were still now, receded.

His nakedness was upsetting, humiliating. Davenhill bent down, and pulled the trousers up to his waist. The buckle was missing, and the waistband was torn. He gently guided the young man's hand until it held the trousers in place. Then he picked up the shirt, saw its condition and abandoned it, then pulled the anorak across his heaving shoulders. The chattering noise had gone. Sobs, irregular and heaving, were the only sounds now.

Waterford came back into the room.

"The back way," he said. "Get him moving." Precise, clipped tones; army manoeuvres. The voice enraged Davenhill.

"You bastard! He'll freeze to death before we can get back!"

"Rugs, blankets in the jeep. He won't freeze—if he runs fast enough!" He glared theatrically at the Russian, who bowed his head, his mouth opening and closing, fishlike.

Davenhill stared Waterford out for a long moment, then capitulated. The man was right—always bloody right. And the Russian had talked. Folley was alive, somewhere in Russia.

And, he realised, they had a witness.

He bundled the young man in front of him, out of the main room, down the corridor, through the kitchen. It was already getting late in the afternoon, and the weak sun low on the horizon, a bleary, tired eye. Waterford went ahead of them, moving quickly, and Davenhill found the gun in his hand again, and he prodded the Russian in the back. He moved like an automaton, and Davenhill snarled, "Pick your feet up!" in Russian. And shuddered as if he had caught some infection.

They almost walked into Waterford, because the man stopped suddenly.

A patrol of four, returning, topping the rise twenty yards away. Rifles, Kalashnikovs, slung over their shoulders, gait weary, relief and tiredness evident in the slouch of the shoulders.

Davenhill had an impression of heads snapping up, of fumbled movements, then the Parabellum roared in the quiet where the only sound had been the labour of footsteps through the snow. The noise banged back from the building behind them, seemed to echo from the low sky.

Then the Russians were firing, even as they split from the tight group; two of them, moving in separate directions, firing from the hip, bent low and running. Two bodies lay on the ground, ugly sprawling things like dark stains.

Then the exaggerated noise again from Waterford—he was in a crouch, hands stiff in front of him, both holding the gun. He was turning on his axis like a doll, spinning like something on a musical box, firing alternately at one then the other. Davenhill saw flame from the direction of one of the Russians, who had paused long enough to kneel in the snow—and the young man in front of him, who had stood stupidly observing events he seemed not to comprehend, was flung back against him. Davenhill clutched the thin body as the anorak came away, and then stumbled and fell, the dead Russian on top of him, an obscene weight, his Walther sticking butt-up from the snow, out of reach of his hand.

Then there was a single shot, then silence. Davenhill lay sobbing, feeling the scream rising in his throat, threatening. It had to be madness, this being buried beneath a dead body naked to the waist and the trousers hanging open across the privates . . .

He heaved at the Russian, as at something loathsome, and staggered to his feet. Waterford was inspecting the bodies. Davenhill plucked his gun out of the snow, and wiped it, attending minutely to the whiteness, the wetness that had gathered on it, and in the barrel. Then Waterford was beside him, his hand on his shoulder.

"Don't sulk," he said, but his voice was without rancour or sarcasm. "I'm sorry the game has changed."

Davenhill felt himself shaking with relief, quivering, and was ashamed. Waterford squeezed his shoulder. Davenhill looked at him; he saw the gulf between them in experience and nature, and he saw the kind of man Waterford was. Yet he saw something akin to pity, too—even regret.

Then the moment was over. Waterford said, "We'll have woken the dead. Let's get moving. We might have to run all the way to Ivalo yet." He looked down at the dead young man whose buttocks were exposed by the broken young trousers as he lay face-down in the snow. "Pity they killed that poor sod. Star witness, he would have been."

Then he walked abruptly away, towards the top of the rise. Davenhill looked at the white buttocks, and the creeping red stain just showing beneath the hip, and felt sick.

"Come on—there are other patrols out, Alex. We *have* to move!"

Davenhill began to walk up the slope in Waterford's deep footprints.

There was an increased tempo of activity. Ilya was certain of it now. While Maxim interviewed a Senior Sergeant in the KGB Border Guard, Vrubel's most senior NCO, he was standing at the window of the wooden hut put at the disposal of the two SID men to conduct their enquiries. It was late afternoon, and Ilya's head was thick with cigarette-smoke and pointless interviews. Maxim seemed to have the stronger constitution when it came to the dead-end minutiae of their profession.

Outside, the pace of footsteps through the packed snow, the number of people appearing from the doors of other huts in the HQ compound of Wire Patrol Station 78, increased. Movement between huts: men emerging into the failing light tugging on jackets—a fur-lined flying-jacket, he would have guessed in one case—the tread of heavy boots audible even through the double-glazing.

He looked once at the Senior Sergeant, a heavy man with a square, passionless face, probably looking a dozen years older than he was—grizzled hair stiff on his head, creased low forehead. The man was glancing over Maxim's shoulder. As his gaze caught Ilya's, he looked promptly back at Maxim.

"Thank you, Sergeant, that will be all," he said on impulse. He saw Maxim's shoulders flex, then relax. He would play along.

"You've been very helpful," Maxim said.

The Sergeant seemed suspicious, then nodded and stood up. The chair scraped on the wooden floor.

When he was gone, Ilya said, "Come over to the window—tell me what you see."

Maxim, amused rather than intrigued, joined him. They were silent for a few moments, then Maxim said in a curious voice:

"The wire which divides Comrade Lenin from Coca-Cola—was that what you wanted?"

"No, idiot. Closer than that." Ilya, too, looked across the six or seven hundred metres of treeless, levelled ground that separated them from the wire and the two visible watch-towers that overlooked it.

"Oh. Mm . . ." He rubbed his chin in mock-thoughtfulness. "Ah—a Border Guard running, is that it?"

"Yes!"

"Unusual, I agree. Shall we put him on a charge? Perhaps he is a follower of Trotsky?"

"Why is he running?"

"Caught short?"

"Lot of people about?"

"Some."

"More than earlier? See that man in the flying-jacket? That's the second I've seen in a couple of minutes."

"Oh, no!" Maxim exclaimed in an assumed falsetto. "It's happening! Finland is invading us!"

"Seriously . . ."

They both heard the sound of rotors quickening, and across the snow from somewhere out of sight a redness was splashed from helicopter lights.

"Where are they off to?" Maxim asked.

178

"I wonder. Let's ask."

He walked swiftly to the door, taking his fur-lined coat from a peg beside it, jamming on the fur hat as he went through the door. The sudden change from the fugginess of the room struck both men—the crisp air after the fumes of the stove.

They walked out into the middle of the open space before their hut. Suddenly, Maxim began to trot, a mere half-dozen steps before he cannoned into a soldier, who lost his balance and fell over. Maxim pulled him to his feet, dusted him down, and snapped:

"What the devil's the rush, soldier?"

"Trouble across the wire, man! All hell's broken loose by the sound of it!" Then he gagged, saw the civilian top-coats, the two strange faces, and backed away. Maxim moved after him, but felt Ilya holding his arm. The soldier was fiddling with the strap of his rifle.

Then all three of them looked up involuntarily as a helicopter, red lights at tail and belly, lifted over the huts, the nearest trees parting like dark waves from the down-draught. Then the soldier, sensing his release, trotted off—looking back over his shoulder from time to time until he was out of sight behind a barrack block.

The helicopter shifted sideways in the air, gained a little more height, and streamed away from them, towards and across the border wire.

"What in hell's name—?" Maxim breathed, watching it.

"Come on!" Ilya snapped. "This is it!" He turned Maxim away from the sight of the diminishing helicopter, a black spot winking red.

"What the hell is *it?*" he asked, in his puzzlement returning to the humour they had shared in the hut.

"The whole bloody shooting-match!" He was looking about him, realising that his voice was raised unnaturally. "*Finland Station!*" It came out as a harsh whisper, just audible above the retreating drone of the helicopter.

The HQ seemed to settle, briefly, then another high-pitched whine of rotors, and, away to their right, where their own helicopter had landed in a clearing, the winking of lights.

"*Finland Station?*"

"Yes, you silly bugger!" Ilya was shaking his arm as he gripped them. "That chopper is *over* the border, in Fin-

179

land. Why? Ask yourself why! It has to be the answer to the puzzle!"

"Oh my—!" Maxim's face went blank, then came back to the present. "What do we do?"

"Where the hell is our pilot?"

"Canteen?"

"On his back reading a naughty book! Where the hell is the rest room—where are their quarters?"

The two young men looked around wildly, feeling the puzzle that the HQ presented.

"He went off that way," Maxim said, pointing to their left.

"He did. A hut down there."

They began to run, feet slipping minutely with every stride on the packed snow. They seemed to be the only people now running in the whole of the camp.

"What about that bloody soldier?" Maxim panted.

"If he's as thick as the usual, he'll spend an hour realising he's given the game away!"

They went on running. Heads turned to look at them, but with the incuriosity of routine. They were part of the retreating wave of activity.

"But if he's not—?"

"Then they know that we know—and up yours!"

"What the hell is over there?"

"Who knows? Hell! *Our* people?" Ilya skidded to a halt, mounted the two steps up to the porch, and wrenched the door open. Maxim crowded into the doorway with him, and Ilya felt the prod of his Makarov automatic in his back.

"Careful!" he could not resist saying. "My virginity."

Their pilot, the young, assured man who had been so unguarded, it had appeared, during the flight from Murmansk, was lying on his bunk at the far end of the small barrack. He was alone. The room was warm, and a record player beside his bunk was tinnily producing Mozart. He lifted his head from the pillow and his supporting arm, smiled—then saw the two drawn guns.

"On your feet!" Ilya barked, then: "You do and I'll blow your hand off! You won't fly again."

The pilot stopped reaching for the automatic in his holster, hung on a peg above the bed with his flying-jacket. He raised his hands, and the recognitions flickered in his face as his thoughts embraced the sequence of half-observed events that had brought them there.

"Yes—we know," Maxim said. The pilot nodded in acquiescence. "Get up."

"Stupid," the pilot observed.

Ilya, the scheme forming desperately in his mind, as a sequence of ill-linked episodes, a badly-edited film, said; "One chance! Only one—but it's there. With your assistance."

The pilot remained seated. "Assistance?"

"Don't drawl, and don't delay! On your feet, and get into that flying-jacket. You're going to take us up, and show us the view!" He smiled. Turning to Maxim, he added: "Ever been to Finland, Maxim?"

"No. Always wanted to, though."

"Great. Let's have a little holiday." He walked over to the pilot, careful to leave Maxim a clear field of fire, and pulled the pilot to his feet. The young man, sensing, perhaps, that an extreme purpose had settled uncomfortably on the room, made little physical protest. Instead, he put on the jacket that Ilya handed down to him, picked up his cigarettes and lighter, and walked slowly to the door, his hands in his pockets.

At the door, a sheepish grin on his face, he said, "And what do we do now?"

"We walk directly to the chopper, and we make it go up in the air, and head west, across the border," Ilya said. "By the way—what's going on over there?"

The pilot shrugged. "Routine patrols. It happens all the time, *this* far from Moscow."

"Balls! No one in their right mind flies routine patrols in those beauties. They're MIL-24s, *gunships!*"

"Clever."

"Only a well-spent Soviet youth, taking a proper interest in the armed forces of our glorious country. Get going."

They crossed the packed snow in a tight group, Maxim walking alongside the pilot, apparently engaging him in animated conversation, with much laughter, while Ilya, the gun in the pocket of his coat, walked just behind them.

The transport helicopter in which they arrived was in the same condition of constant readiness as the MIL-24s that had taken off minutes before, even though it was not required until the following day when it would take an off-duty platoon for forty-eight hours' leave in Murmansk. It sat on a swept concrete square, white-and-yellow striped, in a tiny clearing just big enough to allow it to take off and land. Camouflage netting, now drawn aside, concealed it from the air, and its temporary hangar was erected around it when the weather required. At that moment the corrugated structure was wheeled back under the trees.

The pilot nodded to the two members of the ground crew on duty, and they asked no questions when he climbed aboard. Maxim, then Ilya, clambered awkwardly after him up the handholds on the fuselage. Once inside, they settled themselves in metal-framed, canvas-webbed seats behind the pilot.

"Ask no one nothing!" Ilya ordered, taking pleasure, an almost wild delight in what was becoming for him a daring piece of initiative—an escapade. "Just take off, and follow those taxis!"

"And don't bugger about with the machine, will you?" Maxim added, his tone level, without the slightest humour. "We may be ignorant laymen, but if this thing doesn't behave as helicopters normally do, then I'll make sure you don't live to regale your colleagues with the tale!"

"All right, Comrades. Just like the flying manual says. Strap yourselves in, please." He fitted his headset, settled in his seat, was aware of Ilya craning forward over his shoulder to watch him, and began the checks; hurrying them as much as he could.

As he settled to the task, he began to be less aware of his danger. His stomach settled, and the routines with which he was so familiar possessed him.

He set the turrets on the computerised fuel-flow, then the turbines began to wind up. Ilya was aware, comfortingly, of their increasing whirr. Then the chopper jiggled sideways as the tail rotor started. When there was sufficient power to the main rotor, the pilot released the rotor brake, flickered a switch, and hauled over the handle of the clutch which engaged the drive to the main rotor.

Ilya, seeing the ease, the speed of familiarity, assumed that nothing untoward was in the pilot's mind. The pilot, aware of the gun near his right ear, knew that he could have done a dozen things that Ilya would never have noticed until it was too late.

He settled to fly them. He knew the extent of their

possible discoveries. He did not—he suddenly perceived—have the nerve.

He ignored the whole problem.

When they came back. It would do, then. Then they would be taken care of.

Through the canopy top, Ilya saw the rotor blades begin to turn as the engaged clutch bit, and he heard their swirling beat. Normal. As they achieved proper speed, they became a shimmering horizontal dish.

The pilot gently moved a lever to his left, and the rotor blades changed angle. The engine pitch rose as the engines fed more power to the rotors. The chopper moved off its shocks, the wheels for the moment just in contact with the ground. The pilot gently pressed the rudder bar to counteract any rotation of the fuselage, paused to check his instruments again, then moved the left hand lever slightly higher. The MIL lifted from the square of concrete, and the light suddenly increased as they lifted clear of the trees. It was not yet dark.

The pilot checked the drift caused by the wind, and the chopper swung round towards the border.

"You know the course, don't you," Ilya said. It was not a question. Suddenly reminded of their presence—and Ilya applied the cold barrel of the Makarov to his jaw at that moment—the pilot merely nodded. He moved the control stick, altering the angle of the rotor disc, and the MIL moved over the wooden huts, towards the open ground, snow-covered, and the huge wire.

They passed over the wire at less than a hundred and fifty feet, then the racecourse-like stretch of open ground, then the lower, unmanned fence on the Finnish side, and a narrower space clear of trees, then the forest that engulfed both sides of the border at that point. There was little danger of being picked up; they were too low for radar detection, and the Finns maintained few watch-towers. They relied instead upon regular helicopter patrols—regular as clockwork, risibly punctual. It was a token to independence, designed not to anger the Soviet Union or give the least provocation for a border incident.

They saw the white, winding line of the single road, a parting in the trees, and the further, icy gleam of the river to the south of them. Maxim tapped Ilya's shoulder, and he leaned back.

"What are we going to do?" Maxim whispered. Ilya,

aware of the pilot, stretched his right hand so that the gun rested against the pilot's neck, just where the hair touched the collar of the flying-jacket.

"Don't get any idea," he said. "Sorry if it makes you nervous!"

"Look, Ilya—you're behaving like a kid! What are we going to do, *afterwards?*"

Ilya looked at him, and scowled like a child. The flickering, half-plotted scenario he had felt was in his grasp was not a firm outline. Separate incidents, nothing more, the bulk of his plan already put into operation when the MIL took off.

He said; "We can't go back there." Again he glanced at the back of the pilot's head.

Maxim nodded. "Too bloody true, my son."

"Look—if we—?" He thought, shook his head. Then: "This thing can take us back to Murmansk!" His voice was a breathy whisper.

"Oh, yes? Outrunning those gunships you seem determined to take us towards?" Maxim turned away, looking ahead, past the pilot. The darkening sky was empty of lights.

Ilya was silent, offering after a while only: "I'll think of something."

"You do that. Meanwhile, ask him what *is* going on."

Ilya increased the pressure of the gun against the pilot's neck, sufficient to alarm him. He saw the slight spasm of the shoulders, the wrinkling of the neck as if to get rid of a stiffness. The man was frightened.

"Now, what are we doing here?"

Silence. The steady beat of the rotors over their heads, the dark flow of the forest below, patches of white clearing like baldness, the road like a parting in thick hair. Then, ahead of them, winking red lights, one above and to port, the other to starboard, at about the same height. They were overtaking the two gunships.

"What are they doing?" Maxim snapped.

"Looking," the pilot offered.

"In Finland? What do they want—a wolfhead for the mess wall?"

"No."

"Enlighten us."

A tremor passed through the pilot's frame, as if he were trying to overcome some deep, traumatic block. He

184

was afraid of them, but he was perhaps more afraid of something else. Both Ilya and Maxim, looking at one another for a moment, realised the significance of what the pilot must know.

Then the village whose name they did not know.

"Down!" snapped Ilya, and the pilot pushed the stick forward and the nose of the MIL sagged. Figures moving, light flickering across the snow as torches and lanterns were wobbled in gloved hands—a stream of light from a doorway.

And behind a house, stiff, cold dark spots—too familiar to be anything other than dead bodies.

"What the hell is going on here?" Maxim barked, grabbing the pilot's arm in his shock. The MIL wobbled, slewed sideways, and as the pilot's arm was released and he righted the chopper, he snapped in a high voice:

"Don't touch me! Do you want to kill yourself, you stupid bastard?"

Then the intercom crackled in his ears. The cabin speaker had been left on, and the two passengers heard the pilot of one of the MIL-24s ahead of them say:

"North Star 92 to unidentified helicopter—identify yourself, and state mission."

"North Star 86 to North Star 92—mission to assist search," their pilot replied, the gun digging painfully into the back of his neck.

"Acknowledged North Star 86. What in hell's name have they sent you for?"

"I have troops on board—in the event. Any sign yet?"

"No. Ground radio claims five of our men dead. It should be a sizeable party, but no sign of anything. Over and out."

Ilya released the pressure of the gun-barrel, and patted the pilot on the shoulder.

"Good," he said. "Nice touch, that, about the troops. Now—what is going on?"

"Enemy agents, I should think. Firefight of some kind, not long ago by the look of it. They're looking for the agents."

"This is bloody Finland, not Russia!" Ilya exploded.

The pilot turned his head. Ilya could see the humour around the mouth, the contempt displayed in the nostrils, the eyes. The pilot was pitying his ignorance.

He sat back, the gun relaxing from the pilot's head. It

was—he could not explain the pilot's mood; a frightened man who yet talked as if they were flying over Russia, not a neutral neighbour.

Then, ahead of them, they saw the red lights of one of the MIL-24s dip down below their view.

"Follow him!" Ilya snapped, and pressed the gun back against the neck, which wrinkled with disgust and fear. The cabin seemed to alter its angle suddenly, and the ground moved up to meet them. The road was a ghostly ribbon now, but along it, headlights blazing, an open vehicle was moving at perhaps fifty miles an hour—a suicidal speed.

"What the hell is that?"

"It must be them!" the pilot shouted, his caution swallowed in excitement.

"Who?"

"Enemy agents—the bastards!" It was as if they were no longer with him, or he their prisoner.

Ilya could not believe what happened in the next moment. The MIL-24 which had swept down upon the jeep on the road below them launched two of the small missiles slung beneath its stubby wings, then pulled ahead of the racing jeep.

Flickers of fire beneath the wings, then bright bursts of flame, gouts of snow and packed earth ahead of the jeep —almost in the same instant. It was incredible; his mind refused to countenance what it perceived. He watched the jeep.

It bucked wildly, then swung off the road, leaping like a mad horse across the ditch, and disappeared under the trees. The headlights flickered off. In the moment before it slid under the trees and under the belly of their chopper, Ilya saw a white face looking up, then obscured by something dark held out—and he realised, ludicrously, that the passenger in the jeep was taking photographs of them.

The MIL-24 was flicking round on its course, to make another run at the road. Then the intercom crackled in the cabin.

"You'll have to put your troops down and cut them off!" the pilot said without introduction or call-sign. In his voice there was an aftermath of dangerous elation, and a rising panic. "Follow me!" The MIL-24 slid away from alongside them, stretching to a lead of two hundred metres, flying less than fifty feet above the trees. It was a dark bulk ahead of them, lights flashing, the carpet of trees below them revealed nothing of the whereabouts of the jeep or its two occupants.

A beam of light flicked down from the MIL-24 ahead, bathing the tree tops in white light. They glistened with ice and snow. It was an affecting scene, brilliant and harmless. Ilya shook it off.

"What happens when they find out we have no troops to put down?" Maxim asked.

"We'll have buggered off, won't we!" He prodded the gun into the neck again. "Time to go!" he snarled. "We have a long way to go before any of us gets to sleep tonight."

"Where?"

"Murmansk, brother! All the way, no stops!"

"What?"

"You heard. After all," he added turning to Maxim, "we have a star witness here, haven't we? After what we've just seen, together with what they can get out of him at the Centre . . ." He chuckled. "We're home and dry, eh?" He laughed, infected with the same excitement they had heard in the pilot's voice a little earlier. A pendulum of success had swung in their direction now.

"And what *is* going on?"

"I don't care to think about that," Ilya said flatly. "Someone else can find that out. I don't think it bears thinking about, do you?"

"I agree."

"Right, alter course, Comrade Pilot! Take us just a little south of your HQ—and fly very very low! Understand?"

The pilot nodded. The chopper banked, sliding across the trees to retrace their outward course.

When they were settled on course, Maxim said, "And what are we going to do to make sure that we aren't followed and overtaken by those gunships—or the other two I spotted at HQ? Those aren't fireworks they carry under those silly little wings, you know."

"We're going to fake a forced landing—give our position, and then get the hell out of there while they spend their time looking for us!" Ilya spoke in an intense whisper, his face gleaming with pleasure. He tapped his forehead with the forefinger of his left hand.

"Mm. Do you know, I actually approve," Maxim said,

his face breaking into a rare smile. He was a man not without humour, but who often appeared to lack the necessary facial muscles to smile or laugh.

"I knew you would, you dear old thing," Ilya said.

They flew just to the south of the village, and crossed the border at an unmanned point. They reached the first trees on the Russian side, the MIL flying barely twenty feet above them. They were travelling fast, over a hundred miles an hour perhaps.

He said, "Now, comrade, a little fault is about to develop. Radio in a *convincing* fault that will mean you have to force-land. And radio a position . . ." He reached forward and picked up the pilot's map which lay on a tiny folding rest at his side. He glanced at it, then: ". . . a position on the *other* side of the wire. Understand? Be very careful of what you say."

The pilot nodded, opened the channel, and said, "North Star 86—North Star 86 to base. I have developed turbine surge. I have to set down quick. Repeat—turbine surge, am forced to land. My position is—" The gun pressed more attentively against his stiff neck. He gave the position, and repeated it quickly. Ilya strained to read the coordinates on the pilot's map, gave up the attempt, and nodded to Maxim as if he had checked the position. Neither of them knew that the pilot, who was beginning to sweat with relief, had given their present position.

"Down there!" Ilya snapped, motioning towards a small white patch in the darkness.

"What for, man?" Maxim asked. "We've sent them the wrong way. Let's get going!"

"No! Just in case we're spotted going the wrong way. Sit tight for a little bit, then up and away." Maxim looked doubtful, and Ilya shouted, "We can't afford to cock it up now! As you said, those gunships don't carry fireworks. We can't *afford* to be seen, from the air or the ground!"

Maxim looked down. The chopper was circling the tiny clearing, and its landing light had flicked on. The snow appeared rutted, lunar, beneath them.

"All right. We don't move until they're looking the other way."

"Down!"

The chopper settled slowly, nose slightly up. Snow began to blow in the downdraught, fanning out beneath them, whirling up alongside the cabin as they sank lower. Gently, the MIL seemed to be coming to rest. Fifteen feet, twelve, ten—

The pilot moved the stick suddenly, and the tail boom of the helicopter dropped. It thumped into the surface snow, and there was a tearing sound, the magnified noise of a pencil snapping as the whole tail boom broke away under the impact.

The incident happened so swiftly that Ilya and Maxim were entirely its victims. They were not observers, but sufferers. The pilot, seizing his one opportunity, had sabotaged the helicopter.

The fuselage immediately began to wobble from side to side without the appropriate balancing effect of the tail rotor, in the half-second before it, too, hit the ground at an angle. The undercarriage buckled, and the cabin began to tilt. Then the rotor struck the frozen snow and earth.

The cabin felt like a barrel which was being kicked once a second. The rotor blades churned against and into the ground, hurling up snow and earth as the cabin tilted ever more crazily over onto its side. Then one blade snapped, then another, then a third. The vibration was incredible, seeming to rattle the brains in their skulls, possess their whole bodies.

Maxim felt his whole spine jar against the metal frame of the webbed seat. Then the cabin was completely on its side, and there was a silence. The churned cloud of snow settled, audibly, like a snowstorm, on the Perspex.

Ilya sat stunned, head hanging over towards the ground, the straps of his seat restraining him from rolling against the Perspex which had now become the floor of the cabin. Only the single thought that he was still alive filled his mind. He moved, almost by instinct, fingers, arms, legs. All of them flexed and stretched as they should. Only the pain of bruises.

He watched, without moving, as the pilot killed the switches in front of him, then threw off his straps and began sliding back the canopy above him. He reached up, and pulled himself out of the window. The cold air rushed in, chilling Ilya. The pilot's legs dangled for a moment, then he was smearing the settled snow over Ilya's head as he crawled across the Perspex. Ilya heard him drop to the ground.

Then, and only then, did he move, galvanised as if by electric shock. He clambered on the back of the pilot's seat, lifting his head out of the cabin. The pilot was standing, looking back, only ten yards away. It was as if he felt no urgency, or was perhaps stunned like Ilya. Then they saw one another.

The Makarov was stiff in Ilya's grip, as if the impact of the crash had moulded it to his flesh and bone. He shifted it to a two-handed grip, and leaned his elbows on the Perspex.

"Back inside," he said. He heard Maxim groan below him. "Inside, you clever bastard! You did that on purpose!" His finger tightened on the trigger. His next words were strangely high, almost falsetto. "Get back in this bloody deathtrap before I blow you to pieces!"

The pilot hesitated, and then he turned and began to run through the deep snow, stumbling over the frozen surface, floundering into small drifts where the surface ice gave way.

Ilya felt very tired. He could not run through that. And he felt lightheaded. He aimed, feeling sorry that the pilot was having so much difficulty moving away.

He fired twice, while Maxim's second outburst of moaning drove up his emotional temperature and he hated the pilot.

He watched the sprawled figure on the snow for a moment or two, and when it did not move, he dropped awkwardly back inside the cabin of the MIL, pulling the window shut above him.

Maxim's face was white with strain. His eyes were filled with terror at guessed injuries, and they closed with two spasms of pain even as Ilya watched. Ilya could see each wave leave him weak and terrified, his eyes darting from side to side as if seeking some escape from the next assault.

"What is it?" he asked gently.

"I can't feel my legs. Not at all. Can't feel anything below my waist. Can't move anything . . ." A further spasm crossed his face, crumpling it like a discarded ball of paper. He groaned, teeth clenched. When it passed, he opened his eyes only to see the depth of Ilya's concern. He wanted to avoid the information on the face above his own, and he tried to smile. "Tell me—has my dick dropped off?" As he laughed, the pain came again and he screwed up his eyes.

Ilya winced. Maxim had an impacted spine. He touched the seatbelt. He hadn't been strapped in very securely, and the base of the spine must have been jolted against the metal bar at the back of the seat. He couldn't move him.

He said, feeling the nausea sharp in his throat, "I found it on the floor by your seat. I threw it away."

"Just as well," Maxim muttered through clenched teeth. "Bloody thing only ever got me into trouble . . ." He almost fainted as the next wave of pain took him. "Like being in bloody labour!" he groaned as it passed.

Ilya moved away, rooting in the first-aid box which had remained secure on the wall behind their seats during the crash. He found the flask of vodka and unstoppered it.

Kneeling over Maxim, he poured the liquid against his lips. They opened gratefully, and he swallowed. He coughed once, then motioned to be settled on the floor of the cabin. Ilya released the slack belts, then moved the stiff form awkwardly. By the time he had stretched Maxim on the curving floor of Perspex, he saw he had fainted.

"Sorry," he murmured. "Sorry, sorry, sorry . . ."

When Maxim recovered consciousness, he said, "Why haven't you gone?"

"Where?"

"Anywhere! They will come, won't they?"

"I expect so. I'm not very good at reading pilots' maps. I expect he gave our present position."

"You've—got to go, then!" Maxim moved an arm with difficulty, gripped Ilya's sleeve. Ilya shook his head.

"Not bloody likely! I might as well freeze with you as out there by myself!" And he added a silent prayer that they would come soon, and get Maxim to a hospital.

"Get going! You have to report to the Major—to someone!"

"Bugger the Major! Bugger *someone!*" He poured the vodka against Maxim's lips, and he swallowed with the instinctive guzzling of a baby. "I got you into this, finessing the bloody idea until it didn't work out any more! So —who the hell cares? When they find us, then I'll think about getting out of it . . ." He laughed. "Besides, I need a vehicle—they've got them!"

They talked then, for perhaps an hour or more—Maxim slipped in and out of consciousness, and his lucid moments became fewer. Ilya subsided into a dull monotone which scrabbled for subject-matter to distract Maxim. The only thing, he began to believe, was to distract Maxim from the pain he had caused him.

His first awareness that others had arrived was of the dull concussion of a 122 mm gun mounted on a T-62 battle tank. Its infra-red sighting equipment had picked out the two figures in the now-clear Perspex, the snow having slid away to reveal them. As soon as it was determined that both SID men were in the chopper, the order came from the regimental commander, acting on instructions from Murmansk, to open fire.

Ilya's world exploded an instant after his head lifted in response to the noise of the fin-stabilised shell. He did not hear the second and third rounds being fired.

When the chopper had been reduced to smouldering rubbish, the T-62 retreated again into the forest.

NINE
SAFE RETURN

"Charles—all I wish to ascertain at this time, before my people get back with what I hope will be proof, is this: if I can offer evidence, concrete evidence, of a Soviet incursion into Finland, what will you do with the information?"

Aubrey and Buckholz, Deputy Director of the CIA, had sat in the second-floor office of the American Consulate in Helsinki, overlooking the rock-strewn park of the Kaivopuisto, for almost two hours longer than the American had expected, while Aubrey explained the business he had called *Snow Falcon*. Buckholz, his back to the window, settled deep in his armchair behind the big desk, had said little, rubbing occasionally at the white hair he still wore cropped close to his skull, though now pink skin showed through. Aubrey sensed, almost from the beginning, that he was disturbed, even half-convinced—but that his concern rested on his respect for the teller and not the potentialities of the tale.

Now, in the silence that Aubrey had anticipated after he posed the question, he saw Buckholz as uncomfortable, restless, perhaps even at a loss.

"Kenneth—my standing. That's the problem. I'm going out to grass this year. The Admiral's made that more than clear." Aubrey nodded, unhelpfully silent. "I'm a cold war warrior who embarrasses the Company. Y'know, three Senators have spoken to the President personally, asking he demand my resignation?" There was something affront-

ed, and amused, in Buckholz's voice. "Three liberal Demo-
crats, sure—believers in the Kennedy myth, who've forgotten all the dirty tricks we used to play in those days."
He shook his head—Aubrey thought it only an imitation of
the wisdom of resignation; a hawk's deception.

"I, too, have my detractors, Charles," Aubrey remarked
quietly. "But, arthritis may get me before they do."

Buckholz laughed, a bull-like roaring that sounded as if
it lacked genuine amusement, but which Aubrey knew was
sincere.

"OK. We both got troubles. I'm here to oversee security
for the Treaty signing. Maybe this comes under that
head, maybe not."

"I have lost—"

"Two men, yes. Two *good* men?"

"Yes."

"Your government—they in on any of this?" Aubrey
shook his head, and Buckholz shrugged, as if about to say
something, then relapsed into silence again.

"I have to have proof. But, do you support the hypothesis?"

"It's possible—but unlikely, especially in the present
circumstances."

"Exactly my original thoughts."

"Look, Kenneth—this is the Man's ticket to another
term, this Treaty. Checks and balances that work, *real*
reductions—his social programme can go ahead just as
soon as the ink is drying on the paper. Closer cooperation between the Soviet Union and the West. Man, it's
the *realest* thing in Washington at the moment! And you
want to know if I want to tell him that it may all go
down the tubes? Hell, I don't want to tell him—I want my
pension." He stared at Aubrey, eyes glinting. "But I'll tell
him, if there's anything to tell."

Aubrey sighed audibly. "Thank you, Charles."

"What'll you do if your guys come back with something
—but not enough?"

"Order an overflight—one Harrier, under the net."

"You could do that?"

"I'm sure it can be done."

Buckholz nodded. Then he stretched in his chair.

"It'll have to be good, to convince the White House.
Mrs. Wainright just bought two new fur coats, ready for
the visit to Finland in winter." He laughed. "Why is

Khamovkhin here on a State Visit, if he's planning to ride all the way in a tank?"

"No simple answer—except that he may not know."

"Mm. Hell!" Buckholz slapped his palm thunderously against the desk. "All Joe Wainwright wants to do is rebuild the urban deserts, get the Blacks and the Puerto Ricans educated and in useful work, and solve the energy crisis, and I have to tell him—"

"Perhaps First Secretary Khamovkhin just wants to improve Soviet agriculture, and open up Siberia a little more. One thing is certain—at least to me—someone doesn't want the world ticking like that." Aubrey rubbed his cheeks. "Will you help with this mysterious substitute?"

"Captain Ozeroff?"

"Remember that Ozeroff is dead, Charles. It's the new Captain Ozeroff who interests me."

"Do what I can. You're right—he had to come from somewhere, and he must be known to someone. I'll be checked out."

"Thank you—when we know who, we will know why."

Buckholz stood up. "Drink?"

Aubrey looked at his watch. "Just a small Scotch—no ice."

As he was about to move to the dumb-waiter, Buckholz stopped, and looked down at the still seated Aubrey.

"Hell, don't you long to be legitimate, Kenneth? Just once, to close your eyes to what might be happening, uh?"

"My illegitimacy has weighed heavily upon me of late," Aubrey remarked with a smile. "One knows, or suspects that one knows, so many *nasty* things!"

"For Christ's sake, Alex—swallow!"

Davenhill felt the flask tipped against his lips. As soon as he unclenched his teeth, they began to chatter uncontrollably, and the brandy spilled on his chin and over his chest. Looking up into Waterford's face, he was afraid to question the man. He gagged on the little liquor he swallowed, and then sank back against the seat of the jeep. Waterford's face disappeared from above and beside him —a moment of colder air, if that was possible, and then distant slamming of the door as he sank back into a pain-lit dream where a great dark bird—bird or dragon he could not be sure but it breathed flames and burned his arm

195

—hovered over him as he lay helpless on a smooth white sheet of paper.

Waterford dialled the number of the hotel in Ivalo. He had pulled up on the main road, just outside the settlement—the first time he had halted the jeep since he had stopped under the trees to bind Davenhill's arm, sliced open from elbow to shoulder by a fragment from one of the missiles, just as he had careered off the road and under cover. As he waited for his call to be answered, he drummed savagely on the coin box, though the rest of him —as if all energy had flowed suddenly into his square fingers—slumped against the glass of the call-box. He stared at the ceiling, watched his breath cloud the glass, felt the cold of the night for perhaps the first time; felt the chill of reaction possess him.

"Philipson?"

"Yes?" The voice sounded very distant. He shook his head, and the receiver. "Who is that?" The voice was no louder.

"Where are you, in the bloody bar or the restaurant?"

"Call-sign, please." He realised what it was—Philipson was whispering confidentially down the line. He laughed. "What—"

"Bugger the codes, sonny. We're blown—and we have the evidence to put the Soviet Union behind bars for a long time."

"Where are you?"

"Never mind. Davenhill's wounded. Get the pilot out of his—or anyone else's—bed, pronto. We'll meet you at the airport."

"If he's wounded, then he'll—"

"Forget it! I've got the bloody Indians right behind me. No time to stop. Get there!"

"It'll take more than an hour for clearance—"

"It better be quicker than that. Get moving!"

He slammed down the receiver, and left the call-box. As an instinct, he glanced back down the road the way they had come. Nothing. The emptiness chilled, isolated him. Diminished him in an unfamiliar and frightening way. He winced, as if a helicopter had appeared overhead, or he shared Davenhill's dreams for a moment. He hurried to the jeep.

Davenhill roused himself as they pulled away, opening one vague eye, staring at him as he tried to focus.

196

"Bad, is it?" Waterford asked, seeing the lights of Ivalo as a pale splash low on the sky ahead. They passed a wooden house on his side, silent, a glow of subdued light from behind shutters. The airport was south-west of the settlement—he needed to start looking for a left-hand fork.

"Oh, Jesus-fuck-off—" Davenhill muttered between clenched teeth. Waterford wasn't certain whether the remark was addressed to him, to the pain in the limp arm, or to something else.

"Hold on, son, won't be long now. Philipson's meeting us at the airport."

In the headlights, the road forked. A silhouetted aircraft on a signpost. The jeep slid into the corner, and Davenhill lurched against Waterford. Even as Waterford glanced at him, he saw the spite, even the hatred, on Davenhill's face, and the almost desperate attempt to pull himself upright, away from physical contact. Waterford stared bleakly ahead.

"You—bastard—" he heard Davenhill mutter.

"Save it. You'll get cold, talking and hating. Fold into yourself."

"Your world—" Davenhill began, staring at the canvas roof of the jeep, his head lolling. "Your world—"

"Like this most of the time, son," Waterford said angrily. "No pissing about with bits of paper, conferences, operational planning. This is the sharp end, and you don't like it, rolling in the shit." Waterford watched himself with amusement—part of him was always, eternally angry with people like Davenhill; part of him wanted to take the younger man's mind off his hurt. "You ought to hate me, son. I'm the thing that comes up the plughole, breeds under the stones. Your bogeyman—the one you'd like to think was on the other side . . ."

Davenhill murmured, then began a compulsive nodding of his head, silently punctuating each of Waterford's statements. He was beginning to ignore the self, to attend, listen, absorb.

"Oh, yes—I *liked* doing it to that young Russian. Make no mistake about it. Plenty of instant-result techniques I could have used—just wanted to do that to him." Waterford, obedient to another snow-blown signpost, turned left again, and the suffused lights of Ivalo, creeping alongside them until that moment, slid away. Ahead now there was a paler, whiter glow. Ivalo airport. He hoped Philipson was already on his way. He slowed the jeep, the chains biting as the snow, less compressed, threatened beneath the wheels.

"Liked it," he murmured. "Oh yes. Pull his trousers down, throw a bucket of water over him. Bet you liked that bit, eh, son—bare-arsed boy to look at."

"Balls—" Davenhill murmured. The price of concentration was being extracted, and he was drifting into sleep.

"Yes—I noticed he had two," Waterford replied, and glanced at Davenhill. His eyes were closed, his facial muscles relaxed. Waterford sighed with relief, then tossed his head as if he felt he had wasted valuable time. The piled snow from the plough's passage leaned threateningly over the road on both sides. The lights of the airport were brighter now. Waterford felt tired, but not because of their escape, or because of the driving. He looked across at Davenhill and, as if reasserting some old self, murmured, "Stupid little queer."

"There is no time to go through the formalities!"

"I say we *must*. *Kutuzov* has to be informed at once."

"He will be—eventually. General Pnin will inform him of the escape of these agents. Meanwhile, *Kutuzov* will want to be informed from *this* office that the agents told nothing, that they have been eliminated."

"I'm not so sure. We declare our hand by taking precipitate action here in Helsinki. Are you sure you're not just panicking because of what has happened? Consider the repercussions—"

"Repercussions? The whole thing is turning into a nightmare, and it's up to us to bring some sense back into things. You know we *have* to try and stop a report being made. They attacked agents from a MIL! It is something of a give-away, wouldn't you agree?"

"I'm not sure—"

"Then it's a good job I outrank you. Get onto it at once. Either at the airport, or before they reach either of the two likely consulates. And if you can, take out the man Aubrey as well!"

"Is he going to die?" Philipson asked, leaning over Waterford, staring down at Davenhill's pasty features, gar-

198

ishly purpled by the dimmed overhead light of the passenger cabin of the Cessna. Davenhill was stretched out on two seats, and Waterford was re-dressing the torn arm.

"Don't be bloody soft, Philipson," Waterford replied without changing the focus of his attention. "Just a scratch. Might never be able to play tennis again, but he won't die."

"Thank God for that."

"He had very little to do with it, I imagine—don't worry, there won't be a diplomatic stink about a British Civil Servant dying of his wounds in Finnish Lapland. It won't ruin your career."

"That wasn't my concern," Philipson said stiffly.

"Be a good boy—make sure the pilot's sent that message ahead, will you? I want to be met by *our* side at the airport!"

Philipson hesitated, then moved forward towards the cockpit. Waterford tossed his head, then finished binding Davenhill's arm, his nose tickling at the smell of brandy on Davenhill's breath as he began to breathe more stertorously in drunken, wearied sleep.

Aubrey watched the Cessna seemingly sag out of the lowering sky just after dawn. It touched down as if reluctant, with a waver of the wings, then trundled down the narrow runway towards them. The private airfield at Malmi was almost deserted, but he had come with an armed escort selected from the security staff drafted in by SIS and the CIA for the Treaty visit by Wainwright. At that moment, even as the small plane rolled to a stop, they were searching the airfield and its perimeter, carefully.

There had been a moment, just one, as he first spotted the plane seemingly materialising as it emerged from the cloud, when he had thought in terms of terrorists rather than an enemy security service, and had thought of the RPG-7 anti-tank grenade launcher—even a Dragunov sniper's rifle might have been sufficient. A couple of shots. So vivid was the impression, he could not rid himself of it, could not help but feel that the enemy had lost its best chance.

The Cessna halted less than a hundred yards from him. He nodded to the driver of the Consulate limousine, and climbed into the back seat. The big Daimler pulled silently level with the aircraft, and Aubrey could see the pilot kicking the door-ladder down so that it thumped into the slush at the end of the runway. Quickly, Aubrey got out of the car, feeling the chill of the light breeze suddenly more keenly, sensing the evaporation of warmth in tension. Only now, standing at the foot of the ladder, did he allow himself to wonder how seriously Davenhill might be wounded.

Waterford appeared in the doorway of the Cessna. His face was tired, strained but alert. His eyes suggested the rapid movement of a dreamer, but with specific purpose.

"It's all clear, for the moment," Aubrey called up to him.

Waterford nodded, then disappeared back inside. When he reappeared, with Philipson helping him to support a barely conscious Davenhill, Aubrey was shocked at the waxen, hanging face of the younger man. Philipson he hardly noticed. "Help them get him down!" he snapped at the driver. The driver took Davenhill's waist, and Waterford lowered the upper torso carefully, wearily, down below his own level on the steps. Seeing Waterford using last reserves of energy, Aubrey felt suddenly exposed and vulnerable on the tarmac—defenceless.

"Come on, come on," Waterford instructed in a tired voice. "Get him in the car."

They slid Davenhill into the back of the Daimler. Aubrey saw the bloody bandage on his upper arm smear the trim and the window as they arranged him as comfortably as possible. The breeze, freshening, hastened things.

"You've got it?"

Waterford looked at Aubrey quizzically, then: "Oh, yes—you won't have any problems convincing anyone." He pushed the pack containing the cameras and film into the back of the car. "Now, let's get out of it."

Aubrey sat next to the driver while Waterford took Davenhill's weight on his shoulder and leaned himself against the cold glass of the rear window. All he wanted to do was sleep, and he heard only distantly Aubrey issuing instructions over the radio to the escort.

"Car One—move to the gates, then give us the signal. Car Two, fall in behind us when we move off." Waterford could not be bothered to watch the first of the two Volvos move away from in front of the small terminal building, startlingly white under the grey sky.

"They're just leaving the airport gates."

"What formation?"

"Usual—lead car, then the Daimler, then a second Volvo."

"Very well. Minimum tail, then hand over."

"Sir."

"Anything, Car One?"

The radio sputtered with background then: "Not so far." A Welsh voice—who was that? Aubrey dismissed the question as irrelevant.

"Keep your eyes open. They *have* to try—and I mean that. It will appear *imperative* to stop us."

"Sir."

"Car Two—close up."

"Sir. Nothing behind us—wait!—"

"What is it?"

"Volvo truck—OK, taking the last left, is it? Yes, Relax, everybody."

Aubrey felt irritated at the momentary levity from the trailing car, then dismissed his own nerves. He looked out of the window, still cradling the microphone in his palm. Waterford's breathing was audible from the back seat—but he wasn't asleep. Aubrey had a sense of experiencing something like it before—where was it? Negro tennis player, at Wimbledon? Yes, that was it. Concentrated relaxation, the animal curled up, just for a moment, but ready.

Innocuous suburb—small houses in vivid colours, neat gardens, white fences, all strangely unreal under the grey sky. They were taking a careful, long route, but one which did not leave them far from the main road into the city, in case they were required to make a run for it. Most of the houses too low for the kind of thing a sniper would like as a vantage—

Aubrey dismissed the thought. *A sniper would like to be level with the windows of a closed car.* The glass was reinforced, but impossibly fragile against a Kalashnikov, let alone a Dragunov sniper's special. Would they kill them? Hardly anyone about—the problems of disposal

201

might be minimal—an incident, yes. But for reasons unknown, if they were all dead. Yes, they would do it.

"Car One—anything?" He could see the car, turning the corner ahead. "Go ahead, Car One."

The radio crackled with background.

"Coming your way, Twelve."

"Already got them."

"Go!"

Aubrey had heard nothing. Waterford's breathing, Davenhill's more ragged noise, the humming heater, the background from the radio—enough noise?

The lead Volvo was already burning, and men were moving towards it, cautiously, while others formed a line across the street into which the Volvo had turned. Even as he reacted, he realised that they knew Helsinki better than he did, that the street into which he had turned was a sudden blotch of light industry, old warehouses and grass-usurped, unsold plots.

"Get out—get out!" He cried, even as the driver wrenched the wheel, slid the Daimler into reverse. Aubrey saw the first two holes appear in the nearside wing of the car. Waterford said behind him. "Just move out of it! They don't want prisoners!"

Aubrey felt the draught of air as Waterford lowered the passenger window.

"For God's sake!" Waterford squeezed off three shots from the Parabellum, all of them missing, Aubrey thought, as he craned and crouched in one awkward movement, the scene spinning past the windscreen of the car as it slewed its tail toward the oncoming men. No, one body was sprawled across the road, near the Volvo—one of his, or the enemy?

He banged his head painfully against the dashboard as the Daimler surged forward, and then heard bullets thudding dully into the boot and the reinforcement behind the passenger seats.

"All right?"

"For Christ's sake, I don't want another cucumber sandwich!" Waterford yelled. Aubrey sensed the delight in the voice, the *vivacity*. "Tell *them* to cover us, quickly!"

They were passing the second Volvo which was turning slowly into the wide street. Aubrey saw a face, said into

202

the microphone, "Cover us—but make your way out as quickly as you can."

He saw the window of the Volvo coming down, the passengers in front and back leaning out.

"Take the main road—as quickly as you can!" he ordered the driver, who turned right almost at once, doubling back the way they had come.

"No!" Then the sound of Waterford knocking out the rear window, and the interior of the car like a fridge. "They must have a spotter—that wasn't just luck." Silence, the car merely retracing its journey and the ambush still between them and the centre of Helsinki. "Yes. A helicopter. Fuck it! You know Helsinki?"

"Yes," the driver said.

"Use your judgement—don't listen to the rest of us."

Hesitation, then Aubrey said: "Do as the Major suggests."

"Sir."

"Poor sods," Aubrey heard from behind him. He craned round in his seat, and saw the second Volvo swerving round the corner from the ambush, then staggering across the road as if drunk. It piled against a lamp-standard, and was suddenly still.

The Daimler swerved right again, then left in a second or two. Aubrey, despite the pressure he felt, was amused at the independence the driver had suddenly assumed. Then he thought of Davenhill, and realised, from the way his own heart was beating and his palms felt damp inside his gloves, what the younger man had been through. He looked at Waterford, who was staring out of the shattered rear window, his graying hair plucked by the slip-stream, and said, "You seem to attract extreme circumstances, Major."

"Sure it's not you?"

"How far are we, driver?"

"A couple of miles—as the helicopter flies, sir."

Aubrey sensed the dangerous glamour of threat, of ambush-and-escape, and worried. His own adrenalin seemed to have evaporated with age.

"Your direction, Seven."

"Sir."

"Twelve, you should have let the Volvo go!"

"They spotted one of us, sir—had to."

"Get it cleared up. Any witnesses?"

"No one on the streets—we've got the remains stowed."

"Get out of there, then."

"Sir."

"Where are they now?"

"Down there—see?"

"I see. Who's nearest—Let's see—Four, you're favourite by the look of it—wait, Nine. Nine?"

"Sir?"

"Pick up pursuit. They'll pass you in a minute on the main road—damn!"

"Sir?"

"Forget it! Three—three—move into position Omega, just in case. Four, coming your way again!"

"It's too much to hope they're not still with us?"

"Too true. They're up there, but they're confused. Know what they'll do?"

"What?"

"Take up position as close to the Consulate as they dare. Perhaps anticipate we'll drive to a hospital—how far?"

"Ten minutes, sir—if you give me a straight run."

"Mm. We're inside their outer markers now. No places left for an ambush. Car to car would be—main road?"

"You can see the Stadium Tower over to the right, sir. That's the Eläintarha—straight down to the Mannerheimintie."

"Right—go."

"They're making a dash for it, sir."

"I can see that. Very well—all units. Converge on position Omega. We are into the end-play situation. Don't mess it up! All units to Omega—end-play running."

The Swedish Theatre, broad façade and normality returning as they turned into the Etala-Esplanaadikatu from the Mannerheimintie. The Daimler was suddenly caught behind a tram, and Aubrey, expecting his pulse to begin racing again, was aware that the advert for a soft drink on the back of the tram, the hatted, wrapped-up passengers boarding it, suggested only safety. He accepted the veil that the city centre had put back on the day, on what had happened.

"Watch everything that moves!" Waterford snapped at

the driver, who was watching a leggy young woman in long boots climbing aboard the tram. "When it pulls out, watch the cars, watch the pedestrians."

"Surely you—"

"Mr. Aubrey, when were you last in the field?"

"What do you—?"

"They're into an end-play now—have to be. You might think of driving down to the Soviet Embassy, if you aren't going to expect trouble."

The tram pulled away, and the driver turned the Daimler out into the stream of traffic down the esplanade. The wide street, graceful buildings, trees down the middle of the thoroughfare—Aubrey felt himself resisting Waterford's words, as if they were subversive, or corrupting. Mere hundreds of yards, people everywhere.

"They can blame terrorists—the Provos, Red Army Faction, it won't matter, really. We'll be dead, and they'll have stopped up the leak—*there!*"

The Volvo Daf was innocuous, so was the windowless van which purported to belong to a firm of central heating engineers. Together, they drove, like a closing neck, from different sides into the Daimler. The driver accelerated after a second's hesitation, but he was already too late. The Volvo Daf bounced off the crumpled nearside fender, but the van drove the nose of the limousine round, back into the Volvo. The engine raced, then died. The driver fired it, it clattered, almost caught—

"Out! Out!" Waterford yelled.

"It's what they want!"

"No, shock-delay—move, move!"

They hadn't moved from the van and the car yet. Waterford had minimised the delay by conscious effort, and was out of the Daimler, the Parabellum levelling up at the windscreen of the Volvo Daf—it starred, and the face behind it fell away—ducking or dead, he did not care.

"Get Davenhill out of the back—cross the street!"

He swung to the van as he shouted—the noises of people, acceleration of cars away from the sudden chaos, rising distant whine of a siren—but all distant as he squeezed again. Distant even to the impact of the first bullet, as if his thick clothing was sufficient to stay the passage of the 9 mm slug. All he did was to lean back against the Daimler, as if tired. But he steadied his stiff-arm grip again, and shot both men as they climbed out of the van to finish him.

Screams—eradicate all unnecessaries—siren—*eradicate* —look round, see where they are—driver and Aubrey scuttling across the road, Davenhill between them, body limp—the rest of the scene indistinct, slowed-down like a film—

A man moving faster, crossing the road—focus, check, aim, fire—the man was only yards from Aubrey when he seemed to trip and fall on his face. No one else moving, not towards them—yes, one more, just as they passed out from beneath the lacy, whitened trees—man in overalls, back of the van, probably—difficulty, focus, *focus*—aim, steady, re-align, fire. The man toppled, as if from a wire or ledge, and slid against one of the trees.

Eradicate unnecessaries—impact? Something wet, running down his leg—pissed myself? he laughed. He saw his stomach, and heard a scream that was not his own, but which was on his behalf, and thought he heard pity in it, which for once he did not reject.

How far now?

He had to hold the door of the Daimler—heard the siren, close now, and saw the Volvo Daf pull away quickly. Another car, further away, moving too in a scene that seemed to have frozen.

How far?

He could see the slab of grey that was the corner of the Consulate—thought he saw three figures—focus, *focus*, he screamed at intolerable ineptitude—a lump, three figures, reaching the door, door opening—?

He wanted to say that he wasn't deaf, that everyone should stop screaming, as he let his head drop. The siren, unrecognised, whined down the scale as the police car pulled up only yards away. He saw something in white—might have been overalls—move near the door of the van, and he shot into the puddle of white which might have been snow but he was too old a hand to be tricked like that—puddle that might have been a white-out—

Waterford slumped over the open door of the Daimler, the gun still hanging from his fierce grip, as the police approached his body.

The main doors of the Consulate closed behind Aubrey, Davenhill and the driver before the policeman could remove the Parabellum from Waterford's dead hand.

"Get these developed, would you," Aubrey remarked in a tired voice, indicating the rolls of film and the cameras on the desk of the duty-room. Henderson, the SIS Senior at the Consulate, hesitated as Aubrey returned his attention to the cup around which he cradled his mottled hands.

After a silence, Aubrey looked up into his face with vague blue eyes. "Well?"

"The Consul would like to see you at once, Mr. Aubrey. He has two senior police officers downstairs, and they're getting a little impatient."

The blue eyes sharpened their focus, and the face seemed to collect itself, tidying the sagging folds of skin, etching the lines at forehead and mouth.

"Henderson, I'm sorry that parking regulations on the esplanade have been infringed, and that a certain amount of *litter* has been chucked about—but I am in no mood, nor have I the time, to talk to the Consul or the police. Now, run along and get those films developed, there's a good fellow."

Terrorists, he thought, and nodded his head decisively. And, as if decision brought other thoughts, he grimaced at the tea, got up, and poured himself a large whisky from the bottle on the trolley. Gratefully, he gulped it down, coughed, and then developed his idea. Waterford was a government agent, naturally. But engaged in nothing on Finnish soil. He was obviously a marked man—

That would do, until HMG had spoken in confidence with the Finnish Cabinet, and until he spoke to Buckholz, and he to Washington. The films hardly needed developing—someone had been sufficiently desperate to try to eliminate agents in the middle of Helsinki. Aubrey sighed.

Waterford was dead—he would have to debrief Davenhill, now resting in the tiny consular pharmacy in the basement of the building. An event he wished to postpone, for reasons obscure even to himself. Very well—

He dialled the US Consulate, identified himself by *Dickens Code*, who else but Pecksniff, he thought once more, and Buckholz was on the line in a moment, identified by *Cooper Code* as Natty Bumpo. Buckholz had inherited the code for Deputy Director of the CIA along with the job; Aubrey had retained Pecksniff from the early sixties.

"Secure?"

"Secure, Kenneth. What gives? I'm getting reports of—"

"A vulgar brawl, yes. Us, I'm afraid. One of my people is dead, the other under sedation and wounded. But—the attack is sufficient evidence, I think—?"

"Moscow Centre?"

"A local chapter, but affiliated, I believe."

"Jesus—"

"Helicopter activity, marksmen, and my two car-teams taken out. Two of your men, I'm afraid."

"Hell—OK, Kenneth. Not your fault. It's proof. Look, let me get onto Langley direct with this. I'll get back to you."

Aubrey stared at the telephone for a long time before replacing it. When he did, he thought of Waterford. Then, struck by something else, he thought of Khamovkhin, at that moment touring a pulp-milling complex before doing the rounds of the harbours that afternoon. And he thought of the Ozeroff-substitute.

"Kenneth?"

"Secure. Go ahead, Charles." Aubrey was desperately tired. Davenhill had rambled, and the films had been developed. A little disappointing, but they clarified Davenhill's broken account. As hard evidence, just sufficient to convince of *past* events. The events of that day would have to suffice to arouse suspicion of present, and *future*.

"There's been code-traffic all morning—I've been in conference with Langley and the Pentagon, and the President patched in when we went to satellite comm—"

Aubrey felt too tired for a recital of American technological achievement; unreasonably irritated.

"The outcome, Charles?"

Buckholz continued unabashed. "There's a SAMOS reprogramming under way, and a launch slot later today. The sat can have a look-see. We don't usually have the coverage up here, and the President and the Pentagon won't make any premature moves just on my say-so."

"What will the President *do*, Charles?"

"I told him to stay home." Buckholz chuckled. "He's fixing a dialogue over the red telephone for this evening, our time, with Finland's most prestigious guest of the moment. The First Secretary will be informed of the call at lunch. He'll have to take it in the Embassy here."

"I see."

"What of your people, Kenneth?"

208

"I am sure they would rather not believe it—any of it. But I do think they're worried." Frustration burst out almost as petulance, suddenly. "Charles, are we the only two sane people in the world, or the only two madmen?"

"Hang in there, Kenneth. There's a lot of behind-the-scenes activity in Washington—meetings, dialogues, contingencies, war-games. It isn't being allowed to fall down the back of the wardrobe. There'll be an alert issue by now. Brussels is in constant contact, and I guess we're stepped up to Readiness Two by now."

It sounded a little more reassuring. Buckholz had not been wasting his time, and he could divine the mood in Washington perhaps more clearly than any other CIA officer Aubrey had ever met. Aubrey decided to be conciliatory.

"Very good, Charles. Then we must await developments. One other thing—that trace your people are doing for me—"

"You're worried about that—now?"

"I think it may be more important than ever."

"OK—I won't cancel."

"I'd be very grateful if you didn't. My people in Moscow have come up with nothing so far. I'm onto Africa, Satellites, and Far East now, and its getting urgent."

"Why?"

"You told Wainwright about the twenty-fourth?"

"He laughed—a little. But, he doesn't ignore things. I'll come see you before this evening."

"Very well. I must allocate some people here to the mysterious Captain Ozeroff—or whoever he is."

TEN

PROOF OF INTENT

It was the acceleration of events that tired him so much. Having waited for ten years, it was as if he had adjusted to a somnolent, covert pace, and could not shake off what was now lethargy. In the Diplomatic Lounge at Cheremetievo, waiting to meet a courier, he was confronted by the almost archaic method of communication he had carefully and secretly constructed. And knew that he would have to issue the order in the next twelve hours to switch to radio traffic.

Kutuzov hated feeling a tired old man—but he could not escape, or disguise, the impression his old body forced upon him, the leaden grooves in which his physique seemed to make his thoughts function. Folley, the English soldier—the desperate ambush in Helsinki, after the border incursion—the accident on the road outside Oxford, where Ozeroff's body had fallen into the hands of the SIS —Ossipov's presumptuous destruction of the Khabarovsk KGB Office—

He rubbed his hands down his leathery cheeks. A system of deep-cover couriers transmitting verbal orders and instructions disabled him—broken nerves, failing to transmit in time to the brain, so the hand gets burned, injured, the legs bang into things. The body of *Group 1917* thrashing blindly about like an automaton.

The operation was beginning to develop a frightening

momentum. He had to go to Leningrad, to see Praporovich, even Folley, to establish, if he could, what level of suspicion of half-knowledge had prompted three separate attempts to investigate *Finland Station Six*.

Yet he could not blame them—they had acted on assumptions, and they had acted out of the kind of precipitate confidence he had felt himself a couple of days before —so *close*, he could taste it, feel it against him like another body, the sense of victory. The army induced overconfidence, and the kind of action that had been taken on his authority, without his orders.

When it all came down, in the final analysis, to the word of one old man over the telephone.

He felt chill, and ancient, and imprisoned in the weak, stick-like, hateful body. *Really, was it like that?*

Yes, he admitted, then wondered if anyone in the lounge, especially the security men, had seen him nod absently in concert with the admission—trick of a decrepit, of the senile—

He had to give the order, on the 24th. Valenkov, at Moscow Garrison, insisted on that. Part of the total operation, he had said, part of the whole. Praporovich would give the orders to the Attack Groups at Kirkenes and along the Finland border. Dolohov would give the Fleet its orders. Below them, perhaps a dozen generals to transmit those orders further down, to regimental commanders, to sections of regiments, to companies and platoons—to each tank and rifle and gas-wagon.

His thoughts stung him like an attack of insects; but all the time, with the clarity that pain sometimes had brought him in the past, this emotional infliction cut away at the confusion—and the few small lights upon which his enterprise was founded gleamed brightly and in isolation. But they were small lights, little bulbs strung together— and each one of them dependent upon the others, and he, the fuse that prevented them going out.

Praporovich, Dolohov, Valenkov in Moscow—himself. Millions of men, *millions*—and nothing would happen unless he and those others gave their orders on the 24th. 06:00 to be precise.

He looked at the security men as he fidgeted in his seat and pretended to read a book—there were more of them on duty at Cheremetievo. No, there were *enough* of them on duty, if they knew their targets, to prevent *Rabbit Punch*, and to prevent the overthrow of the regime. Ridiculous, but true.

He glanced at his watch, put down the book, and walked out of the lounge, waving his personal security guard to relax. He went down the steps to meet the courier.

Simple, *simple,* he told himself. They do not know, and there are only fifty-six hours of former days left. Fifty-six hours. And no one knew, no one. Valenkov and the Moscow Garrison would be incommunicado in eight hours' time, until the dawn of the 24th. Praporovich and Dolohov need take no risks, could make themselves unreachable.

And, in forty-eight hours, he would disappear himself.

Simple, simple, *simple*—the litany relaxed him.

He found the courier in the main departure lounge, still in his uniform, and they sat a little apart on a plastic-covered bench set below a panoramic window which looked out over the light-splashed tarmac, the garishly illuminated plumage of the aircraft caught by the lights. The courier read *Pravda,* and he smoked a cigarette as nonchalantly as he could, and drank bad coffee.

When the courier had finished his brief narrative, *Kutuzov* said: "Ossipov cannot be forgiven for attracting attention to Far East District, even though he cannot see where he was at fault. However, on second thoughts, he must continue with the "Exercise Mirror" operations as far as the gas-attacks are concerned—yes . . ." His voice tailed off. The gas was the most necessary. The chemical attack had to be right, and it had to be done without the assistance, in planning and practice, of scientific advice and knowledge. They were soldiers, not research scientists, and the gases they had in sufficient supply in GSFN were unreliable, even unpredictable. And it *had* to be right! Ossipov was too important to be disliked, and his task too important to be postponed, or cancelled. Anger had betrayed him into issuing an order that Ossipov was right to ignore—even though the courier might not understand.

"Very well," he went on. "You have one more trip to make, back to Khabarovsk. You will instruct Ossipov to radio his final report direct to Praporovich—and you will tell him that the SID Major, Vorontsyev, is *not* to be eliminated. He is to be taken and held in custody until— You understand?"

"Sir."

"Very well." He looked at his watch. "They will be calling my flight in a moment." He stood up, and walked immediately away, his cigarette-stub burning in the ashtray where he had left it.

"Goodbye, sir," the young man said to his back, and went on reading his paper.

All the way back to the Diplomatic Lounge, *Kutuzov* wondered what the Englishman, Aubrey, was doing— and kept repeating the litany of time running out. Fifty-six hours, fifty-six hours, *fifty-six hours*. It seemed to settle his stomach, tidy and soothe his thoughts.

Khamovkhin sat at the Ambassador's desk in a spacious third-floor room of the Embassy on Tehtaankatu. With him was the Soviet Ambassador to Finland, Foreign Minister Gromyko, and the head of the duty security team, Captain Ozeroff. Ozeroff stood away from the desk, and its red telephone drawn nearer the First Secretary than the battery of black telephones, as if in deference to the call about to be received, while Gromyko and the Ambassador sat within hearing distance of the amplifier rigged to the "hot line."

Khamovkhin looked at his watch. Eleven-thirty. In Washington, four-thirty in the afternoon. President Joseph Wainwright could call him at any moment. Khamovkhin was nervous. Wainwright wanted answers, assurances that he could not give. There was no way he could bluff convincingly.

The four men in the room heard, distinctly, the connection being made by the Embassy exchange, the slight crackle of the static, then Wainwright's voice as he was instructed to begin his call. The slight delay in the signal, transmitted by satellite, then the illusion that the President of the United States was in the next room, or the next town.

"Mr. First Secretary—good evening."

Khamovkhin gagged on his reply for a moment.

"Mr. President—good afternoon."

And silence, for a long time. Khamovkhin felt, already,

213

a bead of perspiration, standing out on his heavy brow, and his palms damp as he closed his hands into fists in his lap.

A child waiting for the rebuke of an adult.

"Mr. First Secretary—" There was a freezing hauteur about the voice now, a *righteousness,* even. Wainwright spoke from strength. But what followed, surprised Khamovkhin in its cunning, its obliqueness. "I have a suggestion to make to you which I am sure would be in the interests of both of us, and of the world." Khamovkhin shuddered at the grandiloquence which he found rolled so easily from the tongues of American Presidents. He could see Wainwright, dapper, handsome, middle-aged, leaning slightly forward across his desk in the Oval Office, as if to make distinct, unmistakable, each of his words.

"Yes, Mr. President?"

"I propose, as a preliminary to the signing of our Treaty in three days, and as a gesture of faith the world cannot mistake—" A pause for emphasis, for clarity of meaning, for weight of impression, Khamovkhin thought, angry with himself for being concerned to weigh such things, like a theatre critic with an actor's performance. "That we institute, immediately, large and evident troop withdrawals from frontier areas." The clarity with which his situation seemed understood in Washington chilled Khamovkhin, then instantly seemed to raise his temperature or that of the room. But Wainwright gave him no time for thought or reply. "I will order US troops in the Federal Republic to withdraw from forward positions. I will immediately institute the stand-down of strike squadrons in the United Kingdom, and order the US 6th Fleet to a condition of secondary readiness—all of which your satellites and tracking ships can verify in a matter of hours."

Silence—heavy, into which the breathing of the Ambassador and Gromyko dropped like stones, and the static from the amplifier scratched at his attention. He looked at Gromyko, whose face was impassive, without suggestion or support.

"Mr. President, this is a gesture which pleases me, but which I need time to consider." Lame, *lame*—

"What's to consider, Mr. First Secretary? I have satellite pictures here—" A pause, as if an aide had gestured

214

warningly. "I have evidence to suggest that units of the Red Banner Fleet have been recalled to Murmansk. A gesture already on your part, surely? Continue the good work. Stand down forward units in the DDR, or maybe on the Norwegian border, or the Finnish border—yes, maybe best of all. Before I join you in Helsinki."

Satellite pictures—stand down units—Red Banner Fleet—Khamovkhin was appalled, at a loss. He was learning, from the President of the United States, what the Red Army intended. The invasion of Scandinavia? Impossible. *Finland Station.* Not impossible.

"I—have to consult with the High Command of the Soviet Army, Mr. President. I have no room for such a unilateral decision."

"You're reluctant, Mr. First Secretary—at this late hour?"

It was a direct challenge. He could almost begin to frame the rest of the conversation.

"No, no, of course not. But, you expect instant action, Mr. President—"

"My orders have already gone to the Pentagon, and to Brussels, Mr. First Secretary. They need only be confirmed. Now—can you do less than that?"

He was in a trap—he could not even speak to Gromyko. The red telephone, and the amplifier, sat on his desk, a squat toad listening to his thoughts.

"I—I must consult. It will take time to arrange—it is, of course, most desirable—"

"I think that way, too." There was irony now! "Forward units in your northern theatre, to compound your gesture of withdrawing units of the Northern Fleet to port. Can we agree on that?"

"I—in principle, yes, of course—"

"By tomorrow?"

"But—I am not sure it can be done—"

"Mr. First Secretary—unless those units are withdrawn a token fifty miles from the border with Norway and Finland—and by dawn of the 24th, then I will order units of the AMF to go ahead with the cancelled NATO exercise, 'Snowfront Express.' Do I make myself clear, Mr. First Secretary? I will also, in consultation with America's allies in NATO, place our forces on a twenty-four-hour readiness alert, unless I hear from you that withdrawals

215

are beginning. This will happen at midnight, seven a.m. on the 23rd, your time." Another pause, then: "That's all, Mr. First Secretary. Good evening to you."

Static, for a long time, until his hand darted out to cut off the connection, kill the amplifier. Then, only then, did he look up at the other men in the room.

"We seem to have been given an ultimatum, gentlemen."

"A sensible suggestion—" the Ambassador began, then dropped his eyes, lost his voice, and he saw the look in Khamovkhin's eyes. Gromyko remained silent.

"It must be done—he said nothing about coming to Helsinki, you notice. Nothing!" Anger, anger of confidence, he thought. Show them. "Sensible, Mr. Ambassador—of course, sensible. But—demanded, as of right, at this late hour! What kind of thing is that to do, eh? Why must it be done now, at this minute? He talks like a schoolmaster, a dreamer!"

He looked across at Ozeroff, standing stiffly to attention by the door, as if not wishing to draw attention to himself. Inwardly, Khamovkhin quailed. Andropov was right—the 24th. The Americans knew something, something that told them the timetable of *Group 1917*. And they had tested him, and now they knew he was powerless, impotent. And had issued their challenge—put your house in order, or the next war begins in three days' time!

He turned his back on them, looked at the portrait of Lenin above the chair in which he had been sitting. Ozeroff, at attention, had been directing his line of sight there. With little more than a hundred men, Lenin had done it, wrested power from Kerensky and the ditherers. And *Group 1917* had the whole army as a means of doing it!

What was his code? To those faceless men against whom he could make no move—what was his code? *Comrade Romanov?* The idea was laughable, the title apposite.

Get them out, *get them out,* he told himself. He had to get back to Lahti, talk to Andropov in Moscow. Had to. Everything was crumbling in his big, clumsy hands—he had dreamed, hadn't he, a couple of nights ago, of huge hands picking up delicate china cups and saucers, and smashing them with sheer clumsiness. Looking down, he had seen his own body in the dream, and these great shovels of hands sticking out of the sleeves of his coat.

Woken in a sweat—almost crying out, then realising.

He had to talk to Andropov. There had to be *something*, some lead, some identification of the leader, his enemy. Had to be.

"Captain Ozeroff, order the helicopter to stand by. We are returning to Lahtilinna at once!"

"Sir."

Galakhov was smiling as he closed the door of the Ambassador's office behind him. In the morning, he would contact a courier and relay a message to *Kutuzov*. The Americans were suspicious, forewarned. But Khamovkhin knew nothing, feared everything. He would even, as duty officer, hear what was said between Andropov and the First Secretary. The American suspicions would change nothing. Wainwright was bluffing—all the High Command knew he would not go to war for Norway and Finland—it was an axiom of strategy.

He enjoyed Khamovkhin's fear as he went down the stairs to the duty-room to prepare the car and the helicopter.

"So that's it, Kenneth—Khamovkhin isn't behind anything. Right this minute, he's got about as much clout as my Aunt Fanny!"

Buckholz appeared suitably grim, but Aubrey saw the gleam in his eyes, the set of his jaw, and admired, and was amused by, the easy way in which the man had been impressed by the manner of his President's conversation with Khamovkhin.

"I accept your reasoning, and see you are pleased with the President's enactment of your scenario—" Buckholz turned on Aubrey, grimaced, then smiled swiftly, raising his hands in an admission. "However, I am not certain—"

"Not certain of what?"

"How effective it will be. It places us in a position of impotence not unlike that of Khamovkhin himself. We can do nothing more, except sit and wait."

"Tomorrow, we go see Khamovkhin, for openers—"

"Charles, what good will that do? The man knows nothing! Otherwise, this *Group 1917* would have disappeared from sight long ago, into Gulag or the ground or the mental home. Khamovkhin doesn't know who they are, dammit! It hasn't worked out. We can't expect him to move against the High Command, even though we helped put him on the knife-edge."

"Don't come cold water with me, Kenneth. Right now, Khamovkhin is on board his chopper, heading hell-for-leather for his castle on the hill to talk to the Chairman of the KGB!"

Buckholz walked round his desk to confront Aubrey. The round face of an ancient, cunning child looked up into his. Buckholz shook his head, walked over to the dumb-waiter.

"It isn't that I don't want to be optimistic," Aubrey said in a more conciliatory tone. "It's simply a matter of looking at facts head-on, without the squint imparted by the status of representing a super-power. I can do that, having been born into the aftermath of the British Empire, on which the sun has firmly set—" Aubrey smiled as Buckholz handed him the tumbler of whisky. "Your health. No, it is simply that we now have to rely on the efforts of the KGB *for our survival*—as simple as that."

"It won't come to war—they'll back down."

"Khamovkhin would turn somersaults, I agree. But— the Red Army. Will they feel threatened, or simply challenged to a fight—and respond by picking up the gage?"

"It won't come to it, Kenneth."

"In the time that may be left to us, I shall do my best to solve the mystery surrounding Captain Ozeroff—after all, he may know something useful. My surveillance of him begins with the dawn. *And* I have a way of placing him in our hands—do you wish to hear it?"

Buckholz nodded.

"Very well, but bring the bottle first. And I shall tell you what we shall request of Khamovkhin tomorrow." Then, struck by a sobering realisation, he added, "I wonder who the KGB have investigating this matter. I hope it's someone first-class—I really do!"

Vorontsyev stirred in the big bed, reached out, and found Natalia near him. She was still, apparently, asleep, and he touched her only lightly on the arm, not wishing to wake her.

As he came awake himself, there was the groundswell

of urgency, and fear, in the pit of his stomach, making the bed colder, his wife distanced. He had been in Khabarovsk for thirty-six hours, and nothing. Except that they followed him everywhere, and probably laughed as he got nowhere, learned nothing.

Yet he could not move. It was just a case of getting out of bed, stepping on cold tiles in the bathroom—but, literally and metaphorically, he did not want to leave this bed.

He looked at his wife again. They had dined together early the previous evening, and drunk perhaps more than was good for them. Later, they had made love for the first time in months; it had been a natural conclusion to the evening—and perhaps he had wanted to bury his waking, wakeful mind in the temporary dream of sex. It had been as if they were on holiday together, and their behaviour imitated domestic life but with the added piquancy of a new place, a strange bed.

Thus, his reluctance to consider himself a policeman, on an investigation.

A beginning?

He refused to think about that, by an effort of will. Nevertheless, now he had recaptured the mood, there was a deep contentment in him for those few minutes after waking. He had enjoyed eating with her again, and enjoyed the clever, familiar humour they both brought, at one time, to conversation. And their first love-making, hurried and urgent though it was. He had been close to her then, for a few moments—lost in her.

When he had woken her later in the night, then perhaps that had been—more erotic, yes, but not as he would have wished. There was a small wince of shame, of impurity, that ran through his frame; it sprang, he knew, from the kind of puritanism he had inherited from his father, and had imbibed in Gorochenko's house.

In the ecstasy, he had asked her to reassure him, and she had done, telling him over and over that he was better than her other lovers, there was no one like him.

Alexei, Alexei—yes, yes . . .

He felt the stirrings of an erection even at the memory, and the little shame—deeper than the embarrassment at recollected intimacy.

He had wanted her to master him, riding above him, her breasts like fruit just out of reach of his mouth—yes, he had wanted that, and it had seemed real for her as well.

It was himself he disliked a little.

But she had come back to him. And now, while she was still asleep and there could be no contradiction of perfection by anything she did or said, or *they* did or said, he was content again. He felt his eyes pucker at the sense of her nearness, and the weight of memory pressing on tear-ducts.

He got softly out of bed, and went over to the window. He lifted aside the heavy drape; it was a clear day, windy, high-clouded. It would serve for his purpose.

He looked back at his sleeping wife, the bare arm over the coverlet, the black hair massed on the pillow, hiding the small face. Because the moment offered a complete contentment, he had abandoned it. It would be preserved in memory, ready to be returned to. If he had let it go on any longer, it might have passed ripeness. He was afraid, he admitted—as afraid of happiness as he had been of isolation, disappointment.

So, he returned to his job. He looked out of the window again.

The police had rounded up a few suspected Separatists, and he had tried to show a polite interest, but he had known those frightened little people could never have planned to take out the whole KGB Office in Khabarovsk. They amounted to little more than slogan-daubers, boo-ers at public meetings from the safety of crowds.

Which left the Ivanov Charter Company, which rented hangarspace at Khabarovsk Airport, nine kilometres outside the town. Ivanov, or whoever was in charge of the operation, owned two old Antonov high-wing monoplanes, and a helicopter. A small MIL. Which was paid for by, and reserved for, the KGB in Khabarovsk. An economy measure—the lawman's twentieth-century horse in the Soviet Far East.

Ivanov was obviously a local entrepreneur; the charter company was not state owned, like many of the small companies and businesses in this part of the Soviet Union; it was more efficient to allow enterprising capitalists to set up, and fund and operate, such ventures. Ivanov delivered mail to outlying villages, flew missions for the doctors and hospitals, delivered groceries to state-owned outlets throughout the region. And he assisted the KGB in the matter of a helicopter.

Vorontsyev had stumbled across the information by chance. A policeman had referred to the fact that "Old Ivanov was lucky he didn't get blown up too, and his precious helicopter." When Vorontsyev had elicited the source of the reference, he had trembled with excitement. A non-military aircraft; the only successful means of sniffing around the Military District HQ—from the air.

"Have you got any cigarettes, Alexei?" he heard Natalia ask. She was sitting up in bed, her breasts free of the sheets, her arms stretched and she pushed the thick dark hair away from her forehead. Her breasts were taut, inviting. He was almost certain it was an unconscious gesture. Something like the feelings of the previous evening, an ameliorated sense of the erotic mingled with something like longing, came over him. She smiled. He was able to imagine invitation, and a curious innocence and warmth, in the movement of her lips.

He took the packet of American cigarettes from the dressing-table, and threw them to her. Then the lighter. She seemed to weigh it in her hand, and then said:

"We do have the *good* life, eh, Alexei?" She was still smiling. "You and I."

He nodded. "We ought to be able to live reasonably convenient and happy lives." His tone was neutral, carefully so; yet he was inviting her to commit herself. She puffed at the cigarette, leaned back against the headboard, one arm behind her head, and studied him. He was acutely conscious that he was naked, and that the act of her merely looking stirred him.

"We ought—yes," she admitted. Then she stubbed out the cigarette, and murmured, "Come back to bed."

He almost looked at his watch on the dressing-table, to check the time. He smiled at himself, yet there was a tiny sense of disappointment in him, as if her invitation was a substitute; as if he had been reading a great book, and then been told it was superficial, unreal; or involved in a complex puzzle only to be told that the answer was easy, and not worth the finding.

Which was why he stood at the edge of the bed for a moment, just looking at her. She held out her arms to him, her breasts still free of the sheets, and he saw something crude, soiled about the open eroticism of it. He wanted her to be otherwise, even as he wanted her. She smiled as she saw his erection, which for an instant be-

221

came a visible, hated helplessness as far as she was concerned.

Then he ignored the fuzzy complexities of his responses, and got into bed.

It was quick, hungry, abrupt. He did not care whether she came or not; he thought she probably hadn't. He was satisfying himself only. Something to make up for the last months—or to try to indicate his independence.

If Natalia was disappointed, she did not show it. While he telephoned the Innokenti Ivanov Charter Company of Khabarovsk, she sat beside him, smoking another cigarette.

"You want breakfast?" he asked as he waited for the call to be connected to Khabarovsk Airport, where Ivanov had an office and rented hangar-space. Her eyes were closed, and her face tilted to the ceiling, head resting against the headboard.

She nodded. "Will they serve it here?"

"I should think so—hello, Ivanov Charter?"

The voice at the other end was female, middle-aged, gruff and masculine. "Yes—what do you want?"

"I want to check over the helicopter you fly for the local KGB. And I want to talk to the pilot—have him standing by."

"Who is this, comrade?" the voice asked, suspicious but undeterred by the evidence of authority in his voice.

"*Major* Alexei Vorontsyev, Moscow SID. Is that sufficient for you?"

"May be. Bring your ID card, or you don't go anywhere near the helicopter." The woman had to be Madame Ivanov.

"Naturally," he said, not unamused.

"What time are you coming?"

"Shall we say—ten o'clock?"

"Say it if you like. We'll expect you, *Major*."

The receiver clicked at the other end. Vorontsyev stared at the purring instrument in his hand, then burst out laughing. He was still laughing when he called the hotel switchboard and ordered breakfast for two.

The MIL helicopter was an old one, a cramped cabin with canvas seats up front and a dark hole behind for storage space when the helicopter was used by Ivanov himself rather than the Khabarovsk KGB. Which, Vorontsyev was certain, was often. And, he did not doubt, the KGB footed the parts and fuel bills for most of the private trips.

The pilot was young—Ivanov's nephew, who had learned to fly during his army conscription. Since which time he had worked for his uncle, disliked him intensely, shared his passion for business and money, and was obviously waiting for the premature death of his energetic relative so that he could inherit control of the business.

Vorontsyev had been terrified by Madame Ivanov in the cramped, dusty office. She was everything the telephone conversation had promised—large, badly dressed and made-up, coarse, and clever. Her husband was off flying one of the planes down to Vladivostok to collect some freight, she told him grudingly—one of the two regular pilots was ill. She considered, as she told Vorontsyev, that he had a dose, and serve him right.

After a desultory inspection of the chopper, and a conversation with the nephew concerning recent KGB flights in it, Vorontsyev said, "Right, you can take me on a little trip."

"I didn't know you wanted to go up."

"No?" Vorontsyev smiled. Neither did whoever was listening to his telephone calls at the hotel. Nor the car that had tailed him to the airport, and was parked near the terminal at that moment. "No—but it seems like a good idea. Since my company owns it, and there's no one else to use it."

The nephew shrugged. "OK. I'll go and get us cleared. You wait here."

It was half an hour before the MIL lifted away from the airport, and Khabarovsk was spread beneath them and away to the south. The two rivers on whose confluence the town stood gleamed like polished silver in the pale sunlight, and the town, as they ascended, became more and more a diagram of a place where people might live, set out as it was like many towns in Siberia and the Soviet Far East in a rigid, functional grid pattern.

Like American cities, Vorontsyev thought, though he had never seen one except in photographs brought back by KGB men who had spent time in the Washington Residency, or had travelled briefly to America. However, it was as if a child, with his building blocks, had ignored the fact that he required a flat piece of ground if he were

223

to assemble a completely orderly structure. Khabarovsk began to straggle over the three long hills that it had been built upon, losing its firm, clean outlines—looking, he thought, as if it was lived-in after all.

Patches of green, the haze of heavy industry away towards the River Amur—shipbuilding there, oil refining; neat white blocks of offices, colleges; the rural fringes of the town of nearly half a million creeping back, it seemed, rather than being encroached upon.

"Well?" the pilot asked. "Where do you want to go, my Major?"

Vorontsyev turned in his seat, looking ahead. They appeared to be drifting slowly north, towards hills blue and shapeless still with mist, dark with forest where the fog had lifted.

"I want to have a look at army HQ—but only *casually* . . ." He had to trust the man; time was limited, whatever happened, after Ossipov's move against the KGB. He went on: "You know their exercise areas?" The pilot nodded. "Let's overfly some of them, and come back via HQ, eh?"

Vorontsyev settled back in his seat as the chopper seemed to spurt forward towards the distant hills. Already, his attention was impeded by memories of the past twelve hours seeping back. His wife—the tremulous sense of happiness of which he was afraid, and the more stark eroticism that now seemed re-established between them. This flight seemed removed from any useful investigation. He began to wonder whether Military District Far East could in any way reveal its secrets to a whirring speck in the sky.

Just before he left the hotel, there had been a telephone call from Police HQ. Over the wireprint from Moscow had come an unconfirmed report that Ilya and Maxim were missing. Their helicopter had radioed a distress message just before all contact with it was lost. Search parties had failed to locate any wreckage.

He had not known what to make of the report. It had been authorised by Kapustin, but he was uncertain whether it was a warning. He could not believe that the two men were dead, and therefore attempted to ignore the possibility. The report remained as a speck, irritating the mind's eye.

The foothills were below them now, mounting to the

still fogbound clefts and peaks of the mountains. The pilot's voice crackled in his headset.

"Do you want to be seen, or not?"

"What?"

"There'll be a lot of chopper activity soon, when we hit the exercise areas. Do you want to explain what we're doing, or not?"

"Preferably not."

"Then I'll try it as low as I can."

The nose of the MIL dropped towards a forest-blackened cliff face, and the chopper sidled sideways, hugging the tree tops. Vorontsyev craned his head to look down. The dark fir trees flowed beneath the cabin.

"How often do they exercise up here?"

"All the time. Constant readiness. I was stationed along the Manchurian border when I was in. The yellow peril, my Major!" He laughed. "More peril from some of the women in the brothels up there!"

Vorontsyev returned the laughter, settling in his seat, his eyes casting to right and left, and ahead. Small clearings, empty, passed beneath them, then a towering cliff face, bare and grey, threatening the tiny helicopter. Mist rolled beneath them in a deep valley like something alive, or as if flames roared beneath it.

Then the MIL slid across a knife-edged ridge of mountain, and the last tendrils of mist were vanishing. Vorontsyev saw a deep valley, and the Ussuri, a tributary of the Amur, narrow at the bottom of the steep cleft. Snow lying thinly on its banks, ice moving like great grey plates on the river surface. The MIL drove down the mountain side, below the treeline. Then Vorontsyev saw them: an engineer unit had thrown a bridge across the Ussuri, and ZSU self-propelled guns were crossing—a dark-green caterpillar. They swept over them. Further downstream, an amphibious BTR-50 was grinding through plated ice, hurling it aside as it progressed like a green wedge.

"What are they doing?" Vorontsyev asked, pointing down and behind.

"Testing equipment. Some kind of tactical deployment exercise, I suppose. Can you get across a river in winter, or something like."

The MIL followed the line of the Ussuri as it snaked through its lean, deep valley; then the pilot, a straighter, and empty, stretch of the river ahead of him, lifted up and away, past the treeline, the bare face of rock, sliding across another fold of mountain which fell away more gradually on its western side. Deeper shadow here, even at eleven in the morning. Forest, then more open country, stretching to the shore of a spot of blue lake.

In the distance, a winding road, crammed with green vehicles. Vorontsyev used the glasses the pilot handed him. Almost solid—tanks moving in single file. At the head of the snaking column the lighter T-34 tanks and, as if riding herd to the main column, heavy APCs and T-34s in the fields, driving swathes through the long grass, melted snow glistening as it sprayed up from the tracks. Behind the light screen, the heavy JSs and T-62s and -64s. An armoured column, moving swiftly now that he saw them magnified, racing towards the spot of blue water and the sloping forest beyond.

"Do you want to get closer?" the pilot asked. They had dropped below the level of the trees, at the edge of the open land, and were hovering.

"No," Vorontsyev said. "What are they doing?"

"Time trials. How long to move from A to B, or how much can you move in a given time."

"What purpose?" Vorontsyev asked, his eyes still pressed to the glasses.

"You've heard of 'Blitzkrieg,' haven't you? What the filthy Fascists were doing in the war? Well, you can't say the Red Army doesn't learn! One of our intensive practises." He nodded towards the column of dark green vehicles, now simply gun-barrels and turrets above the level of the grass. The grass moved like an angered sea as light tanks ripped through it, moving away from them now.

"Are they doing this all the time?"

"Of course, my Major!" The pilot laughed, the sound hard and deafening in Vorontsyev's headphones. "For when the yellow peril comes boiling across the Ussuri. Practise, practise. It never stops. I sometimes think we keep on doing it just to fool the American satellites—when we finally *do* go, they'll think it's just another exercise."

"All right. Find something else." Vorontsyev said, taking his gaze at last from the fascination of the armour. The MIL seemed to hop over the trees, sneaking away from what it had witnessed like a child crept downstairs to watch adults at their pleasures.

"Why do they practise here, in this sort of country?"

226

Vorontsyev asked as they skimmed the tree tops, leaning up the slope as they did, climbing back towards the ridge.

"What?"

"This isn't like the country in northern Germany—good tank country. Is it? Why the emphasis on armour here? Isn't it going to be infantry and artillery all the way round here? This country looks much more like—" He sensed himself on the verge of a discovery—its momentousness welled up in him so that the thought itself seemed about to be lost in the accompanying mood. Slowly, slowly, he told himself, looking at the terrain. Like, like —The dark trees, the bare rock, over the ridge, slipping along beneath it, the noise of the rotors echoing back to them, amplified. Then he was distracted, almost as he seized upon the realisation.

"What's that?" Vorontsyev snapped, pointing ahead of them. A haze, yellowish it seemed, undispersed. He could not help believing that it was artificial.

"Mist."

"Go *over* it if you go near it."

The nose of the MIL lifted, and Vorontsyev had to crane to see the yellow-painted TMS-65, looking like a petrol tanker with a trailer—the suited men around it like insects, masked heads looking up, spray nozzles in their hands. They were moving beneath a belt of trees.

"For God's sake—pull away from that!" Vorontsyev almost screamed.

The MIL whisked up and sideways, rolling with the violence of the change in the angle of the rotor disc.

"Fucking gas!" the pilot snarled. "What the bloody hell are they doing with it—trying to kill the bloody trees?"

As if to answer him, they flew over a ragged, trailing hole in the forest. Black, naked branches stared at them, a sudden desert. As the MIL followed the defoliated line, it adopted the appearance of a road. Open to the sky, a ragged swathe.

"That's not new," Vorontsyev said. He looked over his shoulder, then smiled grimly at his stupidity. "For— of course! That TMS down there is for decontamination work, isn't it?"

The pilot banked the chopper, and up ahead of them again was the rising, yellowish cloud.

"It is."

"Then—that damage to the trees, what was that?"

"Shelling."

"What with?"

"Gas."

The cloud was rising, gleaming with droplets in the sunlight, steaming out of the tree tops like an exhalation of the ground.

"What is that, then?"

"An alkali fog—I don't know. They didn't give us more than the usual introductory lectures on chemical warfare —how to put your suit and mask on, and what filthy stockpiles the United States had built up! You know the bullshit."

"*Guess* what they're doing—and pull away again!"

The MIL banked sharply. Masked heads followed them —men observing, measuring the effects of the fog that was being sprayed in a widening area beneath the trees. They headed towards the ragged hole in the forest once more, following the narrow road that was its winding central line.

"Guess?" the pilot said after a while. "Maybe—time trials? Could be. Shell the shit out of a definite area, using VX or one of those bastards, then move the men in the special suits in to see how quickly they can clear it."

The MIL lifted away from the defoliated, obscene swath towards the bare, clean lines of a cliff face. Sharp, hard —natural.

"Why?"

"You ask a hell of a lot of questions! Why? Because the army thinks it'll start a war with chemical attacks, and it's practise, practise!"

Vorontsyev, as the MIL lifted clear, into the sun, and the land was spread out suddenly, like something flung from a hand, beneath him—dotted lakes, mountains, deep, narrow valleys, the river—knew he had the answer.

And was stunned, almost paralysed, by its enormity. Yes, yes—He clamped on the thought, the realisation, that had been interrupted, then confirmed, by the yellow cloud. It *was*—it *had to be*—

There *was* a connection between Ossipov and Vrubel, between the Far East and the border with Finland. This mountainous, heavily wooded country below him was the connection. A mirror-image, almost.

Ossipov and his armies were *practising* the invasion of Scandinavia—so the real thing would go smoothly.

A chemical attack to precede an armoured spearhead.

Ilya and Maxim were dead. They must have found out something, and they had been eliminated.

He felt sick.

"Don't look now, my Major—we've got company!" he heard the pilot say at a great distance.

As if from ambush, four helicopters in army camouflage, the red stars bright on their bellies—MIL-24s, gunships, he registered—leapt from the cover of a ridge below and to starboard. They were flying in a rigid formation.

A box to contain their one small helicopter.

PART THREE

THE
RUNNING MAN

22nd to the 23rd of . . . . , 19 . .

"We are passing from the sphere of
history to the sphere of the present and
partly to the sphere of the future."
—LENIN

ELEVEN

THE LIMITS OF DIPLOMACY

There was no call-sign, simply:

"This is restricted airspace over a military exercise area. Your flight is unauthorised, and you are guilty of aerial trespass. You will accompany us to Military District HQ. Acknowledge this message."

After he had automatically done so, the pilot turned to Vorontsyev. Outside, the four gunships jockeyed into their positions; one to port, one to starboard—one flying a little higher, the other a little below them. He could see the helmeted military pilot, and the crewman who controlled the chopper's arsenal, as he looked down through the Perspex of the starboard MIL's cabin.

He craned round, and the pilot said, "They're behind us—one up, one down. We aren't going to be able to slip away from the party." He was unworried. Carrying a major in the SID was surety that nothing bad could happen to him. He would only have been obeying orders from the Committee for State Security.

"We have to," Vorontsyev said quietly, his face grim with strain.

"You're joking!"

"No—I'm not." He looked at the pilot, and was about to continue when one of the gunships slid overhead and took up a position a hundred metres in front of them, at exactly the same flight level. Then the voice crackled again.

"There is no course reference. Simply follow the helicopter in front of you. Acknowledge."

"Message acknowledged. I am following."

The leading chopper immediately banked to port, easing down a grey rock face. The nose of the small MIL dipped and then it imitated the larger machine ahead of it.

"Think!" Vorontsyev snapped. "How far are we from the headquarters?"

"Now?" He glanced at the chart on his knee. "Ten minutes flying time—from here." He looked glum, unresponsive, his assurance evaporated.

"How can you set me down?"

"What?"

"Set me down! Listen—if I'm caught . . ." He had to tell the pilot the truth, but frighten him with it. He went on: "And you're with me, then we'll both of us be quietly removed!" He thought of Ilya and Maxim. Missing. Now he knew they were dead. "We'll have an arranged accident."

There was open fear in the pilot's eyes. It was a situation he could not comprehend, hearing that information from an officer in the most élite section of the KBG. It made no sense whatever.

He said, "You—got to be joking, my Major. They don't kill KGB men, just like that!" And something made his eyes widen more. Vorontsyev knew he was remembering the Separatist terrorism. Then the eyes narrowed in suspicion. "You *are* joking?"

"No, my friend. The army will kill me if it can get its hands on me—after they've checked to find out it's me, and what I might have seen. You—you they might leave alone. I don't know . . ." He shrugged. "But if you're with me, then your life isn't worth a one rouble note!"

They were flying along a valley wall, heavily wooded, dark with firs.

"I can't put you down in this!" the pilot said, as if accusing him.

"Find somewhere where you can!"

They were flying at little more than sixty feet above the trees. The valley widened. Patches of meadow, snow clinging here, dotted houses, and clumps of forest.

"Better," the pilot muttered. He turned to Vorontsyev. "Look, if I drop like a stone, then I can put you down

234

before *they* can get down. But that's no good to you—or to me. It has to be a small clearing—the very smallest, so that they can't get down except by a rope ladder, unless they want to crash on top of us. Then you'll have time to start running." He seemed to beseech Vorontsyev's approval. Vorontsyev nodded. "And, listen, my Major the prize shit—you forced me to do it, at gunpoint!"

"Agreed. I can stand the infamy!"

Vorontsyev looked at the ground flowing beneath them.

"You'll want a map—in the pocket of the door, beside you."

Vorontsyev dipped in his hand. His nails filled with crumbs, or dust, then he picked out a folded, scruffy map. It was local, large-scale.

He said, "How far are we from Khabarovsk?"

"No more than twenty miles."

"Right. The first one you see that's near enough and small enough—drop in it!"

The pilot managed a small grin. "Right, my Major." His smile became more open. "You really are a bastard! Conning me into this flight when you're really a dangerous villain! I must want my brains tested."

"Just look, friend. And—thanks."

"Bloody good luck to you!"

The shallower valley they were following forked ahead of them, and the hills became sheer again. Vorontsyev looked at the map. Villages, not many miles from the valley he could identify. Yes, that was their present position—Khabarovsk more or less south-east, more than twenty miles, he thought. He would need a car, something.

He did not think about what he would do when he reached Khabarovsk. He was under no illusions. Once they talked to the pilot, they would realise that he had seen sufficient to make the guess he had made. He would have to be eliminated. And the whole of Ossipov's army would be pitted against him.

If he got to Khabarovsk, they wouldn't give up. He would be killed, even if they thought he must have passed on a message to Moscow. They would kill him then out of revenge, rage at the loss of secrecy.

He wondered about killing the pilot, once they touched down. He was uncertain. He might not be able to do it, even though it seemed to be demanded by the situation. He decided to compromise, even as the pilot said, "Down there—up ahead."

They were passing over thick fir forest now, in a narrower valley that looked very much like a pen, something into which he could be driven, and boxed. It would have to do. Steep sides to the valley, but no altitude. They passed over the spot in the trees, a tiny clearing, perhaps where timber had been cut for local use.

"What—?" Vorontsyev began. The pilot shoved something into his hand. A small compass.

"You'll need it. Down we go!"

The helicopter stopped almost dead, as if it had struck solid air. Vorontsyev was jolted in his seat. Immediately, the two gunships on either side overshot, and the one following loomed over them.

The helicopter was shuffling in a curious crab-like motion, and descending rapidly, when the voice snapped in the headset: "Maintain position!"

Vorontsyev flicked the switch so that his voice would be heard by the leader of the flight, and he barked. "Get down, you bastard, or I'll kill you now!"

The pilot juggled the MIL level, and the trees slid past the windows as they dropped the last few feet. The clearing was only yards across, too small to accommodate themselves and one of the big gunships. The MIL bounded as the wheels touched, and in the same moment Vorontsyev slid the door open. He looked at the pilot, and saw the suspicion of death in his face.

"Sorry!" he said, and struck him across the temple with the Makarov he had drawn from the shoulder holster. The pilot slumped forward.

Vorontsyev jumped out of the door, his legs buckling as he hit the frozen ground. He ducked under the slowing rotor blades, and in ten paces he was under the cover of the trees. The noise from the gunships overhead was deafening, as if expressing the pilots' anger. The trees swayed in the downdraught.

He had only minutes. He took a compass bearing, turned on his heel, and began running deeper into the trees.

Khamovkhin was in a rage of impotence. There was no part of him any longer able to weigh his words, observe himself, as if at some performance. He did not care that the duty-officer, Ozeroff again, heard him, or would repeat what he had heard to his companions. He could be a laughing-stock—in two days, he might be nothing at all, hardly a memory. Erased.

"I don't want excuses, Yuri—I want *action!*" he raged into the transmitter. He had broken code transmissions during the first conversation with Andropov after his flight back from Helsinki—impatience had become a black animal clawing at his back while he waited for encode-and-decode in order to relieve his feelings.

"I can only offer you a hope, Feodor. Our opponents are close to panic—they have begun to kill, on the least premise. If—*if*, we can keep *our* heads, then we may have a chance."

"That's politician's talk—just farting in the storm! You've got half a million people in your bloody service—what are they doing? Sitting on their backsides in the restaurants you provide for their comfort?"

"My men are doing their best, Feodor—*my* survival, *their* survival, depends upon success."

"Work it out, man! We know who they might be—get rid of them all! If you hit hard enough, the ones we want are going to get hurt—"

"No! I won't do it—not until there is a stronger indication, a stronger proof. Besides, Moscow Garrison is not replying to our signals."

"What? What did you say?" Khamovkhin felt his breath coming as from a distance, insufficient to fill his lungs, keep him alive.

"I said—at six this morning, Moscow Garrison appeared to cut off all contact with the Centre, with anyone. I've had people trying to ring up on all sorts of pretexts—without success. I had a helicopter overfly—and it's as still as the grave down there." Andropov's voice seemed to be coming from a long way away, as if the signal was fading. Khamovkhin flipped the transmit switch.

"Then it's beginning—we're too late."

"Not yet. Nothing happening yet, anyway. The date is the twenty-fourth, remember, Feodor? Someone must have to get through to them before then. This is only part of the operation. We have to find him."

"Do it—do it!"

"We will—" Andropov cut the connection suddenly, so

237

that Khamovkhin thought at first the signal had been lost, then that it had been intercepted, then realised that Andropov was weary of his tantrum. He became aware of Ozeroff behind him, smelling faintly of aftershave, and of the clownish, terrified figure he had cut. And cursed himself.

"You'll see the Englishman and the American now, sir?" Ozeroff asked politely.

"When I've shaved!" Khamovkhin snapped.

Andropov opened the tall window, but did not step out onto the balcony. The early morning air chilled him in a moment, but he remained standing in its draught, feeling refreshed, as if the cold were cleaning his skin, cooling his face of emotion. He hated Khamovkhin, insofar as he was capable of that dark an emotion. A panic-stricken child, an imbecile, a coward. And he the adult, the whole weight of it thrown on him.

In two minutes, he was cold, and he shut the window with hands already slightly numb, and returned to his desk. He hovered, as if about to sit, and then chose to sit in one of the armchairs.

Oh, yes. Kill them all. Group of Soviet Forces North—Praporovich, and Dolohov. Kill them, and stop the invasion of Scandinavia—easy, if you could be sure of finding them out in the open, with their backs turned, easy targets. And you could be sure that that would be the end of it, that they were in sole command, and that whoever was behind the whole thing wouldn't be able to order the invasion anyway—

Or arrest the whole of the Politburo—but, just in case, the Central Committee too, the Secretariat. Only a few hundred, maybe a thousand arrests, just to be on the safe side.

And you were sure that Praporovich and Dolohov wouldn't go ahead anyway.

Find the leader, and stop it all—

As long as you could be certain that Moscow Garrison would not go it alone.

He *wanted* to use naked power. Yes, he understood, complied with, Feodor's reasoning that wasn't reason so much as panic of a threatened animal—because he was a threatened animal, just the same.

But he had to face—as Feodor was hiding from the

fact in rage—had to face the brute, inescapable fact that naked power was insufficient. That there was no complete, satisfactory solution—no way of stopping it, *dead*. A tyranny—it was called that, his service, by the journalists from outside, by the malcontents, the dissidents, even by some of the thugs inside it—a tyranny was impotent, incapable of protecting itself.

A tyranny isn't enough—

He wanted to laugh, except that, even now, he could not find himself an object of levity.

Khamovkhin had changed his clothing—shaved and washed, then a clean shirt, a tie, another suit; for a moment, in the bedroom still darkened by shutters and curtains, he had thought of changing his long underwear. But he could not bear the thought of so literal a nakedness, or the sight of the shivering old body in the long mirror. As he came into the high room, and saw the two intelligence agents waiting for him, near the huge fireplace, their faces lit more by the log fire than the lamps or the light from the distant window, he quailed as if he were an emperor without clothes.

Aubrey received the impression of a warlord in a grey suit; albeit one prey to doubts, and apparently unsure of himself. There was an impression, a patina of confidence overlying a tangible lack of assurance. Buckholz saw a much simpler figure—the representative of an alien system now to be habilitated; and a man to whom his President had given ultimata, and whose representative he was.

"Mr. Aubrey—Mr. Buckholz," Khamovkhin said, waving them back to their seats beneath some unidentifiable armorial crest over the fireplace. There was no one else in the great room; Khamovkhin spoke better English than most of his predecessors, and he would not have admitted lack of confidence by having a security man inside the door.

"Mr. First Secretary, good of you to see us so promptly," Aubrey murmured deferentially as Khamovkhin stood with his back to the fireplace, warming himself. The crest above him—no, Aubrey reflected, there is nothing chivalric about his face, or his posture. A warlord. Buckholz, next to Aubrey, stirred at the diplomacy of tone.

"Of course. You are now accredited representatives of

your governments. You have been—legitimised, mm?" Khamovkhin laughed.

Aubrey dipped his head. "Quite so, sir."

"I have this morning for—my affairs. Please to proceed with your counsel, gentlemen." To complete the spell of confidence, he waved his hands and sat down opposite them, on the other side of the fireplace. The firelight strengthened his square features with shadows and highlights, and Aubrey realised that the effect had been calculated, stage-managed.

"Mr. Secretary—" Buckholz began, bridling at the delicacy of exchange. "This visit is in the nature of a follow-up, if you take my meaning. The President wishes me to discuss—in more detail—matters of importance to both our countries—" He tailed off, as if caught himself in some diplomatic web. Then he added: "You know why we're here, sir."

"Indeed I do." Aubrey caught the hesitation, sensed the man shying from the subject.

"OK, sir. Then we understand each other. I have to make it clear to you, sir, that my country *will* go to war, if that's what it takes. The President, and his allies in NATO, are deeply worried by developments inside the Soviet Union, especially by troop concentrations in the theatre of northern Europe, so close to the date for the signing of the Treaty—" Buckholz blundered on, as if reciting his speech in reverse, throwing away the ultimatum as an opening remark.

Aubrey interjected: "Mr. First Secretary, our combined intelligence services are in possession of information which strongly indicates that the Soviet High Command intend to move troops into Finland and Norway—and perhaps to threaten yourself and the legitimate, *elected* government of the USSR, at the moment when you and President Wainwright would be signing the Helsinki Arms Control Treaty—in two days' time." He paused, and Buckholz, jaw jutting, prow of a nose in profile to him as he leaned in his chair, seemed to have resigned the task to him. Khamovkhin remained silent, but Aubrey was aware of the sense of strain, of the way in which the words, though familiar, inflicted themselves on the Russian.

He pressed on: "What Mr. Buckholz, in his position as representative of his government, and myself, wish from you—is an assurance that these matters are not unknown to you, and that they are being, and will continue to be dealt with successfully."

Aubrey waited. He had given the man a means of admission that would not appear damaging, or impotent. Khamovkhin stirred in his chair, then said, "Very well, Mr. Aubrey. You have been candid with me, I shall be similarly so." He stood up again, and placed his back towards the fire, hands clasped behind him. Irreverently, Aubrey expected a comic policeman's crouch.

"The discontent of the army towards our mutually beneficial Treaty is well known to you, as it is to us. I will not disguise from you the fact that we have long suspected that elements in the Red Army might attempt some kind of—non-diplomatic, non-*democratic* action against the time when the Treaty was signed, and ratified. The security service of the Soviet Union has been assiduous, dedicated, in its investigations—in all parts of the Soviet Union and the territories of our Warsaw Pact allies—into possible centres of discontent and subversion—" He looked at each man in turn. Aubrey saw a quick image of a man hanging wallpaper, and wondered quizzically at the way in which irreverence was creeping into his attitude to his work; even at such a crucial time as this.

"We have had to tread very carefully, as you will appreciate, gentlemen. We had no wish to trigger, prematurely, the very thing we wished to prevent." He smiled —an exercise of the facial muscles. "But, we are now— and I have confirmed this with Chairman Andropov by radio-transmitter only this morning—in a position where the leaders of this conspiracy against peace are clearly identified, their plans known to us—and their *arrests* imminent!" He finished with an actor's flourish, one hand raised a little in the air. Then he closed it into a fist, to emphasise his meaning.

"Your assurances are most welcome, sir," Aubrey remarked smoothly. "We understand that you cannot order the withdrawal of troops—which you so evidently wish to do—until these *dissident* elements have been placed under arrest. I am sure that my colleague—and his government —will be reassured, as I know Her Britannic Majesty's Government will be." He nodded in a little theatrical bow. Khamovkhin watched Buckholz carefully.

"Thank you, Mr. First Secretary," the American began, "for your frank admissions. I will convey your remarks to the President. However, I am sure that he would wish you to know that his sympathies and support are with you—and that he will commit troops to the northern sector at dawn on the twenty-fourth! Unless you can put your own house in order."

Khamovkhin shivered, very slightly, but Aubrey considered it was with suppressed rage.

"I take your President's meaning to heart, I can assure you, Mr. Buckholz. However, the situation you seem to consider with such—*calm*—will not arise. I have told you, the leaders of the conspiracy will be arrested within the next twenty-four hours!" The voice was slightly out of control, and not simply for effect. Khamovkhin had reached the limits of diplomacy, Aubrey considered—and Aubrey understood that it was hopeless; that Khamovkhin's cupboard was bare, his hand empty of high cards. He was simply wishing for the moon.

Aubrey covered the void of the moment, and his own inward quailing, and said, "There is one other matter, Mr. First Secretary. In the interests of your *personal security*, sir, we propose that a new security team, from *our* intelligence services, be drafted to Lahtilinna."

Khamovkhin was visibly disconcerted. "Why is this, gentlemen? My security officers here have been vetted by the Chairman himself." An edge of fear—rank, personal fear. Surprise, anger too.

"Sir, we have a suspicion—no more than that—that you may be in personal danger while in Finland. The thought must also have occurred to you. Considering the possible ramifications of the plot against your government, it is not inconceivable that a move might be made against you—"

"I am to be your prisoner?"

"Our charge, sir. Only our charge."

Silence. Khamovkhin fidgeting, uncertain whether to sit or stand. The fire crackling loudly, and visible restraint against the tiny shock from each of the three men.

"We'd like to move the team in tonight, sir." Buckholz, at last enjoying a small victory. "But naturally, you can have time to think it over. We have the men selected. You will be *safe* with them—with us." The bribe was evident.

"I will consider this—unprecedented step," Khamovkhin said slowly. "In consultation, naturally." A sweep of the

242

arm. "Now, you will excuse me, gentlemen, I have much to do."

"Of course, sir," Aubrey stood up and said, bowing slightly. "Thank you for seeing us."

"Yes—thank you," Buckholz added, as if reminded of his manners.

When they had gone, Khamovkhin stared into the fireplace for a long time, and felt he was looking into a tunnel—he hardly saw the flames, only the blackened back of the fireplace; he was running down that tunnel, and a great train, the monolith of the Soviet Union itself, so it seemed, was thundering and roaring behind him drawing closer and closer.

As they went down the steps of the castle, and their feet began crunching on the icy gravel as they walked to their car, Aubrey said, "Well played, Charles—we should have worked more often as a team."

Buckholz grinned. "Why do you British assume, by divine right, I guess, that you have all the diplomacy, and us colonials only get to be the stooges? Next time, I want to play the smart-ass—you be the dummy!"

"Very well, Charles. Not that it would seem to matter much. Khamovkhin is relying on a miracle—and therefore, so are we."

"Dammit, yes! I know that. What the hell is the KGB playing at? When they got a real job on, they foul up!"

"Never mind, Charles. I think, for the moment, we will interest ourselves in the smaller matter of one man's safety. And the identity of the mysterious Captain Ozeroff. That should be enough for two old night-soil men like ourselves." He paused, then added bleakly, "It should do to fill in time until the twenty-fourth."

The Englishman was near to breaking—perhaps within himself he had already broken. The fierce attention he seemed to be paying to *Kutuzov* indicated a distraction from self, rather than a real awareness, a calculated assessment of his situation. Novetlyn stood beside *Kutuzov*, deferential and silent. The narrow cell with its poor light from one high, barred slit of window, smelt foul. Folley's smell, as if something was rotting beneath the soiled clothes, rotting inside the man.

"Well, Colonel?"

"Sir?"

"Are we going to learn something of value, or not?"

Folley blinked, leaned forward on the filthy cot as if straining to comprehend—or simply to keep himself awake. The body's posture flinched, even while he did it. *Kutuzov* was obscurely moved by the sight, but to no specific feeling.

"Possibly, sir. What he knows, how much he knows— it's open to question." Novetlyn sounded as if he had already done with the Englishman, discarded that particular card. The attitude irritated *Kutuzov.*

"Then I came to Leningrad for nothing?"

"If you came to see him, sir—perhaps."

Novetlyn obviously knew about the border incident, and the escape of one of the agents in Helsinki. Perhaps that explained his indifference. An indifferent interrogator would obtain nothing of value.

"What do they know?"

"Less when he was sent than they know now."

Kutuzov was suddenly tired of the smell, the confinement. Perhaps disturbed, too, though he ignored the feeling.

"Very well, let's go. The Marshal should have arrived by now."

"And him, sir?"

Folley's body looked as if it was pleading; but the eyes, as if overworked, were blank with an idiot's stare; the body might only be an actor's imitation of supplication, or a haphazard arrangement of weary, beaten muscles.

"Keep him here for the moment. We might be able to use him later—in some sort of show-trial." *Kutuzov* seemed pleased with the idea, as if it explained the vague reluctance he perceived with regard to Folley. "Perhaps so. Agent of the Western imperialists—a courier to Khamovkhin's gang. Yes. Keep him alive!"

Upstairs, Praporovich waited in civilian clothes in the main drawing-room of the old house. When *Kutuzov* entered, they embraced, kissed cheeks. *Kutuzov* held the Marshal at arms' length for a moment, smiling, assessing.

"You look tired, Grigory Ilyich."

Praporovich dismissed the observation. "Nothing the twenty-fourth won't put right!" They laughed together. "I was not followed," Praporovich added.

"Nevertheless, this is the last time you must come out of headquarters, until things are under way."

"Perhaps. I will be careful, you know."

"I know it."

"Ossipov, then—?"

"He has been told to radio you the full instructions, timings, everything."

"We need twenty-four hours minimum to deploy and transport."

"Ossipov knows that."

"A pity it's so late in the day—being so important."

Kutuzov settled himself in his chair, studying Praporovich, suddenly wearied by the prospect of argument.

"We could take no chances—chemical warfare training is an *annual event*. Last year, we failed to get it right, and we had to wait. Soldiers *talk*, Grigory Ilyich—and that is something not to talk about. Ossipov's men think they are only carrying out *normal* training—" Praporovich raised his hand.

"Very well, old friend. I agree. Let us not quarrel. As long as the cleaning-up is timed to the minute, I don't worry about it."

"It will be. Radio-traffic for *everything*, using the hourly changes of code, from now on. Tell Dolohov."

Praporovich nodded. "Your part of it?"

"Valenkov's gone underground. The KGB know it, but they can't do anything about it. Valenkov will be ready at 06:00, when I give the order, to move his tanks into the centre of Moscow. They will take up positions around and inside the Kremlin, and in Dzerzhinsky Street—a display of strength. Andropov will be—*collected* at home by a special squad. The Politburo members will be similarly rounded up. As for Feodor the traitor—he will be taken care of."

"He must come back for trial—"

"What else? It is taken care of."

Praporovich nodded reluctantly. "GFSG are still belly-aching about not being in on the action," he observed.

"They *won't* move?"

"No. Marshal Bezenkov will do nothing. '1812' will come to a complete stop at 06:00, as you ordered."

"Good."

Kutuzov stood up, crossed to the drinks cabinet in one

corner, and poured vodka for them both. He raised his glass, aware of, pleased at, the theatricality.

"Your health, old friend."

"Yours, also." They touched glasses, drank off the liquor. *Kutuzov* stayed the Marshal's hand for a moment.

"I have to stay alive, because without me, Valenkov will never order his garrison regiments into the streets of Moscow. *You* have to stay alive, because without you the army has no leader in the north. Remember that when you're tempted to walk the streets today or tomorrow— eh, old friend?"

Praporovich nodded. Then, together, they threw their empty glasses into the fireplace. Praporovich roared with laughter, the laughter of a young man. After a moment *Kutuzov*, too began to laugh.

The senior Helsinki detective had been deferential, almost silent, certainly careful to avoid recognition of Davenhill and the wounded arm he nursed in a sling. He had his orders, evidently, and satisfied his frustrations by enjoying the discomfort that the cold of the city morgue brought to the pale-looking Englishman. Diplomacy, intelligence services, twist justice the way you want—the thoughts rumbled away in the back of his head.

"I'll leave you, if you wish, Mr. Davenhill?" he said, sliding out the drawer of the great metal cabinet that might have contained gigantic files. The expected white sheet with its contours like those of hidden furniture nevertheless shocked Davenhill, made him gag as if the thing under the sheet had rotted.

"Don't you want my identification?" Davenhill snapped.

"Naturally. I meant afterwards—"

"I—"

The detective pulled back the sheet like a conjurer. Waterford's face stared up at them. Davenhill could imagine the eyes beneath the closed lids, glowering, discontented with the *ordinariness*, the boredom of death. Davenhill nodded. Then he remembered his lines.

"Yes—that is Mr. Alan Waterford, of the British Diplomatic Service." It was incredible, even insulting. The detective accepted the blatant untruth, the agreed version of identity.

"Thank you, Mr. Davenhill."

Davenhill was staring into the cabinet drawer. Waterford was neat, tidy. He did not hear the detective walk away, to wait outside for him.

Civil servant—dear God! he thought. At last they had put Waterford in a category, and one he could not threaten or burst from. Waterford the killer, the operator, the desperate man—a *clerk*.

Davenhill could feel nothing more than the irony of his words, his identification. He could not feel that Waterford had saved his life, more than once; he could not apprehend the person that Waterford had been. But he was assailed by a sense of loneliness that had nothing to do with the white room, the ranked drawers, the table with its sluice in the middle of the tiled floor, the gowns hanging up on the door. It was a loneliness that belonged not to himself, but to Waterford. Waterford in life rather than dead.

Stupid tears pricked at the back of his eyes. In an effort to dismiss them, he slammed the heavy drawer shut. It slid smoothly on its oiled rails, and clanged shut. The noise rang from the white walls, from the chequered tiles of the floor.

Vorontsyev sat huddled in a narrow gully, staring at the Makarov 9 mm automatic in his hands. Hands that were clumsily gloved so that he could only just press the trigger-finger into the guard. Eight rounds in the magazine, and three spare clips in his pockets. Thirty-two 244 milligram bullets between himself and the whole of Ossipov's Far East Military District forces. He could not bring himself to contemplate the number of divisions posted at this end of the Soviet Union.

Ludicrous.

His breathing had now become less harsh, and his heartbeat no longer thudded in his ears. He must have been running for miles, for hours.

It had been for nearly an hour. It was twelve-fifteen on the 22nd. In Moscow, eight hours away by jet, it was—what was it? Midnight.

He threw aside the thought with a shake of his head. It did not matter. What mattered more was that he wished he had the larger Stechkin 9 mm automatic, with a twenty-round magazine, better range, more stopping power, instead of the particularly futile Makarov.

He laughed aloud when he considered the uselessness of

247

either gun against a T-54 tank, or even the platoon of men that might leap out of an Armoured Personnel Carrier.

He fumbled the map from his pocket, and folded and refolded it until it revealed his present position. He checked with the sun's position, then the compass, then the shape of the land—here, on the edge of the long knife of forest that had followed the valley as it narrowed. Pointing south.

He was eighteen miles from the outskirts of Khabarovsk.

He crouched instinctively as he heard the beat of a helicopter, coming up the narrow valley from the south. He was just under the outlying trees, in an olive-green anorak and brown slacks, and jammed into a narrow dry watercourse. The beat of the rotors became louder, and he felt his arms against his head throbbing with nerves as he covered his fair hair. The noise was directly overhead, and he could feel the small downdraught. Dirt jumped and quivered near him, and the trees overhead were swaying in the created wind.

Then the noise died away northwards, the way he had come, the pilot and observer in the chopper hoping that their downdraught might part the trees like some green and spiky Red Sea just long enough for them to spot a running man. He waited, not uncurling from his crouch, because he now knew the pattern they were using.

Two minutes later, the second helicopter passed overhead. They could not seriously believe that he had come this far in the time—probably these were the original choppers that had escorted, then lost him.

He stood up. He brushed his trousers free of the little hard dirt that had accumulated, and stepped out of the gully. There was no snow on this side of the narrow valley, facing the sun. The day was almost spring-like, mild. He had even heard insects in the intense silence, above his own breathing.

A vague plan had formed itself in his mind—something akin to a half-dreamed ambition, and connected with childhood. Certainly not a definite plan of action. But it was all he had. It meant getting to Khabarovsk, at least to the eastern outskirts, soon after dark.

He knew he could not enter Khabarovsk, or return to his hotel. He could not even rely on Blinn and the rest of the forensic team, or the replacement KGB officers flown in from Moscow. A tiny force, impotent. He could not attempt to board a plane in Khabarovsk—the airport was outside the town, but it would be patrolled by now, or soon, anyway. He would be arrested, probably on some trumped-up charge and by a GRU detachment, and brought to Military District HQ.

And then, he thought, the light would go out.

Beyond the trees, the narrow neck of the valley opened out. He looked at the map. A small village—Nikoleyev—lay behind the valley, where the mountains and uplands surrendered temporarily to high pasture. A sloping bowl of meadowland, then narrow, radiating valleys again, before the land dropped down to the long hills which cradled Khabarovsk.

In the village, he had to obtain a car. Covertly, or overtly, it did not matter. Probably, there were troops in the village already. It did not matter. He had to get to the village, and he had to have the car. Only by having transport could he hope to make the rendezvous that was already assuming a prominent place in his thinking.

There was some kind of hut on a little rise, perhaps half a mile from where he stood. Not a house, perhaps a store for winter fodder.

He stepped cautiously away from the trees, as if expecting to see the belly of a helicopter slide into view just above the tree tops. He scanned the sky, revolving on his heels until he began to feel dizzy. Nothing. He began to run.

The ground was tussocky with the poor grass, flinty stones unsettling his footsteps. He ran as carefully as he could, his eyes scanning the ground immediately ahead of him, yet his mind screaming at the sense in the back of his neck, across his shoulders, that he was nakedly exposed as he moved with such idiotic slowness across that half-mile of grass and stones.

His breathing became heavier, the steps more automatic, and more laboured. He began to consider the futility of running, of crossing half a mile when thousands of miles separated him from the people who could help him—no, not help now; protect, hide. His breath began to tear and sob, like cloth being pulled apart roughly, something human in him being made into rags for cleaning.

He forced his legs on, his body seeming to bend lower, his face closer to the ground—stumbling more now, trying to shift weight immediately so that an ankle wouldn't give, twist. He could feel the body-heat, rising and breaking out in sweat. There was even sweat on his forehead now. He looked up. The hut appeared hardly any nearer than the last time he had looked up—perhaps one hundred strides ago. No, two hundred at least.

One hand pushing away from the ground as he stumbled, and the tiredness stressed as he tried to drive the legs in a reasserted upright position.

He heard the noise of the helicopter behind him, and it seemed as if the sound was gaseous, unnerving him, causing the moving legs to quiver as if he had already stopped running.

He turned round, staggering as his body shifted clumsily. The small scout helicopter, like the civilian one he had flown in, was fifty feet up, and moving across the grass towards him—a black, insect spot just horizoned above the dark lines of the trees.

He whirled round, stumbling again, and it was now as if he moved through some restraining element. The beat of rotors behind him became louder: he stumbled on, careless of stones and tussocks, waiting for the shadow of the helicopter, the waving of grass as it bent before the downdraught.

The hut wobbled on the rise, joggling in his vision as he looked up. The breath tearing, and the heartbeat frenzied. Above everything, the futility of it, the stupid blind panic to run, to keep running, thousands of miles from safety.

The grass leapt with small stones, flying dirt, near his right foot, then ahead and to his side. Gunfire. The noise of the rotors downed the rifle shots. The helicopter was no gunship, but it carried at least one marksman. Again, flying spots of dirt. He saw the distressed earth scatter on his boot like scuffed sand.

Then his breath was knocked from him, and his shoulder jarred cruelly as he banged into the wall of the hut. He looked up, and the shadow of the chopper passed over him. White plucked splinters of dry wood stung his cheek as the rifleman, with the AK-47 on automatic, loosed a volley before he disappeared behind the overflown hut.

Sobbing, straining to get his breath—one breath, clear and deep would be sufficient, as the blood roared in his ears—he banged against the locked door. Wood splintered —he heard the sound, even as the rotor noise increased again—and he fell into the darkness, redolent of stored fodder, and tumbled against stacked hay bales.

A line of jagged holes, striped across one wall, entry of sunlight in splashes like yellow blood, as the marksman in the helicopter sprayed the hut on automatic. He buried his head, wriggling his body between the spiky, hard edges of the bales. Bullets plucked into the packed earth floor, thumped softly into bales beside him. He put his hands over his ears, terrified.

The noise of the rotors came down to swallow him.

He was unsure low long it was, but he was aware of the changing noises outside. The rotors dying away, then the crackling of a voice, voices, as the helicopter's cabin speaker amplified the calls from nearest units in the search. He was stiff with fear, weak and unable to move.

The door of the hut was hanging open. He had to get out. He pushed himself upright, and staggered stiffly to the door, tugging the gun free of its shoulder holster. A ridiculous little thing, set against the AK-47 waiting for him outside.

He pressed himself against the wall, craning round the door frame. The soldier, in olive-green combat dress, was stepping cautiously towards the door. The small MIL was behind him, its rotors turning sluggishly. The pilot was bent forward over his equipment, his head turned to watch the soldier.

Vorontsyev went into the crouch, arms stiff, gun cradled by two hands. He fired three shots, all towards the centre of the target shape that the soldier had become. The man leapt aside, but a movement without voilition, only the jerk of impact as two of the bullets hit him in the stomach, the other passing through his upper arm as he fell away. The AK-47 spun in the air, catching the sun along its stubby barrel and curved magazine. The pilot was moving to shut the door of the helicopter when Vorontsyev, still in the same crouch, two paces out of the door, shot him. Red hole in the temple, then the head dropping back out of sight behind the body which had been lifted out of the seat, held in some grotesque position of sexual proffering over the seat back.

He turned the soldier with his boot, then bent to pick up the AK-47. Then, he rummaged in the dead man's combat suit for the extra magazines. They were bulky, unsuitable unless he wore combat dress himself. He threw one aside in irritation, and thrust the other into the deepest pocket of his anorak. Then he went to the MIL, moved the body slightly, and only then realised, as the mood of semi-robotic efficiency left him, that he had killed the pilot, and could not fly the helicopter himself.

His legs buckled under him, and he felt tears prick against his eyes as his thinking returned fully. He could have escaped in the chopper, and instead he had killed the pilot.

Voices, querulous and puzzled, demanded reply from the MIL's cabin speaker. Ident codes, positions, movements, details of force strength—spinning in his head.

He looked around. Specks to the west, lifting clear of a rise. Bigger helicopters. Away to the east, down a long slope, as far as a mile away, dots moving across a field, out of the cover of trees. Men on the ground already. A road away to the north of them. Olive-green APCs moving swiftly.

He was watching his encirclement.

Nothing, as yet, south of him, down towards the village of Nikoleyev that he could now see, nestling in gentler folds of country; not as flat as he had thought from the map, better for him. Dotted clumps of trees. He began to run again, the unfamiliar AK-47 banging against his thigh. The tussocky grass seemed longer on this long downslope—something to do with drainage, he wondered incongruously—and it seemed to wrestle with his tired legs, continually throwing the body too far forward, out of balance.

Bending low as he ran, he watched the sky. Only the air concerned him for the moment. Nothing on wheels or afoot was close enough.

Except that he knew they would put men down in Nikoleyev now. If they hadn't already done so.

Something had happened to him, however. Probably a result of the killing he had done, the evident superiority given him by two dead bodies that belonged to the enemy. He no longer thought ahead more than minutes. He had no sense of distances other than the little way to the village, the seventeen or eighteen miles to Khabarovsk. No promises, none of the luxuries of larger thought. Only the body moving, its imperatives occupying him.

He paused behind a rock, near the bottom of a stretch down from the hut. Below him, the road into the village wound through a shallow defile, cracked with frost, icy puddles in the shadows of trees. Empty. He paused long enough to regain something like casual breath, then jumped down onto the road. The hard earth jarred his legs and spine, and he groaned. More in fear of injury than in pain.

He crossed the road, which was lined with dark trees, and began to trot carefully, under their shadow, towards Nikoleyev. He stopped only once, hearing behind him the dull thump of an explosion. He knew what it was, and shuddered with knowledge. The first gunship at the hut had destroyed it with rocket fire. Probably simply because of the dead pilot, and the olive drab spot of a body below them. Incensed anger transmitted to firepower before reason could interfere. He consciously stopped the trembling of his body.

The road dropped down into the village—a straggle of houses, peasant dwellings of wood, single-storeyed and ramshackle. He bit his glove as his hand wiped his face. A car—*there?* It was like a grainy photograph from some old album; from Gorochenko's pictures of his peasant origins on the steppes. Chickens flicked across the road, and a cow ambled between two houses. Straggling dead gardens, patches of dark, cultivated earth marking the properties, darker than the packed earth of the village's one street.

He looked for a store.

Yes.

He breathed deeply, as if he had gained some kind of victory. There had to be some kind of delivery van. Unless they still delivered by cart.

He waited, his body eager, the legs quivering with the need to move; but he had to be sure of troops, yet the longer he waited the more surely they would come.

As he stood up, caution finally satisfied, an olive-green APC rolled up and over the rise at the other end of the village street. Groaning he dropped back into the shadow of a fir. He had waited too bloody long!

TWELVE

THE TRAIN

The APC rolled to a halt at what the driver considered the centre of the tiny hamlet. There was almost a contempt about the reluctant way in which the vehicle slowed, then stopped. It was a BTR-152, standard model without roof armour. Vorontsyev could see the heads of the troops it carried, bobbing up and down, two rows of flattish Red Army helmets, like mushrooms or Chinese straw hats painted green.

When it stopped, the gun mounted at the front began to swivel threateningly. There was no one on the street. Only the officer stood up, a Stechkin automatic in his hand. His movements were lazy, confident. Either he hadn't heard about the two dead men, or he had accepted the unchanged, sleepy parameters of the scene before him. Nothing could happen there, in the precise middle of nowhere.

Eventually, he barked an order, and the soldiers began to dismount from the back of the personnel carrier. Vorontsyev clutched the AK-47 tighter, as if it were a talisman.

There were twelve men. Some women, one or two old men, began to emerge from the low wooden houses. The officer spoke to one of the women, who seemed undeterred by his tone of voice. A large woman, great bosom and dragged-back hair, wiping her hands on a check apron. Vorontsyev, relaxed by the slow place of the scene, the indifference of the troops who fanned out slowly, and the NCO who was already smoking a cigarette, watched the encounter. He could almost see the scowl on the woman's face.

The officer walked away eventually, then questioned another villager, an old man; he shrugged repeatedly, and appeared simple-minded. The officer's step expressed frustration as he rejoined the NCO. He gave his orders with a deal of arm-waving, and it was as if the projector showing a film had slipped into another speed. The whole scene speeded up. Men went now from house to house with a purpose, and much noise. The officer and the NCO stood by the APC, where they were joined by the driver, who also lit a cigarette. The officer, as if the habit was somehow beneath him, walked a little apart, watching the search.

It took little more than ten minutes. Then, at an order from the NCO, the men doubled back to the APC. For one moment, Vorontsyev thought he might be given the unbelievable luck of their leaving the hamlet of Nikoleyev.

Then he saw that they were detailed to fall out, except for individuals posted one at either end of the village, on the road. There seemed, then, nothing more to do, and the officer cast about, his head turning like that on a doll. Vorontsyev thought he must be looking for a drink, or a chair.

He had to move now. Soon, the men would drift towards the store, which might proffer food, or something to drink. The officer would, having absorbed the motionless innocence of the hamlet, allow them to relax as the afternoon wore on. They were obviously detailed to remain in the hamlet, and until they received new orders they were no longer part of the search.

He studied the land immediately round the village. He could, by moving carefully around the southern perimeter, use such things as wood-stacks, outhouses, to shield him. Only if one of the villagers saw him would he be in danger.

He stood up, let his cramped legs relax, then moved off to his right through the thin belt of trees until he was overlooking, from a slight rise, a stack of logs behind the most outlying of the poor wooden houses. This one appeared deserted, he could see a cracked window and there was no smoke from the thin chimney. Cautiously, he moved out of the trees and half-slid down the slope, resting only when he was concealed by the logs.

A few moments, then he raised his head cautiously. Here, he could not see the APC nor the soldiers. He fished out the map, and studied it carefully. The nearest village was three, perhaps four miles away, and in the wrong direction. He looked at his watch and made a swift calculation. He would not have enough time, unless he took a vehicle of some kind from Nikoleyev.

He considered, uselessly, the APC. He could not overpower twelve men, an NCO, a driver and an officer, not even with surprise and an AK-47. The store had to have some kind of van.

He looked at the roads on the map, fully marked even to farm tracks. He thought he could see a way of keeping away from any road that might be carrying troops, or have a road-block in operation. He would be safe from everything, perhaps, except aerial patrols. Which might, or might not, investigate a civilian vehicle.

But, the APC . . .

He wished he had taken the dead soldier's grenades.

How could he leave, without being followed, and captured? It was an impossibility, so impossible that his body became weak, his mind irresolute. He sat with his back against the wood, its rough bark pressing into him, the rifle upright between his legs like a prop—he gripped it tightly.

Stupid, stupid.

The soldier who had come to relieve himself behind the pile of logs was as surprised to see Vorontsyev as the KGB man was to be stumbled upon.

It was a ridiculous moment. The soldier's hand was in his flies, and his rifle was over his shoulder. He was helpless, his mouth opening and closing like that of a fish. He appeared at every instant to be about to cry out, but no sound would come. Vorontsyev himself, moving as if through a great pressure of water, or clinging nets, moved the gun to his hip, turned his body so slowly, levelled the gun, and squeezed the trigger. The soldier jumped back, his hand and his penis appearing from his trousers, and then he lay still on his back.

A single, loud shot.

This time Vorontsyev scrabbled in the combat dress, and unfastened the two RGD-5 fragmentation grenades the man carried. He could hear, at a distance, shouted orders, and perhaps the soldier's name being called. He ducked behind the logs again, then leaned forward, caught hold of the dead man's boot, and pulled the body awkwardly towards him, out of sight.

Twelve men.

Ridiculous.

They came at the run, disorganised and unprepared, because they might have been mistaken and the officer was evidently panicking and they had had to throw away cigarettes—

Vorontsyev raised his arm, swung back and then foward, and lobbed the grenade into them. Then the second one. Five of them, not bunched, but the grenades, more like fat tins than pineapples, carried heavy charges and an effective fragmentation radius of twenty-five metres. The first one exploded, and he heard something thud into the logs on the other side. The second explosion. A thin scream, then he was on his feet, all but head and shoulders masked by the logs, and firing at the two men still moving, staggering though they were. He did not miss.

He could hear one of the wounded men behind him, screaming something incoherent and terrible about his guts, and then he pressed against the wall of a house twenty yards away, his head bobbing round the corner of the house, cheek rubbing against the rough board— and the APC, a background to the stunned officer and the NCO, who looked white, was fifty yards from him.

Then the officer screamed rather than shouted some confused orders. It was as if he did not realise that his force had been cut to half, and he no longer had sufficient men to perform the demanded tasks.

Vorontsyev grinned. Death, violent death, and winning, even temporarily, charged him with new energy. It was one he would despise later, if he lived. But not now.

One soldier came at a reckless run, because his officer was screaming behind him, down the earthen alleyway between two of the larger houses in the hamlet. His boots pounded on the packed, dark earth, cracked by frost. Vorontsyev waited until he was level, then fired. There was no thought of silent disposal—noise was a part of it, part of the electricity that now galvanised him. It was as if the man had been shoved in the back—arms thrown out, legs going, then face down in a chicken run. Vorontsyev wanted to laugh, because that, too, was a source of energy, of destructive confidence—ways of dying. *One man burying his face in chicken-shit, another pulling his pisser out as he died.* It had to be *good,* that.

He ran up the alleyway, seeing the officer confronting him, the NCO already moving away towards the place where the grenade had exploded. He could see no one else now—a face at a little window, barely glanced as he raced past it, then the stutter of the AK-47 on semi-automatic, forty rounds a minute, quicker than single, aimed shots. Vulgar, untrained destruction.

The officer was sliding down the side of the APC even as the NCO dived into the hard dirt of the street. Both of them were dead. He trained the gun, trigger pressed against the back of the guard, until he was sure they had been hit repeatedly. He was ten yards from them, still in the narrow alleyway. Eight dead, and the driver, who had been climbing back into the seat of the APC, perhaps to move it forward, clutching his leg, still bent as if to mount the side of the carrier, knuckles of the hand gripping the rung above him turning white with the pain, and the effort of hanging on. He was afraid to drop on the wounded leg.

Vorontsyev felt the dangerous energy flag. He had known the mood only once before, in a brief KGB firefight with a hijack team surprised in their warehouse headquarters. He had killed two of them, and received a commendation. It had helped to obtain his transfer to SID. He felt exhausted now, as if slipping into sleep or coma. There was little time left, as if the effects of some drug were wearing off.

He dashed to the APC, and bundled the driver out of the way. The man screamed as he fell on his wounded leg, and Vorontsyev saw the hand red with gouted blood. He hauled himself up and tumbled into the body of the carrier, brusing his ribs against the hard edge of a seat.

Bullets puckered and whined against the side of the APC. But he was safe now, the armour of the vehicle protecting him. As he lifted his head cautiously, he saw a soldier's head peer from behind a wooden wall, and he pumped four rounds, heard the scream as the high-velocity bullets passed through the two walls of the building that met at the corner concealing the soldier and hit their target; then the rifle clicked twice.

He tore the magazine off, and struggled with the one in his pocket, which threatened to snag awkwardly. Then it was clipped in, and he raised his head again.

The street was empty.

He felt desperately tired.

With his back against the armoured side of the APC, he raised his head and shouted into the silence of the street:

"Everyone else is dead! How many more of you are there—four, five? You won't get close enough to throw a grenade in! Give it up. Let some other bastard take me on!"

He listened. Nothing, for a long time.

"You bastard!" he heard someone shout, away to the left of the APC. "You killed all our mates, you bloody terrorist!"

He wanted to laugh. They were dying, and prepared to die, for the same fiction that had killed the KGB team in Khabarovsk—the Separatists. And then he hated Ossipov. Not the men out there, but Ossipov.

He tried to think coolly, because the mention of grenades had been deliberate. There would be only a few moments more of cold logic, before thought became muddy, indefinite.

He shouted: "Give up, you stupid bastards! I'll kill the lot of you unless you do!" Then he raised his head. The right arm, half the frame, of a soldier had appeared, hand raised with a grenade. The soldier moved to get a freer throw, and Vorontsyev fired. The arm disappeared, and the grenade bounced twice, then exploded. He heard a scream.

They would have used grenades anyway. He had made them try on his terms, in the moment of his choosing. He did not know how many he had killed or disabled. Probably two.

"Come out, you stupid bastards!" he repeated. "Give yourselves up!"

It had to be now, in the next few seconds, while their minds clogged still with the number of the dead, with their own lack of safety in diminishing numbers. Had to be.

From one side of the street, two soldiers appeared.

Across from the APC, another. One of them was holding a bloody, torn sleeve. He must have been behind the others when the grenade went off. They ostentatiously dropped their guns. The wounded driver wriggled on the ground.

Vorontsyev stood up, almost swaying with weariness. He motioned with the gun.

"Come on!" he barked. "Get in! Get in or I'll kill you!" He should have done, but he was beginning to be appalled at the slaughter. It was no longer a gratuitous feeling, but wrenched at his stomach. There seemed a stench in his nostrils. The perspective he had rigidly bound in the toil of action loosened and came free, and he was still eighteen miles from the only airport, and thousands of miles from safety. He waggled the gun down at the young peasant faces. Men on military service, without sophistication or great intelligence. Badly frightened automata, shocked out of their normal machine-like operation, their officer dead.

"Get in!" he barked. "One of you drive!"

They seemed to hold a silent debate, and then one of them climbed into the driving-seat.

"Pick him up!" he shouted, pointing at the wounded figure on the ground. They did so, bundling him gently into the back of the APC, the double doors opened. One of them examined the wound, and took out a field dressing, binding the calf that had been torn by a bullet. "Get moving!" Vorontsyev called, sitting down next to the driver in the officer's accustomed seat, turning so that he could watch the two men and the driver, and the wounded man supported in one of the seats.

"Where?" the driver asked, his hands gripping the wheel to still fear.

"Turn round—back the way you came. I'll give directions."

The APC's engine roared, and then they turned on the dirt of the street, picking up speed as if to leave the carnage behind. Vorontsyev felt the weariness leave him, feeding instead on the shocked, stunned faces of the men he had captured, lifting himself up from the level of their self-abnegation. Now they did not even hate him. They were feeling nothing.

The APC left the village behind. Still no one had come

out of any of the houses as they bumped over the rise and the village dropped out of sight. Within a quarter of a mile, Vorontsyev barked, "Right here!" They turned off the road, down a narrow dirt track. The driver appeared puzzled. The rifle prodded against his arm, which quivered as at the touch of an electrode, and he changed down. The surface of the track was pitted with craters, in some of which icy pools remained.

Vorontsyev watched the sky, and the road ahead. It would be some time before the men became dangerous again with renewed hatred; and by that time he would have dumped them, and the driver. He would not kill them. He would simply leave them, in the middle of nowhere, on foot.

During the short afternoon, as they wound slowly, methodically along tracks and lanes, often screened by trees or high hedges and walls, always heading generally eastwards, the sky darkened swiftly and heavy cloud pressed down on them. A wind, too, sprang up; the weather had been deceptive in the morning. When it began to snow, large flakes driven into their faces, pattering against the sides of the APC, he knew he had been given the kind of luck he needed. The weather closed in on them. He worked from the map and the compass as the scenery was blotted out by curtains of rushing snow.

No air traffic.

Eventually, he abandoned the soldiers. They feared him, momentarily, but hatred was already beginning to make them calculate recklessly. They were beginning to be dangerous to him. They climbed out of the APC reluctantly, hauled out the wounded man without tenderness, and stood beneath the trees, sheltered from the worst of the weather, looking up at him in a murderous little knot of faces. He almost abandoned his plan to take the uniform of the man nearest him in build—but he knew he had to disguise himself if he was to drive the APC the rest of the way.

The man did it, shivering with rage and cold as he stripped to his underwear, then donned Vorontsyev's sweaters and anorak and slacks. He seemed to hate the still-warm clothes, but he was forced by the temperature to put them on quickly. Vorontsyev bundled the uniform into the cab, jumped in shaking with cold, and drove off. He drove until the wind and temperature made it difficult to hold the wheel or use the gears—then he stopped, dressed in the chilly uniform, and swigged from the vodka in the first-aid kit.

Gradually, warmth returned. He had abandoned the men at least three miles from the nearest dwelling. They wouldn't die, but it would be a long time before they could describe what had happened.

He drove on, ten miles still from Khabarovsk, having covered nearly eighteen miles of country tracks and lanes. It was already beginning to grow dark with evening rather than storm.

He picked up the first of the roadblocks in the gleam of the headlights, only yards ahead of him. He had skirted Khabarovsk as best he could, keeping to the east of the town, but eventually, after three hours, he had had to join one of the main roads, which would take him through the outer suburbs to cross the river. He wanted to be south-east of Khabarovsk, and time was running out.

The roadblock was thrown across the approach to the bridge, a red-and-white pole, bollards to close the traffic flow down to a single lane, armed soldiers. He slowed behind the cars ahead of him as the brake lights went on, glaring in the falling sleet. He put out the cigarette, adjusted his uniform to some impression of tidiness, and waited to creep forward, or for them to come to him. He tried to shake off the narcosis of the journey. He had thought about nothing, made no plans beyond getting to the destination he had decided upon—even when he began running it had been there, a means of escape more like a child's dream than a plan. But, it had settled itself, apparently, and he had made no conscious effort to rid himself of it.

As the soldier marched down the little rank of waiting cars, he realised the mistake he had made. The sleet shifted aside for a moment, and he could see an army truck up ahead, in another lane. He had ignored the sign he had passed a hundred yards back redirecting priority traffic—which meant any army vehicle. Quickly, he wound down the window.

The cold flowed in, sleet peppered his face. The soldier looked up at him. He believed, in that moment, that they knew who he was—even though the chances of the soldiers

262

he had abandoned getting to a telephone had been almost zero. They might, might just have run into another army unit—

"What the hell's the matter with you?" the guard asked, his face old and flat under the helmet. "Can't any of you buggers read?"

"Sorry—" Vorontsyev murmured, thickening his Muscovite accent, not able to trust himself to assume another way of speaking; he made himself more stupid, uneducated. "Nearly asleep—been driving this bloody thing for hours."

"Papers?" The guard held up his hand lazily. He didn't want to listen to anyone else, had his own grouses about being on duty so long his feet had gone numb and his back ached.

Vorontsyev handed over the papers as nonchalantly as he could; sensing a situation developing even as the heavy mittened hand took them, flicked a torch on them. Perhaps it was the click of the officer's boots coming down the line, or the fact that the car ahead of him pulled away, its boot having been slammed down after a perfunctory search.

"Where's the bloody picture, then?" The guard held out the ID papers. "And your movement orders—in the cab?"

"Picture fell out," Vorontsyev mumbled, looking sheepish.

"Sent it to some tart, I expect."

Nothing, nothing yet—

"What's going on here, Boris?" the officer said, and Vorontsyev saw the soldier wince at the use of his first name by the younger officer.

"Nothing much, sir. Silly bugger—sorry, sir—this man pulled up in the civilian queue—and he's lost the picture in his ID card."

"Has he? You, where's your picture? Have you reported this to your officer?"

"Sir—he said he had more important things to worry about."

"Mm. From Moscow, are you?"

"Sir."

"All as thick as cowpats, they are, sir," Boris offered, obscurely in league with Vorontsyev now that the officer was present.

263

"It says here you're from Tallinn."

"Lived in Moscow for years, sir. Mother's from Tallinn—"

"Bloody conscripts for you," Boris murmured helpfully.

"Why are you driving around on your own. Where's your officer, the rest of the platoon?" the officer snapped, then strolled to the back of the APC. As Vorontsyev leaned out of the cab to answer, Boris winked up at him. The officer glanced into the back of the vehicle.

The blood—there had to be blood—

A car horn hooted at the delay caused by the APC. Vorontsyev saw the young officer's back straighten, his attention fixed on the offending driver.

"You watch this," Boris muttered, grinning and showing bad, stained teeth. Vorontsyev could smell the tobacco on his breath. "All bullshit, he is. Don't worry, mate—he won't keep you long now."

The driver of the car behind had wound down his window. The officer was half-swallowed by the interior of the car, his words muffled as he remonstrated with the driver, his tone evident. Then he re-emerged from the car, and it pulled meekly over to the side of the road. The officer strode back towards the APC's cab, Vorontsyev's papers in his hand.

"You—why are you alone?" he snapped, his face red with outrage and cold.

"Sir? This is going to the depot for repairs—new gearbox needed, seems like. I was detailed to take it."

"Then you're not—?" The officer was confused.

"Not what, sir?"

"Never mind. Oh, get on with it—get moving. Boris, come with me!"

As Vorontsyev wound up the window again, Boris winked again, then swaggered off briskly behind the officer, towards the hapless driver who had expressed his impatience.

Vorontsyev felt weak, and grateful that he had been able to sit through the last few minues. It was an effort to depress the clutch, get the APC into gear, pull forward to the pole. It went up, out of his view, and he was through and onto the bridge across the Amur. He dared not look in the rear-view mirror, nor the side-mirror. He sat as if there was nothing behind, only the rutted slush on the bridge. As he pulled off the other side of the span, he slumped more in his seat, tried to relax, to pretend that his weakness, his quivering arms and legs, was due to tiredness and not fear.

The track lay below him, gleaming icily in the moonlight, the white, snowbound fields spreading away below the steep, inclined embankment the tracks followed. It was ten o'clock. The storm had lasted until only an hour earlier, and then had been brushed aside by the mounting wind which now swept the last rags of high cloud across the night and howled across the expanse of lower land between the eastern hills and Khabarovsk.

Vorontsyev lay in the shelter of a rock ledge which overlooked the main line between Khabarovsk and Vladivostok. It had been his destination all that day, since the killings in Nikoleyev certainly.

He had abandoned the APC in a steep-sided gully, beneath dark trees. It had ploughed into a snowdrift below, wheels spinning, engine racing. Then it had collapsed on one side, like something dying, and then the engine stopped. Silence.

That had been six miles and three hours before. He had struggled across open country, the snow deepening as he followed the lines of hedges and walls, and passed from clump to clump of thin trees as best he could. He had stayed away from all roads, all traffic. The flask of vodka from the APC was almost empty.

He was chilled to the bone, even the uniform fatigues hopelessly thin and useless now. His feet, he thought, must be frostbitten, and there was little feeling in his hands. His face, where he had been unable to keep it masked by his hood, he had rubbed periodically, feeling the flesh deadening as he walked or rested, the wind-chill removing all feeling.

Clumsily, he unscrewed the stopper on the flask, and poured the last of the vodka into him, burning his throat. He felt it like a dribble of molten metal, thin and scalding, tracing its way to his stomach. Then, as if a light going out, its effect dissipated and was gone. He shivered. If the train did not come soon, then he would be asleep and dying as he crouched there.

He kept himself wakeful, at least fitfully so, by concentrating his feelings on two objects—Ossipov and his own wife. It generated a mental life, to swing now between

265

what had become opposite poles of experience. He did not consider that he might have falsified either or both of them. They became devil and angel to him, and the dynamism of his responses kept his mind alive, and his body less insistent to succumb to the cold.

Khabarovsk was a minefield for him; he had known that from the beginning. He had to get to Vladivostok, and to the KGB Resident there. He had to communicate with Moscow, because what he knew about Ossipov, and the fact of his escape, thus far, meant that whatever was going on—and it was the invasion of Finland—would be moved forward. As would the coup, if that was intended, as it had to be, to coincide with the invasion.

He began to despair—not of his escape, but of its being a trigger. They had no idea, in Moscow, just as he had no idea, who was involved, which of the High Command, if not all, and which of the Politburo and the Central Committee and the Secretariat. They were no nearer arrests, or prevention, than before he arrived in Khabarovsk.

How could they get Ossipov or one of his senior officers into a KGB office, and make him talk? Impossible.

He made himself not think about the larger perspective. His survival depended on the importance of what he had discovered, not its limitations. He *had* to live, to get to Vladivostok, and perhaps then to Moscow. What he knew was priceless.

He thought of his wife. He would have to call her, when he got to Vladivostok. He would have to tell her he was safe.

The deep bellow of the train hooter reached him through thoughts becoming foggy. He roused himself. It was hatred that was required, not love. In thinking of his wife, he had been betrayed almost to sleep. He tried to stand, staggered against the rock, and began to pummel frantically at the weary, numb legs. He beat his fists against them, and that action seemed clumsy and ineffectual. He almost wailed with anguish at the thought of failing to get on the train.

He hobbled out of shelter, into the force of the wind which pushed him backwards. He raised his hands as if to ward off physical blows, and forced himself to place one stiff leg before the other, bending his body as if approaching an assailant.

The hooter of the train roared again, its noise loud even above the wind. A couple of miles further up the track, the line branched south and entered the Khakhtsir Mountains. The train would be slower there, but it would have been impossible for him to have reached them.

He scrabbled down the slope, his feet numb brakes which seemed unable to stop him. He jolted his elbow, then he was brought up jarringly short by the packed, snow-covered gravel lining the track. The cutting was very narrow. He heard the train labouring, and looked down the track. Great gouts of steam billowed against the black sky. He pressed back against the wall of the cutting, the one tiny outcrop of rock that lifted above the level of the country, and which had given him shelter. He began to run, to force his legs to move, as if he were being pursued by the train.

He was out of the cutting, struggling up the embankment, a couple of hundred yards ahead of the train. Its noise now drowned the wind. He lowered himself down the embankment until his head was below the level of the tracks. The huge engine crashed past him, pistons churning as it laboured up the slope. He stood up. It was unlikely that anyone on the train would see him, not from the high windows of the carriages. He began to run alongside the train. He forced his legs to move, trundling forward in a hideously slow jog, stumbling more than once and almost losing his footing. The carriages slid past him, accelerating away from him because of the labours of the huge locomotive. Patterns, squares of light gleamed over him, slid on, gleamed, slid on—each one marking the passage of a window. Too quick. He wondered how many windows to a carriage.

Then, suddenly, he was laughing. He lifted his head, and remembered the childhood hobby that had brought this train to mind. If he had *dreamed*, then, staring at the picture books, that he would one day run for his life alongside the great Trans-Siberian Express, trying to board it . . .

It was a fulfilment. He drove on, counting now the moments it took for each carriage to pass, and looking back to check down the remaining length of the train. The guard's van, last carriage. Observation platform, or hand rails. He had to board this train.

He was sheltered from the bitter wind by the bulk of

the express. He ran on, his speed, untiring now, nowhere matching that of the labouring train, but making the difference of speed more acceptable, less deadly.

The last carriage still took him by surprise. The corner of an eye, and moonlight and a snowbound field—he swore he could see them *behind* the train—and then he leaned into the train, grabbing for the handrails at the side of the guard's van. His arms seemed wrenched from their sockets, and his strides leaped out until they were great lunar bounds, then one foot on the step, then the other.

He was clinging to the side of the Trans-Siberian Express, like someone in a film, and he wanted to laugh because he was certain that somewhere down there on the track his child-self had watched it all, laughing with glee, and clapping hands and wanting to imitate the man he had become.

He stepped up onto the narrow observation platform. It was only then that he understood that a steam engine would no longer be used on the Trans-Siberian, and that the last carriage would not be the guard's van, but an observation coach. He wasn't on the Trans-Siberian at all. He laughed, loudly and almost hysterically. He had saved his life only because of a fantasy. It wasn't real. This was just a local train. Even the timetable he had scrupulously dredged out of the past was out of date, and no longer applied. Which was why the train had been late. It was the wrong train.

He sobered, realising how near to some kind of frozen death he must have been during the last hour.

He gripped the handle of the door, almost wrenching the Makarov free of the shoulder holster. He had abandoned the AK-47 in his rush for the train. Which train? He opened the door, stepped inside, and closed it behind him with a bang.

The guard was a little man, perhaps nearly sixty, with grey hair plastered across a bald dome. He was sitting with his uniform jacket unbuttoned, the tiny room foggy and heady with the heating. A mug of tea was raised to his lips. When he saw Vorontsyev, and the gun, his eyes widened helplessly, and the mug quivered in his grip. Some of the dark tea slopped onto the grimy wooden table.

"Where is this train going?" Vorontsyev asked. It

seemed the most important question at that moment, to satisfy the strange sense of disappointment he felt, as if awakening reluctantly from a pleasant dream. He shook his head as if to clear it.

The guard's mouth moved for a time without sound, then: "Night-sleeper to Nakhodka."

"Vladivostok?" He moved threateningly closer, the gun levelled at the little man's face. "Does it go to Vladivostok?" Somehow, it *had* to go there. The little man nodded, carefully putting down the mug as if aware that he might drop it. Vorontsyev sighed, and almost slumped against the wall in his relief. He felt the train speeding up, having reached the top of the incline. "When?" he asked, more gently; tiredly. "When do we arrive?"

"Four in the morning." The little man could cope with that kind of enquiry.

"Good." Vorontsyev sat down in a hard chair, on the other side of the unvarnished wooden table from the guard. He reached into his pocket, and took out his wallet. Flipping it open, he passed it to the guard. Vorontsyev could already feel the skin on his face pricking with returning feeling, and the numb feet hurting as if thrust into a fire.

The guard looked up from his inspection of the ID card. For him, all was satisfactorily explained. A KGB officer had boarded his train. It was not permitted to ask why, or to question the peculiar method of boarding. Or the army uniform. His face was smoothed to indicate attentiveness, and efficiency. He said, "What can I do, Major?"

"Is there a KGB man on the train?"

"Yes, Major. One of the stewards. Levin. Shall I fetch him?"

"In a moment." His feet and hands were burning now. He put down the gun. "Has this train been searched in Khabarovsk?" he asked.

"Yes, Major. From end to end. It is why we are late."

Vorontsyev did not bother to observe the additional luck that had come to him. He said, "Who carried out the search?"

The little man shrugged, as if indicating Vorontsyev, then when he saw him shake his head, he said, "Then they must have been army, Major. There were some in uniform."

269

"They were—looking for me," Vorontsyev said. "Are there any on the train—any *late* passengers?"

The guard looked puzzled, and frightened. He glanced at the ID card in the wallet, then swallowed. He said, "There were a few—all men."

"Very well. You will do as *I* say. You know enough to know what SID is?" The guard nodded. "Then I need say no more to you, comrade. The people who searched the train are—*traitors*. Naturally." He watched the guard glancing over his dishevelled clothes, then at the ID card again. Then the little man nodded.

"You would like some tea, Major?"

"Yes. Then fetch this Levin. I have orders for him."

His eyes felt heavy. The man bustled to pour tea, cleaning a mug with his woollen slipover, out of politeness, deference. Then he sugared it well, and placed it before Vorontsyev. Vorontsyev nodded his thanks.

When the little man was at the door, to run his errand, he said, "When does the Trans-Siberian cover this stretch of track?"

The guard appeared surprised. He said: "Two days' time, Major."

Behind him, as he closed the door, Vorontsyev was laughing helplessly.

A postal van, drab and windowless, met the train at Vladivostok, usurping the normal mail-collection. It drove onto the platform, and its open doors masked Vorontsyev's passage into its rear compartment from the guard's van. Inside was the Resident, Svobodny, and two other armed KGB men—one of them seated next to the driver —and a doctor. Even as the van drove furiously out of the station, the doctor began to attend to Vorontsyev's frostbitten fingers and toes.

Vorontsyev felt stretched, worn—he had had a couple of hours of uneasy sleep on the train which had not refreshed him; he was unable to consider the fate of his fingers and toes. It didn't seem to matter, especially when the Resident, without expression on his flat, Mongol features, said, "What the hell is going on, Major Vorontsyev? I have to pick you up from the rear of a train, just after getting a Blue Call from Moscow Centre!"

"You what?" Vorontsyev was on the point of asking

270

about the secure channel to Moscow, and Aeroflot flights. Now, with a sick wrench that might have been hunger, he sensed that his questions no longer mattered.

"Yes—Blue Call. That's stand by to destroy all records, and make your own way out. It's never been used *inside* the Soviet Union before, has it?" Svobodny was frightened, and bemused. He had come to collect Vorontsyev personally in order to find answers, allay fears. But Vorontsyev's face indicated ignorance, and shock.

"I know what it means," Vorontsyev murmured. Then he asked, very slowly, "When was the message timed?"

Priority messages from Moscow Centre were always timed according to a code. The almost mythical Blue Call, used in normal circumstances to warn cells, units, or bases outside the Soviet Union, would be timed so that the recipient would understand the deadline of the call— the hour of maximum danger.

"06:00, on the 24th—tomorrow."

Vorontsyev slumped in his seat, so evidently that the doctor looked up from his feet, reached for his pulse. Vorontsyev brushed his hand aside.

"I'm too late—too bloody late!"

"What's the matter?" Svobodny was anxious, but almost indifferent since realising that the SID Major could provide no answers to his own fears. "We might all be too bloody late, Major!"

"I can't get to Moscow in time—I *know* what they intend doing!"

"Who?"

"The bloody army—they're going to invade Finland and Norway—I know it, and it's too bloody late to tell anyone!"

"What the hell are you talking about, Major?"

"Wait—what time is it in Moscow, now?"

Svobodny looked at his watch for an interminable time; Vorontsyev could almost see the wheels and cogs in the gold case moving, and imagine them moving in Svobodny's head. It didn't seem to matter to the man, or was too difficult for him.

"Four in the afternoon—yesterday."

"The 22nd?"

"Yes."

"Eight hours' flight—when is the first plane?"

271

"Seven."

"You're not going anywhere, Major," the doctor said, now examining Vorontsyev's left hand.

"Are you going to amputate anything?" The doctor shook his head.

"You have to rest."

"We can all do that after we're dead—seven, seven—eight hours, going backwards. I'd get to Moscow before I started, wouldn't I?" Svobodny nodded. "Three in the afternoon here, three in the morning there. I can do it —I can do it!" He moved his bandaged feet, and groaned. The doctor looked at him as if at an idiot.

"It gives a little over twenty-four hours before the deadline. What will you do with it?"

"The Blue Call concerns an attempted coup—"

"What—?"

"Listen! By the army—but I know who's behind it. It's obvious—the same men who are behind the invasion they're planning—Group of Forces North. Praporovich, Marshal Praporovich. We can get him!"

"Oh, yes," Svobodny observed. "Just like that—hands up, the Red Army."

Vorontsyev missed the evident irony. He was flexing his fingers, trying to move his toes, as if in preparation for some extreme physical effort. One thought now possessed him—that he had an answer, *some* answer which was better than ignorance, and he had to communicate it to Andropov personally.

"Use the transmitter and stay here," Svobodny said. "It's not Moscow, but there are things, to do."

"In the time that's left, you mean? No—your transmitter will be intercepted, I'm sure of that. Tell them—*you* speak to them, only what you can tell them without giving the game away. Don't attract attention. Use a low-grade code—warn them I'm coming, but don't give details." Svobodny nodded.

The engine of the car was switched off.

"We're here, Chief," the driver called back.

"Any tail?"

"No."

"Good." Svobodny looked at Vorontsyev. "So, the world's falling round our ears—I'll get you a ticket, and get on the radio."

As he limped out of the back of the van across the courtyard behind the KGB building, Vorontsyev thought—they must think I'm dead of the cold by now. They must think I'm dead.

By six-thirty he was at Vladivostok Airport, looking out over the windy tarmac to the Aeroflot Tupolev Tu-154 which would take him to Moscow. He was dressed in a dark woollen suit borrowed from one of the KGB staff, and a heavy overcoat. He carried a briefcase, and some luggage had been sent onto the plane ahead of him to further enhance the cover he possessed as a civil servant in the Bureau for Industry and Construction. His new name was Tallinn. He would be met at Cheremetievo by an armed escort, and taken straight to Andropov's office.

If Kapustin understood the simple code.

He had become more and more confident that by now Ossipov and his staff would consider him dead. No one outside the KGB knew otherwise. Levin and the guard had been removed from the train before it left Vladivostok —no one could ask them questions. Before the mistake could be discovered, he would be in Moscow.

He knew he should not call his wife.

He walked slowly, getting used to the unaccustomed stick, his feet aching and his gloved hands sore and prickly, towards the telephone booths. Eight hours, and he could call her from Moscow. Eight hours, and Svobodny could tell her.

He barely understood the compulsion, or why the compulsion made the risk seem minimal. It had to do with almost dying as he waited for the train, and the narrow mental life, almost obsessional, of those hours. And it had to do with the burden of knowledge he carried, the sense of isolation that it gave him. He had to talk to her. Whatever—she had to be told *now* that he was safe.

Or perhaps he required her comfort now, because it had been unavailable earlier. He dialled the operator, using a pen in his gloved hand, and asked for the hotel in Khabarovsk. She would be there; eagerness to hear her voice overrode any remaining reserve, as the line hummed and crackled with static, then buzzed with the connection.

"Madame Vorontsyevna," he said. "Room 246."

273

He waited. The operator came back.

"I'm afraid that Madame Vorontsyevna is not in her room. I'll have her paged, if you'll wait."

"Very well."

It was only after the operator had gone away again, and he could distantly hear the tiny noises of the switchboard, a mumbled voice, then the tannoy call for Natalia, that he realised how long it was taking. A minute to make the connection with the room—now how long to find her?

He should ring off—just in case. Then he heard her.

"Alexei! Alexei! Thank God you're safe! Where are you?"

She seemed breathless, but he could not be sure. Then his mind stopped investigating her.

"Never mind. I'm all right. I called to tell you I'm all right."

"I was so worried—!" she said, her voice thick with emotion. It warmed him, yet he looked at his watch. Six forty-seven. In a few moments, they would be calling his flight. She could probably hear the sounds of an airport coming down the connection—stop it, stop it! he pleaded with himself.

"It's all right, darling. It's all right. Look, I'll be in touch. Don't worry—it's all right now."

"Alexei—where are you, darling? *Where are you?*"

And there was no mistaking the imperative in the voice. Someone behind her had shaken his head. The trace was not completed, despite the fact that they would be working back through the Vladivostok exchange. She was being encouraged by a waved hand and an imploring face to keep the conversation going. He knew that. He did not know or care how he knew it—but he did. Just as certainly as he knew that she was helping whoever it was voluntarily. She was not being coerced.

As a last chance, he said, "Can you talk freely?" And he prayed that she would give the right answer.

She said, "Of course, darling. What's the matter with you? Where are you, Alexei? I'll come right away!"

He prayed for control over his voice.

"Sorry, darling—must go now. I'll be in touch soon!"

He slammed down the receiver. When he took his hand away from it, it was quivering. There was perspiration on his forehead, and he wiped it angrily, miserably away.

They knew he was speaking from Vladivostok, but they hadn't completed the trace. He looked at his watch. Six fifty. They were calling the flight, he realised. He settled the briefcase under his arm, adjusted the stick, began to walk.

He tried very hard not to understand that his wife was working for Ossipov, and the people who had tried to kill him. And behind that fact, there was another terrible possibility, which he could more easily bury—because he simply had no desire to entertain it.

But—boarding a plane? he thought as he crossed the chilly tarmac slowly. *To give the service twenty-four hours to round up the army?* His wife's final infidelity dragged at his purpose, tried to diminish and ridicule it; told him to turn round, give himself up, or get away with Svobodny and his team. Stupid, *stupid—*

The steward at the door of the Tupolev noticed how white and upset Mr. Tallinn looked as he boarded the plane for Moscow. His eyes were unduly wet, too, for someone who had merely walked across the tarmac in the wind.

THIRTEEN
THE COURIERS

The passengers boarding the Moscow flight travelled from the terminal building across the windy stretch of tarmac to the Tupolev accompanied by a military truck. There were four soldiers with Kalashnikovs thrust upright from between their knees, and three officers in fur hats and great-coats. In the distance, Vorontsyev could see the olive-green and drab brown vehicles and knots of men that signified the military presence at Khabarovsk Airport. The Moscow flight from Vladivostok had landed at Khabarovsk, a scheduled stop of twenty minutes, less than an hour after taking off. It was a return to the hub of the search for him that Vorontsyev could not avoid.

With the tension mounting within him, he involuntarily fingered the papers in his pocket that declared him to be Tallinn, and a member of the Secretariat. They were good papers, since they were KGB, but the passport photograph on his identity visa—which he had to use for internal air travel—was a hasty affair. And it looked too hastily affixed to the ID card. The other papers would pass inspection.

He wondered who amidst the cold little huddle of passengers climbing the gangway had been detailed by Ossipov to travel on this flight—or had Ossipov decided that a search would be sufficient? He hoped so.

Vorontsyev was travelling first class, as befitted a civil servant visiting the Soviet Far East on state business.

There were only a handful of fellow-passengers, including one KGB officer from Vladivostok—a tough, capable looking individual with a broad stomach and a bandy-legged walk—loaned to him for his protection by Svobodny. The man had boarded the plane separately, and gave no sign that he was in any way connected with Vorontsyev.

Vorontsyev turned. The man was looking out of his window, studying the ascending passengers. His only real concern would be with anyone who was to travel first class.

Then the great-coated officer, a colonel, pushed aside the curtain from second class, nodded as the passengers, with one accord, looked up into his face, and said, "My apologies for any delay and inconvenience, comrades. An inspection of documents is necessary. If you please."

He was a tall man, his thin face reddened with the wind, then the abrupt change of temperature inside the Tupolev. His eyes were grey, and keen. He waited to be obeyed.

Slowly he moved down the narrow aisle, checking each passenger's papers. He was methodical, and scrutinised photographs carefully, comparing them with faces. Once or twice, he held papers up to the light, as if looking for some watermark of authenticity. Vorontsyev, watching him as unobtrusively as he could, did not see him make any comparisons with a photograph he might have possessed. Perhaps Natalia—he remembered her perfidy with a sick lurch of the stomach—had no picture of him. Perhaps there was only a spoken description.

His hair was tinged with silver at the temples, and he had acquired some padding in his cheeks so he appeared fatter-featured. It was a hurried and partial job—Svobodny had clicked tongue against teeth in disparagement at the effect—but it might just defeat a spoken description of an apparently younger man.

The Colonel stood at his side, his hand extended. Vorontsyev passed him the small bundle of documents with an assumed confidence. From the second class compartment, masked by the curtain, came the sound of stifled argument. An irregularity. For some reason, it steadied Vorontsyev. The Colonel looked over his shoulder, momentarily distracted.

It seemed an age until the papers were handed back. The Colonel tipped his fur hat with his gloves, and clicked his heels.

"Thank you, Comrade Tallinn. A pleasant flight."

Vorontsyev was the last passenger in first class to have his papers scrutinised. The soldier turned on his heel, and clicked back through the curtain. Vorontsyev breathed deeply, and returned his attention to the window. After a few minutes, he saw the detachment of soldiers climb back aboard the truck, which pulled away from the aircraft, followed by the passenger gangway and the bus.

No one had entered the first class compartment. Vorontsyev could hardly believe his luck. The "No Smoking" notice flicked on at the end of the compartment, and the voice of the steward instructed him to fasten his seat belt. He did so, amused at the quiver in his hands; a record of a past tremor. It was over now. He settled back in his seat as the Tupolev turned out of the taxiway onto the long runway.

The steward entered the first class only minutes after the Tupolev had reached its cruising height and speed, taking orders for drinks and breakfast. Vorontsyev decided at first against a drink, then relented and ordered whisky rather than vodka, but no food. He could not feel hungry, even though the steward had hovered at his elbow until he ordered at least a drink. He had again succumbed to the sapping imagery of Natalia's betrayal.

The steward went away. Vorontsyev, as if for distraction, glanced behind him at the KGB man. He was apparently sleeping, head lolling on the shoulder of a good-looking girl, who appeared reluctant to enjoy the experience, reluctant to move the greasy-haired head. As if she knew the man's occupation. Probably she had seen the ID card.

Natalia. The betrayal went to his loins, to his head; touches of hands and lips, but now cold, revolting. He felt sick, and cursed the feverish imagination she had always encouraged whenever he thought about her. It was not time now to fall to pieces, to dissolve like a snowman into the comfortable seat. He had to be strong, he told himself, tears pricking behind his eyes, and his nose seeming to run. He sniffed like a child, loudly.

He could not believe they had forced her to do it. That was the trouble. He knew she had agreed, that she had only come with him to watch him, to—distract him. He could see her, vividly naked, even when he opened his eyes and

278

tried to concentrate on the dazzle of sunlight off the cloudbase below the wing. Her arms out to him.

He hated, too, the thought that someone else, other than her, knew him well enough to exploit his weakness, his stupid, pleading, childish desire for her. That, perhaps, since all things seemed to return to himself, more than anything; that he was *known,* and his weaknesses were sufficiently understood to make him a tool, a pawn, in someone's operations.

He coughed, the bile of anguish in the back of his throat choking him. More than anything, the *impotence*—the lack of secrecy about his deep self.

The steward proffered the whisky on his tray—soda in a tiny bottle. He looked up in surprise, then seemed to come to himself, and nodded. He wanted the drink now. The steward smiled, the tray with its ringed white cloth waiting for his money. He pulled out his wallet, then, clumsily, fitted the glass into the socket attached to his seat. Then he juggled the bottle from hand to hand, trying at the same time to open his wallet on his lap. He fumbled for money, as if he had just been awoken from sleep, and saw his SID identity card staring up at him. He looked up at the steward, hastily closing the wallet, a ten rouble note gripped in his free hand.

The steward had noticed nothing. The suspicious quality in his behaviour was that there was no flicker of increased deference in his manner. Simply the bland, smiling features of a young man who saw nothing. Vorontsyev passed him the money, and raised the glass to his lips. Then things happened confusingly, and his only impression was of the steward being elbowed aside and his lap getting wet as the whisky was spilled. He leaned out in his seat. The steward was on the floor, and a heavy body was astride his, a gun—a big Stechkin—was at the steward's temple.

"What's going on?" Vorontsyev asked, standing up, wiping foolishly at the wet lap of his suit.

"This little bastard put something in your whisky, comrade. I was going to tell you after he went—but you couldn't wait for your reviver!" There was a certain contempt in the voice, as well as delight at the KGB man's own prowess.

"In the drink?" Vorontsyev asked stupidly. He looked

279

round at the other passengers, all of whom were moving out of shock into calculated lack of attention. Except the girl. She seemed relieved that the KGB man had left his seat. With a delicate but angry movement, she wiped at the shoulder of her coat where his head had rested. Vorontsyev returned his attention to the tableau in the aisle.

The KGB man had dragged himself and the steward up-right—then he pushed the slight figure in the white uniform jacket into an empty seat. The Stechkin was again thrust against the temple. Vorontsyev, studying the steward for the first time, could see an evident fear, and behind it something that appeared like confidence. It was as if he had the gun, or he were protected by the kind of power and organisation the KGB man had on his side. Puzzling.

"What was it?" the KGB man asked in a harsh voice. The steward said nothing. The KGB man slapped him across the face, then forced his head back with the barrel of the gun, and roughly searched the steward's pockets. The steward did not resist, but even when the KGB man held up a small phial, empty, in his big hand, the steward showed no fear, no terror of discovery. "What's this?"

The steward did not reply.

"You know who I am?" Vorontsyev said quietly, and the deference that had been missing seemed automatically to reappear in the other KGB man. The steward stared at him unblinkingly.

"Answer the Major!" the KGB man snapped. Silence.

"Who are you?" Vorontsyev asked.

"Boris Vassiliev—a steward, as you see." Something had happened to the steward; the deference that was part of his function seemed to have been removed by the surprise with which he had been assaulted, discovered. But nothing else had gone, in the face of the gun and the threats. Now he tried to reassume the mask of ordinariness it fitted incompletely, letting the strong personality they had already seen glance out.

"Who gave you the order to dope my drink? It was lethal, I take it?" Vorontsyev was fascinated now. There was no reaction to the attempt on his life—shock or hate or anger. Just the aroused, challenged curiosity. "Who gave you the order? Is that why no one boarded the plane, because you were here already?"

"Answer the Major!" The gun pressed beneath the jaw. The face distorted, but only because of the pressure. Still was there no real, shaken fear.

Ideas tumbled through Vorontsyev's head. He needed a shape to contain them, a process to undergo.

"Watch him," he said. "Don't hurt him—yet." Then he walked forward, towards the galley and the door to the flight-deck.

As he opened the door, the flight-engineer, sitting side-on to him and to the rear of the two pilots, glanced up, and said, "Please return to your seat at once."

Vorontsyev showed him the ID card. The flight-engineer studied it suspiciously, then spoke into his microphone.

"Captain—Major Vorontsyev, SID, would like to speak to you . . . ?" Vorontsyev nodded. "Now, I think."

"Take control, Pavel," the captain said to his second officer, and then released the control column. He took off his headset, and squeezed past the second officer, to confront Vorontsyev. He seemed surprised at the man's youth, being probably fifty, Vorontsyev estimated. A bulky, solid individual, still in command on his own flight-deck.

Vorontsyev said as they confronted one another, "Captain, what do you know about your steward. Vassiliev?"

Immediately, the captain appeared puzzled. His mouth opened, and even the flight-engineer, looking up at them like a wondering child, smiled at the question.

"Know about him?" the captain said. "The little—he's one of yours, KGB!" He seemed unwilling, even defiant, about concealing his dislike of Vorontsyev.

"He's not," Vorontsyev said. "I would have known that. The officer from Vladivostok travelling with me would certainly have known it. Why do you believe it?"

"He has the proper authority, Major," the captain said stiffly, as if his dignity had been afforted. "I have flown with Vassiliev on board a number of times. He has always presented himself to me as KGB Airline Security."

Vorontsyev nodded. "Thank you, captain. You may leave the matter in my hands. How soon before we can talk direct to Moscow?"

The pilot appeared puzzled.

"A matter of hours yet, I'm afraid. However, anything you wish can be relayed ahead of us . . ."

"Thank you for your cooperation. Tell me, you say that Vassiliev has travelled with you many times. He is your regular steward, then?"

"Not really. It doesn't work like that. We draw from a pool of available stewards and stewardesses, for internal flights. They're always changing flights and journeys with one another—proper little capitalist enterprise, Major!" There was a smile in the blue eyes, and round the mouth. "They very much suit themselves—especially the ones who are in your organisation. They fly where they want, and when they want."

"I see. But Vassiliev flies this route regularly?"

"Quite often. When I come aboard, I don't expect to see the same faces. But his—yes, quite often."

"You always thought him—one of us?"

"Yes—his arrogance." The pilot was cool, even amused. Vorontsyev smiled, and saw in his mind the face of the young steward. Yes, he could be KGB. Certainly not a steward.

Working for Ossipov—travelling all over the Soviet Union. Not frightened by the KGB, even masquerading as a KGB man. Pleasing himself which destination—changing his travelling arrangements at the last moment, perhaps.

Vorontsyev was quivering with excitement. He knew what he had caught.

"Leave—this matter in my hands, captain." He had to make him talk—had to! "Captain, I must ask you to descend to a level where the pressurised cabin is not needed!"

"Must you, hell!"

"That is an order! Disobedience to that order may be construed as treason!" Vorontsyev was in no mood to trifle, to bargain or persuade. His face was grim with determination. He would not need to touch the gun in his holster. He knew the power of SID, even on people like this experienced pilot.

It was a moment only. Then the pilot, with ill grace in his voice and impotent, angry contempt in his eyes, said, "Very well. What are you going to do, throw the little sod out?"

"Threaten to. You understand, captain. This aircraft is effectively under the control of an officer in the SID. I shall not interfere, more than is necessary, with your

282

flight-plan or your authority. But I *must* have your complete cooperation!"

"Very well," he replied surlily. "Very well, Major Vorontsyev." He leaned to speak into the flight-engineer's microphone. "Pavel, descend slowly to flight level seven-zero. And tell no one." Then he straightened up. "Will that do you? Seven thousand feet. It will be bloody cold, so don't leave the door open too long, will you?" There was an acid humour in the voice, the truculence of forced assistance.

"Thank you, captain. And keep her steady, would you? I have no wish to fall out somewhere over Siberia!"

He closed the door behind him, the jubilation of the humour of his last words bubbling in him. He had the answer, a mouthpiece now, if only he could force it to speak.

A courier.

The missing piece of the puzzle; *the communications network.*

Using the resources of Aeroflot, the network of the internal airline services, to transmit their messages—from Moscow to the Far East and who knew where else— by jet airliner; by stewards who rendered themselves virtually secure from interference by posing as members of the KGB. It would work, too. He stood looking into the first class for a moment, as the thoughts resolved themselves. He could feel the airliner descending, not rapidly enough to arouse the passengers—but descending.

The couriers would know to whom they spoke—they would even know the man or men behind *Group 1917* and *Finland Station.* He had an almost physical longing to shake the information from the steward, now seated upright, the KGB man alongside him, the gun evident between them. The other passengers were consciously inattentive.

Messages transmitted by word of mouth, within hours. Simple, and effective. If there was a KGB man on the flight, Vassiliev—and the others, for there had to be others; *twenty, thirty, how many?*—would simply not reveal his assumed authority. If not, and always as far as the flight crew were concerned, he was KGB. Who would think to check?

"Bring him!" he snapped.

The KGB man hauled Vassiliev out of his seat, and prodded him along the aisle until all three of them were jammed into the tiny galley. Vorontsyev could smell rank sweat. It was the KGB man, not Vassiliev. He glared into the confident young face—no, there was an ashen tinge to the cheeks now that they were so close to him, or now he was alone with them.

"Listen to me, Boris Vassiliev. I know what you are." The steward still appeared confident. He straightened his tie. "I know about *Group 1917* and *Finland Station*. Which is why you had to kill me. But I know what you are, and I'm going to know what you know. You are a *courier* from the top men . . ." The eyes bolted, as if seeking escape. The KGB man, as if on cue from Vorontsyev, thrust the gun into Vassiliev's back. The steward gasped.

"You see? I know, and I want to know what you know. Everything. As no doubt you will have noticed, the aircraft is descending. When it has done so, I will open the passenger-hatch opposite us . . ." He watched the steward's eyes stray towards the locked hatch; it was a movement the man could not control. "And if you don't then tell me everything I wish to know—I shall throw you out!"

The barely furnished room was icy cold, even in the middle of the afternoon. He had removed only one glove in order to dial without making a mistake in the number. The telephone had been freed of bugs; it was the first of his secure lines, in a flat in a northern workers' suburb, part of a grey block of cement with tiny, slitted windows.

His breath smoked in the room. He sat at a rickety table which was smeared with the marks of mugs and plates, and gritty with sugar, on one of the two upright chairs that constituted the remaining furniture. It was an apartment that was officially occupied, but in fact had been empty for some weeks, and the superintendent of the block of flats had kept it so at his instruction.

Kutuzov was there to make one telephone call. He had travelled by metro from his house, smug in the confirmation that even now, with Andropov and the KGB so desperate and short of time, he was not being followed. Naturally, he had planned that it would be so; but the relief was still very real, and the sense of success—omen of greater success—warming as he had ridden the metro.

His finger was icy. He dialled the number—only he possessed it. The central switchboard at Moscow Military District HQ outside the city would register the number, and the call would be diverted to Valenkov, commandant of the Moscow Garrison regiments. Moscow Garrison was cut off from the outside world—but it would accept his call.

Finger numb—he fumbled the glove back onto his thick hand, the telephone tucked between cheek and shoulder. He wanted action, quick, vivid *decision*, as he listened to the sputter and clicking of the connection. Valenkov had to be handled carefully, he told himself. Carefully—

"Good afternoon, sir." Valenkov himself, twenty years younger and knowing who must be his caller.

"Dmitri. Good afternoon. I'm still here, as you can hear." He held his breath, trying to sense telephathically the mood of the younger man. The heavy joke seemed to delay in the wire, as if too indigestible to travel down its gut.

"Yes, sir." Nothing. No commitment.

"I need cheering up, Dmitri," he tried again. "So I called you."

"Sir."

He was angry—Valenkov was behaving like a stubborn, idiot corporal. He had expected the call, since it was part of his agreement with Valenkov that he should report his safety at intervals before the final call at six on the twenty-fourth.

So that Valenkov would know he was still alive, he thought with contempt.

"Tell me again—your final decision."

"Airborne assault on the Kremlin, at oh-six hundred. Tank assault on Dzerzhinsky Street, special squads to round up the designated targets." Valenkov sounded as if he were reciting a lesson—one that bored him.

"Excellent, excellent!" *Kutuzov* enthused, watching his breath curling up to the low ceiling—seeing the ring of smoke-stain round the light-fitting—and noticing the ice forming diamonds on the windows. "How long do you estimate the whole operation will take, Dmitri?"

"Forty minutes."

"Excellent. Dmitri—?"

"Sir?"

"When it's over, promise me one thing?"

"What—would that be?"

"That you will *smile!* Show a little enthusiasm for our great enterprise."

He waited for the reply, listening almost as if he could hear the man wrestling with his conscience, hear its grunts as he twisted it to what he thought of as treasonable shape; all for him, for *Kutuzov,* he reminded himself. *He* was the talisman, the ikon.

"If you give me the word, *personally,* to move against the Kremlin the day after tomorrow—then I will smile, sir. As I have said, sir, I will make no move against the Politburo or the KGB without knowing you are safe and will assume control after the operation."

"Very well, Dmitri—!" he spluttered angrily. Then, more calmly: "Very well. You will hear from me. Good-bye, Dmitri!"

When he put down the telephone, his hand was shaking. The weight of the promise he had given Valenkov seemed heavy on him. It was as if he had promised to run far and fast, or be young once more—

He slapped his hands on his thighs, and thought of the long underwear beneath the trousers of the formal suit, looked down at the high boots he had taken to wearing since he had slipped on ice-bound Ministry steps last winter and broken an ankle. And he hated it.

He could hear his teeth grinding, in the room and inside his head, in the blank silence. Freezing outside the grimy windows, the dirty diamonds of the ice thick on the panes. He was a monarch in exile, the forgotten hero about to return.

The fictions comforted him. His surroundings were not epical, but his purpose was. And though it was linked by a piece of wire to a frightened soldier, by his very voice he could change the world. Valenkov would *obey,* when the time came.

He fiddled with a loose button on his overcoat, looking down at the garment as it swelled over his ample stomach. It had once been a hard body. Now all that was left was the hard mind, the stubborn, dedicated clinging to an ideal.

He remembered the death of Lenin—the grief of

young manhood. The great leader had never recovered from the assassination attempt by Churchill's agent. Then the years of Stalin the pig, the death of Trotsky in exile, murdered by the NKVD in the hands of the butcher-king, Beria. Socialism in one country, the filthiness of the Purges—the point of counter-revolution being reached—and the Fascist invasion saving Stalin from what he deserved at the hands of the people. Pig-Stalin had used, relied on, the greatness of the Russian people to save him while they saved their country.

And since then only the decline of force, the collapse of will. Trading with the capitalists for the trinkets, the worthless things—the Soviet Union being bought like a whore.

The rush of thoughts was like volcanic activity, or the gases of indigestion. They discomfited him, even as they filled him with a shallow rage. He could hardly control himself while the procession of his own history, the history of his country and his ideology, passed through his awareness.

Look, his hands were quivering now. He clenched them, and banged them on his thighs as if they were the witnesses of senility or imbecility. He breathed deeply, the exhalations seeming to roar in his ears in the room's silence.

Nothing could stop them—whatever had gone wrong, whatever was known—nothing could stop it.

Vorontsyev.

He *was* dangerous—though he knew nothing, knew nothing.

Frightening. Because, in the last few days, it had come down to a few old men—Ossipov, Praporovich, Dolohov, Pnin and the other generals. And a young man—*two* young men, he corrected himself. One in Helsinki, and the other flying back from the Far East.

He was thankful that Vorontsyev knew nothing about him, in no way threatened him. He knew about Ossipov's exercises, and guessed the invasion. But he did not know about the coup, and he did not know about *Kutuzov.*

He was grateful for that. He was only an old man in a dirty bare room, and feeling very old, as he did at that moment, he could not but be afraid that the young man would find him.

Which was why Vassiliev would kill him, aboard the airliner.

Thirty-nine hours seemed a very long time to wait—to hide.

"What height are we at now, Boris?" the voice asked him softly, insistently. "What does the altimeter read? Are we low enough for you to survive the fall?" And the voice chuckled in his ear, a dry, pitiless sound. Boris was even able to perceive how the menace of the voice had grown during the last—how long? And that was not the quality of the voice; it was his fear.

He was hunched in a forced, doubled position on the cold floor of the baggage compartment. His buttocks were numb already, and the cold had ascended to his stomach, his genitals. He desperately wanted to urinate. The SID officer had held him at the closed hatch opposite the galley, in first class, until he was shivering with fear—then they had blindfolded him. Down the aisle, brushing past the rough curtain, its material against his face, through second class. The click of locks, and the door closing behind them. Their breath, eagerly harsh—his own, barely controlled.

Then they had forced him to sit, dragged his arm between his knees, and the click of handcuffs, tightened so that they hurt. Then something to strap his ankles tight together. Then they had lifted him, and now he was close to the fuselage. He knew that. He thought—could not avoid thinking—he was placed close to the baggage door. If it was unlocked, folded back—it would take one small push to tumble him out over the Yablonovny Mountains, or Lake Baikal. A shudder went through him.

He had rehearsed what he knew in his own mind in the early moments, or minutes—not hours?—before the sense of his isolation pressed down on him. There was the faintly creaking silence of the baggage compartment and nothing more for a long time, before the voice began to speak to him. The handcuffs had hurt then. Now, he could not feel his hands. They might have rotted on the ends of his wrists for all he knew. His stomach churned at the thought, and he hated the weakness that allowed such ridiculous imaginings to take root.

He knew some things, but not all. What could he tell them, what keep back? If he told them, would it help *them,* or himself?

It was the blindfold, of course. And the numbing cold.

Deprivation of sense; so easy to achieve. He had lost the ability to know his surroundings, and the space around him expanded and contracted like something malleable. He could retain no firm hold on his environment. It was, at the worst moments, like falling from the plane.

They would not kill him, they would not kill him.

"You are a brave man, Boris. Many would have already broken. But not you." He clung to the voice, now at his other ear, pathetically. It told him he was not alone, that he was still in the baggage compartment. Then someone moved a heavy weight across the floor, a deep scraping noise. He twitched, as if the door had opened and the sub-zero air outside had flowed over him. "I don't think you will tell me what I want to know." He felt proud of that. "I shall dispose of you, then. You can be of no use to me."

Then, silence.

He wanted to cry out, but they had gagged him as well with an evil-tasting woollen scarf. It filled his nostrils with the smell of cheap hair-oil. He wanted to cry out—it was too late, he realised. He shook his head, then nodded it stupidly, like a moving doll, and tried to wriggle his numb limbs about. To show them he was alive.

He could not tell them, if they didn't take off the gag!

Desperately, he worked his mouth on the gag, trying to chew at it, his mouth full of the strands of wool. He couldn't get his teeth outside the great wrap of the scarf —if only he could do that. He tried to pull his arms back to his face, but he must have been tied in such a way that he wouldn't—couldn't move them . . .

His one chance lay in getting the gag off, crying out. They could not see his eyes, he could not move his arms. He could not show them how much he wanted to talk— that he did not want to die.

Someone laughed, a distance away. So disorientated was he, that it could have come from beneath him. He moaned, and could not even hear the noise he made.

Cold air—he swore it. The click of a lock—he bent his body towards the sound, straining to hear it. Then the arms round him, moving him so that he was against the bulkhead. Gratefully he pressed his head against its solidity. Then the door slid back—*he was against the door!*

The air—freezing. The wind, terrible. He screamed, and screamed. He was falling, he knew he was falling . . .

At that moment, some sensation at the back of his

289

head. The blindfold was coming off! He passed out, gratefully. He did not want to see the jagged mountains, the endless lake towards which he was falling.

Vorontsyev stood against the luggage, securely strapped except for the one chest they had used to make a noise, just before opening the hatch. He was smoking a cigarette, the feeling just returning to his hands and feet and face, despite the fact that he had worn gloves, and wrapped his scarf around his cheeks when they opened the hatch. The gale that had blown on them had terrified him, and he understood a little of what Vassiliev had undergone.

He had no pity for him; he had had to break him, and quickly. They were half-way to Moscow, possibly, and due to refuel at Novosibirsk before very long. That respite in his agony would have given Vassiliev the strength to hold out, perhaps.

Besides which, Vorontsyev knew and accepted without qualm that he was avenging his private betrayal on the steward who was also a courier. It served the man right. They had used his own wife against him.

He drew deeply on the cigarette, watching the KGB man—Tikhon—as he revived Vassiliev. The trick now was to appear friendly, reconciled. The heavy coat was loosely buttoned around Vassiliev, and the handcuffs and the strap had disappeared. There was vodka in a flask. Tikhon poured some against Vassiliev's blue lips. The man spluttered, and his eyelids echoed the movement.

Then he was staring at Vorontsyev, who smiled at him, took out his cigarette case, and offered Vassiliev a cigarette. They had moved the steward so that he was sitting on a strapped pile of luggage, Tikhon holding him almost in his arms, the vodka flask tilted towards the man's lips. It was as if two other people had come and rescued Vassiliev.

"Well, Boris?" Vorontsyev said, coming to sit beside him, so that all three sat like children on a wall, legs dangling free. Vassiliev coughed on the cigarette smoke. "Tell me about it." It was important not to mention what he had been through, or to indicate that it might recur. He would remember vividly and know.

"I—I wanted to, didn't want to . . ." Vassiliev stuttered, his eyes rolling in his head.

"I know, I know. But that is over now. Just tell me. Shall I ask you questions? Will that make it simpler?"

Vassiliev stared in silence at the closed cargo hatch, checking minutely that the locks were fully shut. He drew on the cigarette—a bout of nausea gripped him, lurching his stomach sideways. He gagged on the vomit, then lay back, the sharp edges of a case digging into his spine. When Tikhon offered him the vodka, he guzzled at the narrow neck of the flask, and the liquor burned down into his stomach.

It seemed to settle him. He sat up again, and nodded. "Yes. Ask me."

Vorontsyev knew he could not take long. Vassiliev, after his experience, would retreat progressively into a grudging silence. There would be some recovery of the will, enough to lead to lying and prevarication. The truth would come only at first.

"Who is your superior? Who recruited you? Who is behind *Group 1917?*"

Vassiliev appeared disappointed that he could not answer the question. He said: "I—don't know . . ."

"You've never met him?"

"A few times—to report directly to him."

"And?"

"It was always at night. He kept his face away from the light. Just an old man, with a dog."

"Where were these meetings?"

"Usually in the 'Field of Virgins,' near the Tolstoy statue. You know it?"

Vorontsyev nodded. He did not consider the information. He said, "What is his code-name?"

"*Kutuzov,*" Vassiliev replied, still at the point of being eager to help.

Vorontsyev smiled. "A liking for heroic figures," he commented. "So have you, no doubt. How many are there like you?"

"Perhaps thirty—no more than that."

"You will write down all the names you know, when we have finished talking. Now—Ossipov is the dry-run for the invasion, is he not?" Vassiliev nodded. Vorontsyev stifled his sigh of relief. "Who will command the invasion?"

"Praporovich himself."

Vorontsyev had known, of course. It had to be the Commander of Soviet Forces North. Nevertheless, the information was like a blow that expelled breath, left him winded. He was silent for a time, then he said, "His entire staff is involved?" Vassiliev nodded. Vorontsyev forebore to call them traitors. "What do his staff *know?*"

"Some of them have the complete picture, but most believe it is—sanctioned by the Kremlin." There was a contempt in the voice. "Dolohov is involved, too," Vassiliev offered confidingly.

"Yes, he would have to be." He lit another cigarette, then said: "When is it to happen?"

Vassiliev was silent. Vorontsyev wondered whether he was already becoming truculent, considering evasion and lies. Then: "I have been relieved of my job as a courier. It must be close."

"How are they communicating now?"

"Secure telephones."

"*Kutuzov* is in Moscow?"

"I suppose so."

"What of the coup?" It was difficult to keep the excitement from his voice.

"To coincide with the invasion of Norway and Finland. Exactly."

"*Who* is involved? *When* does it take place?"

The cold silence of the baggage-compartment seemed interminable, seemed to press upon them. Then Vassiliev said, "I do not know. It is the truth. I carried messages concerning *Finland Station*, but not the coup. I do not know how, or when."

There was hesitation in the voice, but Vorontsyev did not think he was lying. With a nauseous certainty, he knew that Andropov knew as much already as he was able to tell him—the 24th. It had to be. He forced himself to consider only the interrogation. In an attempt to enlarge the innocence of the atmosphere, so that Vassiliev might volunteer any remaining information, Vorontsyev said, "We should be at normal cruising height and speed by now—unless we are already descending to Novosibirsk."

It was the observation of a seasoned passenger, nothing more, but it affected Vassiliev. He felt an inexplicable rush of gratitude to his interrogator. He said eagerly, "There is an Englishman, in Leningrad. At the safe house. He was captured in Finland."

It was not what Vorontsyev had expected; nothing like. He drew on his cigarette, then asked, "What use would he be?"

"He spoke to *Kutuzov*, I was told."

Vorontsyev stubbed out his cigarette on the metal of the floor, and stood up. He looked at Vassiliev, then said to Tikhon, "When he has given you the names—every name he knows, take him back to first class." Tikhon nodded. Vassiliev looked grateful, and dog-like. But the eyes were staring, and tired. He would be little more use. Tikhon had already taken out a notebook, and pen, offering them to Vassiliev. The numb hands hung from the swollen wrists, apparently useless.

"He will write for you," Vorontsyev said kindly, and went out, closing the door behind him.

When he entered the flight-deck again, the captain turned his head, and scowled. Yet there was a gleam in his eyes. He evidently did not care what had happened to Vassiliev, but his dislike for Vorontsyev was unmistakable.

He said, "It's snowing in Moscow. We refuel at Novosibirsk, then fly on to Sverdlovsk. We'll hold there until it clears." He knew the information would anger Vorontsyev.

"You'll hold at Novosibirsk until I've talked to Moscow!" he snapped. "Radio ahead. I want to talk to the KGB man in the Tower. I want to arrange a secure channel to Moscow Centre."

The snow was thickening outside the window of the restaurant. *Kutuzov* had watched it throughout his meal. When he had finished his coffee and a glass of Ghorilka spertsem, Ukrainian vodka with peppers in it, he went to the telephone booth—it had been checked for security that afternoon by someone posing as a KGB telephone engineer—and dialled Valenkov. When the man came on the line, *Kutuzov* said, "What if it is snowing on the morning of the 24th, Dmitri?"

Valenkov seemed surprised, even insulted, by the question: His voice was testy as he said: "We have contingency plans for that eventuality, sir. A special airborne detachment will travel by APC to the Kremlin. A plan I personally prefer—except that you seemed always to favour the *Blitzkrieg* of airborne assault."

It was a just rebuke. *Kutuzov* laughed, and again: "Forgive me, Dmitri. I am in your hands. Goodbye."

When he came out of the booth, he was shaking with anger at himself. A stupid, nerveless old man! That was all he was becoming. All through his meal the falling snow had nagged at his stomach like indigestion.

He went back to his table. One of the GRU men in the restaurant, as his special guard, settled back in his seat as *Kutuzov* ordered another Ukrainian vodka. He felt cold. There was no word from Novosibirsk concerning Vorontsyev, who should be dead by now. He would have to make a call from secure line four later if there was no message.

He swallowed gaggingly at the peppered vodka.

Vorontsyev stared up at a street map of Novosibirsk as Kapustin, at the other end of the radio-link, digested his first bout of information. He was in the KGB duty-room at the aiport. He had never been to Novosibirsk before, the third largest town in the Soviet Union, a vast industrial complex spurred to enlarge its industrial capacity ten times after the evacuation of industry from European Russia to Siberia during the war against the Fascists.

There were more than a million people in Novosibirsk. Vorontsyev cared about none of them. The map of the city that lay to the south of the airport, divided by the River Ob, was simply a distraction. It bore no relation even to the sprawling mass of lights he had seen beneath the wing as they made their descent.

The temperature outside the plane had been minus five degrees centigrade. Mild for the time of year, milder than Moscow at that moment. Already he had been told that the weather was closing in outside the windows of Kapustin's office, where he and Andropov listened to the tinny, strange voice with its apocalyptic messages. Vorontsyev knew he would be unlikely to get into Cheremetievo or any other Moscow airport that day, or night.

He felt impotent and frustrated.

"How were these men recruited, Vorontsyev?" It was Kapustin again.

Vorontsyev felt unreasonably angry, as if his superior was simply tinkering with unimportant parts of the machine instead of ripping out its wiring, stopping it.

"My assistant was told by Vassiliev that he was an army reject—though there was no reason given at the time he applied for a commission. Then, after a time, an approach was made to him. He believes all of them were recruited in the same way—high-grade officer material rejected, then picked up for this *special* work . . ."

He was interrupted by Andropov's dry tones. He was surprised that he could catch the full acid superiority of the voice, even at this distance on a satellite radio-link.

Andropov said, "Read me the full list of names again." Vorontsyev did so, slowly, spelling out many of them. There were seventeen in all. When he had finished, he said, "What will you do now, sir?"

"Aeroflot will be informed. KGB men inflight will make immediate arrests—the others will be collected on arrival at destination. From them we will build up the complete picture."

Vorontsyev said urgently, "Sir, you don't seem to understand the urgency . . ."

"I understand, Vorontsyev. What would you have me do—order the KGB Resident in Vladivostok to go and arrest Ossipov?"

"No, sir—I simply . . ."

"What else have you for us, Vorontsyev?"

"There is an Englishman at the Leningrad safe house they've been using. He can identify *Kutuzov*—at least, he is supposed to have seen him!"

"An Englishman?"

"A soldier—sent to Finland to verify some infra-red photographs. He is, apparently, still alive."

"Then we shall have him." There was a silence, as if Andropov had turned and looked out of the window. Then: "Can we trust anyone in the Leningrad KGB? The address of the safe house is an address used by the KGB. What is your opinion?"

"I don't know, sir. It seems to be mainly GRU—Vassiliev is vague. He doesn't know very much of the whole picture."

Another silence, then: "We can't fly in a team from outside. At least, not from here. You will do it from there. Understand? I will speak to the Resident at Novosibirsk, and place you in charge. Can we trust them, do you think?"

"Again, sir—I don't know. But it's a risk we have to take . . ."

"I agree. Select a team, and brief it to take the safe house. Then catch the first available flight to Leningrad. The weather is fine there, I believe." Vorontsyev sensed the irony, even thousands of miles from the grey face, the thin lips that would have been slightly curled as the words were spoken. Someone had once called Andropov a demonic bank-clerk; Vorontsyev could not be sure now whether it was a notorious dissident or someone in SID.

He shook his head slightly, and said, "Sir, is the object to get the Englishman, or everyone we can?"

"Everyone—but the Englishman most importantly."

"What about Praporovich, sir?" He was nervous of reminding the Chairman; yet it seemed encumbent upon him. There was an arid vagueness about the conversation, akin to the atmosphere of an academic exercise.

"Yes. There is one man in Leningrad we can trust absolutely." Vorontsyev knew that would be the Department "V" operative, a man unconnected with the official hierarchy of the Resident and his staff. He would have a job, a family, a normal civilian life. The KGB assassin in Leningrad. "The man will be briefed to report to you before you take the safe house—after the *accident* has occurred."

"Sir." Vorontsyev thought, then: "Will that stop it, sir? The invasion, I mean?"

A silence, as if he had gone too far, enquired too nearly into matters beyond him. Then, as if admitting his right to know, a reward of unprecedented confidence for the man who had broken Vassiliev, Andropov said, "I do not know. Dolohov in Murmansk is a different matter. He cannot be got at so readily. However, the same kind of operation is necessary there. I—will come back to you on that, Vorontsyev. Meanwhile . . ." Andropov went on as if talking to himself. ". . . we need time, Vorontsyev, time in which to assure loyalties. We have no time left!"

"No, sir. Sir—don't you think—I mean, it has to be the Moscow Garrison, doesn't it? If they're going to make the coup effective . . ."

"I agree. What do you suggest?" Again the trace of irony, distinct as the odour of tobacco. "We arrest the whole Garrison?"

"Sorry."

"No. Your task is to get a team to Leningrad before tomorrow morning—find the Englishman, and identify *Kutuzov*. If we have him, and Praporovich and Dolohov are dead—then there will be no order for the invasion, and none for the coup. Do I make myself clear?" Andropov was without pleasantry or obligation now. Simply efficient. "*Kutuzov* is the key. We must have him!"

When he had broken the radio link, Vorontsyev sat in the swivel chair before the set for a while. In his mind he could see, quite clearly, a picture of an old man in the park known as the "Field of Virgins," walking a dog. In only one respect did the picture differ from anything conjured by Vassiliev's information. In the image in Vorontsyev's mind, the old man and the dog were accompanied by a child.

FOURTEEN
BEYOND DISCUSSION

"Just in time to catch the post office before it closes," Philipson observed to the driver, who was too dulled with the cold to reply. The observation car had been parked opposite the Central Post Office in Station Square for less than fifteen minutes, but already Philipson had to keep wiping the windscreen to clear the mist that was freezing —he rubbed now with his heavy mitten until a scratchy little patch of clear glass allowed him to check that it was Captain Ozeroff entering the glass doors of the post office.

"All units," Philipson said into the car radio, now that he was certain, "subject has just entered the post office. No one is to follow him in—I'll go. He hasn't seen me." He looked at Greaves, the driver. "Come on, old son. Let's go and see who's been writing to our friend."

The driver merely grunted. Outside the car, the wind cut instantly through Philipson's sheepskin coat, and the snow struck through his fur-lined boots. He wondered whether a centrally-heated office had made him soft, then thrust his hands into his pockets, and crossed the Mannerheimintie from the railway station, careful with his footing as he dodged the last of the home-going commuter traffic heading north to the suburbs.

He went up the steps, suddenly aware of the unfamiliar gun in the small of his back, tucked into his waistband, as if the temperature of its butt had suddenly dropped. He avoided a woman in a tent-like fur coat, then went through the revolving doors into the delusory warmth of strip-lighting in the high ceiling. It was warmer—*where was he?*

Philipson had only a vague idea of why Aubrey was interested in Captain Ozeroff of the Soviet security team at Lahtilinna. But, as surveillance jobs went, he had done a good one, in his own estimation, especially since Ozeroff had been off-duty and in Helsinki for most of the day, and surveillance of a slow-moving, undistracted subject was more difficult, and wearing. Ozeroff had been to the Ateneum Art Gallery, the Parliament building, the National and Municipal Museums, and down to the harbour in a taxi—plenty of open spaces, and plenty of confined spaces. But the surveillance, it appeared, had remained unsuspected.

Philipson had had to shuffle men, monitor everything; enjoy the organisation and be bored to tears by the passing, monotonous hours.

Ozeroff was over by the mail collection counter, talking to a grey-haired assistant, explaining in affable terms and halting Finnish—by the look of the smiles—what he wanted. Philipson sensed the little tug of excitement in his belly—something? Or nothing; the answer came like a breath of the outside air through the revolving doors. Greaves had taken up a watching position behind him, filling in some interminable form—perhaps for a Finnish driving license. Ozeroff was fifteen yards away. Philipson, pleased with himself, confident of security, moved towards Ozeroff, and stood as if forming the first of a queue behind him at the counter. He tried to appear bored—recalled the hours and the scrappy sandwich lunch, and had no difficulty in looking uninterested in the conversation.

"Your aunt—naturally. A strange name to come from Karelia," the old man behind the counter was murmuring, half to himself. "However, you have the little warrant, there is no difficulty." He turned to search in the alphabetically-labelled pigeon holes behind him. Philipson caught an impression of the edge of Ozeroff's jaw, tight with muscle, and his hand resting on the counter, hopping like a bird—suspicion, tension? Silly old bugger, Philipson thought as the old man pulled out air mail letters and inspected them carefully through his thick glasses before putting them back.

"You're not from Karelia, are you?" the old man asked conversationally, without turning round.

"From the Russian part—we had to learn Russian at school." Ozeroff was reluctant to reply. Philipson admired the story, but that small feeling was swept away as the feeling of delight overcame him. Ozeroff was here, pretending to be someone else. He concentrated on not moving, then on allowing all the tension of his frame to flow into a desultory shuffle of his feet, as if he was bored with waiting. Ozeroff did not look round.

The old man turned from the pigeon holes, and held out a letter to Ozeroff—Philipson watched as the hand came out, almost in slow-motion, to take it, then speed up as it was pocketed.

"Thank you," Ozeroff said. "She will be pleased to hear from her sister."

"A pleasure," the old man replied, staring at the breast-pocket into which the letter had gone, as if envious of it or its Russian stamps. Philipson stepped aside as Ozeroff turned away and headed for the door. The old man adjusted his glasses, put his head on one side, and was about to ask Philipson what he could do for him.

Philipson said, "Who was that letter addressed to?" The old man was taken aback. "Quickly." Philipson held out the Helsinki CID card that identified him as an Inspector, so that the old man adjusted his glasses once more, stared at the photograph that matched the face of the man in front of him, nodded a couple of times, and cleared his throat, as if he were about to utter a solemn promise of prayer.

"Ah, Inspector—a letter for the young man's aunt. I think the man is Russian, but he could be from Karelia, eh? The Russian part. Lots of people have crossed the border in the last—"

"He hasn't got an aunt from Karelia. Now—who was the letter for?" Philipson tried to be neutral, because the old man ought not to remember him too clearly, for any reason—and he was staring attentively at him now, enjoying a sense of conspiracy.

"A strange name—probably a Jew, mm?"

"How would I know—you haven't told me yet."

"Oh, sorry, Inspector. I hear myself in my head most of the time, living alone. Think I've spoken when I haven't.

Fanny Kaplan—that's her name. Strange, isn't it? Fanny Kaplan."

"Thanks. And keep this to yourself, uh?" There was no hope of it, but it had to be said.

"Of course, of course—"

The old man watched Philipson join the man filling out the form and both men as they went out of the doors, shaking his head with puzzlement, and excitement, all the time.

Outside, Greaves pointed out Ozeroff's retreating back.

"He's probably heading somewhere he can read that," Philipson remarked. "Unless he already knows what's in it. Let's go."

As he went gingerly down the frozen steps, he considered the addressee of the letter with the Russian stamps. There was something familiar about the name, but he could not remember what it was. And it had nothing to do with espionage—he had a ridiculous idea that it had something to do with sixth-form history lessons. Ridiculous, of course.

"Fanny Kaplan—"

"What?" Greaves said, stepping carefully alongside him, a hundred yards behind Ozeroff.

"Look, I'll report this over the radio. Aubrey might as well know at once. You follow our chum, and I'll pick you up in the car."

"Don't be long, then," was all Greaves said by way of reply.

As he crossed the Mannerheimintie, Philipson tried to remember where he had heard the name before—but all he could think of was getting drunk after the school fifteen had beaten the old boys' strongest side in his last year. The history master had played at wing-forward, being an old boy. Fanny Kaplan—he could almost hear him saying it now.

Praporovich stared down from the gallery at the huge map-table. He had come out of the glass booth where the computer-operators were feeding in movement reports and dispositions, because the atmosphere seemed unreal in there. The glass had become that of a soundless fish tank, and the events registering down there on the board of no more interest than gawping faces staring into the tank.

Out on the gallery, there was still little noise. Each of the staff-officers round the table wore headphones and throat-mikes, and their murmurs were indistinct and desultory. But it was more real—the lights glowed more brightly, and he could see through them to the tanks and guns and ships they represented.

Pnin was across the border, taking up concealed position prior to the attack on Ivalo and the capture of the airfield. He thought of Pnin because of the trouble his rehearsals had almost caused—the other Finland Stations were also in position. Attack Force One was massed on the Kirkenes road, right up against the border with Norway. Dolohov's Red Banner Fleet units were putting to sea from ice-free Murmansk—troop-carriers and their submarine and destroyer escorts. And the submarines—the big ones, were in position at the mouths of the principal fjords all the way to Tramsø. Further to the east on the map, well inside the Soviet Union, GSFN airborne troops were being moved up to forward positions; they were less than an hour behind schedule, well within the tolerances they had set.

The *size* of it—the *reality*—ran through him with the effect of an electric shock. He could not help his features assuming a fierce smile, as if he had been confronted with some massive present in childhood, or some anticipated sexual joy as a young man. There, there—

Ships, tanks, APCs—the chemical platoons, because Ossipov had got it right in time and the computer programme for the use of the VX gas on each of the target areas had been transmitted to GSFN HQ. Ships, tanks, guns, men; regiments, battalions, divisions, armies; concepts, words, little pictures from old army exercises rolled through his mind in the jumbled image of a dreamer.

Tomorrow—

"Very well—Kapustin, order the eliminations to be carried out! You have the list."

Andropov watched Kapustin's back until the Deputy Chairman had closed the door behind him. Then, just as clearly, he seemed to watch his own features, though there was no mirror before him and no reflection from the polished surface of his desk. Something was happening to his face, and he could see it clearly, as if each muscular twitch and movement was a brush-stroke on the wall in front of him. His face was collapsing into a mirror of fear.

It was like a nightmare—he put up his hand to remove his glasses, because he was sweating around the eyes, then put his hand hastily away because that nakedness would have further reduced his face to a frightened blob. He remembered his trick of making the light catch his spectacles, so that his eyes disappeared into two moons of light—but there was no one to see the trick, so it would not work. His hand, then—

Trembling. He put it away, sitting on it with his thigh; and he could feel the quiver in his thigh.

Yuri Andropov, Chairman of the KGB, sat on his hands, his body hunched forward in his chair, as if he had been caned at school and was trying to still the throbbing. Yuri Andropov's face was out of control, sliding into an expression of terror at what he ordered, and its now undoubted consequences. He had just ordered the deaths of a dozen men. Yuri Andropov hated himself.

When the men died, the invasion would not be stopped. It would begin. He had used the only weapon he had, murder, and it was insufficient. Just as his face was insufficiently endowed with muscular control to present another look than the one of terror he knew it was assuming.

The coup would go ahead—they knew nothing, nothing.

Vorontsyev—Major Vorontsyev. A few men, raiding a house in Leningrad. How could that stop anything? He, as Chairman, could stop nothing by ordering the deaths of Praporovich and Dolohov and a dozen generals—

It could not come to good. They had left it too late. Too late. He realised, as his body calmed, and the persistent image of his collapsing features went away, that he was a fatalist. They had played and they had lost. Temerity, poor investigative technique, over-confidence—it did not matter what the reason was. They had lost.

In accepting that fact, he told himself, there is a kind of strength. Certainly, *he* felt calmer, stronger—

"Sir—a message from your daughter."

"What—now?"

"Yes, Admiral."

"Very well. What is it?" Dolohov could not resist being amused, even on the point of leaving for Praporovich's headquarters. His own work was done—the units of the Fleet were at sea—and, yes, there was time for his only child to ask him what he would like for his birthday, or to tell him that she would be staying for supper so what did he want her to cook for him—?

He would be sorry to tell her that he would not be home for the next forty-eight hours.

"It's your wife, sir. Apparently, she's been taken to the hospital."

"What? When?"

"Your daughter found her, in the kitchen, sir. She had collapsed—"

"How is she, man?"

"Your daughter says she's all right, that you're not to worry, sir—"

"Worry? How can I not worry? Dammit—which hospital?"

"Sir—she's feeling much better, just a dizzy spell—"

"Which hospital? I must go and see her."

Aubrey stood at the tall window of the study in which Khamovkhin had first received him and Buckholz. There was no warmth from the huge fire behind him, and he was aware of the cold striking through the frosty glass. He wondered why he had come away from the fire at all, except that, he had wanted to see the light of a cigarette from down on the snowbound paths and lawns, the flicker of torchlight from the security team on duty. Silly. But, the news was deeply disturbing. He turned again to Anders, Buckholz's chief aide.

"You're certain of this ident, Anders?"

The tall American was little more than a bulky shadow on the far side of the fireplace.

"Yes, sir. We're sure." The voice seemed to come out of the firelit shadow, and Aubrey had to force himself to attend to the mere words, not their dramatic delivery.

"And Captain Ozeroff is nowhere to be found, you say?"

"Sir, Mr. Buckholz checked every one of the Russians himself. Our man wasn't one of them—he's gone AWOL, Mr. Aubrey."

"Damn!" He turned to Anders then, as if he felt his back suddenly exposed to the window, turned back again. "Ilarion Vikentich Galakhov, Lieutenant, GRU. One-time

Intelligence Adviser to Cuba—you're sure about that suspicion of attachment to Cuban Intelligence, are you?"

"One of our senior Latin American analysts was on the wrong end of that attachment, sir," Anders replied without expression. "Mission curtailed—and his successor in the field."

Aubrey looked down at the message in his hand. It had been delivered to Lahtilinna over the radio, in a simple code, and been broken down for him by an operator drafted in from Copenhagen earlier in the day as part of the replacement security team. The message scribbled in a bold, quick hand on the message form was from Philipson, and it was originally timed some hours earlier. By the time he had it, it had been too late to arrest the substitute Ozeroff. He had disappeared—probably triggered by the letter with the Russian stamps.

"Fanny Kaplan," he murmured.

"Begging your pardon, sir?" Anders murmured deferentially.

"You know your immediate post-Revolutionary history, Anders?"

"Some."

"Remember Fanny Kaplan?" He wished Anders would not remember, as if that might make his own conclusion less real. Ozeroff had reported back to Lahtilinna from his day off, had spent less than an hour in his room before the official hand-over of security duties had led to his being required to report to Buckholz—and had calmly disappeared. So completely that repeated searches of the castle and the grounds had not unearthed him.

Anders was silent for a long time, so long that Aubrey thought he was bemused by the question.

"Yes," he said eventually.

"I ask you again—you are certain about Galakhov's role in Latin America, and his real function while acting as adviser to Cuban Intelligence?"

"Yes."

"Then the letter was a trigger—it probably contained blank paper. Perhaps even a black spot, mm?" Anders seemed not to understand. "It meant simply—go underground, carry out your mission. Isn't that the final signal in a Department 'V' operation?"

"Often it is, sir."

"Fanny Kaplan! She killed Lenin—shot him up so bad-

305

ly he never recovered. My God, but these people in *Group 1917* love their recent history!" Now he turned to Anders. "I must see Khamovkhin—and cut through the bluff and the bull. He has to be made to realise that *he* is the target for Fanny Kaplan—" His words died suddenly as a thought struck him. "I think we may have been extremely stupid to have taken over security here, Anders."

"How's that, sir?"

"Because, if Khamovkhin *now* comes to harm, it will be our fault. And a perfect excuse for our friends in *Group 1917* to make war on the murderers of the Soviet First Secretary!"

"Mr. First Secretary," Buckholz spluttered, losing patience at last, "we're way beyond any *performance* here! You could be on the verge of rounding up the so-called ringleaders back home—though I doubt it—but we're talking about your life!"

"Very well, Mr. Buckholz!" Aubrey could see that Khamovkhin was shaken by the outburst as he was by the threat, which he had seemed capable of absorbing in some way, as if digesting it. "Very well. However, your men have now completed the take-over. One of them will be on guard outside the door of any room I occupy until you give orders otherwise. What more can I say or do to please you?" The square features were defiant, the thick eyebrows seeming to bristle, the jaw to jut like a prow.

"You're a prisoner here, sir—I have to make that clear to you, and you must make it clear to your people, and to the world, that you are unwell. That's why you have had to cancel your speech to the conference tomorrow."

"And what about President Wainwright? Is he ill, too?"

"Weather delay. Washington's snowbound."

"Fortunate."

"He'd have found another reason."

"Very well—I will have a communiqué drafted, for the conference and for the President of Finland."

"I have it here," Aubrey said quietly, holding it out. Khamovkhin took the sheets of paper and studied them. Then he removed his glasses, nodded at them, and walked out of the room.

"Sweet Jesus Christ," Buckholz breathed, slumping into the chair opposite Aubrey. "What is it with that guy? World War Three is about to happen, his life's in danger

306

—and he spends his time offering us drinks and making small-talk!"

"He's beyond consideration of his predicament, Charles. He can't bear to think about it. A condition that is going to get worse."

"Hell. Is he kidding when he tells us the ringleaders are on the point of being arrested—Andropov says so?"

"I should think so. Killed, perhaps, but not arrested. *If* the Chairman's men can get at them in time."

"In time for what? They could *start* the whole thing!"

"I realise that, Charles. I was trying not to think about it. Just like the First Secretary. I consider that the scenario doesn't bear thinking about!"

Buckholz looked at his watch, then into the fire.

"The first units of the AMF should be landing at Bardufoss about now, Kenneth."

"Please don't remind me."

Ilarion Vikentich Galakhov looked up at the window of the first floor study. A thin strip of light where the curtain had not been closed properly. Probably the security men, Aubrey and Buckholz, were still discussing his disappearance.

He cursed *Kutuzov* for the romanticism of the letter from Moscow. All the way, since the beginning of the operation, he had argued against any final signal to Helsinki. But the old man had been adamant. There had to be a back-up, a contingency. Withdraw—abort—go ahead. A range of signals indicated by the arrangement of the stamps and their denominations on letters addressed to "Ozeroff" care of the post office—or the final signal, the "kill" alert indicated by the addressee—Fanny Kaplan. Nothing had come for the man he was pretending to be, but that afternoon there had been a letter for Ms. Kaplan. Stupid game-playing—he was going to kill Khamovkhin anyway.

He adjusted the rifle over his shoulder, and clapped his hands to his sides as he felt the cold of the night. He heard footsteps behind him, smelt cigar smoke on the freezing air.

"Anything?" the American asked him.

"Not a thing," he replied in English. He might have been Norwegian with his accent. "Quiet as the grave."

"As long as it's not your grave—or *his*," the American

commented, tossing his head to indicate the lighted window above them.

"He's safe now," Galakhov said lightly.

"Let's hope so. If anything happens to him, old man Buckholz will put my ass in a sling!"

Galakhov laughed, the American puffed a wreath of smoke up against the hard stars, and walked on, his footsteps crunching like the sounds of a child eating a hard biscuit as he moved on the snow-covered gravel. "Keep your eyes peeled!" he called back.

"Sure," Galakhov replied.

When the American had gone, he grinned to himself. Easy. Simple and easy. Become Norwegian, join the hunters. A fox in a pink coat, riding a horse, he thought. The image amused him.

Fanny Kaplan, the envelope had said. *Fanny Kaplan*. Khamovkhin was a dead man. The only problem would be getting away alive, afterwards.

The nose of the huge USAF Galaxy transport plane opened even as the dying roar of the reverse thrust from its engines still hovered at the edge of audibility. The ramp of the cargo-hold thudded against the cleared runway of Bardufoss, northern Norway, and almost immediately a camouflaged truck rolled onto the ramp, then another and another, out into the landscape which glinted a ghostly silver in the moonlight. Exhaust rolled in white clouds behind them as they moved away from the hard-lit, ribbed interior of the transport plane towards their assembly point.

Two RAF Harriers roared over the airfield, a deafening wave of sound succeeding them, only to be followed by a lesser wave which lapped against the low surrounding hills as a flight of Wessex helicopters circled the perimeter of the field. Then another Galaxy, which disgorged field artillery, then a Luftwaffe Transall carrying tanks, and an RAF Hercules which contained Royal Marines, landed in swift succession, settling their bulks into the iron-hard airstrip.

From the tower of the air station, a group of senior NATO officers watched the arrival of the first units of the Allied Mobile Force, the lynch-pin of any NATO first-stage land defence against a surprise attack.

Among the officers, and the most senior of them, was

Major-General Jolfusson, Commander Allied Forces Northern Norway. As the succession of whale-like transport planes disgorged their cargoes of men and war machines, he was unable to take any satisfaction from the sight. His staff were also subdued. This was no NATO exercise—and it was happening all over the north of Norway that night—or would happen the following morning and afternoon. Especially at Kirkenes, where the main thrust of the Soviet attack would come. Jolfusson was due at Kirkenes, then Tromsø, before midday.

Major-General Jolfusson had never expected to see the day. Never. The unthinkable was happening. On both sides of the border of his country, the world was massing to begin the next war. And it was all but too late to avoid the first clash. His orders stated oh-six hundred, tomorrow, the twenty-fourth. That was when the invasion would begin.

It *was* too late. He looked at his watch. Already, it was four o'clock on the morning of the twenty-third.

PART FOUR

KUTUZOV

"I do not welcome venerable gentlemen . . .
because in their wake, in their footsteps,
springing up like sharp little teeth, are these dark
young men of random destiny and private
passions—destinies and passions that can be
shaped and directed to violent ends."
—PAUL SCOTT: *A Division of the Spoils*

FIFTEEN
THE TWAIN MEET

Admiral Dolohov walked as quickly as caution would permit up the steps of the Murmansk Central Hospital. All the time, he watched his feet on the icy steps. And he kept his head bent because he was worried, and disturbed, and feeling small and vulnerable because of his fears for his wife, and did not wish anyone to see the look on his face.

He glanced up only once, as he reached the top of the steps. The glass doors of the main public entrance were directly ahead of him—and he could see a white-uniformed nurse crossing the well-lit reception lobby. A man bumped into him, and he lifted his head again, almost taking his hands from his coat pockets to right his balance. He did not catch even a glimpse of the man's face —noticed only the soft exhalation of the gas from whatever cylinder the Department "V" operative carried, before his breath seemed snatched away as if by a wind, so that he gagged in surprise, then in fear, then terror as his breath would not come.

The operative was too far away by the time he staggered for him to fall against him, and he began to lean drunkenly backwards—glimpsed the lit corridor beyond the reception lobby, the imposing façade of the hospital which he had always thought more like a museum, then the starlit sky, then a street light—which had been behind him?—then he tumbled down the icy steps, his heels ringing in a distressed, irregular pattern.

The woman at whose feet he rolled to a halt, on the pavement at the bottom of the short flight of steps, dropped her little plain paper bag of fruit and clutched the collar of her fur coat round her throat before she began to scream.

Army General Sadunov, commanding Attack Force One at its temporary headquarters near Pecenga, almost on the border with Norway, and less than fifty kilometres from Kirkenes, complained of indigestion almost as soon as his senior staff-officers, with whom he had dined, began passing round the good Ukrainian vodka. Reluctant to miss the bout of drinking—at least so much of it as was concomitant with respect from his officers—he decided that a short walk outside would cure his complaint. He bantered and laughed with his staff while he was helped into his grey winter great-coat, and while he donned his fur hat.

Outside, the night was fine, starlit and cold. Immediately, and for a few moments, he felt better, attending to the chill of the air in his lungs, to the noises of his army—hum of generators, wind-up of helicopter engines, clicks of tested artillery like the snapping of iron twigs.

He was thinking that perhaps he should not have eaten the *bliny* after the beef Stroganov, certainly not after the *krasnaya ikra*, when the pain surged through him, starting in the pit of his stomach and reaching into his chest like a burning hand, spreading its fingers as it reached upwards. He had time to half-turn, as if to call back into the wooden building on the steps of which he stood, before he tumbled outwards, falling on his side in the snow. He rolled on his face for a moment, as if trying to put out the raging fire in his stomach by rubbing it in the snow, then lay still.

They were lined up to see him board the helicopter. General Pnin, commanding Finland Station Six, already in position south-east of Ivalo, across the border with Finland, was pleased and gratified by the sight. He shook hands with each of his headquarters staff, who would join him only after Ivalo was taken and secured, and they snapped into salutes one by one—like a row of clock-

314

work soldiers, he thought, then dismissed the unkindness. Good men.

He ducked under the rotors when the last man had been saluted, and climbed into the MIL helicopter. His aide saluted, and proceeded to strap him into his rear seat in the passenger-compartment of the command helicopter. Then Pnin nodded that he was secure, and comfortable, and the aide spoke into the microphone.

Immediately, the beat of the rotors increased, and Pnin, twisting his head to look out of one of the ports, saw his staff retreating to a distance where the downdraught would be less distressing. He raised his hand once more in salute. The noise of the rotors reached a whine, and there was that little fearful moment as the whole helicopter wobbled as it first left the ground. Then it rose slowly, its lights—he could see them reflected through the port— splashing redly on the snow of the take-off pad. He could see the upturned faces of his staff, caught by the light, hands holding onto fur hats—

Then the seat seemed to lift quicker than the rise of the whole machine, but he could not be sure because the scene in the MIL turned from shadow into orange into whiteness and he could see nothing. He could feel, just for an instant. He was being pulled apart, and scalded and deafened.

The staff officers below saw the MIL stagger, then rip like a tin can, belching flame, spit off bits of molten metal and chunks of rotor blade and fuselage—before they began running to escape the debris as it sagged then drove down towards them.

Marshal Praporovich had not heeded his own warning, nor that of *Kutuzov*. He was faintly amused, rather than disturbed, by the knowledge. And tickled at the idea that, while he had made love to the young lady whose apartment he had visited, two of his officers had stood guard outside the door—another two had been posted outside the entrances to the apartment block.

A risible occasion—but he could not help but be smug about his performance. Not that he had been impotent— no, never that. But—disinterested, certainly unenthusiastic. And he could not explain why the study of the map-table, the digestion of the innumerable movement and disposition reports, the smiles and confidence of his staff-officers

—why those things had concentrated themselves in a genital itch which blossomed into lewd images, a vulgarity of mental language that had surprised him, gratified him.

And the girl's call—that had come at just the apposite moment. He had not thought it strange, only convenient —even mystically appropriate. And, laughing, he had collected his little team of bodyguards, and as if they had all been Suvorov cadets they had passed round a flask of vodka in the staff car, and there had even been jokes and vulgarities about occasion and performance and community of indulgence—which he had allowed, so satisfied had been his mood.

He studied himself in the long mirror in the bedroom, touched his fur hat with his gloves in mocking salute, glanced at the sleeping girl in the round bed under the mirror in the ceiling—that, too, an innovation he had submitted to, enjoyed—then turned on his heel, went out through the lounge where the empty glasses stood next to the champagne bottle, half-empty. He let himself out of the apartment. He acknowledged with a nod the evident interest in the eyes of the two young aides on duty outside the door. They followed him with indisguised smiles to the lift.

The house was on the island of Krestovski Ostrov, between the Bolchaia and Malaia Nevkas (The Great and Middle Nevas). It was in a tree-shrouded suburb off the Morskoy Prospekt, amid old and spacious houses. The nearby Maritime Park of Victory and the Kirov Stadium were both masked by the trees—gaunt though they were in the cold pre-dawn as Vorontsyev paced the pavement near the Volga saloon in which he had sat for most of the night.

The house was at least a century old, pre-Revolutionary, lavish, perhaps the retreat of a wealthy businessman or landowner. It had been taken over as a subordinate office and interrogation centre by the Leningrad KGB; just as many of the big houses in those quiet streets had become offices, clinics, kindergartens.

Vorontsyev ground out the cigarette with his foot, and looked at his watch. Five minutes before six. The sky was dark, but the stars were fading. He was cold with the hours of waiting. The pavements and the road were bright with rime, silver in the light of the few street lamps. Two other cars were parked in this quiet street—containing the team he had selected and briefed from the resources of the Novosibirsk office. The men were bored, yet eager. They had come through visa control at Leningrad airport at midnight, as a party but unconnected with Vorontsyev ahead of them in the short queue. They were noisy, and apparently drunk. The local KGB man wished them a successful and drunken leave in the city.

The cars had come from Intourist—a waspish woman woken from sleep in her flat above the office who was immediately, ingratiatingly humbled by the ID card he showed her. If there was a connection between Leningrad KGB and the group of traitors—he thought about them consistently in that way now—then the Intourist woman would be unlikely to possess sufficient suspicion of SID to pass on the information that an alien KGB *apparat* was in the city.

He had a reasonable, thought undetailed, impression of the interior of the house. If this one—three-storied, double-fronted, deep with rooms—worked to the general pattern, then the Englishman would be in the cellar. The cellar would have been converted to interrogation rooms and cells.

He was still dog-tired, he admitted, yawning. He had slept deeply on the five-hour shuttle Aeroflot Tupolev from Novosibirsk, via Sverdlovsk, Perm, Kirov and Vologda—but a sleep interrupted when he was jerked out of the unconsciousness each time the plane landed.

He would have felt more comfortable with his own men —he remembered that Ilya and Maxim were dead—but he had no special fear of these strangers. They would not fail. He had chosen young men, men who reminded him of his own team. Most of them were graduates of a university as well as one or other of the KGB training schools, and all of them were ambitious. He had chosen them partly because of their ambition. To work with SID was a privilege, something which would assist their careers. It mitigated the sense they must have of working against comrades. At least, he hoped it did.

He returned to the car, held out his hand, and the driver, trying to look wide-awake with bleary eyes and bleached cheeks, handed him the radio microphone. They had set up a HQ for radio or telephone traffic to be relayed to them from Moscow at another KGB safe house —one due for redecoration in a few weeks and therefore empty. One of their team had been left there with a radio and telephone link.

" 'Father' to 'Son'—are you receiving me, over?"

The voice was faint, tired and bored. "Receiving you, 'Father'—over."

"Any more Moscow traffic?"

"Three reports for you, 'Father,' from Centre. Priority One."

"Very well. Make them brief—over." The young driver was looking at Vorontsyev with wide eyes. The highest priority for KGB radio traffic, for a young Major in the SID. He was impressed.

" 'Sailor' is dead." Admiral Dolohov. " 'Soldier Beta' also dead." Sadunov, he thought, the army General commanding Red Army units in the Kola sector of GSFN— part of any invasion; the most important part. " 'Apostle Four' also dead." Four—four, who was that in Andropov's little code? Pnin—yes, one of the Finland Stations. Vorontsyev squashed a half-formed image of an enraged and wounded animal lashing out blindly, murderously. It had to be done, had to, he told himself. No other way.

"Anything else?"

"Request for message concerning 'Soldier Alpha' as soon as available. And good luck, and instructions to take all alive, if possible." "Soldier Alpha" was Praporovich himself. The Department "V" executioner would report to Vorontsyev, and his message would be relayed to the Centre.

"Very well. Over and out."

He handed back the microphone. The driver clipped it beneath the dash, then said: "Are we waiting for the mortician to show up, chief, or are we going in now?"

Five past six. Vorontsyev considered, rubbing his chin. He wanted sleepy, unresisting people. There would be fewer than a dozen people, perhaps only three or four, on the premises. But they had to be taken alive; and they all had immediate access to guns. And he knew Andropov would be waiting for the message concerning Praporovich.

He was a little man. It was almost six-forty when he arrived. The sky was perceptibly lighter now. There was no traffic and few lights in the quiet street, since there were few houses still occupied by tenants or owners. It was a daytime street. He came on foot, in overalls as if coming from a night-shift somewhere, wispy hair jammed under a fur cap, scarf hiding most of his face, dirty overcoat open in front. A totally anonymous man.

His face was pinched, mean-looking. Grubby with whatever mechanical job he did. He smiled at Vorontsyev, and his teeth were sparse in his mouth. Vorontsyev wondered how old he was. All he said was, "I've taken care of your embarrassing little problem, Comrade Major. I'll be off home now. The wife will have breakfast for me." He began to walk away, perhaps towards the metro, which must have been how he came there.

"How . . . ?" was all Vorontsyev could find to say in the face of such undemonstrative behaviour.

"How?" The little man rubbed his chin. "A car accident. The Marshal was leaving the apartment of a young lady. A rather silly affair, I would have thought. He's practically impotent. A car mounted the pavement, skidding on the ice, I expect, and he was knocked down. He only had a hundred yards to walk to his staff car which was waiting for him. Two of his junior staff officers were injured, too. One of them must be dead, I would have thought."

"I—see."

"Well, Major, I'll be off now." He raised his hand in salute, turned, and walked off down the street. Vorontsyev watched him go, then bent to look in at the driver.

"Did you get that?"

"Sir." The driver's eyes bulged comically.

"Send it, then. 'Alpha' has met with an accident. Then we go in."

The driver spoke into the mike, then listened while Vorontsyev, picking up a torch from the rear seat, flashed it in the direction of two cars parked well down the street. Doors opened, and overcoated figures got out, moved down the street towards him. The driver said, "Sir—another message. 'Apostles One, Two and Seven all eliminated.' "

"Hell—is it really only the dream of a few old men—is that all we have to worry about?" He banged his hand absently on the window-ledge of the car. It seemed impossible. It could not be easy, not as easy as that. Kill some old men, and stop a war?

He thought about *Kutuzov*. The unknown face; the mystery man. Unless he was stopped, then the Kremlin

319

regime, the entire Politburo perhaps—certainly the KGB —would be ousted.

One old man, with a dream of passion. If he wasn't found, then he would succeed. Again, he punched the side of the car with his fist.

"Let's go," he said.

The other four men were opposite them now, crossing the frost-rimed road. Four heavy dark shapes. The driver shut his door quietly. Vorontsyev looked at them. The tiredness of being awake, or only fitfully dozing, all night was now only slight smudging beneath their eyes. Their faces were tight with tension.

"Right. You know what to do," Vorontsyev said. "You two to the back window you spotted earlier—break in if it doesn't give in ten seconds. Understand?" They nodded. "The rest of you, the front with me. We'll have to break in, and quickly. You two take the first floor rooms, you downstairs . . ." He addressed the driver with this remark. "Be careful. I don't know who, or what, is in there —except that you can bet a bloody alarm will go off as soon as we break in." One of the men grinned. "But we're experts. We know what to expect. You try to *hold*, not kill." He paused for a moment, then: "But you kill rather than be killed. Understood?"

He looked at each face in turn. Each man nodded. Then he walked ahead of them, briskly, towards the house. Their footsteps behind him seemed to clatter on the frosty pavement. He watched the curtained, blind windows as carefully as he could.

Nothing seemed to be awake, or moving, in the house. There appeared to be no duty-staff. Which would be consistent with the house being only an occasional office for the KGB. And, he thought, perhaps consistent with the timing of the *Group 1917* and *Finland Station* operations. If they were only a day away, then there was little need to secure a safe house like this one.

He suddenly wondered whether the Englishman was still alive. His interest, and importance, must surely have passed?

The house was surrounded by a high, dark hedge, behind which was a short gravel drive. They kept to the lawns that flanked it, their feet crunching through the stiff grass, their trouser-bottoms wetted by the frost. Still the house seemed empty, or dead. Vorontsyev pulled the

Stechkin from his holster—he had exchanged the Makarov for the heavier gun with the larger clip in Novosibirsk.

They paused, of one mind, at the edge of the lawn. The gravel drive surrounded the house like a stony moat. Vorontsyev motioned the two men detailed to the back of the house to move off. They trod with comic stealth and lightness along the gravel drive as it curved to the rear of the house. Vorontsyev studied the windows at the front of the house, as he had done earlier in the night. The door was stout, but the downstairs windows were not barred. The Leningrad office must have decided not to draw attention to the house by such methods of increasing security. Fortunately.

They crossed the scuffling little space of the gravel, and gathered in a little knot by the window, a large bay whose sill was at the level of their heads.

Vorontsyev said; "Office, or bedroom, or lounge?"

"Probably lounge or rest-room, sir," one of them volunteered—the driver.

"Agreed. Up on the sill—have a look at the catch." As he was helped up onto the sill, Vorontsyev inspected the window frame. Not the original, but a standard wooden frame; sash-cord. "Well?" he said, looking up.

"It's wired, sir."

"Can you open it quickly if you smash the window?"

"Yes, sir."

Vorontsyev looked at his watch. Thirty seconds for them to reach the back window they had chosen, then ten seconds. He waited, then: "Smash it!"

The driver punched his gloved fist through the pane of glass, just above the catch. The noise was horribly loud in the cold air. Then he said, "Up and away, boys!" Two of them, Vorontsyev and another man, heaved at the window, and it slid up protestingly. The driver dropped into the room, gun out, and pulled back one curtain.

Vorontsyev clambered over the sill, then turned to help the last man in. There was sufficient light for them to see the door in the far wall. Only then, when they were all inside, did Vorontsyev notice the alarm ringing deep in the house somewhere. It galvanised him.

"Let's go!"

He ran across the room—a frail-looking chair with spindly, glossy legs spun out of his way as his overcoat caught it. He opened the door, and peered out. A big hallway, wide stairs leading up into the darkness. There was a gleam of light, probably coming from under a door, up on the first floor. He prodded the two detailed men, and they took the stairs in a run. The light increased, as if a door had been opened. A voice called out.

Vorontsyev heard "Hold it, friend!" No more than that. No shooting, yet. The instruction "Watch him!" then more footsteps.

The driver had crossed the hallway with its chequered tiles, and was opening the door of a room. His head ducked round the door, then he was back out.

"Nothing," he called, and set off towards the rear of the house.

A shot from what must be the second floor—but towards the rear of the house. The back stairs, the old servants' stairs probably, which meant the two men had broken in and made for the second floor.

Where was the door to the cellars? For a moment, the size of the house defeated him. Then he realised he should have entered at the back of the house. Only the servants would have needed to enter the cellars—and the door would be in the kitchens. No—ground floor reception rooms here, left and right, that door to the kitchens, butler's pantry—and cellars. He followed the direction taken by the driver.

The body thudded on the lowest stairs, and rolled almost gently onto the tiled floor. Dark overcoat, fair hair, hidden, broken face. One of the two men from the second floor search. Someone had thrown him over. He heard faint shots, and a distant cry.

He was losing impetus, he realised. How many seconds had now passed? He burst through the door at the rear of the staircase, and stumbled down three steps, into the huge, gloomy kitchen. A door at the other end of the room was open—the kitchen was some kind of dining-room as well, it appeared. Scraps of food on a table, washing-up in an old sink. Dirty plates. There was no sign of the driver.

He opened two cupboards before he found the door to the cellars. He should have noticed the light beneath the door. It was on, showing the wooden steps leading down. He hesitated, then stepped onto the topmost stair.

A scuffle of footsteps, a muttered voice, sharp with feverish command. He went down the steps quickly. They

322

twisted half-way, almost doubling back. A man in civilian clothes, but carrying an army rifle, was facing him in front of an open door. There was a narrow corridor behind him, and rows of metal doors. And the atmosphere of a prison where once there had been racks and bins of wine.

He fired before the man had time to challenge him. He had been alseep, was leadenly awakening still, for the alarm sounded only as a muffled buzz down there. He fell against the door, a stupid, open-mouthed look on his face.

Vorontsyev was still at the bottom of the steps when he saw the other man, a thick dressing-gown tied with a cord, his greying hair ruffled from sleep. He was opening one of the doors, and there was a gun in his hand.

"Halt, or I fire!" Vorontsyev snapped, and the man's head lifted with a jerk, as if he had not noticed the gunshot that had killed the guard.

Somewhere in the house, two more shots. They seemed to startle the man in the dressing-gown as much as Vorontsyev's order. He had a bunch of heavy keys in his right hand, which he was using to open the door, and the gun was evidently awkward in his left hand. Vorontsyev watched the gun, and then the right hand turned the key in the lock, and the man's body began to disappear into the cell he had opened, Vorontsyev fired twice, but missed.

He ran. The pain in his toes came back. He had forgotten the frostbite, even when he patrolled the street outside during the night. A dull ache he gave none of his attention to. Now these few steps hurt. He cannoned off the wall, opposite the open cell door, and then saw the man in the dressing-gown lying by the wall, the gun waveringly pointed at something inside the cell.

Vorontsyev kicked out at the wrist, and the gun flew up and away. The man turned to look at him, evidently afraid now that his concentration on killing the Englishman had vanished. And the fear turned to pain. There was a dark stain spreading across his shoulder; he must have been hit by a lucky ricochet.

Vorontsyev dragged at the collar of the dressing-gown, and the man winced with pain. Novetlyn, having failed in his attempt to kill Folley, realising that it could only be a break-in to rescue him—somehow the Centre knew about Folley—was now desperate to sink into unconsciousness. His shoulder ached crazily, more than any wound had any right to, and he moaned aloud as he was pulled backwards out of the cell. The image of Folley heaped in a foetal plea on his filthy cot disappeared. As the man who had shot him tried to jerk him to his feet, Novetlyn passed out.

Vorontsyev let the body drop again to the floor. The man had passed out; and more, he'd given up trying. Vorontsyev knew the look. The wound would keep him out of the game. He stepped over the still form, into the cell.

Even though the door of the cell had been open for more than a minute, the stench of urine and body dirt assailed Vorontsyev almost tangibly. In a corner, perhaps ten feet from the door, something was crouched on a narrow cot, a blanket wrapped around it. Vorontsyev could hear the chatter of teeth. Cold or terror—or both.

He felt a lurch of what might have been pity, or disappointment. The man of the cot had evidently been broken. The body suggested it—abject, displayed almost as if it had been physically broken and poorly reassembled. He had seen men, and women, crouching like this in the Lubyanka—before he went to SID. Since then, he had never visited the prison complex behind the Centre in Dzerzhinsky Street.

"Who is it—who is it?" A querulous voice, speaking English. Yes, he had been broken. No cover now, nothing but a pleading not to be hurt or questioned any more. Vorontsyev crossed to the cot.

The Englishman's shirt was filthy. He had urinated in his trousers more than once. Vorontsyev, in appalled fascination, lifted the thin blanket. The man's feet were bare and white—where they weren't filthy. A white globe of a face looked up at him with an idiot's stare. The fair hair was matted. A hand was held out to him; perhaps in supplication, or to ward off some unknown terror. Vorontsyev swallowed gagging on the stench.

"I've told you everything!" the voice said, querulous, old, ashamed. The head was already hanging, admitting the failure, prepared to answer more questions.

"I've come to help you," Vorontsyev said softly.

The head stayed still, but he heard the Englishman mutter. "*He* said that."

Vorontsyev understood. His interrogator; perhaps the man outside the door. He said, "I shot him. Do you hear me—I shot him. I've come to help you." Vorontsyev spoke in English, with a heavy accent, which he cursed silently

324

as if it was the only barrier now between them. Folley looked up. His eyes tried to focus.

"Not English," he said.

"No—I'm a Russian." Folley cringed. "But I have come to help!" His voice was earnest. He moved a step nearer, and the Englishman backed against the wall behind the cot, the blanket held under his chin in both hands, as if to protect nakedness; or to comfort, child-like.

Vorontsyev knew he was using the methods of a policeman. He could not be simply human, or humane, towards this man, because he needed information from him. Closing his mouth, breathing shallowly through his nostrils— the stench was vile—he sat on the edge of the cot, and put away the Stechkin. Then he touched the man's leg; the flesh seemed to crawl under the touch.

The Englishman tried to make himself as small on the cot as possible, shrinking from contact. Vorontsyev calculated that the moment was right, then said, "I have come to take you to safety. It will have to be the United States Consulate, I am afraid, because your government maintains no official presence here—nor is there an SIS unit here, as far as I know." He spoke conversationally, lightly. All the time his hand patted the Englishman's, leg, stroking gently much as he would have done to a dog or a cat, to still its fear.

The Englishman was little better than an animal— worse, if the capacity to keep oneself clean was taken into account. Vorontsyev could see that he hadn't been beaten—if he had, then the beating was a time ago. This man had been broken by isolation—by the utter loneliness he had suffered. Vorontsyev had seen it work before. The collapse of the will, crumbling like stale cake in the pressure of fingers. Because the fingers that held him were omnipotent, omnipresent—and no help would come. That was how it was done.

Just to find out what the West knew about *Finland Station*. Vorontsyev shrugged. The Englishman was having difficulty with what he had heard. Vorontsyev, easing as much gentleness as possible into his voice, repeated himself.

"The United States Consulate—I will take you there, as soon as you are ready to go."

And then he wondered, as the man moved, seeming to release a more gagging odour from his armpits or crotch.

Perhaps he had been unable to control his bowels, realising that he might be safe. Beyond hope, safe. Wondered.

What *would* he do with this Englishman?

"You—you . . . Why?" Folley found it difficult to speak, as if his voice had gone rusty; or he had not wanted to use it because of the things it had said, confessed, revealed. He tried to look at the Russian, read what was in his mind in the white mirror of the face. He couldn't tell—did not trust . . .

Vorontsyev saw the distrust, riddled deep in the man. Yet, thankfully, he saw the mounting hope; a quiver to the lips that was not cold. He could not help hoping—beyond shame, unworthiness, despair. He would be feeling all those things, or felt them already. But he could not help hoping.

His interrogators had never offered him hope. They had used despair. Therefore, the weapon of hope was his.

"Yes, my friend. Frankly, you are an embarrassment to my government. You were captured on neutral territory —your government *knows* you are alive." Disbelief was swept away by gratitude. Vorontsyev breathed a sigh of relief. The Englishman could not accept him as an ally— but now he could believe in him because he spoke of others knowing, his own government, the people who had sent him. He had not been abandoned, after all.

Vorontsyev had no idea whether the British knew this man was alive; it did not matter. It served. He said, "I am to take you directly to the United States Consulate. I have a car outside. You will make yourself ready to go, just as soon as you have helped me a little."

The flash of fear again, returning like a stain ineffectively erased; and cunning, a re-adoption of an earlier self, the early days of his interrogation. Vorontsyev guessed at the dazed, damaged mind of the Englishman. He was busily erasing his abject defeat, his failure. Now he knew his friends were working for his release, he only had to hold out. He had told them nothing. He would tell them nothing.

Vorontsyev said, "I know you told them nothing, my friend. What *I* want to know is who they were. That is all. Nothing about you. Only about who came here. They were traitors, you understand—understand? *Traitors.* That is why they hurt you."

He stroked at the man's leg still, comforting, lulling

him. Then, on an impulse, he lifted the hand, and held it out to Folley. There was a long moment, and then the Englishman grabbed at the hand, pressing it to his face, bending the head to do so. Vorontsyev felt the stubble, and the filthy hair on the back of his hand. He prevented himself from shuddering.

Then Folley looked up. "Traitors?" he said suspiciously, as if he had been accused.

"Of course! Why else were they in Finland? My government does not wish a war at this time. A—conspiracy in the army. That is why you were questioned by army men—uh?" Folley nodded. Vorontsyev had guessed luckily—no, not so luckily. It was likely that GRU would handle Folley. "What is your name—don't tell me if you don't want to!"

"Allan," Folley said after a while. The hand was still against his cheek. No one had touched him, not since he was beaten. Perhaps even the guards had avoided any physical contact. Touch-deprivation. It was an accustomed technique, one of the devices of alienation. Perhaps this man, Allan, had begun to doubt he had a physical shape any more. Had begun pathetically touching his body in the dark, to be certain. And revolted by his own filthiness, become even more desperate.

"Allan. Mine is Alexei." He gripped Folley's weak hand more tightly. He felt wetness on the back of his hand. Folley was crying silently. Stifling impatience, and distaste, he reached out with his other hand and stroked the matted, greasy hair. Folley moaned like a lover, and leant against Vorontsyev.

The driver came through the door, and stopped, mouth open, as he saw in the gathering light from the tiny high grille in the wall, Vorontsyev and his prisoner in each other's arms. Vorontsyev waved him out with a flip of his hand, and the driver winking knowingly and irreverently, mouthed his satisfactory status report. Then he went out. Folley did not appear to have heard his approach.

"Tell me, Allan," Vorontsyev said, rocking to and fro slightly, as if cradling a child. "Tell me about the men who questioned you—all about them. Then we can catch them. Begin with the one I shot, outside the door . . ."

It was as if he had turned on some tap in the Englishman. At first a trickle of rusty water; then an increasing flow. Patiently, he listened, attending to only one thing, which did not come. Desperate not to hear it, yet knowing he had to ask.

Folley was still in his arms, and he was brushing the matted hair and patting the shaking shoulder, when he appeared to have finished his self-purgation, self-justification.

Then, in the sudden and unfamiliar quiet, Vorontsyev said, "Wasn't there someone else, Allan? Perhaps he only came once, so you forgot him. I don't know when it was—but I know he came to see you. An—*older man . . . ?*"

Folley was quiet, like a child thinking in the arms of a parent. Then, after a long while, he said, "But he didn't—interrogate me."

"No, he wouldn't," Vorontsyev said. Or not seem to, he added to himself. "Tell me what he looked like."

"Is he a traitor too?" It was direct and unfeeling as the question of a child. Piercing.

"Yes—he is," Vorontsyev said quietly.

And then he listened. He did not, he was sure, draw breath once until the Englishman had finished. His hands plucked nervously at the stuff of Folley's shirt, and he perceived a despair more real than he had ever felt before.

He could envisage the features that were being described; the clothes, too, betrayed the picture. It was as if an outline that he had deliberately blurred were redrawn, etched then coloured and shaded.

Mihail Pyotravich Gorochenko, Deputy Foreign Minister of the Soviet Union, and his own adoptive father—was *Kutuzov*. What he had suspected when Natalia had tried to betray him in Khabarovsk—the man had sent her with him to the Far East—and what he had seen in his mind as Vassiliev had talked, was now confirmed. There could be no mistake about the face these two words confirmed. Gorochenko was *Kutuzov*.

The despair of acknowledgement welled up in him; he could not prevent the tears, though the tears now were slow in coming, an emotional condition already abandoned by the rushing brain.

He sensed Folley moving a little apart from him, but took no heed of it. His thought at that precise moment—of a moment before it had been to kill Folley, silence him—was that no one else must hear what he had just heard. For whatever reason he had come to the cellar room,

328

whatever confirmation he had sought—now he must act. He must bury the truth, and find Mihail Pyotravich.

He would not kill Folley. He would do as he had promised, take him to the US Consulate on the Grodnensky. They would take him in, and he would be safe there; as Gorochenko might be.

He snapped at Folley: "Are you ready to leave now?" The Englishman appeared confused, sullen even. He stared dumbly at Vorontsyev. "Get up! Where are your shoes?"

Folley doubled over, peering under the cot. It would have been stupidly comical, had not Vorontsyev felt the insistent urgency of the passing moments.

"Quickly!" he snapped. Folley shrugged. There were no shoes. "Come with me!"

He caught hold of Folley's arm, and hurried him out of the cell. Someone had dragged the man in the dressing-gown away from the doorway. He pushed Folley up the cellar stairs in front of him.

The small group of exhausted men were gathered in the kitchen. There were three men, in various states of undress, against the wall. Standing. Only the man in the dressing-gown appeared to be wounded. His face was gray with weakness and pain, and he slumped against the wall. Around the table were the driver, one of the men who had entered from the rear, and the two who had searched the first floor. One of them was wounded. He nodded to them. Only one dead.

"What do we do now, sir?" the driver asked, staring at Folley, who hovered behind Vorontsyev.

"Mm? Now?" Vorontsyev was ready to leave; this was a delay. He snapped, "Use the radio—then take these men to the safe house. Keep them there until arrangements can be made."

"What about him, sir? Shall I report him?" The driver was nodding in Folley's direction.

"What? Yes. Now, have you brought the cars round?"

"Yes, sir."

"Very well. I shall be going. Don't waste time getting this little gang under cover!"

They all wished to question him, it was evident. He felt guilty, caught out. He hoped they would not ask. The driver said, "Aren't you—?"

"Don't question me!" he snapped "Report in when you get to safety!"

They sat stiffly in their chairs as he turned his back on them. He had not congratulated them, thanked them. They had done well—it did not matter; was irrelevant. He had to get rid of the Englishman now, and get the first flight to Moscow.

How long did he have?

He had no idea. It might be only hours.

The thought pressed in his back, almost expunging breath. He opened the front door, and pushed Folley onto the steps. One of the Volgas was parked by the steps.

"Get in!" he snapped. Folley stared at him dumbly, as if retreated into some catatonic escape from his situation. "Get in!"

Vorontsyev slammed the door, fitted the key in the ignition, and then looked at his watch. Six fifty-nine. Nineteen minutes. Was that all?

He stared at the dashboard in a blank moment, then switched on. The tires squealed on the frosty gravel as he pulled out from the drive into the still empty street. Again, he looked at his watch. Seven.

Twenty minutes to get to the Consulate, bang on the door until a marine opened it, or perhaps the doorman in pyjamas—then allow another forty minutes to get to the airport and through the controls. What time was the early-morning flight to Moscow? Eight? Nine?

Eight-thirty.

He would be in Moscow by ten.

And by that time Andropov would be looking for him, just as he would be looking for Gorochenko.

"Gone—what do you mean, gone?" Andropov's face darkened, and he held the telephone a little from his freshly-shaven cheek as if suspicious of it. He had felt comfortable, pleased with the initial report from Leningrad, having shaved and washed to rub away some of the sleepless night's grime, and the residue of his panic. Then this. Vorontsyev was not available. "Where is the Englishman—not dead, I hope?"

"Comrade Chairman," replied the voice with punctilious respect, "we assumed he had orders from you. Major Vorontsyev left before us, with the Englishman."

"Had he questioned him?"

A slight delay, then: "He was alone with him for at least ten minutes, Comrade Chairman."

330

"And he left hurriedly?"

"Very—sir."

Andropov was silent in his bemusement for a moment, then remembering there were certain courtesies required, he said abruptly: "Very well. Well done. I shall despatch a team to take over from you. You will all be commended for your work, and the commendations noted on your files. That is all."

"Thank you, Comrade—" He put the receiver down quickly. His first action was to look at his watch. Nine twenty-five. The early flight from Leningrad would already have landed.

Why had that occurred to him?

The more proper enquiry was—why had Vorontsyev disappeared and where was he now?

A stupid return to logic—he already knew the answer. He had disappeared because he had discovered the identity of the ringleader. *Kutuzov.* Vorontsyev had found out who *Kutuzov* really was—

Andropov watched his hand on the desk slowly opening and closing, like a small, independent, grabbing animal. And he felt the excitement of knowledge.

Vorontsyev would do that because—

For only one member of the Politburo. One hitherto trusted, unsuspected, almost senile member of the Politburo—

Andropov savoured not pronouncing the word in his thoughts, even the way in which he refused to countenance an image of the old man. Instead, he picked up one of his battery of telephones and dialled the duty-room on the ground floor of the Centre.

"Andropov. Alert the security team at Cheremetievo. If Major Alexei Vorontsyev lands, he is to be detained and brought to me here." He broke the connection and pushed his glasses more firmly onto the bridge of his nose. Then he dialled a second extension. "Records? Bring me Major Alexei Vorontsyev's personal file, at once. And the file on Mihail Pyotravich Gorochenko—yes, the Deputy Foreign Minister."

He put down the phone and looked at his watch. Vorontsyev might have passed through visa control already. If he had done, where would he go?

The two personal files he had requested might tell.

He felt a twitch of fear. The night's fatalism had disappeared not so much with the dawn, but with this sudden knowledge, and the danger offered by the disappearance of Vorontsyev.

They could not have known, of course. He allowed himself to think that, quite clearly and precisely. Even now that he knew, it was hard to believe, hard to *elevate* the shambling has-been Gorochenko to the level of arch-plotter, overthrower of the state. A broken-winged nag who'd toed every line ever pointed out to him, whoever owned the pointing finger. Army, yes—they'd spotted that right away, but that was during the war, and he'd gone straight back into government. A good man with paper, patient on committees, a good right-hand for Gromyko. Never any trouble—

As Andropov rehearsed the innocuousness of the Deputy Foreign Minister of the Soviet Union, the confidence that the KGB had been rightly and unavoidably fooled became the hollow laughter of the hoaxer. He could almost hear Gorochenko laughing at the manner in which they had been taken in for thirty years—by a *caricature* of the third-rate Party man!

He closed hands into fists, one containing the other, and the knuckles whitened as he squeezed. He had played the booby, and taken them, Beria and himself. *His very spotlessness should have been sufficient proof!*

He released his hands from the mind's grip, and rubbed them, as if washing.

Concentrate on Gorochenko. Think, *think*—forget Vorontsyev, concentrate on Gorochenko. Find him—stop a coup. He reached for the telephone. There would be time to tell Khamovkhin at Lahtilinna later, when he had given his instructions. Perhaps they had as much as twenty hours—

A tyranny is sufficient, he thought. He is ours already.

Kutuzov sat in his study. He concentrated on each item of furniture, each painting and photograph, even the grandfather clock which told him it was almost nine-thirty, as if in valediction. He felt very tired. He had been unable to sleep—who would have done, in his situation?

Twenty hours to go. Only twenty.

He stared at the telephone. Praporovich dead, Dolohov dead, Pnin and other generals—dead, too. He put his head in his hands for a moment, then shrugged and made himself sit upright in his chair. He was angry, and would not accept, not for a moment, the image of defeat such a slumped posture would portray. An angry movement of his hand, as if brushing something aside, rattled the bone-china cup and saucer on the delicate little table with the leather surface at the side of the chair. He glanced at it, then replaced the base of the cup firmly in the centre of the saucer.

He was all will-power; a strong man. He had always known that. He had needed it, all of it, then, as he had listened to the report from Leningrad. Or, most of all perhaps, when he had been told that Vorontsyev had talked to the Englishman, and then disappeared.

He stood up. There, he could do it steadily, betraying no reaction from the news he had received. It was as if he were aware of some audience. He laughed, a deep, almost threatening noise. Yes, he did behave as if for an audience, a great deal of the time. He was his own audience now. Once, the audience had been Kyril Vorontsyev, Alexei's father. Then Alexei himself. Not usually his wife. She, though he had sometimes loved her, occasionally needed her, had borne with him as he was without make-up and a role to play.

Yes, Alexei would know by now—would have talked to the Englishman, primed by Vassiliev as to what to look for. And he would know about the stupid bitch, Natalia, and how she had been used against him. There was a moment of admiration for his adopted son. He was clever, and brave, and dogged.

And now, doubtless, would be coming for him. And, even if he had not told Andropov—he might not have—Andropov would have guessed.

He crossed to an escritoire, opened a drawer, and took out a Makarov automatic. He checked the mechanism, and inserted a full clip. Then he put two more clips in his coat pocket. He closed the drawer again.

The invasion—that may have been stopped. But the coup—that would proceed. Oh, yes, that would proceed. He swept his hand through the air in a slicing motion. That, and *Fanny Kaplan*. The Kremlin gang and their secret police would be swept away. Valenkov would obey him, as long as he was free to make the telephone call at six the next morning.

The traitors to the Revolution would be swept from

power, from life. Andropov and his gang of thugs and leeches. The KGB—Beria's gift to Russia, descendant of the MVD, the NKVD, and OGPU, the Cheka—the Cheka alone might have been necessary. The others were sores and lice on the bear.

He went to fetch his overcoat, and a small bag he had packed. He would only come back after it was all over. He paused for a moment before a photograph on the wall, of a young man, which he had draped with black crêpe. He shook his head, and left the study. He had the city of Moscow in which to hide, and only twenty more hours to hide.

"Alexei—!" he cried involuntarily, ashamed of the sound in the moment he uttered it. He tugged on his coat stiffly. Then he picked up his bag, heard the dog snuffle at the closed kitchen door, and went out into the below-zero temperature of Kropotkin Street. He stopped at the gate for a moment, and looked back at the restored house. Then he walked away, upright, his stick clicking on the icy pavement.

Galakhov looked up at the window of Khamovkhin's bedroom as if studying a target or an obstacle in his path. He was on the point of being relieved of duty. He would disappear until the following night, when his return to duty would provide him with the opportunity of killing Khamovkhin.

Kill him—for what? A part of him he did not wish to acknowledge asked the question in a precise, cool mental voice. Kill him, now that they *knew* who *Kutuzov* was? And the generals were all *dead*?

It has been a long night, after he had heard the gossip of the radio traffic coming in from Moscow—a longer early morning after Andropov's last message, the one they had relayed direct to Washington and London—the ringleader, code-name *Kutuzov*, has been identified and is on the point of being arrested in Moscow. Subject identified as Mihail Pyotravich Gorochenko, Deputy Foreign Minister of the Soviet Union. *Subject identified—*

Kill Khamovkhin, who had laughed like a bully-boy when he heard the news, so the rumour said? An American CIA agent had told Galakhov, and sounded relieved, and then spat into the snow cursing all Russians for bastards.

334

Security was relaxed—except that they still worried where "Captain Ozeroff" was. He *could* kill—but why?

He saw a guard hurrying along the path to relieve him.

Kill him for revenge—do the worst you can. Kill him because it did not work, he told himself.

SIXTEEN
ANNA DOSTOYEVNA

Vorontsyev let himself into the empty house with the key that he had been given on his sixteenth birthday—an inordinate time to wait, he had thought as a youth, before Mihail Pyotravich Gorochenko had let him come and go as he pleased. But he had always kept the key, and now it enabled him to enter the house silently by the front door.

The dog barked from the back of the house as he pushed open the door. He knew the house was empty, and that Gorochenko had left the dog. Vorontsyev laughed— of course he had left the dog. He intended coming back— the next day, or the day after that.

He pushed open the kitchen door, and the big, over-weight bundle of red fur was planted against his chest, the pink tongue slobbering for his face. He lowered his head and let himself be licked, ruffling the fur, bunching it in his hands as memory assailed him, making the small incident perilous with allusion.

"Down, boy," he said softly, pushing the dog away. The great paws left his chest, and the dog ambled beneath the kitchen table, curling in its huge basket which was still too small. Brown eyes stared up at him, tongue lolling out, breaths wheezing. It was always hard to realise the dog was old.

Like Gorochenko.

He looked at the sink-unit. A cup filled with water, a

single saucer and plate. A slight smell of the breakfast that had been cooked remained. Gorochenko was not long gone, and he had left in no particular hurry.

Swiftly, after closing the kitchen door behind him, he searched the rest of the house. He did not go near the room he had once occupied himself, nor the room that had confined his adoptive mother in the months before her death. It was evident that no one else had yet searched the place and he became anxious, having frequently to shrug off the slow-motion that memory imposed, to complete the task before he was surprised.

He found that the gun was missing from the drawer of the escritoire. And that it was nowhere else in the house. It was a realisation that filled him with foreboding. He was sustained by a certainty that he would find Gorochenko, sometime that day or night, and to know the old man had a gun depressed, worried him. Apart from the gun, there was little missing. The dog had been given only one meal, and he had already guzzled half of it.

It was certain, then. Twenty-four hours. No more than that. The old man had perhaps one fresh shirt, his shaving tackle, his heavy overcoat, galoshes. All in the small bag he had had since the war. The bag had belonged to Kyril Vorontsyev. He had been told that the first time he had asked Gorochenko why such an important man used such a shabby old bag. A soldier's luggage, had been the unsmiling reply.

Talismans to ward him off—the old bag, the old dog—?

He had not asked himself what he would do when he and Gorochenko came face to face—had not asked on the plane, that sleepless hour, nor as he showed his papers at Cheremetievo, his palms tacky and his forehead beating as he waited for them to arrest him. But he had been too quick, just a little too quick, and the word to bring him in had not then been issued, he realised.

What would he do?

The answer, of course, was simple. Why else was he on his own, the decision to dump Folley at the Consulate and catch the first plane to Moscow already made before he had consciously analysed the matter? He wanted to find Gorochenko *by himself*. Stupid knight-in-shining-armour idea. No—an idea prompted by the weight of the past on him, which he could not ignore or overcome. If he could

337

find Gorochenko, he could stop the coup—that would be his duty.

Find Gorochenko. Find, like an order to the dog. Find, but not kill—

Gorochenko must not be put on trial, and executed, no matter that he had used Natalia against him, ordered Ossipov to kill him; ordered the deaths of Ilya and Maxim. Tried to kill him in the *dacha*, with the booby-trapped corpse. He must not be caught—

The telephone, suddenly ringing next to him as he stood indecisively in the study, caused him to jump. His hand came away from the blotter on the desk as if it were electrified. With simple reflex, before his thoughts could interfere, he picked it up.

"Yes?" he asked, caution catching in his throat like phlegm.

"Is that the Gorochenko house? Who is that speaking?" Masked, official tones.

He slammed down the telephone. He glanced round the study once, realising that it oppressed him with a weight of obligation. He moved to the door, and noticed for the first time the portrait of his father, dressed in uniform, a photograph taken in the last year of the war, perhaps just after the patriotic army had entered Germany. It was the picture of his father he had liked best as a child—slim, youthful, laughing, a tank and its crew behind him. The picture was surrounded, carefully, by black crêpe.

Which made Vorontsyev run cold for a reason he could not understand. His father—the anniversary of his death had been six months before. He touched the black crêpe gingerly, as if he half-expected a seaweed sliminess, then shook his head.

He ignored the dog in the kitchen, and let himself out of the house. There were a few parked cars, but none of them suspiciously occupied. He closed the gate behind him, and heard the faint barking of the dog from the kitchen. Its tone seemed plaintive. He shuddered as if cold and hurried away from the house where he had once lived.

Aubrey was, reluctantly, becoming adept at conversation with Khamovkhin. Now that the Soviet First Secretary was no more than a problem in security, he had lost a great deal of his interest in the *Snow Falcon* operation, as he still termed it—which meant he should have been bored. The fact that he was not was yet another indication that he was getting old.

They were walking on one of the terraces of the Lahtilinna, overlooking the slaty-grey expanse of the lake. The sky was a pale blue, with little cloud, a spring day without the temperature to sustain the illusion. Buckholz was on one side of the Russian leader, Aubrey on the other. They walked with the slow pace of statesmen or pensioners.

Khamovkhin was relieved, it was evident—and confident in Andropov's security machine. Aubrey thought it the over-confidence of a man driving a car that has never broken down before. The knocking in the engine—not possibly something wrong, the car never goes wrong. Any fear he had was a personal one, that assailed him at moments, for his own safety. Which was smaller, more agreeable, than the emotions aroused by the potential cataclysm the Soviet leader now considered impossible.

"I do think you should spend only the minimum of time out of doors," Aubrey said stiffly, and disliked the old-maid manner of his solicitation.

Khamovkhin's eyes sparkled. "Your concern for me is very touching, Mr. Aubrey." He enjoyed the pursing of Aubrey's lips. "You have much of the manner of our own security service." Aubrey's face went suddenly like a chalky mask, and Khamovkhin realised that his joke had touched some secret nerve of loyalty or righteousness in the small old man beside him.

They came to the end of the terrace walk. Buckholz placed one foot up on the low wall, leaned an elbow on his knee.

"Tell me about this Gorochenko, Mr. First Secretary. Our files seem to be as bare-assed as yours as far as he's concerned."

"Perfect for the role of leader of a military take-over," Khamovkhin observed, rubbing his mittened hands together, and nodding. "Yes—war hero, immensely loyal throughout the Stalin period—or so it appeared to Beria and Stalin. You had to be loyal to survive the periodic—*changes?*—in the Politburo in those days. And even more loyal to survive in the army. But he did it. I suppose that was cleverness." Khamovkhin was speaking to both, and neither, of them now. He stared out over the lake, but

339

observed an internal landscape. Then anger suffused his face, colouring it despite the cold. "I should have had him watched more closely!" It was the anger of a man outwitted by a sharper mind. "He played the semi-senile old goat too well!"

Aubrey smiled. "So it would seem. However, you appear very confident, sir, that his arrest is imminent."

"Yes—he won't get away."

"And we have nothing to worry about—?"

Khamovkhin looked at him sharply, as if the Englishman had unsuspected knowledge that Moscow Garrison was off the air and primed to begin the coup. He could not know that.

"No, we have not. Chairman Andropov will order the Chief of the General Staff and the Defence Minister to begin the stand-down of border units this afternoon. You will have confirmation as soon as it has been done."

"As soon as our satellites can see it happening," Buckholz commented drily.

"As you say," Khamovkhin observed frostily, aware that the honours were now firmly with the two foreigners.

"Unless you are killed," Aubrey said. "If that happens, then everything could escalate again—" He raised his hands, as if to imitate some explosion. "I think, for that reason alone, we should not prolong our exercise further. Shall we go inside?"

"Very well."

Galakhov lay on the narrow bunk, smoking a cigarette. On the bedside table was a plate with a few crumbs and a smear of grease. It had been easy to collect a late breakfast from the kitchens and bring it to one of the unoccupied security team bedrooms in the east wing of the Lahtilinna. He had not quite possessed the bravado to occupy the room he had been given as Ozeroff, but it was on the same floor and corridor. The Finns doing the cooking had taken little notice of him, nor had the few off-duty Englishmen and Americans still eating. It was unlikely that anyone would disturb him before nightfall, when he could act as if on-duty again.

It was ridiculous, and ridiculously simple. Everyone assumed he *should* be there. As with Ozeroff, drafting in a security team whose members were strangers to each

340

other had a fatal flaw—who could tell who should not be there? He had dyed his hair so that it was lighter in colour, combed it another way—he had been wearing the hood of his parka all his duty-spell anyway—slipped in contact lenses that changed his eye colour, padded his cheeks slightly, and made sure that he walked with much more of a shuffle. He was certain that, in anything but the best light, he could walk past someone holding his picture—that passport picture they had issued, the one from his Heathrow disguise—and not be recognised.

He blew a contemptuous funnel of smoke towards the high, cream-painted ceiling. If they searched, he would be asleep, or reading. He was one of them, and they would not bother with him.

He stubbed out his cigarette, and opened the door of the bedside cabinet. He took out a sketch plan made from his own observations of the castle, and a large-scale map of the surroundings of the Lahtilinna. The problem of making his escape had begun to concern him in an immediate, pressing way, so that when he thought of it, as he seemed to do with increasing frequency, his palms seemed to grow damp, his whole body just that infinitesimal amount out of his control.

He began to recite to himself, using the sketch-plan, the litany of the moves that would end with the assassination of Khamovkhin.

The mere presence of Defence Minister Druzhinin and Chief of the General Staff Pavoletskii in his spacious office gave Yuri Andropov a renewed sense of authority, command. He perceived that his worst moments during the past days had come while he was alone—without the challenge of possible enemies or the satisfying obedience of subordinates. The two men before him now, both elderly and in uniform, might be enemies—though he did not think so—but since they were tangible and present, they could give no more sense of threat than their bulk, or medals or features.

And they looked old, and rather ordinary, with turkey-necks of loose skin just above the collars of their green uniforms, just above the V-shapes of their rows of medals, and framed by the heavy square shoulder-boards. Gold rank, green cloth, and the bronze and gold of med-

341

als. There they were, he thought—his reaction was tinged with contempt—the old stories—both of them wearing the medal commemorating the thirtieth anniversary of the Soviet Army, both of them the medal for Heroic Work during the Great War of the Motherland; both with the medal for the Liberation of Berlin. Pavoletskii with the Medal of Valour, and the Medal for the Defence of Leningrad—Druzhinin with the Medal for Battle Merit, and the Defence of the Caucasus.

Parade uniforms, parade minds, parade behaviour. Old soldiers. He weighed his words carefully.

"It is necessary, at this time, to stand down certain of the border units—especially those that have undertaken *unauthorised* movements and dispositions during the past week." He watched their faces, just as Kapustin, standing a little way behind the two soldiers, watched him. Andropov was already assessing future loyalties. His remarks had challenged the two visitors to take sides, declare themselves.

It was Pavoletskii who spoke first. He cleared his throat as if the words stuck there.

"I speak personally, Chairman Andropov," he began, glancing at his companion, "When I say that I learn with surprise, even horror, of the charges you have levelled against certain senior officers in the Soviet Army—"

"And I—" Druzhinin interrupted, but as if on cue, "I am saddened to hear of the—*accidents*—that have befallen those same officers who have fallen under suspicion from the security service."

Then there was a silence. Andropov felt an unexpected anger welling in him, and pressed his palms on his thighs, as if to restrain the emotion. But he was unable to prevent his outburst. The anger forced his body forward, made his face thin with rage.

"He is one of you! Gorochenko is one of you—an *army man!* Don't pretend you didn't know—" He saw Kapustin's face darken with warning.

"You have no *proof* that the Deputy Foreign Minister is involved in a conspiracy against the state involving sections of the armed forces," Druzhinin remarked levelly, his stare seeming to read Andropov's thoughts.

"Proof?" Andropov asked mockingly. "We have all the proof we require to arrest him for questioning—" Each of the two soldiers flinched in contempt. "Now I ask you again—will you issue the necessary orders to units in GSFN and the Red Banner Northern Fleet?"

After an interminable silence, Druzhinin said, "I will request Marshall Pavoletskii to draw up new dispositions for the units who may have adopted *provocative* frontier positions."

"And the Moscow Garrison? Something must be done."

Pavoletskii's eyes gleamed, and Andropov realised that the dialogue had been rehearsed, that he had been led, rather than been leader, thus far.

"When you have taken Deputy Foreign Minister Gorochenko into custody, then I will order the stand-down of the Garrison and the arrest of Valenkov."

Suddenly, the furniture of the room, gloomily heavy to eye and hand, seemed unsubstantial to Andropov.

"You refuse?"

"No. There is nothing to accept or refuse. I will comply with your request when I am presented with proof that the Moscow Garrison is involved with Comrade Gorochenko in a conspiracy against the state."

"Where is Major Vorontsyev, who you say has such proof?" Pavoletskii asked silkily, unsurprised even when Andropov stood up, leaning his weight on white-knuckled hands on the edge of his desk.

"Get out! Get out!" was all he managed to say. The two soldiers, as if the years had lightened, stood up together, put on their caps and saluted like junior officers. Then, as one, they turned to the door, and went out.

Kapustin watched Andropov for a moment. "You handled that very badly," he observed.

"Don't tell me that—what are you, a bloody theatre critic?" Andropov screamed. Kapustin took one step towards the desk, then halted as Andropov succumbed completely to his fury. "They're all in league! Those two, they're just standing back to see who will be the winner! They will watch as you and I are swept away like dirt, or flushed down the lavatory. Don't you understand—they *know* what's going on! And they will do nothing about it!"

"They will order the invasion troops to stand down from frontier positions. What else did you expect?"

"Valenkov is all that's required for the whole thing to succeed!"

"I know that. We have to find Gorochenko before tomorrow. *And* Vorontsyev."

"Find them, then—find them!" Andropov raged, the sweat bright on his forehead, the light from the window catching his spectacles so that he had no eyes for a moment and looked hollow and incomplete. "Find them— find them!"

Vorontsyev dialled the unlisted number of the telephone on his own desk in the Frunze Quay office. The glass of the public telephone on Gogol Boulevard fogged swiftly, so that he could no longer see the people waiting at the bus stop, staring up at the public TV screen at the head of the bus queue. The opaque glass of the booth became a mirror of the tension which had built with every step from Gorochenko's house. So far, he had not been followed.

He listened to the ringing of the telephone, his other hand tugging compulsively at the cord as he waited. Then, thankfully, Alevtina answered.

"Office of Major Vorontsyev."

"Alevtina, can you talk freely? It's me." The anonymous admission sounded coy and unreal from an SID officer. The girl gasped audibly.

"Major—they've been here," she stammered. "Kapustin himself is looking for you. We're supposed to report if—"

"Alevtina, will you help me?" It was a plea. His isolation, his dependence on this single telephone call, assailed him. He was naked before what threatened him, and he could not assume the strength to order or impress. Alevtina was silent for a long time.

"What can I do, Major?" It was not a bluff, or a delay while they put on a trace. Vorontsyev knew it was something more than obedience—and for the first time he was grateful for the girl's romantic feelings towards him, which he had studiously ignored. He was greedy for affection, suddenly.

"I have to have the file—on my father."

"Your—the Deputy Foreign Minister? I heard there was a panic on, and *he* was part of it—"

"He *is* it," Vorontsyev said slowly. "Didn't they tell you? He's the ringleader of *Group 1917*."

"Oh-my-God," the girl breathed softly. Vorontsyev envied her the simplicity of the shock.

"Yes. And I have to find him—*me*, no one else. You understand, Alevtina? I need that file. Is it still there?"

"What—oh, yes. A copy was taken by the Deputy Chairman, but there's still our office copy——" She had retreated into a secretarial neutrality.

"Er—yes. My lunch-hour is due in a few minutes. Where?"

Cautiously, Vorontsyev said, "The café—where we used to meet my wife after rehearsals. Yes?"

A pause then: "Yes. Give me half an hour."

Vorontsyev put down the clammy Bakelite of the receiver. The air outside the opaque of the booth seemed colder, a sudden shock of water flung in his face. He had to have that file. The fact that the girl would help him, at least sufficiently to bring him the file, was a small warm place in his chest.

The TV screen at the head of the bus queue was showing a repeat of Khamovkhin's address to the Finnish Parliament. Vorontsyev ignored it.

The café was in a small street off Sverdlov Square, which contained the Bolshoi Theatre, and it specialised fairly cheaply in Georgian cooking. Vorontsyev had not been there for some time, and most of the waiters were unfamiliar. He sat in a dim corner towards the back of the café, knowing that one avenue of escape via the urinal at the back was quickly available. It was risky, moving as openly as he must round the centre of the city—he was the KGB's best means of finding Gorochenko.

He combatted his tiredness with dark coffee, and stilled hunger by devouring heavily spiced chicken *satsivi* with brine-pickled cabbage and red peppers. The overpowering flavour of the food refreshed him, gave him a sense of normality; it did not evoke memories of any personal life.

While he was drinking more coffee after the meal, he saw the girl framed in the square of light at the doorway. He raised his hand, and she joined him.

"Were you followed?"

"I don't think so. I tried to be clever——" There was a pleasure in conspiracy about Alevtina, and a deeper concern for him in her green eyes. She was concerned for him, wanted to help him—and somehow was pleased with

345

his isolation and helplessness. "At least no one saw me removing this, sir."

Vorontsyev nodded, and pushed his coffee cup aside. Then he took the file from its envelope and opened it. He leafed through the entries, uncertain now that he had it what use it would be. Then he looked up, putting it back in the envelope.

"Now I have to go." He placed a ten-rouble note on the table.

"Sir—can I help?" Vorontsyev saw the eager, brave look in the girl's eyes, and shook his head. He was refreshed by her concern, but wanted no more of it at that moment.

"No, Alevtina. You may be in trouble already. *I* have to find my father. If anyone questions you, say I tricked you into this—" The girl shook her head.

"Don't worry about me, sir."

Vorontsyev took his overcoat from a chair, put it on. Then scarf and gloves.

"Leave first, will you? Just in case."

"Sir. And good luck, whatever that means."

"Thanks, Alevtina. Don't worry about me—" He motioned the girl towards the door. She stared at him, as if to remember, then went out, turned to the left, and was out of sight. Vorontsyev gave her a few moments, then turned up his collar because the café was more crowded now with office workers and shoppers, and he could not be certain of the faces that bent over food or were masked behind newspapers and clouds of cigarette smoke.

He stood in the doorway of the café, watching the street, and the few parked cars, and the turning into Sverdlov Square. Then he headed for the nearest Metro station.

From where he stood, sipping coffee he had poured from a flask into the plastic beaker that was its screw-top, Mihail Pyotravich Gorochenko could see, at the other end of Red Square, the hideous bulk of St. Basil's Cathedral. A slight shift in his stance at the tiny, dirt-coated window and he was able to see the towers and pinnacles of the Kremlin. Should he care to, to alleviate the tense, wearing boredom that must at some time assail him, he could recite the names of each tower. For the moment, he stared over the bare trees, seeing some distant parts of the gardens.

The bare trees, the ordered borders of now bare earth, the patches of thawing snow on the grass, the straight, rulered walks.

What was it Ivan the Terrible had done to the architects of St. Basil's he wondered as he shifted his gaze. Blinded them so they couldn't build another? Something of the sort.

He sipped noisily, the coffee wetting the upper lip and the thick moustache. Far below him, the lunchtime crowds huddled along the square, the trolleys sparked and flashed, and shoppers hurried in and out of GUM. The serpentine queue outside the Lenin Mausoleum, all of whom appeared to be dressed in black, or dark-brown, waited patiently for admission.

A few people sat on the benches in that corner of the Alexandrovski Gardens that he could see from his high window.

The waiting was, he admitted, taking its toll. His eyes wandered over Red Square endlessly, like those of a drunken man lying on his back, not daring to focus for too long in case the room began to spin. Yes, like that. As if he could not look at any one thing out there for too long, in case his moral surroundings began to lurch sideways. He could not even look over the walls of the Kremlin for very long—he could not see Khamovkhin's office from where he stood—despite the hatred that it caused in his breast, hot, fiery like a cardiac pain.

Yet he had to go on looking out over the square, down at the tiny figures bustling—seeming to be blown by the wind that whistled at the grimy window. If he did not, then the megalomania assailed him—that or the fury of rage at still waiting, at the distant threat of Dzerzhinsky Street and his adopted son.

It was strange, he thought, that megalomania, a word in history books or psychologists' reports, was palpable like this. A mounting feeling like phlegm in the back of the throat, or extra air filling the lungs so that the chest strained out. A lightness in the loins. No mirrors, but the eyes seeing from just behind the head, shaping the figure consciously from that angle. He did not enjoy the feeling. In fact, he was ashamed of it, and feared it. If anything, he wished for the purer megalomania that might have been more readily available to a religious man. He was not. His purity of motive had to do with ideology, with politics—and they were not *visionary* like a religious faith, however desperately he had clung to them over the years.

But the megalomania—the strange sensations, the brimming—no, swelling of the brain in its case of bone—did not come when he looked down at the tiny, insignificant people, or even at St. Basil's, or the Kremlin. It came when he did *not* look at them. When all he had was the perspective of the small, bare dusty room full of unopened crates and a small table on which resided a dust-free telephone whose wire ran across the bare boards to the wall-socket that had been fitted for him—when that was his only perspective, then it was no bigger than himself. He inflated, weirdly, to fill the room, like a balloon.

The people, the buildings, in the street, gave him *scale*, perspective. And he had to have scale—otherwise he had *no* sense of anything outside himself, nothing but ambition, greed, love of cold power.

He had never thought himself like that, having those qualities. Only in a little way. He had tried, and succeeded, to think of himself as a servant, a *conscience-keeper*, an acolyte of his own ideology.

Was that a more dangerous megalomania, masked in humility? That would be a religious megalomania, perhaps? Sainthood, willed and purposed. Was that what he was?

He shuddered, and concentrated his gaze downwards, watching one old—man or woman? He couldn't tell from that angle, in those swaddling lumps of clothing. One old *being*, walking slowly and with difficulty, the wind plucking at coat-tails. He tried, very hard, to say—for you. For *you*.

It did not work.

He looked, instead, at the serpent before the gates of bronze—he smiled at the vivid rhetoric. The queue of the faithful waiting to look on the mummified remains of V. I. Lenin in their glass box; too luridly lit, he had always considered. There were hundreds of them, even in winter. Nearly sixty years on.

For you, he said to himself. For *you*. There were more of them, a bulk of people, representative.

For you.

It seemed to ease the constriction in his chest, to free his breathing. He inhaled the dusty, prickling air and almost sneezed. He swallowed the last of his coffee, and looked over his shoulder at the telephone. There was a renewal of purpose. The destructive sense of his own motives had gone like a bout of nausea. But he felt stronger now, not weaker.

One telephone call. He could do it with one telephone call, at six the next morning. Valenkov, who had been a close friend of Kyril Vorontsyev—and who had been with him, as a junior officer, from Stalingrad to the outskirts of Berlin—he would answer the telephone, and receive the command, and in his turn issue the commands to the Moscow Garrison ...

One telephone call and—he looked across the Kremlin walls—he would start again. *It* would start again. The new beginning.

He closed his eyes in satisfaction, and was alarmed when an image jumped at him out of the red-spotted darkness behind his lids. Of Alexei Vorontsyev, as a child, holding his hand. The boy had bright red plastic boots, and was kicking up gouts of snow, and laughing.

He shook his head to clear it, and open his eyes. The image retreated obediently.

Where was he? Where was Alexei now?

The apartment was in a block of Vosstaniya flats on the Kutuzovsky Prospekt, near the Ukraina Hotel, an elaborate wedding-cake, and the Comecon building a modern grey slab, hard-edged against the pale blue of the sky. The apartments had been built during the time of Stalin, when Anna Dostoyevna had been Minister of Culture and had had much to do with the design of the new city centre. She had chosen to live in one of the apartments in the Vosstaniya because her ministry had been connected with their design. When she had been allowed to resign quietly from the Politburo after losing Stalin's favour, she had remained in the apartment.

Vorontsyev remembered her from his childhood—a big, powerful woman with a deep voice, who frightened him. And he disliked her, too, because she seemed to occupy a place in Mihail Pyotravich's private world that should have belonged to his adoptive mother. He sensed, rather than knew, that Anna Dostoyevna was not Gorochenko's mistress in the conventional sense. Rather, she possessed an ideological bond with him, shared an intellectual community from which Gorochenko's wife was excluded.

Vorontsyev had found her name in the files, and remembered the intellectual intimacy that had once bound the two of them. And he had felt he might have found the answer.

He had digested the information in the files, as well as he could, in the washroom at the Komsomolskaia Metro Station, locked in a chilly cubicle, hearing the footsteps across the chequered tiles outside, the whistling, the splashing of water.

When he had reduced the file to a list of possibilities, he had torn each sheet into shreds, then the file itself into scraps of blue card, and flushed them away. It had been a setting free of Gorochenko rather than a dismissal.

He had travelled on the Metro all afternoon, moving from station to station, making only one, or at most two, calls from any one place. Slowly, he had crossed through all the names on the list, all the places Gorochenko might be, until he had come to the apartment on the Kutuzovsky. Prospekt.

Because it was the last name, and he was dog-tired now, and crazed with futility, he was certain that Gorochenko would be there; yet knowing that he would not be with anyone whose name was in the file under "Known Associates." Yet, caught as he now was in the pattern of this action, from file to contacts to the elimination of possibilities—he was unable to envisage other possibilities, other patterns.

He did not even know, he realised, what Gorochenko was any more. He was a collection of facts and observations that led nowhere. His Surveillance Log was impeccable—he simply could not be, without additional information, the man *Kutuzov*. Further back, in the thirties and forties, he was a natural survivor, along with Molotov and Gromyko, in a Politburo periodically purged and decimated by Stalin's psychotic suspicions. When had he changed, when achieved another, and radical, view of the Revolution?

Vorontsyev had abandoned the attempt to understand Gorochenko.

He pressed the doorbell of the apartment. Would she explain his father to him? Would she know where he was?

Vorontsyev realised that the former question had become more pressing—that the afternoon had left him barren of investigatory technique or desire. He only wanted to understand.

He was dangerously in sympathy with Gorochenko now, he perceived; it might prevent him ever finding the man.

She was shrunken, but perhaps he had expected the child's perspective, to have to look up into the strong face. She was perhaps five feet ten, dressed in a sweater and cardigan and a drab skirt of thick wool. Her stockings were thick and dark, and her shoes stout. She looked like a schoolteacher. Her eyes behind the wire-framed spectacles were sharp with a glistening suspicion.

He showed her the ID card, and she involuntarily backed half a step, and her hand gripped the edge of the door so that the fingers whitened. He said, "Comrade Dostoyevna—might I speak with you?" She was suspicious of the careful neutrality of tone, the implication that she possessed choice.

"What is it, Comrade Major?" And old inflection, one she must have used many times during the years when Stalin let her live on in anonymity. "What do you want?"

Involuntarily, as if without will, she had opened the door a little more. He stepped forward, and she seemed to retreat silently from the door, spectrally backing towards the lounge. He closed the door behind him, looking at her all the while as at an old film. Cheka, NKVD, MVD, KGB—they were all the same, her posture informed him.

The lounge was sparse yet comfortable. A great many books, one or two blunt, square pieces of statuary and furniture that was old but which had been carefully repaired and recovered. She had never married, he knew. On one low table near the sagging sofa there was a big metal ashtray such as might have come from a bar or restaurant, full of stubs and ash. And one smoking cigarette she picked up with a quick, swooping gesture as if he might have appropriated it.

"What is it?" she said, standing in front of a packed bookcase of dog-eared Russian paperbacks. It lent her solidity, and he suspected that she knew it. Her mind had always been formidable; the books were an assurance of her personality and her past. She was nervous, but seemed calmed to some degree by his quiescence.

351

"May I sit down?" She gestured to an armchair recently re-covered in a floral pattern of browns and golds. A threadbare patch of carpet seemed to have slid out from beneath it. He said, "I want to talk to you about—my father . . ." It was the only way to inject a sincerity, a lack of officialdom which would cause her to close like a shell, into the room. "Not Kyril—Mihail Pyotravich."

"What—is the matter with him?" It was a selfish question, he saw. Her hands brushed her body, as if admitting its age, as if only illness and infirmity could involve someone she had known a long time ago.

"He is not ill," he said. She seemed to resent it, and puffed at her cigarette. He noticed that the cardboard tube of the cigarette had been flattened by the pressure of anxiety. "No—I have to find him, Anna Ilyevna." He recalled her patronymic from the files. "I have to find him very urgently."

"To do with your job? You're SID." Suddenly, the idea seemed to seize her. "Your own *father?*"

"Please understand," he began, realising he was being rushed, was losing control of the conversation. "It is not official. Yes, *they* are looking for him. I—want to help him." He hated the clichés. She was evidently suspicious now.

"Help?" She was younger, an old habitual scorn came back to her face and voice.

"Yes!" he blurted out, feeling himself younger also—too young. He had, suddenly, to commit himself. "Look, I don't know how often you see him, or speak with him, but he—he's into something very dangerous. And they know he is, and they want him very badly! I have to get to him before they do!" There was a plaintive note in his voice, and he was sure his habitual identification with Gorochenko, used with emphasis in that way, had damaged his argument. It would appear to her little other than a transparent deceit.

She looked at his face, then lifted her stretched, dry skin in a look of scorn. She puffed at the cigarette again, and he noticed that now it was held delicately in her fingers.

"He was always fond of you," she said, staring at the ceiling. Then the face seemed to subside into its stiff, wrinkled lines again, and the eyes were dark points.

"And I of him!" he said. "You must know that if you know anything."

"Perhaps."

He realised she had taken control of the situation; he thought she must believe him to some degree, otherwise she would not have had the temerity to seize the initiative.

"Do you know where he is?"

She was silent. She paced the worn carpet, circling the furniture, as if she had ambushed the room and its occupant. He saw the power of the mind and will in the frame, and sensed the kind of magnetism such a complementary nature must have had for Gorochenko. Then she looked at him, emphasising her words with little stabs of the cardboard tube.

"I have not seen Mihail Pyotravich for almost two years." His stomach seemed heavy and his breath constricted. He knew she was telling the truth.

"What has happened to him?"

"In what way?" Interrogative, sharp.

"He—he's organised a coup!" Her eyes sharpened, gleamed with some inner knowledge. "He's on the point of success or failure. I have to find him before—before . . ." Weakly: "Before they do."

"But will they find him?" She was amused now, and allied with Gorochenko. He wondered how much she had been his mentor.

"Yes, they will!"

"I wonder."

He saw the mind shut like a handbag, almost heard the metallic click of the clasp. She had retreated from him again. He was a stupid policeman and his quarry was Gorochenko. The muddle of his own motives, no doubt plain to her, did not justify answers. She would not help him.

"Don't you see?" he said. "I have to stop him. He has to be stopped."

"Why?" The challenge was almost sexual, and she might have been a young woman; but even as he looked at her she became ancient and decayed, and delighting merely in the strength of impotence. Someone she knew, her age and experience—not put out to grass as she had been. Affecting things. *Breaking* things.

"Because it will not work any more. Everyone who has helped him has been put aside. There's only him."

"No. You would not be worried if he was alone."

He admitted the truth by dropping his eyes.

"Yes." He felt stupid and childish now. And futile.

"Then he *will* do it!" she whispered.

"You—you persuaded him!" he cried.

She looked at him with contempt, moving a step closer to his chair, her presence more powerful now. Sitting, she loomed over him in the perspective he had anticipated when she opened the door.

"I did nothing, you stupid adolescent. Once I quarrelled with him—quarrelled all the time because he seemed to accept Stailin and Beria and the NKVD and all the *filth* that went with it!" Her eyes gleamed fiercely. He saw a dab of spittle at one corner of the mouth. The dentures moved in an approximation of speech, but seemed not to diminish the force of her words.

"But he did *not* accept!" She clasped her hands to her heavy bosom like a young girl. "All the time—all the time . . ." She seemed unable to make her feelings coherent.

"But you—you fell from favour with Stalin. He didn't. He was loyal to Stalin, until his death. Then to Kruschev, and to Brezhnev." He couldn't understand anything, he decided. *He* was in the KGB—Mihail Pyotravich had made sure of that, even getting him transferred to SID. Now this old woman was talking as if all the time Gorochenko was a traitor to the Soviet Union, had always been.

"All the time it was a game," she said. "It must have been a game to him! Waiting his chance." Then, with regret, she added: "I had little or nothing to do with it—" Finally, shame. "I accused him of toadying to save his skin. Long ago I did that. I didn't understand him, I suppose."

She sat down, and seemed to resolve everything into silence, as if her mind was dying away like her words. It was as if she had indulged in some physical exercise belonging to her youth, and it had tired her to the extent that now she felt very old. She had relived some of her political life, some of the intellectual passion with which she had loved Gorochenko, and now it had passed, and she was spent.

"Tell me where he is?" Vorontsyev asked quietly. When she looked up at him, her eyes were vague. She had retreated almost as if he had interrogated her. She shook her head like a stubborn child. He did not know whether she was refusing, or admitting ignorance. Suddenly, he was tired of this cat-and-mouse game with an untidy old woman. He was bone-weary, at the end of his patience.

"Tell me where he is!" he ordered, and her eyes snapped shut, then opened attentively. A voice had spoken from thirty years before—the voice of command and terror.

"I don't know where he is." Her voice almost whined as it pleaded with him.

"But you can guess—you know him better than I do. Where would he go? To whom would he turn? Where would he hide?" She mistrusted him again. "I *have* to help him—I have to be *with* him—don't you understand that?" Now, she was confused by the smeared emotions, the apparent contradictions, as if he had taken on a multiple personality. "I want to be *with* him, Anna. I'm his *son*."

He saw intolerable pressure in her eyes. She was lonely, she was guilty towards Gorochenko, wanted to do something for him, make some gesture of atonement for the years in which she had despised him.

"He wants to change the history of Russia—just as Lenin did," she said, concentrating.

"Is that a clue to help me?" he asked, forcing himself to smile, stifling his impatience. He had broken through, had only to sustain the artificiality—and ignore the cold part of his head that mocked his anxiety to learn the ignorant guess of a half-senile old woman who lived alone. "Give me another clue, Anna?"

She had adopted that almost foetal position of consciousness that prisoners under interrogation often discovered and utilised. A child knows nothing. The interrogators call it "Hide-and-Seek." He would have to continue with the game.

"He would want to watch it—whatever is going to happen, he would want to watch it." She was staring at the carpet just in front of her feet as she spoke. Of course! So bloody *obvious*! She did know Gorochenko better than he did.

Red—Square—his mind spelt out carefully.

"You think so?"

"Oh, yes."

A room with a view of Red Square. Vorontsyev closed his eyes, tried to be a rooftop camera, and to sense the best perch a camera might adopt. Where best—? Then he had it.

The History Museum!

He was in the History Museum!

"To change the history of Russia," the old woman murmured again, Vorontsyev trembled with understanding. Gorochenko would have chosen his vantage-point cleverly, and with fitting, appropriate irony. A room at the top of the History Museum, watching Valenkov's tanks make history.

He was about to pat her hand with his own, as if to wake her from some light hypnotic trance, about to speak, when the doorbell damaged, broke the silence. Anna Dostoyevna's eyes went bright with immediacy, then her face collapsed into a look fossilised from thirty years ago. Terror. She glanced at him, then at the door of the lounge, then back to him, her eyes wide with guilt and fear.

"It *is* them," he said, dropping the words like pebbles into the distressed water of her awareness. "Hide me. Quickly!"

SEVENTEEN

YOUNG AND OLD

The doorbell rang again, longer this time.

"Where can I hide?" he asked.

"What?"

"Hide!"

"The bedroom—please don't make a sound. Yes, I'll hide you . . ." She started for the bedroom, eager to propitiate him, as if by so doing she was pleasing the people at the door.

He entered the dim room, banging his shin against the leg of the bed as he took his third step. She opened a cheap fitted wardrobe, a thin sheet of plywood poorly stained—he could perceive its quality as he flicked on the light, then switched it off again almost immediately. The doorbell rang again—three separate summonses.

"Quick, quick!"

He stepped into the wardrobe, his face brushing against an out-of-fashion dress that reeked of tobacco, and the rough material of three skirts on the same hanger. The door squeaked to behind him.

"Pull yourself together or you'll kill us both!" he barked. He heard the sob of fear in her throat. Then he reached into his jacket and unholstered the Stechkin. He pumped a round into the breech, and slipped off the safety.

He heard her open the door, and a man's voice. He leaned against the cheap, thin plywood, listening to the voice as it moved nearer, down the corridor until its quality changed, unconfined in the lounge. It was Kapustin himself.

His mouth was dry, and he sucked spit from his cheeks. He found it difficult to distinguish what was being said, but he could sense the different voices, even apprehend the changes in tone that coloured each voice.

Kapustin had another man with him—there was a murmur of introduction—but only two voices continued the conversation. Kapustin was looking for Gorochenko. There was no mention of himself at the outset, at least.

Strangely, he experienced little fear beyond imagining the physical sensations of a light being switched on, the thin door being pulled back noisily, a man with a gun motioning him out—or opening his eyes and mouth with bleak fear as he saw Vorontsyev's own gun, before it deafened him, Perhaps some residue of office clung to him—he knew the man in the next room, and was a trusted subordinate. It was difficult to consider such familiar concepts in the past tense. Moscow Centre was his place of work; he was not an ordinary Soviet citizen.

The face of his watch glowed as he moved his wrist to inspect the time. Perhaps five minutes had passed. An interrogative colour to Kapustin's voice, and Vorontsyev strained to catch the tone in the woman's reply. It seemed satisfactorily neutral, and he hoped the question had been about himself.

Another ten minutes passed. Filled with awareness of an itch in his left calf, the texture of clothes against the skin of his hands and face, the smell of moth-balls, and the dry mustiness of old flesh; and the reek of stale tobacco in the clothes. He was appalled, gradually, and felt revulsion that he should be confined in the woman's wardrobe. It was as if he had seen her naked, or made love to her, the proximity of scents and odours that were hers.

"Come out."

He heard the woman's voice, whispering like the rustle of paper, and incautiously he slid back the door. She had not switched on the light and he said, "They've gone?"

"Yes."

"What did they want?"

As he joined her in the lounge, he saw how drained she appeared, the skin taut as stretched hide, grey with wasted health. She seemed unsteady on her feet, and he took her elbow and guided her to the sofa. It sagged as she sat, as if in imitation of the bonelessness of her posture. He thought she might fall sideways at any moment, like a small baby.

"Thank you," he said. She looked at him vehemently.

"Leave me alone!" she breathed venomously, her hand fiddling with the stuff of her woollen jumper, clutching it into a third breast, releasing it again in creases. She was badly frightened. Kapustin had a quality of quiet menace, and authority to make the threat real.

"What did he say to you?"

"I told him nothing!" she cried desperately.

"I know that, Anna." But, whether Kapustin had believed her or not, he would have posted at least one man somewhere in the foyer of the building, or outside in a car.

Vorontsyev got up and went to the door. Then he looked back at the old woman. She seemed quiet and self-possessed, and only the movement of her lips indicated the furious mental activity as she tried to rid herself of her recent experiences. He knew it would not be long before she was able to do it. He looked at his watch. Almost five. The museum closed at five-thirty. He would have to hurry.

He opened the front door of the apartment carefully, and looked out. No one in the corridor. He slipped out. The narrow hall of each floor of the block, much like an hotel corridor, was uncarpeted. Lino squeaked softly under his shoes as he crossed to the window at the nearer end of the ill-lit corridor.

As he had guessed, there was a fire-escape passing the window. Ugly ironwork already frosty in the light of a street lamp a little further down the Kutuzovsky Prospekt. He unlatched the window, and slid it up. It protested, and his head spun round as if he had been shouted at. The corridor was still empty.

He heard a child coughing behind a nearby door. And, even as the cold air flowed on his face, he smelt cabbage cooking. He had not noticed before. He swung one leg over the sill, touching his toe gently on the platform of the fire-escape. Then he stepped out, shutting the window behind him.

He paused for a moment, looking down. One or two cars, and a lot of traffic on the Prospekt, already heading out of the city; trolleys and buses mainly, some cars.

Congealing on the road which was shining with frost. He could see no one in wait for him, and he clattered down the first flight of steps. Three floors down was the street. Three minutes, if he ran, to the Metro. His feet slipped, and he clutched the icy rail of the fire-escape to steady himself. The clutter of sound rang above the noise of the traffic. He paused, then hurried on, the few moments of swift movement down the steps becoming an imperative, a surge of action like flight.

"Identify yourself!" The order came from below him—a dark shadow, the light behind it, seen through the trellis-work of the last twist of the fire-escape. "Come down slowly!"

Vorontsyev could not see the gun, but he knew it would be there. It had been too easy. Kapustin had left a man in the foyer, and a man near the fire-escape. He prayed it was no one he knew; not one of his team . . .

He knelt, firing through the gap between two steps, into the centre of the dark shape. The gun was very loud in the cold air, seeming to halt the traffic. Something plucked away from the rail beside his head in the same moment as there was a little spit of flame from the shadow of the man's coat. Then a purpled face as it caught the light of the street lamp, and the body falling backwards, something metallic skittering away across the frosty concrete of the path. He clattered down the last flight, the Stechkin making separate flat concussions as he held it and the rail in one gloved hand, steadying himself.

He did not bother to inspect the form on the ground, but ran away from it, his feet uncertain, the momentum threatening to spill him on the ground at any moment. He skidded round the side of the flats into the wall of lights and noise of the Kutuzovsky Prospekt. He thought he had heard a summons behind him, but could not be certain. He slipped the gun into the pocket of his coat where he could reach it easily, and weaved his way through the thick flow of traffic. In front of a bus, the lights glaring in his face, then a car screeching as the brakes were applied—suddenly the traffic coming from the opposite direction, and a moment of disorientation. Then three lanes of halted traffic, and he was a minute from the Kievskaia Metro station.

He began to walk, head bowed, fur hat settled firmly on

his head, hands in the pockets of his thick overcoat. He was on his way home, an ordinary citizen.

Behind him, the dark stain of the overcoat lumped on the path had decided everything. Now, he was irrevocably determined upon a course of action. He was an outlaw now, a murderer. The single act gleamed in his confusion like a beacon. It did not matter, his moral assessment of the act. This had moulded his mental proportions like the hands of a potter; he had to find Gorochenko, and stop him, and help him escape.

He passed through the barrier, a marble bust of Lenin in a small alcove just beyond it, and descended the escalator to the platform. The station was crowded with home-going workers, and he saw the KGB men, two of them, eyes swivelling hopelessly as they tried to identify and assimilate each face that passed them. They would know that now, for perhaps an hour and a half, they had very little chance of sighting him and making a positive ID.

He stood against the wall on the platform, the crowd washing in front of him, bunching like seaweed moved by a gentle sea, keeping warm, staring at the map of the metro on the opposite wall, reading the paper, talking. They were only, in his eyes, camouflage. Only *he* was real in the scene.

The train sighed into the station, strips of bright light from the crowded, fuggy carriages elongating, separating as the carriages slowed. The doors slid open. He glanced swiftly along the platform in both directions. He was so far ahead of them, there was no disturbance. Even though, by the time he reached Revolution Square station, they might have sealed the exits.

He had no time to worry about it. The doors slid shut behind him.

A woman, against whom his side pressed as the train jogged, sensed the imprint of the gun for what it was, and looked up at him. His face was set, his eyes staring, and she knew that he must be KGB. She never looked at him again. Rather, she tried to edge a little from him in the packed compartment.

Darkness—Arbatskaia—darkness.

No evidence of special, concentrated activity. They were slow, too slow. The violent death of the man on watch had caught them unprepared. Anna Dostoyevna was a name on a long list, and they were looking for Gorochenko there. Instead, they had found him, and he had killed one of them. Orders were needed. Kapustin was in a car somewhere, being fed the information that a KGB man at the Vosstaniya flats was dead, and had undoubtedly been killed by Vorontsyev. Units all over the centre of the city would have to be alerted.

He bent his knees slightly, as if urging the train to greater speed, his body suddenly possessed by his race against the unwieldy net closing round him.

A bright glare of platform lights, and the name sliding as if in oil past the window—Revolution Square. He grimaced at the appropriateness of his destination. He pushed to the door, panicking momentarily as his arms were jammed into his pockets by the pressure of bodies. Someone glanced round at the pressure of the Stechkin's ugly shape, then looked ahead as they saw his eyes. He stumbled onto the platform, hemmed in by the crowd, a bobbing mass of fur caps and hats and woollen scarves ahead and alongside him.

He turned left with the crowd's momentum, then broke from them as they passed through to another platform, for another train. He looked up. A few individuals, strung loosely like irregular beads on the necklace of the escalator. He stepped on, watched his feet as the stairway froze into steps, and then kept his eyes ahead of him, up the long steep flight towards the exit. He could feel the colder air of the street above, and the gun was hard in his hand.

He walked up perhaps a dozen steps, until he was close behind a middle-aged man with a battered briefcase and woollen mittens, and a woman in a shapeless brown coat. Then the stairs smoothed to a run, and he was on the tiles of the foyer. Slowly, it seemed to him, he moved behind the man and the woman towards the exit, a narrow space between two glass booths. The occupants of the booths wore metro staff uniforms. There was no policeman at the foot of the steps to the street.

Perhaps, moving back into the centre of the hive, he had wrong-footed his pursuers. They would expect him to flee outwards on the metro, flung off from the hub by the centrifugal violence of his action.

Then, as he passed his ticket to the unseeing man in the booth, he saw Alevtina's face in front of him, as if the girl had stepped out from behind some screen or appeared like

362

a camera trick. She was with another man from the Frunze Quay whose name Vorontsyez could not recall. Her mouth opened in a greeting that changed to sudden despair as she remembered her quarry and her duty. Her hand went to her waist, and Vorontsyev saw the holster, and Alevtina reaching for a gun. Someone bumped Vorontsyev in the back, and he turned as if attacked, seeing the bent-headed individual slip past him, a curse on his mouth, rubbing his arm from the collision. By then it was too late.

Alevtina had the Makarov out of the holster, and the other man, moving to one side, was drawing his automatic.

"Please, Major——!" the girl said, her eyes wide with desperation. It was a selfless plea. Vorontsyev, his own gun still buried in his clothing, caught on the lip of the pocket, hurled himself against her, easily knocking her off balance. In the same moment, the gun came free and he fired from behind Alevtina at the man. Someone screamed as the gun went off, and went on screaming as he fired twice more. The man was flung over the barrier near the glass booth, somersaulting backwards into an untidy, graceless heap on the other side.

He heard Alevtina say, "Put down the gun—*put down the gun!*" It was a high-pitched voice, shocked and appalled. Vorontsyev looked at her, half-up from the tiles, the gun levelled at him. And he knew he could kill her.

Instead, he ran for the exit, leaping the few steps. Behind him, and distinct from what followed, he heard the explosion of the gun above the screams that were coming from bystanders.

Then his leg went, and he lurched against the wall, gripping the iron gate folded back from the station entrace to support his sudden weakness. He looked down. Nothing. Yet his sock felt wet, and he was certain the shoe squelched as he tried to walk. Pain shot through his leg, burning into thigh and groin. Alevtina had shot him. He whirled round, stumbled, and a man stared at him uncomprehendingly as he passed. She was standing at the foot of the steps.

Vorontsyev shot her twice. The girl seemed surprised rather than hurt. Then she was unmistakably dead. He turned away, stifling the sob in his throat, the extended gun warding off pedestrians. He limped badly almost at once, and the numbness of the bullet's passage had already gone. His nerves shrieked with the pain of his own weight on his left leg.

Across the street, the lights of the Moskva Hotel reached into the darkening sky. He put the gun away. It was as if he had donned a disguise. Now, only the fact that he lurched against people unsteadily attracted their notice. Forty yards from the entrance to the Metro, he was anonymous again.

Even when the siren of the police car seemed to point him out as it wailed past, heading for the scene of the incident. Somewhere in him, he felt a part of him sliding into emptiness, as if he had received a physical blow to the head, and his consciousness lurched sickeningly; but more insistent was the pain in his calf, and the icy wetness in his shoe—the strange sensation of the trouser leg clinging wetly—and more imperative was the lighted bulk of the Historical Museum across the square from him.

It was five-twenty. He was too late, they would already have closed the entrance and be shunting out the last visitors—perhaps another five minutes for a respected academician or historian. But no one would be going in now.

At the traffic-lights of the pedestrian crossing from the Lenin Museum corner to the History Museum, he felt chilled and weak and purposeless. And then he remembered it was a Wednesday. The museum closed at seven, Wednesdays and Fridays. He leaned gratefully against someone's back as relief flooded him. The woman turned her head, and he touched his fur hat in apology, trying to smile and realising how unwell he looked; as if his face had been mirrored in hers.

A green silhouette on the pedestrian lights, fuzzily unclear to his eyes. He stepped out, then was bundled back again as another siren screamed up the scale and a police Zil tore past them, round into Revolution Square. Then the crowd moved forward again, warily watching the stationary traffic.

He leant against the wall of the museum for a moment, as if recovering his breath. He inspected his shoe and ankle. A tiny pool of darkness seemed to well round the sole of his shoe as he watched, and he looked stupidly back to the gutter and the pedestrian crossing, convinced he could see the betraying spots. He shook his head. No, nothing. Moving the injured leg with both hands, as if it were a wooden limb, he smeared the little pool, and stepped forward. No one seemed to notice him. Probably they would think him drunk, or ill, if they did.

He moved swiftly—at least the pain seemed to come in quick gouts now, suggesting speed of movement—his limp comically exaggerated. The main façade of the museum overlooked Red Square, a long flight of grandiose steps up to the pillared entrance. A mock-Russian style, designed by an Englishman. He saw the steps before him with pain rather than relief. They were almost bare of people—one or two loungers, near the bottom, a few students passing in or out of the doors, some figures bent with study and the very weight of history. And the glass, revolving doors in the shadows under the pillars of the porch.

Slowly, careful of the treacherous early frost, looking back every few seconds, he mounted the steps. He was leaving only the occasional blood-spot. He had left two or three footprints clear in his blood after he had paused in the street, but not now. His leg ached more familiarly, as if with cold—except when he placed his weight on it. He kept close to the balustrade, using the handrail to assist him, swinging the wounded leg before him. He concentrated on the immediate task, narrowing his awareness; that way, he did not think of Alevtina, dead like Ilya and Maxim, but killed by her own superior. Yet he did have a vague sense of living beyond the immediate future, living beyond a new expansion of consciousness in which he would perceive, in a pitiless clear light, the moral nature of what he had done, what he was doing. The puritan in him was poised to reassert itself.

It would have to wait, he told himself, gritting his teeth—I have to get to the fucking toilet and bandage my bloody leg!

The coarse, blunt language, the simple demands from the time and place, eased aside the looming shadows at the back of his mind. He straightened up, walking slowly so that his gait might have a little normality, he pushed through the revolving doors, seeing a man's wizened, clever face moving past him on the other side, nodding in greeting. Vorontsyev did not know him. It was a gesture without suspicion. He stepped away from the doors, heading swiftly through the turnstile, hardly pausing to pick up his twenty-five kopeck ticket. The door of the male lavato-

365

ry was near the entrance to the museum, he remembered.

At the door of the lavatory, he turned his head. The chequered pattern of the floor seemed unstained, but if he looked carefully he could see one or two faint smears, perhaps a spot or two. Even as he looked, he saw the shoe of an attendant smear one spot out of recognition, and nodded in satisfaction. He closed the door of the washroom behind him, then locked himself in one of the three cubicles. He slumped wearily on the seat, his strength seemingly drained entirely.

The thought kept hammering in his head like a migraine. He had killed Alevtina—killed her. He hardly envisaged the flung corpse, arms wide, or felt the initial pain in his leg. Merely the moral position, a whirl of abstracts in his mind. Killed Alevtina, a member of my team.

He was dizzy, too, with the lost blood. Carefully, he bent over, his awareness spinning like a drunk's, and rolled up the sodden trouser leg. The bullet from the Makarov had passed through the flesh and muscle of the calf, a neat hole at one side, a darker, cratered wound on the other. His sock was soaked with blood, and he decided not to remove his shoe.

Clumsily, he fished the leather-bound flask of vodka from his hip pocket, and wetted his handkerchief with the spirit. Then he washed around the area of the wound, which seemed to have eased its bleeding since he had begun to rest it. Then he wetted the handkerchief until it was soaked, and dabbed it against the wound.

He cried out once, then clenched his teeth in quivering weakness to still the further cries the pain prompted. Then he pulled his shirt from his waistband, and tore off a strip of it. Then he knotted over the wound, waiting without breathing to see if the material became dyed. A spot bloomed, but did not spread far. He leaned back against the cistern, grateful, his trouser leg still rolled above his knee, his fur hat askew on his head.

Almost at once, inattentive to the world beyond the cubicle as he was, the mental landscape asserted itself. The brief future—where was Gorochenko? Had he made a mistake in coming? If he was locked in, and the old man wasn't there, hadn't he wasted the last night before the coup? Where would he hide until the museum closed?

And the past—the dead sprawled overcoat on the frosty path near the flats; the dead Alevtina with her face twisted into the dust coating the tiles of the Revolution Square Metro station. The man, whose face he barely knew, did not figure in the flash of images.

And his own death; inescapable, boiling certitude of ideas, raging as soon as he touched on them, an opened box of his world's ills. For he was committed now, irrevocably. Not in the eyes of others, of the organisation or the state he would be judged to have betrayed, but in his own eyes. The death of Alevtina had revoked all extenuation in his own severe judgement.

He had to be strong—he looked at the gloved hands before his face, and he could see them quivering—if he was to finish it now. Nothing definite formed in his mind concerning the final encounter, but he believed that there had to be one. He needed safe darkness for a while. He could not let the whirl of imagery, its mad dance, control him.

He longed for unconsciousness as he might have longed for sleep before a difficult task.

He stood on the leg, rolling down the damp trouser leg, testing his weight. Pain shot through his thigh and side. He sagged against the wall of the cubicle, then unlocked the door, opened it, and stepped out. He limped to the single washbasin, and cleaned his hands.

As he left the toilet, idling his way as unsuspiciously as he could towards the stairs to the level below ground, and the boiler-room where he would hide, he wondered how large the night-duty team would be. Two or three, perhaps. He did not know whether or not they were armed. He thought not. But they would have an alarm system rigged direct to the nearest police station, perhaps even to the Centre in nearby Dzerzhinsky Street.

But he would need a plan of the building, or a guide.

He eased himself down the steps, treading softly and nursing the aching leg. He hoped the boilerman had gone off duty. He did not want to kill him.

He noticed a returning calm, as if his severely limited view of circumstances and needs forced other considerations aside. He was glad of that.

Physical acts. Through a door marked "Private," then along a dusty corridor roofed and walled, it seemed, with lagged pipes. A hollow but muffled click of footsteps, tangible irregularity of movement. He limped on, quicker. Take the gun from the pocket, hold it in both hands for a moment of steadying, left hand clutched round the stub of barrel, right hand on the moulded butt. Then left hand to turn the doorknob. Unlocked. He pushed open the heavy door, and the boiler-room was in darkness. He flicked on the light, glanced swiftly round the low-roofed, dusty room with its landscape of huge pipes and the squat old boilers. He switched off the light.

He stepped fully into the room and closed the door behind him. He did not think the night staff would lock the boiler-room, rather use it for warming themselves, since it was likely that the regulations disallowed the whole building to be heated overnight.

He tried to picture the room. A faint radiance from windows high up near the ceiling aided him. He limped cautiously across the open space he had registered, turned left, left again. His hand reaching forward all the time, then connecting with the rough surface of a wooden crate. A stack of them, against the wall beneath the small high windows. Careful not to bang against them with his left leg, he eased himself behind them, and lowered himself, like an invalid might do into a bath, to the dusty floor. The concrete was warm, the wall against his back also warm.

He settled himself, the Stechkin on the ground immediately by his hand. The luminous dial of his watch indicated five fifty-five. An hour, or a little more.

But he would have to find a plan. The History Museum contained forty-seven halls and rooms and who knew how many store-rooms, cellars, repositories. Gorochenko could be anywhere. The dry, dusty heat insisted that he would be found. Vorontsyev found his head nodding forward, as he was relaxed by the safety of his hiding place, eased by its silent warmth. A gurgle of pipes, the muted roar of the boilers, but no noises.

He knew he would find Gorochenko. He would find him. Find him.

His tiredness was too imperative. There was no real need for him to be awake before say eight or nine at the earliest. The KGB would not make a thorough search, his fuddled senses reasoned. And he was tired—drained.

He slept.

Kenneth Aubrey had decided on a policy of genial attentiveness to detail as a method of auto-suggestion. He had tired of conversation with Khamovkhin, even of badinage or recollection with Buckholz. Bored with the world of diplomacy, he wished to re-create a sense of the secret world, his own covert life. Thus, armed with the files and reports of the duty-team drafted to Lahtilinna, previously in the care of Anders, he retired to his room, took off his jacket—the central-heating was more than adequate—poured himself a large whisky, and began to read.

Slowly his mind seemed to unstick—perhaps a more appropriate image, he thought, might have been of an oil-calmed sea through which now thrusts the spars and wreckage of his secret life. He did not feel quite so old, hardly felt useless at all—and enjoyed the jagged, broken bits of reality jostling on the calm waters of diplomacy. After all, he was not employed by his masters to baby-sit the Soviet leader while everyone waited on the KGB, nor form a human wall through which no bullet might reach Khamovkhin. Since the crisis seemed to have passed, he had felt diminished by his occupation, just as he had felt enlarged in importance perhaps five or six days before. But this, this—his hand waved over the apparently untidy heap of papers as if to indicate something to an audience—was what still, apparently, satisfied him most, and most consistently.

There, he thought, turning back a page. What a scratchy account! A boat had been discovered four miles up the lake from the castle. Some attempt, it seemed, had been made to hide it. Aubrey picked up the form, as if checking for some watermark of authenticity. It was a Duty Report Form DRF/22B, which he had issued to Andres for the purpose of collating all duty-team reports. This one was more than a day old—part of an initial wide-sweep search for the missing Ozeroff. At the bottom of the report, the column for "Diagnosis" and that for "Prognosis" both remained blank. Aubrey clicked his tongue against the roof of his mouth. The boat was still there—it had been disabled by the report-maker, and left. Obviously not important because it was still there.

Aubrey continued reading. It was two hours before he came across another report on the boat, then another. All of them with the same indifference to speculation. It irritated him that the duty-teams should have been so unused to search operatons that they had covered the same ground three times in a space of hours. By that time, anyway, several other items in the reports had irritated him, then begun to disappoint him, then turn his mood slowly to dissatisfaction.

Meal times were slack times, agreed. Sleep or rest periods were undisturbed. Patrols seemed efficiently organised—he picked up a series of duty-change items, and saw Anders's bold hand scoring through names—on three different sheets—because he had forgotten the names, or had been wrongly informed who was going on or coming off duty. And the individual reports—he reached further across the desk for a handful of them, the light from the standard lamp catching the shiny baldness of the top of his head—these were sloppy in the extreme. He began to read one aloud in a stage-Cockney accent, to ridicule it.

"Ah took owver from this geezer a' ayt-uh-clock. Tall blowke, pahka on. Don' know 'is nayme." He snorted, then added: "What use is this sort of thing? None whatsoever!"

Once he began to look—there was some sense of anti-Americanism in the exercise—he saw signs of it everywhere. Then he had the justice to admit that the substitute duty-team, drafted in from half a dozen countries and belonging to two or three different security services, had been his idea. He mentally apologised to Buckholz, leaned back in his chair because he had suddenly lost interest in mockery which had turned to self-mockery, rubbed his eyes so that he pushed his half-glasses up onto his forehead, and stared at the ceiling.

His mouth opened like that of a fish, as if he could not catch his breath. Immediately, he sat upright, fiddling his hands across the sheafs of papers as if playing a piano or uncertain of what he wanted. Then he pressed both palms down flat and hard on the paper, as if a wind might disturb them. It was in there—it was in there!

He looked at his watch—almost three. *Three?* Three in the morning, and the date was the twenty-fourth.

He picked up the telephone, dialling Anders's extension. The voice, when it came, was drowsy but unruffled.

"Yeah?"

"Aubrey here."

"Sir—anything wrong?"

"I'm not sure. I've just been reading over your collated reports and roster stuff here—"

"Yeah?" Now the voice was that of a civil servant and anticipating some ministerial displeasure.

"No, not a rocket for you, dear boy—just a thing that struck me, looking at the thing overall, as it were."

"Something wrong?"

"Possibly. Tell me one thing—how many of the names can you recollect, just off-hand?"

Silence, then: "Maybe seventeen, eighteen—why?"

"I can't recall all SIS personnel here, either. To me, they were names Shirley supplied from London, or Philipson here, or other Station Heads. All we worried about was getting sufficient *bodies* here. Our little friend. 'Captain Ozeroff-Houdini'—he relied on a similar situation, didn't he?"

"He had papers, and records must have been altered—"

"Yes, dear boy—but, they didn't know his face, did they? As long as they expected the face that turned up, no one there would recognize him as someone else, would they? Now, if you take that a stage further—?"

Anders digested the idea in a moment.

"I'd better wake Mr. Buckholz!"

"I think you'd better wake everybody—and we'll do a spot-check of everyone who is *inside* Lahtilinna at the moment—then those outside can come in and be recognised!"

Galakhov looked at his watch—three-o-two. He was standing in the darkened kitchen of the castle, the moonlight slicing through tall narrow windows. He had stayed long enough to make himself a cup of coffee, even turning on the lights while he did so. But, assailed by a sense of approaching crisis, he had switched them off as soon as the mug was in his hands, the coffee on his lips. He had been on patrol round the castle grounds, only occasionally meeting other duty personnel, exchanging a word or two with them, they leaving amused by something he said, he secretly revelling in the ease with which he was able to remain at Lahtilinna while the hunt for him went on.

He finished the last of the coffee, put the mug in one of the huge enamel sinks. He paused for a moment, a shaft of moonlight weirdly illuminating his narrow young face, as he visualised the sketch-plan of the route to Khamovkhin's room. Softly, softly, he told himself, a smile on his lips. In and out, and then back on patrol, to slip off when he was alone in the grounds. So simple.

He let himself out of the kitchens, and took the stairs to

the main hall. From the furthest point of the corridor, he could see that there were lights on in the hall—off-duty men at the billiard table? Hardly likely they were watching Finnish TV—especially at that time? Cautiously, he approached the archway into the hall.

There were perhaps a dozen men already there, and he could see others coming along the galleries above, or down the staircase. Most of them were in dressing-gowns, some with coats over the pyjamas all of them were wearing. He saw Aubrey, in shirt-sleeves, and Buckholz in dressing-gown and pyjamas, fur boots on his feet. Anders was dressed, and looking extremely wide-awake and efficient. He listened to his opening remarks and then, as if by reflex, about a complete head-count, and the men staying where they were until everyone was accounted for, went a long way away because he had understood their intention at once. What he wanted was an alternative route to Khamovkhin's bedroom.

Anders's voice faded behind him as he returned down the corridor, fur-lined boots silent on the stone floor. At the end of the corridor was a flight of stairs—servants' route to the master bedrooms on the floor above. He listened—a distant, muffled burst of laughter cut short in the hall, but nothing closer than that. Galakhov felt the urgency press him, and he ascended the stairs as quickly as he dared.

He paused on the landing, feeling time running ahead of him. He had to move swiftly now—the job was nothing in itself, occupying no more than a minute. He looked up the next flight of stairs from the landing. Shadow, but lights from a corridor beyond and to the left.

He was almost at the top of the stairs when the sleepy man with disarranged hair and silent slippers bumped into him—and recoiled at the still-cold touch of his parka and the barrel of the rifle. A Finnish copy of the Kalashnikov, issued by Anders.

"Sorry," he murmured.

"What the hell's going on?" the other man muttered, rubbing his arm where he had bumped the gun, yawning. Galakhov could have driven the rifle butt into his face—but he would only waste precious moments.

"Some sort of identity check, I think."

"What? Jesus—what a waste of good sleeping time!"

He tossed his head, rubbed his hair more into place, and began to descend the stairs. Then he paused, and looked up quizzically, taking in Galakhov's outdoor clothing and the gun. And perhaps the face he had not seen before. Galakhov cursed that he had not killed the man—now, he could not reach him, and dare not fire a shot. Then the man seemed satisfied, nodded, and went on down the stairs.

Galakhov ran along the corridor, his footsteps thumping on the strip of carpet. Up one more short flight, stopping just before the turn into another corridor, well-lit, and a man on guard at the door of Khamovkhin's room. The man in the dressing-gown, going now perhaps into the hall. If Anders or one of the others was still speaking, he might wait before he mentioned the man in outdoor clothing, armed, too, that he had passed on the stairs. But he might have thought about it—

He looked once. The guard was sitting on a chair, alert but comfortable. Then he took the last step, two strides to the middle of the corridor—fifteen yards. He fired twice, and the guard, only then looking at the intruder, hand hardly moved at all where the gun rested on his lap, was flung off the chair and slid across the corridor, a piece of carpet rucking up beneath him, a vase tumbling with a hideous noise from a delicate table whose legs were snapped by the impact of the body.

Fifteen yards—his hearing was coming back now as he ran to Khamovkhin's door. He fired another two shots at the lock, then kicked in the door. The bedroom was dark, but Khamovkhin had left one lamp on in the sitting-room. Galakhov saw his quarry, impotent and foolish in striped pyjamas in the bedroom doorway, and pointed the rifle at the middle of the figure. Khamovkhin was frozen with terror.

And Galakhov cursed. Shots, shots. The guard had been despatched noisily, now he was going to kill Khamovkhin with more noise. Because he had passed one sleepy-eyed, half-awake Englishman on the flight of stairs, and the adrenalin had worked, time seemed to escape him, and he had bludgeoned his way to this moment. He listened.

Nothing, but his hearing was still ringing from the explosions of the rifle.

"Get dressed—get dressed, or I'll kill you now!"

Khamovkhin, as if slapped by the voice, went back into the bedroom. Galakhov crossed to the door as Khamovkhin switched on the light in order to dress. He pushed it wide, and leaned against the door-frame, his eyes flickering from the figure of the Soviet leader as he dressed to the outer doorway which yet remained free of shadows.

"Hurry up—hurry up!" Adrenalin running away again, and panic-thinking. He wasn't going to kill Khamovkhin now, he was going to use him as a hostage to get out. Something had decided that—the same stupid animal in himself that had used the gun because time seemed about to run out. "Hurry."

Khamovkhin looked up at that. Galakhov saw the flicker of cunning hope in his eyes. Then the man pulled on his jacket.

"That'll do!"

"My jacket—my topcoat. You don't want your hostage to freeze to death, do you?" He turned to the wardrobe, and reached in for his coat.

What was that—noise on the stairs? Someone must have heard! Then Khamovkhin, tidying the collar of his topcoat, donning his fur hat, as if on his way to some public appointment in Helsinki, was standing next to him—a look of amusement in his eyes. Galakhov jabbed the rifle into his ribs, making the old man's breath exhale in a gasp. But the look in the eyes did not change from their damned superiority, their amusement. Galakhov was baffled.

"Go to the door," he ordered. Khamovkhin did so, then waited, pausing as if for some stage entrance. Enter the statesman—Galakhov placed the rifle against the old man's spine, then he called out.

"You're there, of course—Mr. Aubrey and Mr. Buckholz?"

Silence.

"Galakhov?" They knew his real name, then. "Mr. First Secretary—are you unharmed?" Aubrey, the Englishman.

"Yes, Mr. Aubrey. I am afraid that—who did you say, Comrade Galakhov?—I am his hostage, shall we say?"

"Shit!" Buckholz or Anders.

"I'm taking him out *now*! If you listen very carefully, you'll hear me switch to automatic. Kill me, and he dies anyway."

"I know how rifles work, Galakhov!" he heard Buckholz say.

"Then don't take any chances." He jabbed Khamovkhin in the back. "He's coming out first—and the rifle is placed against his spine. Clear a path for us. Right—move!"

EIGHTEEN
THE 24TH

Vorontsyev awoke with a start, his head jerking upwards so that he banged it against the wall. He had opened his eyes, but there was a deep blackness in the room, deeper than he remembered. Frantically tugging back the cuff of his coat, he stared at his watch, the luminous figures slowly swimming to an approximation of a circle of numbers. His mind tried to reject the information, but the body groaned with realisation. Three-twenty—no, three-twenty-five. He had slept, undisturbed, for nine hours.

His back ached, and his neck was stiff. He moved his left leg, and the pain shot through him, seeming to erase the restorative sleep in a moment. He rubbed the back of his neck, groaning softly to himself. It was too ridiculous to contemplate, the unforgivable slide into sleep when he needed to be strong, alert.

He climbed upright, hands pressed against the wall behind him, until his left leg stuck out awkwardly, and his frame was shaking with the effort. He banged his palms against the wall in impotent fury. Gorochenko—he had perhaps two hours, no more than that.

Forty-seven halls, countless store-rooms and cellars. He could be anywhere!

He dared not consider that he might not be in the building at all.

He bent clumsily and picked up the gun, gripping it tight as if in an affirmation of purpose. He hurried now, banging against the edges of crates, then slurring his foot across the concrete. Despite the remaining warmth of the boiler-room, he was cold, and shivered. It was dark because the street lights in Red Square were out. He groped along the wall until he found the doorknob, cool under his hand. He turned it, holding his breath.

Still unlocked.

He went down the passage, rubbing the sleeve of his coat against the lagging of the pipes, tasting the dust he disturbed as he breathed in. Then the outer door, open, closed behind him. The flight of steps, lit by a frosty moonlight, chill and ghostly, the imitation marble glinting in flecks, as if frost-covered. He leaned against the wall, and pushed himself up each step, hurrying, oblivious to the pain—perhaps encouraging it as a punishment for his dereliction of purpose, the weakness of the physical organism—swinging the leg forward, leaning the body-weight on it, then upright, back to swing the leg again.

He was breathing raggedly, and there was a chill sweat across his back, and his brow was damp. The shoe seemed to squelch loudly again, noises like the slapping of a wet rag against a dirty windowpane. He waited until the panic of his blood died, then he looked up, and studied the high, pillared hall which contained great lumps of statuary, the rows of glass cases containing the earliest history of Russia—ivory, stone, pottery. High windows let in the deceptive frosty moonlight, seeming to render the hall into monochrome and chill him.

He shuffled as quietly as he could across the hall, towards two doors in the far wall, near the stairs ascending to the first floor of the museum. When he reached them he ran his fingers over the little brass plates as if reading braille. "Private." The gun pressed against his chest, his body close to the door from beneath which came a strip of yellow light, he turned the handle, and pushed. He almost fell into the room, gripped tight to the door handle, and stood upright. A small room, fuggy with the warmth of an electric fire and a *samovar*. Slightly hazed with cigarette smoke—he was sure it wasn't his eyes because the tobacco smell was pungent. Two faces looking up from steaming mugs. He must have caught them just after a security patrol. He closed the door behind him, and leaned back against it. Neither of the two men had moved more than a half-turn to face him. After the slight, surprised scraping of chairs, there was silence, except for the faint noise of the *samovar* in the corner.

Two men, both in their late fifties or sixties. They seemed two aspects of one personality—medium height, he suspected, medium build, greying hair, thin. For all they interested him, they might have been twins. They were simply hands, reaction-times, and a lack of guns. He said, because somehow it seemed an inevitable remark, "Where is he?"

Because *that* was what he had seen in the moment when they were real, and separate, before his clogged him and furious purpose dissolved their identities; he had seen them glance at one another, as if in knowledge.

There was a silence. He thought he had imagined it, was wrong. Then one of the men—he distinguished him, with difficulty, as the one with the broader face, the thicker grey hair—said quietly, "He said—if you came, we were to take you to him."

Vorontsyev sagged visibly against the door, the gun dropping to his side. Ridiculous. He had only to ask for an interview with his father. Crazy. They had been waiting for him. Without consciously considering the action, he reached into his coat and holstered the gun.

One of the men nodded.

"Where is he?" Vorontsyev asked in a thick voice, still leaning against the door.

The smaller of the two men, his wispy hair stranded across his head, said, "Above us. He's safe." He looked at the trouser leg, and the smudge of dirty red around the heel of the shoe. "You're wounded," he observed dispassionately. He spoke like a policeman. Vorontsyev did not bother to consider how they had been suborned by Gorochenko. Now, all he wanted to do was to come face to face.

The man who had answered him first stood up. Surprisingly, he was taller than Vorontsyev. "Come with me." He turned to his companion. "Check he has left no traces—just in case." He turned to Vorontsyev. "Where have you been in the museum?" It was off-hand, yet meticulous.

"The toilet . . ." The man still seated nodded.

"I told you," he said. Then they had expected him. The remark about his wound was confirmation of a previous theory.

"And the boiler-room."

"We deliberately did not search," the big man said, standing now only a foot or so from Vorontsyev's face. His breath smelt of some spicy sausage. "Why has it taken you so long?"

"I—fell asleep." Vorontsyev felt ashamed as he made his confession. He watched the big man's face, but there was no sign of amusement.

"Shall we go?" he said. Vorontsyev nodded, and backed out of his way.

The big man opened the door, and walked ahead of Vorontsyev.

"The lift?" Vorontsyev asked, struggling to keep up, his leg hurting with each impact with the tiled floor. Their footsteps echoed now, it seemed.

"Shut off—the power." Vorontsyev did not believe him, but felt unable to demand. He was to be made to use the painful flights of stairs. He found himself accepting it as some kind of retribution—for his reckless sleep in the boiler-room or the death of Alevtina, he was uncertain.

The attendant who was, effectively, Gorochenko's bodyguard, unarmed though he was, went steadily ahead of him; a taskmaster who proceeded at what seemed the exact pace to wear and pain him without ever being more than half a flight ahead of him.

First floor—the moonlight opening spaces of glass cases, long dusky corridors hardly coloured by the pale light. He knew from somewhere in his memory that the exhibits concerned the popular uprisings through history, and he grimaced with the irony as much as the nagging, reiterated pain in his calf—he noticed that the pain was becoming localised, though a more intense stabbing sort of hurt.

The footsteps strange and intrusive in the silence. Then the next flight of stairs, and Peter the Great's minutiae. Vorontsyev felt like an old man, and coughed as if with asthma. The attendant stopped, looked back and waited patiently until he was only a few steps behind. Then he moved on again.

French standard from 1812. And, almost at the head of the flight of stairs, a life-size dressmaker's dummy in the uniform of Kutuzov as general commanding the Russian forces in the war against Napoleon. It was so sudden, turning at the head of the stairs, lifting his head from his study of each careful step, and the irony was so obvious, his breath was expelled in a noisy rush, as if he had come unexpectedly face to face with Gorochenko.

It was not a lucky guess, it was inevitable that he should be here—in this building of all buildings in Moscow. He said, his words echoing hollowly, "I wonder my father hasn't borrowed the uniform."

The guide's footsteps went on without pause, then clicked more heavily as he began to mount other stairs. Vorontsyev groaned at the thought of the continued effort demanded of him, and gripped the stone of the balustrade more urgently.

Captured French colours from the awful, icy retreat from Moscow, scraps of partisan unit flags, swords, carbines. Moonlight glinted from metal, sombrely outlined the stripes and shapes in flags and colours. He felt heavy with effort and the weight of history, which had come alive for him as never before. His journey was allegorical, he could feel that palpably. Perhaps Gorochenko had intended it—a kind of first interrogation was the only parallel he could conceive. A softening-up. Gorochenko saying—he could almost hear the voice—this is what we are going to talk about. This what is at stake.

He shook his head as if to rid it of the buzzing of a fly. He would not listen. Siren-song. The first bite of the drill on tooth's enamel. He had to steel himself.

At the top of the next flight—pause—stiff clutter of footsteps, his own—then another flight. He began not to attend, to attend rather only to the feet he placed carefully one after the other.

So he came to the last hall, the inevitable last one. 1917. Arms, banners, clothing, like 1812. And, in glass cases, the writings of Lenin and others—just as his corpse was under glass in the Mausoleum. The storming of the Winter Palace—great indistinguishable portraits and crowdscapes on the walls.

Gorochenko had brought him here often, as a boy. He remembered now. And the memory completed some circuit, fulfilled a pattern. Gorochenko was consistent, credible throughout his life—no strange dislocation here. This always had been the shrine.

He sobbed quietly, knowing that the guide would take it as an expression of effort or pain.

The guide unlocked a small door—they were at the end

of the last hall, and switched on a light. Another flight of stairs, narrower. He motioned Vorontsyev inside, and now lent him his arm for support. Squeezed together, they mounted the stairs to a narrow wooden corridor, uncarpeted. Here, the guide knocked on another door, one of many set in the long, dim corridor that smelt of must and unseen, stored things. Vorontsyev heard the voice and, as if at the study door of a feared pedagogue, blenched.

"Come in."

"He panicked," Aubrey whispered as he crouched next to Buckholz at the head of the stairs, both of them peering round the corner at the open doorway of Khamovkhin's suite—and the heaped-up tangle of flesh and wood where the guard had collided with the table. The pieces of the broken vase looked like stiff petals surrounding the still form. "I don't know why, but he went at it hammer-and-tongs, when no doubt he expected to kill quickly and quietly, and get out again. In this mood, self-preservation will be high, but he won't be entirely rational. He might kill just because someone's breath smells."

"So—we line up in a fuckin' parade and wave him to the door?" Buckholz was in a mood to blame everyone, principally himself, and the mood was one he hated.

Khamovkhin appeared in the doorway, then stepped boldly into the corridor. Aubrey heard behind him the rustle of a rifle placed to a shoulder. Acute angle, he thought, almost rising his hand in warning—but Galakhov was already behind the Soviet leader, gun jammed into the spine. Aubrey stood up, and moved slowly out into the corridor. Galakhov saw a rather dishevelled old man in a shirt with its stiff collar detached. Aubrey looked like a plucked bird, except that the eyes were bright and alive, seeking an opportunity.

"Get back!" Galakhov ordered, making Khamovkhin twitch involuntarily as he jabbed him with the rifle.

Aubrey raised his hands innocently. "Very well, Comrade Galakhov. I saw some evidence of your efficiency as an assassin just outside Oxford—" Galakhov was puzzled, but he knew what Aubrey was doing with his relaxed, studied, almost hypnotic words. Delay.

"Never mind the talk. Get the stairs cleared. My guest and I are leaving."

"I am sorry, Mr. Aubrey," Khamovkhin remarked. "I hope we shall meet again—"

"Get moving!"

Aubrey stood to one side, and Buckholz retreated from the head of the stairs. Galakhov realised that urgency alone would serve him now. He had to increase the tempo, disturb any arrangements and dispositions being made. They were slowing the whole thing down. Again, he futilely cursed the tempo inposed on him by the scene in the hall and the man on the stairs.

He looked down at knots of upturned faces, trellised by gun barrels, as armed men jostled each other on the narrow staircase. None of the guns was pointed at him. Increase the tempo, he told himself again. Whatever they're setting up, you can outrun it.

"Should I say that you won't get away with it?" Aubrey remarked at his side.

"I have a ticket to anywhere in the world," Galakhov replied, and saw the discomfiture of the Englishman. "You," he added to Buckholz, "can you drive?" Buckholz was silent. The rifle dug into Khamovkhin's spine. Aubrey suddenly felt the atmosphere rise in temperature, until the four of them were standing in the heavy heat of a greenhouse—just the four players, surrounded by silent extras, or an audience. "Can—you—drive?" Galakhov said precisely, emphasising each word with the gun in Khamovkhin's back.

"Yes," Buckholz replied sullenly.

"Good. You will drive us away from here." Galakhov looked from the American's face to that of Aubrey. The Englishman had made his features bland, inexpressive. Galakhov wondered whether he had not made a mistake, leaving behind to organise some counter-measure the more brilliant and ruthless of the two intelligence men. He had no time for second thoughts—he opted for bulk, and physical menace, which meant that Buckholz would be neutralised by having to drive the car. "Come!"

He pushed Khamovkhin down the first step, and the men fell back in front of them. Turn at the stairs, and the long corridor down which he had sprinted—that might have been the moment when the mental pulse had outrun him—and the security men, silly and innocuous, despite the guns, in their pyjamas and dressing-gowns, or coats thrown on over pyjamas. One in his vest and pants, even less dangerous. Buckholz was two paces behind him, and he did not know where Aubrey was. Not that it mattered. Every face he passed was distraught, angry, frustrated. He had them beaten, and he was going to make it.

A moment of shame—an image of *Kutuzov,* looking in disapproval, as he had done when ordering the death of Vrubel. But they had *Kutuzov,* and it was all over, and he had been stupid and found himself trapped, and there was no other way he could act—he *couldn't* squeeze the trigger and kill Khamovkhin, because he could feel the bullets of their reply—he could feel his skin crawling and wincing with the impact of their bullets. The imperative of survival had established itself like a disease.

Stairs again, then the corridor to the hall—everything done in silence, until Buckholz said, "I have to have a coat, man."

They stopped, like toy men whose mechanisms have run down. Galakhov half-turned, and snapped, "Someone give him a coat." Then he pushed Khamovkhin on, through the kitchen, out into the cold night. As if the other men were party-givers seeing off last guests, they came no further than the door. Their footsteps were loud after all the silence, and their breathing suddenly visible in the moonlight—breathing had been almost the only sound they had heard all the way from Khamovkhin's bedroom. Galakhov let Buckholz walk ahead, so that his gun covered both of them, until they came to the garages.

"Something powerful," Galakhov said as Buckholz dragged open the doors. He peered into the darkness. Buckholz switched on the lights, and Galakhov flinched as if a searchlight had suddenly been turned on him.

What was he doing here? Where were they going? He suddenly wanted to call back at Aubrey that they must supply an aircraft, in Helsinki—where was he to go? Anywhere—literally anywhere, with such a passport?—

He quailed inwardly. Nowhere, *nowhere.* The moment he let Khamovkhin from his grasp, he was dead. He would have to spend the rest of his life with a rifle against the Soviet leader's spine if he wanted to stay alive. Anywhere —New York, London, Moscow, Cairo, Tunis, Rome, Rio—somewhere, a man with a gun would remove him, as soon as there was sufficient daylight between himself and the Soviet leader—Siamese twins.

"Get in—get in."

Buckholz seemed surprised at the tone of his voice, then smiled grimly in satisfaction. "Beginning to understand, uh, kid?"

"Get in, get in!" The gun waved in Buckholz's direction.

"OK. You're the boss." The irony was a slap across his face.

Galakhov pushed Khamovkhin before him into the rear seat, made him slide across, got in himself. Buckholz turned round.

"Where to, bud?" He was almost laughing!

"North—follow the lake, north!" Galakhov tried to snarl, but the words came out as the utterance of someone without direction. Buckholz turned away, and switched on the ignition.

The guide opened the door, then stood aside. Gorochenko was seated at a rough table, his overcoat and fur hat on, his hands gloved. He was smiling in welcome. Vorontsyev lurched into the room, dizzy with weariness, and the old man rose anxiously from the chair, a spasm of pain on his strong face. The guide caught him, lowered Vorontsyev into another hard chair. Then he saw Gorochenko shake his head, and the door closed, leaving them alone in the room with its blacked-out window and small, shadowy lamp.

The silence seemed interminable. Vorontsyev stared at the edge of the rough table, feeling the aching in his left leg dying to discomfort. He did not move the leg. His sock was stiff with dried blood. All the time, he sensed Gorochenko studying him.

Then the old man said, "You're hurt, boy. Do you want it looked at?" Vorontsyev waved his hand on the table in a small, impatient gesture. Then he looked up, his eyes burning.

"You betrayed me!" It was intended to recriminate, to express hatred. Instead, uncontrollably, it was a wail of anguish, even though he did little more than whisper.

"I never did that," Gorochenko replied.

"Natalia—Ossipov in Khabarovsk—the dead man wired with a bomb—Vassiliev on the plane—each time you were trying to kill me!" Vorontsyev, in the presence of the old man for minutes now, was unable to react in any other

384

way. He realised that he did not know, any longer, why he was there, what imperatives had driven him to this meeting. Perhaps only some sense of dramatic climax. He had no policeman's motives left to voice.

"I—ordered *none* of those, Alexei." There was little softness in the voice, no apology. Yet there was a desire to be judged innocent. "Your wife is a whore, I agree I used her." The judgement was almost prim rather than patriarchal. Vorontsyev ground his teeth together. "She was intended to watch you, and report to me. I—blackmailed her . . ." The sense of authority that was natural to him was clear in the neutrality with which he confided his actions. "I would ruin her career, even have her arrested if she did not go with you, and report to me, via Ossipov. It was Ossipov who used her."

"No, it was you. And you who killed Ilya and Maxim. They are dead." The scorn fell dully in the room, as if something in its cramped, ill-lit confinement deadened sound. Vorontsyev had the unnerving sense that, whatever had driven him here, whatever humanity he had brought, it had been stilled in him. They were two almost disembodied voices discussing distant matters.

"Yes, they are dead. But—you sent them to *Finland Station*. What they witnessed left my—colleagues, no alternative." A sudden spurt of emotion, violent as the cutting of an artery. "They were KGB! What do you think they would have done to me if their report had been made?"

The contempt now evident in the voice was like a hand which had been shading the light, suddenly taken away. It stung Vorontsyev, but before he could respond, the room's deadness seemed to settle on him once more. He said, almost sullenly, "They were just pawns in your game. Of no value. Like Vrubel."

"No. But Vrubel wanted to get rid of you. He could not believe he was safe from a jealous husband in SID . . ." A flicker of hard amusement on the lips, then: "He killed the substitute—an actor, by the way—and tried to kill you."

Implacability. Vorontsyev had seen it before, but confined by the minor problems of a parent's unheeded authority. Now his father disposed of lives much as he might have upbraided him for poor marks at school.

"Ingratiating act—father," Vorontsyev observed, and

385

was pleased as the old man's face winced as from the taste of lemons, hollow-cheeked suddenly. "I'm only grateful."

"Only natural in a son," Gorochenko remarked coldly. Then something in his eyes seemed to decline, a light or a fire. He said, seeming ill at ease with a softer voice, "I always knew that you would find me. If anyone were to do it, it would be you."

"You had me transferred to SID—what did you expect?"

"Don't be ungracious, boy. I agree, however. I created my own Nemesis when I did that." The powerful shoulders sloped forward, the head stretching to him in emphasis. "I did it to *protect* you."

"Protect me? How?" The room seemed to have lightened as a force on his frame and voice. Or perhaps it was only that Mihail Pyotravich was less oppressive as a presence.

"The safest place in this police-ridden state of ours is—in the police. Especially in the SID. How else could I be *certain* that you would never have to suffer?"

"Why? What would I have suffered?"

A pain seemed to glance across Gorochenko's face, and he said, "It does not matter. I wanted to protect you, and that is the way I chose to do it."

"Why did you do all the other things?" Vorontsyev asked, responding to some contact re-established between them. "Why? *You*, of all people!"

It was as if Gorochenko could no longer control himself. Even muscular control of his features seemed to lapse, and his mouth worked silently. One side of his face, as if he had suffered a stroke, was still, but there was a tic near the right eye. His strong, veined hands curled and uncurled on the table. When he spoke it was in a sudden shout like an exhalation of all the rage of his life.

"Me! Why *me*? Boy, you are a cretin, an imbecile! Who else would it be but *me*?" He got up, as if obeying a summons, and paced back and forth on his side of the table. "How many times did I bring you here—how many times? Didn't you listen to *anything* I said?" He was a pedagogue, and Vorontsyev had shrunk in his own perspective. He had seen imitations, pale substitutes, of this anger before in Gorochenko. He had never been patient with weakness, with intellectual failure. "*1917!* It was all for nothing! Stalin was something from the Middle Ages, with a savage dog he let off a chain. Beria. Even now I can smell that man and what he did, like a stench in my nose! Do you know that, eh? A *stench!* Everything came to nothing. One prison, from one end of the Soviet Union to the other. A bloody, dark, infested prison!"

He paused. Vorontsyev saw him venting the rage he had never expressed, not as wildly. All the years of silence, of compromise, of acceptance, had burst like a boil.

"And I'm a policeman!" Vorontsyev said. "You made me belong to something you hated so much. Why?"

Gorochenko was calmer, passing from fire to ice in a moment, it seemed.

"I have explained that to you already. Didn't you understand? I never sought political sophistication in you, Alexei. But I never expected stupidity." The tone was hard-edged, gleaming like a blade. The very exercise of contempt seemed to calm Gorochenko. An anodyne drawn from his own superiority. Vorontsyev saw the cold, aloof ego of the man, and he understood that he had always feared Gorochenko in some way. Perhaps this was why. Some secret sense of the qualities in him that had made him into *Kutuzov.*

"Never mind. It doesn't matter—not that part. But, you wanted to start a *war!*"

"I agree," Gorochenko said frostily.

"Right was on your side, of course?"

"Naturally." Vorontsyev searched the face as if seeking some other, deeper confirmation. As if his gaze was a blow, he saw the face crumple into softer outlines. The deep lines at the side of the mouth, habitually cast in an ironic frame, became shallower.

"Just listen to me, Alexei." His hands were flat on the table, as if in declaration. "I—became *Kutuzov.* All the years I worked for it, using my standing with the army, with old friends who had risen high—I knew what the price would be." Again the rasp of certainty. "And I was prepared to pay the price of a—change of leadership. I knew that the army wanted, *needed,* a limited war in Europe. Scandinavia was their prize for assisting me."

"And it would end there?"

Gorochenko shook his head.

"Of course not! Nor should it. Stalin is the one who decided the revolution should end at the borders of Russia!" Again the contempt for political ignorance or incertitude.

"How can I be here, *debating* with you?"

"Because you have to know *why* I am the man you have searched for, why I have done the things I have done."

"Is that all?"

"Of course. You will not stop me."

"I—have no ..." Vorontsyev, as if threatened, let his hand move from the table.

Gorochenko smiled. "No you won't, Alexei." His eyes hardened their gaze. "Look at yourself. You have spent the last ten years working your way up in an organisation you have not questioned, whose nature you have largely ignored. That, and being an emotional spendthrift at the expense of a tart. You have no capacity to stop me—because you have no perception of any concerns larger than me. You came to *save* me. Admit it. Perhaps from my own foolishness, perhaps from your organisation. The one thing about which you are certain is that I must go on living ..."

It was the experience of being told of your contemptibility by a beloved, the revelation of despite where he thought there was love. Like Natalia's flaunted lovers. Perhaps deeper.

He flinched away from it. Get back to the debate. He said, "You are beaten, Mihail Pyotravich. Praporovich and Dolohov have been eliminated. How can you do *anything?*"

Gorochenko looked at the telephone, the only object, other than his big hands, on the table. He said, "There is all the power I need. One telephone call—and the change of leadership occurs today, the conquest of Scandinavia is only a matter of time."

"You mean to go on, then?" Vorontsyev was appalled, despite the fact that he knew Gorochenko was unyielding, determined.

"Of course. As I said—it is a simple matter of a telephone call."

"I won't let you make it!"

"How will you stop me, Alexei? You have no moral or political reason for doing so. Have you? What is it? Loyalty to the state? To the KGB?"

"Perhaps."

"Foolish. You have no loyalties. Your work has been an anodyne, an escape from your personal life. You are just a bureaucrat disguised as a policeman. A clerk."

"Are you *so* certain?" He was pleading. Gorochenko despised him, and he could not bear it.

"Yes, Alexei. I love you, you are my son. But you are not a man of vision or faith. Which is why you cannot stop me. You have nothing to outweigh the love you have for me, the debt you owe me. I don't say this in contempt, but in understanding." He reached his hand forward across the table, but Vorontsyev snatched his own hand away from the gesture like a sulking child, shaking his head as he did so. He was near to tears, and hated the truths he had been told, the hollowness his own father had exposed; hated the way in which his ego had been assaulted, and the superiority his father had displayed. He could not admit all those things, could not.

"Why are you doing it—why?" It was a distraction, and he saw that Gorochenko knew it.

"I *believe*. Do you understand that? I believe in the old dream of revolution. That is why."

"You want power—that's all. Just greedy for power they never gave you!"

"Stupid," Gorochenko murmured, but two spots of colour appeared on his cheeks. "You do not understand. To have been alive in the twenties, and to see the whole country turned into a shit-pile by Stalin and Beria and the NKVD! Terror as the normal experience for millions! Can't you see any of it, Alexei?" He half-rose, then sat down heavily, as if winded. But his voice was clear as he went on. "I swore, every time I saw an empty chair at a Politburo meeting—every time I heard of another purge, every time a new, subservient face appeared on a committee or in the Secretariat—I *swore* I would survive, and I swore I would do what I could, when I could. I have waited a very long time. But now it will be done, for all those who died." He clenched his fist. "The people were at his throat when the Fascists invaded Russia! He was almost finished!" His voice cracked, then, more calmly: "It has taken me another thirty years. A long time."

"Stalin died thirty years ago."

"What he did to weaken the Soviet Union did not die,

Alexei. Now we have *détente,* another way of dying slowly."

Vorontsyev was appalled. He seemed unable to absorb the successive shocks of his father's obsessive determination. None of the previous revelations immunised him against those which followed. It was a drill breaking through to the living nerve each time.

"You're mad." Gorochenko smiled. Vorontsyev felt rage boil in him at the continuing superiority that smile symbolised. He drew his gun, and it lay heavy and black on the edge of the table. Gorochenko looked at it unflinchingly. "I'm going to stop you. I'm arresting you." Then he added, lashing out like a child: "And you're not my father!"

Gorochenko rubbed at his cheek, as if the blow had been a physical one. He looked at his watch.

"I have only a little time left to wait. And you are not going to arrest me." He seemed so *certain,* of everything.

"I am! I am! You're a traitor! My father—my *real* father—would have hated you for this!"

Gorochenko groaned, and passed a hand across his face. But it was as if he was afraid of something in himself, rather than of the rejection Vorontsyev proffered.

"No, he would not, Alexei."

"He would, he would!" Vorontsyev was no longer conscious of his grotesque approximation to the voice and manner of a child. He crowed: "My father was a hero! He would have despised you for what you're doing. You're a traitor!" The clichés comforted and strengthened him. They gave him a sense of existence to some purpose. An armour against Gorochenko's words.

"Alexei!" It was a command. Vorontsyev watched him, shamefaced. Gorochenko seemed engaged in some silent debate, then to relent to some inner decision. "Very well," he said. "Very well. I swore—perhaps an oath as solemn as the one I took every day of the Stalin years—never to tell you this. But I will."

"What? More bogeymen?" Vorontsyev sneered.

"If you like." The old man's face was ancient now, filled with bitter wisdom. He reached into a breast pocket. Vorontsyev watched the hand carefully. It came out holding a letter—an old, stained letter with fluff in the creases where it had been folded for years.

390

"Read this," Gorochenko said carefully. "It's from your father."

"Where is he now?" Aubrey flipped the transmitter's switch, and heard the crackle of the radio in the spotter helicopter.

"A couple of miles outside Heinola, still moving fast."

"You're experiencing no difficulty in keeping track of him?"

"None at all, sir." Philipson was up in the Finnish Police helicopter which had picked up the fleeing Volvo less than ten miles north-east of Lahti only minutes before. The helicopter had been based in Lahti—a piece of good fortune for which Aubrey was grateful. He glanced at his own map.

"Where can he go when he gets there?"

"North again."

"Very well. Alert ground units—talk direct to the Police Chief via their channel. No *interference*."

Aubrey switched the set to receive, and turned round in the operator's swivel chair to face Anders. He appeared like an abandoned, betrayed child, or a worried parent. Aubrey could not decide which, but his concern for Buckholz was evident.

Anders was staring at the set. "You want to try Moscow again, sir?"

"Not after the last little snub, thank you, Anders. If Chairman Andropov is unavailable, he will remain so. He'll tell us soon enough if he's succeeded in finding Gorochenko."

"He hasn't succeeded, has he?"

"No Anders—I'm afraid he hasn't. All we can do is hope the coup will fizzle out—or he's got Druzhinin or somebody to order other units into defensive positions—" Anders was scowling. "I agree, Anders. It does seem unlikely."

"So—what the hell does Khamovkhin matter?"

"He is the *elected* head of the government of the USSR," Aubrey said with no trace of irony. "He must be kept alive. We simply cannot afford to let him be killed. Your President has made that more than clear." He looked at his watch. Four-forty.

"The more he runs, the more that guy is going to realise he has nowhere to go," Anders observed.

"I know that, Anders!" Aubrey snapped. He studied the map. "Now, where can he go? Get my driver in here."

The smile on the driver's face was inappropriate, but Aubrey recognised it not as self-importance or amusement, but derived from the experience they had shared escaping from the ambush in Helsinki—when Waterford had been killed.

"Quickly, Fisher—tell me where they could go. They're here at the moment."

Fisher bent over the map, studied it briefly, then said, "If you let him get beyond Heinola, to here—" His finger traced a minor road. "This cross-roads gives him choice again—and if you let him go either left or right, then he's into deeper forest, and you might lose him."

"Are you sure?"

"I spent a holiday up there, fishing and walking. Very *private* country." Fisher grinned with memory. "It would take hours, maybe days, to root him out. And who's going to be alive by then, I wonder?"

"Yes—thank you, Fisher. One other thing—is Philipson anything of a shot?"

"Handgun, not bad. Never fired it in anger, I don't think. Rifle—?" Aubrey nodded. "Nowhere near good enough, sir."

When Fisher had been dismissed, Aubrey looked directly at Anders, his hand raised to signal the police helicopter.

"I have little or no choice in the matter."

"I realise that, sir. I just hope that helicopter has a marksman in it."

Aubrey flipped the switch.

"He might stop in Heinola. We must hope that he does." He bent to the microphone. "Philipson, come in, Philipson."

"Sir." The voice seemed very far away, and unreal. And it was hot again in the radio room, just as it had been in the corridor, earlier. Just hot flushes, he thought.

"Is there a trained marksman among the helicopter crew?"

"Pardon, sir?"

"Have you a trained marksman on board?"

A protracted silence, then: "Yes, sir. Just the one, and he's out of practice—"

Aubrey looked at the map, measuring distances with his finger and thumb, shaking his head.

"No car could get far enough ahead of them—do we know what's out there, Anders?" He stabbed his finger north of Heinola.

"Some cars, but keeping out of sight—local police from Heinola. We haven't got anything out that far by chopper, and nothing from Helsinki."

"Then he will have to do," Aubrey commented. His finger went on tapping the map, as if he were trying to influence something in the place to which he was pointing, trying to cast some spell over it by mental suggestion. Then he said into the transmitter, "Very well—fly ahead of the car. Warn local units in Heinola to keep clear of it, but to keep an eye on it. *You* find a good vantage point for the marksman. Then set down."

"What—do you want him to do, sir?"

"The usual—engine-block, tires—" He glanced at Anders. "And the car must be stopped dead—understand? You must place police near the road, and they *must* get to the car in time to prevent any retaliation whatsoever. Is that clear?"

"Jesus Christ," Anders breathed.

"You do not need to be told that the driver must not, repeat *not*, be killed. Understand?" Anders appeared relieved. "You use Vehicle Arrest, Method D, Philipson— understand?"

"But—"

"Understand, Philipson?"

"Sir."

"Leave this channel open from now on."

"Sir."

Aubrey stared at Anders. The man was evidently concerned, but Aubrey had checked the anger and disgust that had been welling in him when he thought Aubrey intended killing Buckholz. Aubrey smiled slightly. Method D of Vehicle Arrest called for the wounding of the driver— death if the quality of marksmanship was not sufficiently high—in stopping of any fleeing vehicle. But Anders, not privy to the Marksmanship Manual of SIS, did not know it.

"Let's hope this policeman spends a lot of time hunting, shall we?"

He looked at the crackling radio.

It was simply an old letter. There was no dramatic dried and faded blood, it seemed stained by time rather than tears or despair. It was almost falling apart, of course, Vorontsyev saw as he tried to consider it forensically, detached from its words. Heavy creases full of pocket-fluff, the writing faded—done in pencil that must have been licked a hundred times before the short account was complete. Perhaps the dirty fingers that had held the rough paper—it *was* writing-paper, not packing-paper or toilet paper, so God knew where it had been obtained. Those hands had pressed the paper down on some wooden table, gripped the pencil stub stiffly because the mittens didn't really keep out the cold.

The letter is simply old, he tried to tell himself forensically.

Then Gorochenko was speaking, and he listened, even while he turned the letter in his hands. He heard every word, even though he did not want to listen.

"Your father was a hero in the war against the Fascists. He was—arrested by the NKVD twelve miles from Berlin, when he was part of Zhukov's army group. It was for letters he had written home to your mother, describing the conditions at the front, and expressing sympathy for the refugees he saw every hour of every day. And criticising the way the war had been run from Moscow."

Vorontsyev suddenly glanced up from the letter. His eyes were wide, but he could say nothing. "He was tried, and sentenced to hard labour. He went into the camps—one near Moscow, at first. Later, he was transferred to Siberia, to the Kolyma region in the north-east. When he was arrested, your mother was pregnant, carrying you. She bore you, weaned you, then killed herself because she knew she would never see your father again. She knew by then that he would not take even his freedom from them. I was to be your guardian, your adoptive father."

There was no question of denial, even though the hot rejections rushed to his throat. He knew Gorochenko had spoken the truth. He was dumb, while his mind whirled crazily out of its accustomed orbit. He felt, with a sense of literal truth, that he was going mad.

"It is not that she did not care for you," Gorochenko said softly, "but his arrest and imprisonment destroyed her. She lived for him. He, once he knew that she was dead, became ever more reckless with his life. He smuggled out accounts of their treatment—the filth, the cold, the starvation diet, the beatings, everything. Each time they caught him, he was punished. And his sentence was lengthened. And then he died in 1952, the year before the Beast himself—still fighting them." He looked at Vorontsyev, saw the dull eyes and sensed the mind retreating behind their opaque surfaces. He bellowed, "Don't you understand? Your father wasn't killed in the war—he was alive until you were eight years of age—a *zek,* one of the inhabitants of the Gulag archipelago! Stalin had him imprisoned just for what he thought and felt and said!" There was a spittle of foam on his lower lip. He grabbed Vorontsyev's hands across the table, clutching them as if to squeeze truth through the pores of the younger man's skin. "I *loved* your father—loved him!

"And they killed him—the NKVD, the MVD, the KGB. They're all the same—filth! Scum! Pigs who wallow in the dirt they make of life! Can't you see that? I tried to save you from them by hiding you *inside* the organisation!" He paused, wringing Vorontsyev's hands, his face distorted with pain. Yet Vorontsyev still failed to respond. Gorochenko wanted nothing but to see him weep for the death of his father; it was a moment without calculation. He said, "Believe me. It happened to millions—and it's still happening, I want revenge for your father, for Kyril Mihailovich Vorontsyev, and for all the others who are dead or dying. *That* is what I want."

Vorontsyev looked at him, and what Gorochenko saw made him afraid. There was something like hatred in his eyes for a moment, then the returning blankness. Gorochenko had the sense that he had failed in some inexplicable way. He had not persuaded, perhaps not even immobilised Vorontsyev. He reached out and pulled the telephone towards him, watching Vorontnsyev's gun all the time.

"No," Vorontsyev said, looking up at him.

Gorochenko lifted the receiver, and began to dial the number. He was too early, but Valenkov would act. He *had* to act, just as Gorochenko had to telephone, now in the next few minutes, before Vorontsyev—

He dialled the third digit of Valenkov's number.

"No," Vorontsyev said again.

"It's crazy! One dumb Finnish cop with a rifle—you got the Soviet First Secretary out there, and the Deputy Director of the CIA! You can't mean to go through with it!"

"Be quiet, Anders!" Aubrey turned his back on the American, and spoke into the transmitter. "Your man has a clear field of fire, Philipson?"

"Sir. We're just back in the trees, on a slight rise. He'll see the car about a hundred yards before it draws level with him, then another hundred and fifty after that. It's the best we could do."

"Early warning?"

"A spotter with an R/T, quarter of a mile down the road."

"Where are the others?"

"Thirty—forty, fifty yards beyond me."

"Move two of them closer."

"Sir." Philipson's voice could be heard faintly as he spoke into a handset. Otherwise, Aubrey was aware only of Anders's eyes staring into his back. Aubrey concentrated on the face of the transmitter, because there was nothing else to be done. He was shuffling pieces on the board, but he knew as well as Anders his practical impotence. He was relying on one policeman whose name he did not know, on a moonlit road thirty miles away from him.

There was no sense of satisfaction—something he had felt on past occasions when he moved the wheels of the political world a fraction by his own hand. Nothing except the dreadful possibilities of what he was attempting.

Anders loomed behind him like the keeper of his conscience, or an arresting officer.

"In position, sir. We're ready." Philipson did not sound confident, not at all.

"How much time do we—?"

"Sir, he's in sight. Spotter has him picked up now."

"Tell me everything, Philipson—you have no orders to give. Tell me."

"Sir. Passing spotter—*now*, travelling at approximately fifty mph—spotter has him on the bend—*now*." Philipson's voice was mounting like mercury in a thermometer. The end-play was going critical. "We have him in sight, sir—here he comes—"

Aubrey glanced up at Anders, who had moved closer to the transmitter, as if threatening it. Aubrey could see the clenched white hand at the man's side as he turned back to the microphone. But he could say nothing. Spectator—radio commentary, as if he might be listening to a horse race—

"Drawing level—*now!*" Aubrey strained—he heard the noise of Anders's other hand rub his stubbly jaw, tried to hear the shots—two, three, four tinny, unsubstantial clicks —static or gunfire?

"What's happening, dammit?" His voice was squeaky.

"The—car's stopped. Two shots through the engine-block, no fire—car swung off the road—"

"The driver?" Anders bellowed.

"The passengers—where are your policemen, Philipson?"

"Two more shots, sir, into the car—"

"Jesus living, get *down* there, you dumb bastard!" Anders roared, flipping the switch to transmit. Aubrey took the microphone from his white hand.

"Find out what has happened, and report back, Philipson."

He flicked the switch, and there was nothing but static. And the static went on, and on, until it was like white noise being used to empty their minds, reduce their will. Aubrey felt himself crumbling inside, so that he was spent and empty and wanted to sleep. The static went on and on.

"You bastard—oh, Kenneth, you're a bastard!"

It was Buckholz.

"Khamovkhin?" Aubrey snapped, as if coming out of deep hypnosis. Then he flipped the switch, remembering. "Khamovkhin?"

"*Alive*—you lucky son of a bitch! Shaking like a leaf, but alive."

"Galakhov?"

"Got his from the cops who rushed the car. Banged his head on the head-rest behind me, and Khamovkhin wrestled with the gun until someone blew his head off. Khamovkhin will bill you for a new coat and a bath. Galakhov's brains are all over him."

Aubrey shuddered, as was intended.

"You're not hurt?"

"Of course I am. You knew I would be—isn't that the way it works. Only the arm—your man aimed as far away from my body as he could, I guess—at the wheel." A

397

silence, then: "You bastard, Kenneth—you *ass-hole!*" Finally: "Thanks."

Aubrey held out the microphone to Anders, and saw that his hand was shaking. But then, so was Anders's big hand, and he was a much younger man. Much younger.

Gorochenko stopped dialling. There was a strange light in Vorontsyev's eyes, and he was afraid of it. It looked like madness, and he silently cursed himself for what he had done. The miscalculation of arrogance, or desperation—or even anger. Break Alexei, then rebuild him. Perhaps he had overloaded him—*buried* him in truths?

How would he dig himself out? He dialled two more digits swiftly. His eyes flickered to the gun, once, just as he paused before the final digit.

Vorontsyev saw the old man resume dialling, and understood only that the truth about his father was just another ploy—like Natalia, like Vrubel, like Ossipov. Gorochenko had used everything—everything *sacred*—against him. Especially his father. He had used his father's memory to stop him.

He lifted the gun, and heard Gorochenko say, "Stay calm, Alexei." The dial of the telephone purred back to rest. He focused his gaze on Gorochenko's free hand—tapping on the edge of the table, the drumming muffled by the glove, the anxiety clear in the movement. He attended to the face. It was clear in his strangely foggy vision, and seemed wizened, shrunk. The cunning eyes were transfixed by the levelled gun. It was a hateful, arrogant face.

"Put down the phone." Vorontsyev said, the gun pointing at Gorochenko's forehead. "Put it down. You're under arrest."

Gorochenko appeared surprised. Then he said into the telephone, "Valenkov? Where is he—get him to the phone, at once!"

The telephone was a little way from Gorochenko's ear, and Vorontsyev could hear a distant, tinny voice referring to the caller as *Kutuzov*. Obeying the order. That name, though—

The traitor. The man who had tried to kill him. *Kutuzov*, the conspirator.

A long moment of silence, in which Gorochenko seemed to concentrate utterly on the telephone. Until he looked up at the gun, and at Vorontsyev's face, and whatever he saw there caused a spasm of fear to cross his features. Vorontsyev felt himself inside a dream or a concussion, and he was simply doing his duty. He concentrated on the hand, the telephone, the shape of the jaw, the dark coat. Only physical things.

He could not kill his stepfather—but he would stop him. He was afraid that there would be an answer from Valenkov—an aide scurrying through corridors, ringing out on another line—just as Gorochenko, he could see, was beginning to fear that Valenkov would ignore the call.

Vorontsyev had buried his appalling misery for a moment. He felt clear-headed in a kind of delayed shock.

It was an endless moment for Gorochenko. He sensed that Vorontsyev was trying to excise areas of reality, concentrate only on the stupid inadequacy of his duty. He stared at his son for a long time, then he heard the receiver at the other end being lifted from a desk or table. He pressed the mouthpiece close, made as if to speak.

Before he uttered a sound, Vorontsyev did his duty. There was no time for thought or passion or memory. He shot Gorochenko through the head, twice, neatly. The body flew backwards out of the chair under the impact of the heavy 9 mm bullets, and the telephone clattered onto the floor squeaking tinnily.

As he sat there, the gun now resting on the table, he appeared from his angle of vision to be alone in the room. So he sat quietly, without moving his head. Not even slightly.

He had done his duty.

Because there was nothing else. Gorochenko had taken away everything else, except his duty, his loyalty to the State.

He grasped the heroic fiction of the moment. He had prevented the coup. Then he abandoned speculation for a dream-like emptiness. Perhaps he would go and look at the body in a little while. But not yet, not just yet. At the moment, it was sufficient just to sit quietly in the silence of the dusty, cold little room. The telephone, its connection broken, buzzed like a distant insect. Everything else was quiet.

It was five forty-six on the 24th.

ABOUT THE AUTHOR

CRAIG THOMAS was born in Wales and educated at University College, Cardiff. He is the author of six previous novels: *Firefox* (also made into a highly successful film starring Clint Eastwood), *Rat Trap, Wolfsbane, Snow Falcon, Jade Tiger,* and *Sea Leopard.* Craig Thomas is married and currently lives in Lichfield, Staffordshire, England, where he is at work on a new novel.

LION'S RUN
By Craig Thomas
(25824-9 • $4.50)

"When it comes to keeping the story moving and stoking up the excitement, Mr. Thomas knows his business."

—*New York Times*

"He knows how to make a chase scene drive the reader from page to page ... A damn good read."

—*Washington Post Book World*

"Not to be missed."   —*London Daily Mirror*

Sir Kenneth, Director-General of British Intelligence, is the victim of an elaborate and brilliant KGB plot. At its heart is the murder of a British agent. Having discovered his role in it, the Soviets have found the one weapon against which Sir Kenneth cannot defend himself. The truth will convict him.

Time is running out as the KGB moves to bring Aubrey to Russia where he will quietly disappear. There are only two slender hopes for Aubrey's survival, one a persistent friend who refuses to believe the worst, the other Aubrey's bodyguard, who is only one desperate step ahead of the KGB assassins who are attempting to track him down before he can find proof of Aubrey's innocence.

In LION'S RUN Craig Thomas has created a masterpiece of suspense, a thrilling novel of intrigue, friendship and betrayal that has all the ingredients of a major Craig Thomas bestseller.

Also from Craig Thomas:

THRILLERS

Gripping suspense . . . explosive action . . . dynamic characters . . . International settings . . . these are the elements that make for great thrillers. And Bantam has the best writers of thrillers today—Robert Ludlum, Frederick Forsyth, Jack Higgins, Clive Cussler—with books guaranteed to keep you riveted to your seat.

Robert Ludlum:

☐	24900	THE AQUITAINE PROGRESSION	$4.50
☐	26011	THE BOURNE IDENTITY	$4.95
☐	26094	THE CHANCELLOR MANUSCRIPT	$4.95
☐	26019	THE HOLCROFT COVENANT	$4.95
☐	25899	THE MATARESE CIRCLE	$4.95
☐	26430	THE OSTERMAN WEEKEND	$4.95
☐	25270	THE PARSIFAL MOSAIC	$4.95
☐	26081	THE ROAD TO GANDOLFO	$4.50
☐	25856	THE SCARLATTI INHERITANCE	$4.50
☐	05905	THREE BY LUDLUM	$12.95

a Bantam Omnibus edition including:
THE AQUITAINE PROGRESSION
THE PARSIFAL MOSAIC
THE BOURNE IDENTITY

Frederick Forsyth:

☐	25113	THE FOURTH PROTOCOL	$4.50
☐	25526	NO COMEBACKS	$3.95
☐	25522	DAY OF THE JACKAL	$4.50
☐	26490	THE DEVIL'S ALTERNATIVE	$4.95
☐	25224	DOGS OF WAR	$4.50
☐	25525	THE ODESSA FILE	$4.50

Robert Littell:

☐	05097	THE SISTERS, a Bantam hardcover	$16.95
☐	25416	THE DEFECTION OF A. J. LEWINTER	$3.95
☐	25457	MOTHER RUSSIA	$3.95
☐	25432	THE OCTOBER CIRCLE	$3.95
☐	25547	SWEET REASON	$3.50

Prices and availability subject to change without notice.

Buy them at your local bookstore or use this handy coupon for ordering:

Bantam Books, Inc., Dept. TH, 414 East Golf Road, Des Plaines, Ill. 60016

Please send me the books I have checked above. I am enclosing $_____ (please add $1.50 to cover postage and handling). Send check or money order —no cash or C.O.D.'s please.

Mr/Mrs/Miss _____

Address _____

City _____ State/Zip _____

TH—11/86

Please allow four to six weeks for delivery. This offer expires 5/87.

Special Offer
Buy a Bantam Book
for only 50¢.

Now you can have Bantam's catalog filled with hundreds of titles plus take advantage of our unique and exciting bonus book offer. A special offer which gives you the opportunity to purchase a Bantam book for only 50¢. Here's how!

By ordering any five books at the regular price per order, you can also choose any other single book listed (up to a $4.95 value) for just 50¢. Some restrictions do apply, but for further details why not send for Bantam's catalog of titles today!

Just send us your name and address and we will send you a catalog!